THE MYTH-ING OMNIBUS

THE
MYTH-ING
OMNIBUS

Robert Asprin

A LEGEND BOOK

Published by Arrow Books Limited
20 Vauxhall Bridge Road, London SW1V 2SA

An imprint of the Random Century Group

London Melbourne Sydney Auckland
Johannesburg and agencies throughout
the world

This Legend edition 1992

Printed and bound in Great Britain by
Cox & Wyman Ltd, Reading, Berkshire

ISBN 0 09 914991 5

ANOTHER FINE MYTH

Robert Asprin

This book is dedicated to

Bork The Indestructible
(Known to lesser mortals as George Hunt)

whose gruff but loyal friendship has seen me through
many crises in the past . . . and probably in the future!

Chapter One:

"There are things on heaven and earth, Horatio, Man was not meant to know."
—HAMLET

ONE of the few redeeming facets of instructors, I thought, is that occasionally they can be fooled. It was true when my mother taught me to read, it was true when my father tried to teach me to be a farmer, and it's true now when I'm learning magik.

"You haven't been practicing!" Garkin's harsh admonishment interrupted my musings.

"I have too!" I protested. "It's just a difficult exercise."

As if in response, the feather I was levitating began to tremble and wobble in midair.

"You aren't concentrating!" he accused.

"It's the wind," I argued. I wanted to add "from your loud mouth," but didn't dare. Early in our lessons Garkin had demonstrated his lack of appreciation for cheeky apprentices.

"The wind," he sneered, mimicking my voice. "Like this, dolt!"

My mental contact with the object of my concentration was interrupted as the feather darted suddenly toward the ceiling. It jarred to a halt as if it had become

1

imbedded in something, though it was still a foot from the wooden beams, then slowly rotated to a horizontal plane. Just as slowly it rotated on its axis, then swapped ends and began to glide around an invisible circle like a leaf caught in an eddy.

I risked a glance at Garkin. He was draped over his chair, feet dangling, his entire attention apparently devoted to devouring a leg of roast lizard-bird, a bird I had snared I might add. Concentration indeed!

He looked up suddenly and our eyes met. It was too late to look away so I simply looked back at him.

"Hungry?" His grease-flecked salt and pepper beard was suddenly framing a wolfish grin. "Then show me how much you've been practicing."

It took me a heartbeat to realize what he meant; then I looked up desperately. The feather was tumbling floorward, a bare shoulder-height from landing. Forcing the sudden tension from my body, I reached out with my mind . . . gently . . . form a pillow . . . don't knock it away. . . .

The feather halted a scant two hand-spans from the floor.

I heard Garkin's low chuckle, but didn't allow it to break my concentration. I hadn't let the feather touch the floor for three years, and it wasn't going to touch now.

Slowly I raised it until it floated at eye level. Wrapping my mind around it, I rotated it on its axis, then enticed it to swap ends. As I led it through the exercise, its movement was not as smooth or sure as when Garkin set his mind to the task, but it did move unerringly in its assigned course.

Although I had not been practicing with the feather, I had been practicing. When Garkin was not about or preoccupied with his own studies, I devoted most of my time to levitating pieces of metal—keys, to be specific. Each type of levitation had its own inherent problems. Metal was hard to work with because it was an inert material. The feather, having once been part of a living thing, was more responsive . . . too responsive. To lift metal took effort, to maneuver a feather required subtlety. Of the two, I preferred to work with metal. I could see a more direct application of that skill in my chosen profession.

"Good enough, lad. Now put it back in the book."

I smiled to myself. This part I had practiced, not because of its potential applications, but because it was fun.

The book was lying open on the end of the workbench. I brought the feather down in a long lazy spiral, allowing it to pass lightly across the pages of the book and up in a swooping arc, stopped it, and brought it back. As it approached the book the second time, I disengaged part of my mind to dart ahead to the book. As the feather crossed the pages, the book snapped shut like the jaws of a hungry predator, trapping the missile within its grasp.

"Hmmmm . . ." intoned Garkin, "a trifle showy, but effective."

"Just a little something I worked up when I was practicing," I said casually, reaching out with my mind for the other lizard-bird leg. Instead of floating gracefully to my waiting hand, however, it remained on the wooden platter as if it had taken root.

"Not so fast, my little sneak-thief. So you've been practicing, eh?" He stroked his beard thoughtfully with the half-gnawed bone in his hand.

"Certainly. Didn't it show?" It occurred to me that Garkin is not as easy to fool as it sometimes seems.

"In that case, I'd like to see you light your candle. It should be easy if you have been practicing as much as you claim."

"I have no objections to trying, but as you have said yourself so many times, some lessons come easier than others."

Although I sounded confident, my spirits sank as the large candle came floating to the work table in response to Garkin's summons. In four years of trying I was yet to be successful at this particular exercise. If Garkin was going to keep me from food until I was successful, I could go hungry for a long time.

"Say, uh, Garkin, it occurs to me I could probably concentrate better on a full stomach."

"It occurs to me that you're stalling."

"Couldn't I. . . ."

"Now, Skeeve."

There was no swaying him once he used my proper name. That much I had learned over the years. Lad, Thief, Idiot, Turnip-Head, though derogatory, as long as he used one of these, his mind was still open. Once he reverted to using my proper name, it was hopeless. It is indeed a sorry state when the sound of your own name becomes a knell of doom.

Well, if there was no way around it, I'd just have to give it my best shot. For this there could be no half-effort or feigned concentration. I would have to use every ounce of my strength and skill to summon the power.

I studied the candle with a detached mind, momentarily blanking the effort ahead from my consciousness. The room, the cluttered workbench, Garkin, even my own hunger faded from view as I focused on the candle, though I had long since memorized its every feature.

It was stout, nearly six inches across to stabilize its ten-inch height. I had carved numerous mystic symbols into its surface, copied painstakingly from Garkin's books at his direction, though many of them were partially obliterated by hardened rivulets of wax. The candle had burned many long hours to light my studies, but it had always been lit from a taper from the cooking fire and not from my efforts.

Negative thought. Stop it.

I will light the candle this time. I will light it because there is no reason I should not.

Consciously deepening my breathing, I began to gather the power. My world narrowed further until all I was aware of was the curled, blackened wick of the candle.

I am Skeeve. My father has a farmer's bond with the earth. My mother was an educated woman. My teacher is a master magician. I am Skeeve. I will light this candle.

I could feel myself beginning to grow warm as the energies began to build within me. I focused the heat on the wick.

Like my father, I tap the strength of the earth. The knowledge my mother gave me is like a lens, enabling me to focus what I have gained. The wisdom of my teacher directs my efforts to those points of the universe most likely to yield to my will. I am Skeeve.

The candle remained unlit. There was sweat on my forehead now, and I was beginning to tremble with the effort. No that was wrong, I should not tense. Relax. Don't try to force it. Tenseness hinders the flow. Let the energies pass freely, serve as a passive conductor. I forced myself to relax, consciously letting the muscles in my face and shoulders go slack as I redoubled my efforts.

The flow was noticeably more intense now. I could almost see the energy streaming from me to my target. I stretched out a finger which focused the energies even more. The candle remained unlit.

I couldn't do it. Negative thought. Stop it. I am Skeeve. I will light the candle. My father. . . . No. Negative thought. Do not rely on others for your strength. I will light the candle because I am Skeeve.

I was rewarded by a sudden surge of energy at the thought. I pursued it, growing heady with power. I am Skeeve. I am stronger than any of them. I escaped my father's attempts to chain me to a plow as he had my brother. My mother died from her idealism, but I used her teachings to survive. My teacher is a gullible fool who took a thief for an apprentice. I have beaten them all. I am Skeeve. I will light the candle.

I was floating now. I realized how my abilities dwarfed those around me. Whether the candle lit or not was inconsequential. I am Skeeve. I am powerful.

Almost contemptuously I reached out with my mind and touched the wick. A small bright ember appeared as if in answer to my will.

Startled, I sat up and blinked at the candle. As I did, the ember disappeared, leaving a small white plume of smoke to mark its departure. I realized too late I had broken concentration.

"Excellent, Lad!"

Garkin was suddenly beside me pounding my shoulder enthusiastically. How long he had been there I neither knew nor cared.

"It went out," I said plaintively.

"Never you mind that. You lit it. You have the confidence now. Next time it will be easy. By the stars, we'll make a magician of you yet. Here, you must be hungry."

I barely got my hand up in time to intercept the remaining lizard-bird leg before it smacked into my face. It was cold.

"I don't mind admitting I was beginning to despair, lad. What made that lesson so hard? Has it occurred to you you could use that spell to give you extra light when you're picking a lock or even to start a fire to serve as a diversion?"

"I thought about it, but extra light could draw unwanted attention. As for starting a diversion, I'd be afraid of hurting someone. I don't want to hurt anyone, just...."

I stopped, realizing what I was saying, too late. A heavy cuff from Garkin sent me sprawling off my stool.

"I thought so! You're still planning to be a thief. You want to use my magiks to steal!"

He was towering in his rage, but for once I stood my ground.

"What of it?" I snarled. "It beats starving. What's so good about being a magician, anyway? I mean, your life-style here gives me so much to look forward to."

I gestured at the cluttered room that was the entirety of the hut.

"Listen to the wolfling complain," Garkin sneered. "It was good enough for you when the winter drove you out of the woods to steal. 'It beats sleeping under a bush,' you said."

"And it still does. That's why I'm still here. But I'm not going to spend the rest of my life here. Hiding in a little hut in the woods is not my idea of a future to look forward to. You were living on roots and berries until I came along and started trapping meat for the fire. Maybe that's your idea of a wonderful life, Garkin, but it's not mine!"

We glared at each other for several long moments. Now that my anger was vented, I was more than a little afraid. While I had not had extensive experience in the field, I suspected that sneering at magicians was not the best way to ensure a long and healthy future.

Surprisingly enough, it was Garkin who gave ground first. He suddenly dropped his gaze and bowed his head, giving me a rare view of the unkempt mass of hair atop it.

"Perhaps you're right, Skeeve," his voice was strangely soft. "Perhaps I have been showing you all the work of magik, but not the rewards. I constantly forget how suppressed magik is in these lands."

He raised his eyes to meet mine again, and I shivered at the impact. They were not angry, but deep within them burned a glow I had never seen before.

"Know you now, Skeeve, that all lands are not like this one, nor was I always as you see me now. In lands where magik is recognized instead of feared as it is here, it is respected and commissioned by those in power. There a skillful magician who keeps his wits about him can reap a hundred times the wealth you aspire to as a thief, and such power that. . . ."

He broke off suddenly and shook his head as if to clear it. When he opened his eyes again, the glow I had seen burning earlier had died to an ember.

"But you aren't to be impressed by words, are you, lad? Come, I'll show you a little demonstration of some of the power you may one day wield—if you practice your lessons, that is."

The joviality in his voice was forced. I nodded my agreement in answer to that burning gaze. Truth to tell, I needed no demonstration. His soft, brief oration had awed me far more than any angry tirade or demonstration, but I did not wish to contradict him at this time.

I don't believe he actually noticed my response. He was already striding into the large pentagram permanently inscribed in the floor of the hut. As he walked, he gestured absentmindedly and the charred copper brazier scuttled forth from its place in the corner to meet him at the center of the pentagram.

I had time to reflect that perhaps it was that brazier that had first drawn me to Garkin. I remembered the first time I peered through the window of his hut seeking to identify and place objects of value for a later theft. I had seen Garkin as I have seen him so often since, pacing restlessly up and down the room, his nose buried in a book. It was a surprising enough sight as it was, for reading is not a common pastime in this area, but what captured my attention was the brazier. It hobbled about the room, following Garkin like an impatient puppy that was a little too polite to jump up on its master to get his attention. Then Garkin had looked up from his book, stared thoughtfully at his workbench; then, with a nod of decision, gestured. A small pot of unidentified content rose from the clutter and floated to his waiting hand. He caught it, referred to his book again, and poured out a dollop without looking up. Quick as a cat, the brazier scrambled under his hand and caught the dollop before it reached the floor. That had been my introduction to magik.

Something wrenched my attention back to the present. What was it? I checked Garkin's progress. No, he was still at work, half hidden by a floating cloud of vials and jars, mumbling as he occasionally plucked one from the air and added a bit of its contents to the brazier. Whatever he was working on, it promised to be spectacular.

Then I heard it again, a muffled step outside the hut. But that was impossible! Garkin always set the . . . I began to search my memory. I could not recall Garkin setting the protective wards before he started to work. Ridiculous. Caution was the first and most important thing Garkin hammered into me, and part of caution was always setting wards before you started working. He couldn't have forgotten . . . but he had been rather intense and distracted.

I was still trying to decide if I should attempt to interrupt Garkin's work when he suddenly stepped back from the brazier. He fixed me with his gaze, and my warning died in my throat. This was not the time to impose reality on the situation. The glow was back in his eyes, stronger than before.

"Even demonstrations should give a lesson," he intoned. "Control, Skeeve. Control is the mainstay of magik. Power without control is a disaster. That is why you practice with a feather though you are able to move much larger and heavier objects. Control. Even your meager powers would be dangerous unless controlled, and I will not teach you more until you have learned that control."

He carefully stepped out of the pentagram.

"To demonstrate the value of control, I will now summon forth a demon, a being from another world. He is powerful, cruel, and vicious, and would kill us both if given the chance. Yet despite this, we need not fear him because he will be controlled. He will be unable to harm us or anything else in this world as long as he is contained within that pentagram. Now watch, Skeeve. Watch and learn."

So saying, he turned once more to the brazier. He spread his hands, and as he did, the five candles at the points of the pentagram sprang to life and the lines of the pentagram began to glow with an eerie blue light. Silence reigned for several minutes, then he began to chant in a low mumble. A thread of smoke appeared from the brazier, but instead of rising to the ceiling, it poured onto the floor and began to form a small cloud that seethed and pulsed. Garkin's chanting was louder now, and the cloud grew and darkened. The brazier was almost obscured from view, but there . . . in the depths of the cloud . . . something was taking shape. . . .

"Isstvan sends his greetings, Garkin!"

I nearly jumped out of my skin at the words. They came from inside the hut, but not inside the pentagram! I whirled toward their source. A figure was standing just inside the door, blinding in a glowing gold cloak. For a mad moment I thought it was the demon answering Garkin's summons. Then I saw the crossbow. It was a man, alright, but the crossbow, cocked and loaded in his hand, did little for my peace of mind.

Garkin did not even turn to look.

"Not now, you fool!" he snarled.

"It has been a long hunt, Garkin," the man continued as if he hadn't heard. "You've hidden yourself well, but did you really hope to escape. . . ."

"You dare!?!" Garkin spun from his work, towering in his rage.

The man saw Garkin's face now, saw the eyes, and his face contorted in a grotesque mask of fear. Reflexively, he loosed the bolt from his crossbow, but too late. I did not see what Garkin did, things were happening too fast, but the man suddenly disappeared in a sheet of flame. He shrieked in agony and fell to the floor. The flame disappeared as suddenly as it had come, leaving only the smoldering corpse as evidence it had existed at all.

I remained rooted to the spot for several moments before I could move or even speak.

"Garkin," I said at last, "I . . . Garkin!"

Garkin's form was a crumpled lump on the floor. I was at his side in one bound, but I was far too late. The crossbow bolt protruded with silent finality from his chest. Garkin had given me my last lesson.

As I stooped to touch his body, I noticed something that froze my blood in its veins. Half-hidden by his form was the extinguished candle from the north point of the pentagram. The lines were no longer glowing blue. The protective spell was gone.

With agonizing effort, I raised my head and found myself gazing into a pair of yellow eyes, flecked with gold, that were not of this world.

Chapter Two:

"Things are not always as they seem."
—MANDRAKE

ONCE, in the woods, I found myself face to face with a snake-cat. On another occasion, I encountered a spider-bear. Now, faced with a demon, I decided to pattern my behavior after that which had saved me in the aforementioned situations. I froze. At least, in hindsight, I like to think it was a deliberate, calculated act.

The demon curled its lips back, revealing a double row of needle-sharp teeth.

I considered changing my chosen course of action; I considered fainting.

The demon ran a purple tongue over his lips and began to slowly extend a taloned hand toward me. That did it! I went backward, not in a catlike graceful bound, but scrabbling on all fours. It's surprising how fast you can move that way when properly inspired. I managed to build up a substantial head of steam before I crashed head-first into the wall.

"Gaahh. . . ." I said. It may not seem like much, but at the time it was the calmest expression of pain and terror I could think of.

At my outburst, the demon seemed to choke. Several

11

ragged shouts erupted, then he began to laugh. It wasn't a low menacing laugh, but the wholehearted enthusiastic laughter of someone who has just seen something hysterically funny.

I found it both disquieting and annoying. Annoying because I had a growing suspicion I was the source of his amusement; disquieting because . . . well . . . he was a demon and demons are. . . .

"Cold, vicious, and bloodthirsty," the demon gasped as if he had read my thoughts. "You really bought the whole line, didn't you, kid?"

"I beg your pardon?" I said because I couldn't think of anything else to say.

"Something wrong with your ears? I said 'cold, vicious. . . .' "

"I heard you. I meant what did you mean."

"What I meant was that you were scared stiff, by a few well chosen words from my esteemed colleague, I'll wager." He jerked a thumb at Garkin's body. "Sorry for the dramatics. I felt a touch of comic relief was necessary to lighten an otherwise tragic moment."

"Comic relief?"

"Well, actually, I couldn't pass up the opportunity. You should have seen your face."

He chuckled to himself as he strode out of the pentagram and began leisurely inspecting the premises.

"So this is Garkin's new place, huh? What a dump. Who would have thought he'd come to this?"

To say I was perplexed would be an understatement. I wasn't sure how a demon should act, but it wasn't like this.

I could have bolted for the door, but I did not seem to be in immediate danger. Either this strange being meant me no harm, or he was confident of his ability to stop me even if I tried to flee. For the sake of my nervous system, I decided to assume the former.

The demon continued to inspect the hut, while I inspected him. He was humanoid; that is, he had two arms, two legs, and a head. He was short but powerfully built, a bit broader across the shoulders than a man, and heavily muscled, but he wasn't human. I mean, you don't see many hairless humans with dark green scales covering their body and pointed ears lying flat against their head.

I decided to risk a question.

"Ah, excuse me."

"Yeah, kid?"

"Um, you *are* a demon, aren't you?"

"Huh? Oh, yeah, I guess you could say I am."

"Well, if you don't mind my asking, why don't you act like a demon?"

The demon shot me a disgusted look, then turned his head heavenward in a gesture of martyrdom.

"Everybody's a critic. Tell ya what, kid, would you be happier if I tore your throat out with my teeth?"

"Well, no, but. . . ."

"For that matter, who are you, anyway? Are you an innocent bystander, or did you come with the assassin?"

"I'm with him," I hastened to reply, pointing a shaky finger at Garkin's body. That bit about tearing my throat out had me on edge again. "Or at least I was. Garkin. The one who summoned . . . him! . . . I'm . . . I was his student."

"No kiddin'? Garkin's apprentice?" He began advancing toward me, reaching out a hand, "Pleased ta . . . what's wrong?"

As he moved toward me, I had started backing away from him. I tried to do it casually, but he had noticed.

"Well . . . it's . . . you *are* a demon."

"Yeah. So?"

"Um . . . well, demons are supposed to be. . . ."

"Hey, relax, kid. I don't bite. Look, I'm an old buddy of Garkin's."

"I thought you said you were a demon?"

"That's right. I'm from another dimension. A dimension traveler, or demon for short. Get it?"

"What's a dimension?"

The demon scowled.

"Are you sure you're Garkin's apprentice? I mean,

he hasn't told you anything at all about dimensions?"

"No," I answered. "I mean, yes, I'm his apprentice, but he never said anything about the demon-suns."

"That's dimensions," he corrected. "Well, a dimension is another world, actually one of several worlds, existing simultaneously with this one, but on different planes. Follow me?"

"No," I admitted.

"Well, just accept that I'm from another world. Now, in that world, I'm a magician just like Garkin. We had an exchange program going where we could summon each other across the barrier to impress our respective apprentices."

"I thought you said you were a demon," I said suspiciously.

"I *am*! Look, kid. In my world, you'd be a demon, but at the current moment I'm in yours, so I'm a demon."

"I thought you said you were a magician."

"I don't believe this!" The demon made his angry appeal to the heavens. "I'm standing here arguing with some twerp of an apprentice. . . . Look, kid."

He fixed me with his gaze again.

"Let me try it this way. Are you going to shake my hand, or am I going to rip your heart out?"

Since he put it that way . . . I mean, for a minute there, when he lost his temper and started shouting, he sounded just like Garkin. It gave credibility to his claim of friendship with my ex-teacher. I took his extended hand and shook it cautiously.

"I'm. . . . My name is Skeeve."

His grip was cold, but firm. So firm in fact that I found it impossible to reclaim my hand as rapidly as I would have liked.

"Pleased ta meetcha, kid. I'm Aahz."

"Oz?"

"No relation."

"No relation to what?" I asked, but he was examining the room again.

"Well, there's certainly nothing here to arouse the

greedy side of his fellow beings. Early primitive, enduring, but not particularly sought after."

"We like it," I said, rather stiffly. Now that I was over being scared, I didn't like the sneer in his voice. The hut wasn't much and I certainly wasn't overly fond of it, but I resented his criticism.

"Don't get your back up, kid." Aahz said easily. "I'm looking for a motive, that's all."

"Motive?"

"A reason for someone to off old Garkin. I'm not big on vengeance, but he was a drinking buddy of mine and it's got my curiosity up."

He broke off his inspection of the room to address me directly.

"How about you, kid? Can you think of anything? Any milkmaids he's seduced or farmers he's cheated? You've got an interest in this too, you know. You might be the next target."

"But the guy who did it is dead." I gestured to the charred lump by the door. "Doesn't that finish it?"

"Wake up, kid. Didn't you see the gold cloak? That was a professional assassin. Somebody hired him, and that somebody would hire another one."

A chill ran down my spine. I hadn't really thought of that. I began to search my memory for a clue.

"Well . . . he said Isstvan sent him."

"What's an Isstvan?"

"I don't . . . wait a minute. What do you mean, I might be the next target?"

"Neat, huh?" Aahz was holding up the gold cloak. "Lined, and completely reversible. Always wondered how come no one noticed them until they were ready to pounce."

"Aahz. . . ."

"Hmmm? Oh, didn't mean to scare you. It's just if someone's declared open season on magicians in general or Garkin specifically, you might have some. . . . Hello, what's this?"

"What's what?" I asked, trying to get a look at what he had found.

"This," he said, holding his prize aloft. "It seems I'm not the only demon about."

It was a head, apparently the assassin's. It was badly charred, with bone showing in several places. My natural revulsion at the sight was compounded by several obvious features. The chin and ears of the head were unnaturally pointed, and there were two short, blunt, horns protruding from the forehead.

"A devil!" I exclaimed in horror.

"A what? Oh, a Deveel. No, it's not from Deva, it's from Imper. An Imp. Didn't Garkin teach you anything?"

"Come again?" I asked, but Aahz was busy scowling at the head.

"The question is, who would be crass enough to hire an Imp for an assassin? The only one I can think of is Isstvan, but that's impossible."

"But that's who did it. Don't you remember? I told you. . . ."

"I thought you said 'Isstvan.' "

"I did! Wait a minute. What did you say?"

"I said Isstvan. Can't you tell the difference?"

"No," I admitted.

"Hmmm . . . must be too subtle for the human ear to detect. Oh, well. No matter. This changes everything. If Isstvan is up to his old tricks there's no time to lose. Hey! Wait a minute. What's this?"

"It's a crossbow," I observed.

"With heat-seeking armor-piercing quarrels? Is that the norm in this world?"

"Heat-seeking. . . ."

"Never mind, kid. I didn't think so. Well, that tears it. I'd better check this out quick."

He began to stride into the pentagram. I suddenly realized he was preparing to leave.

"Hey! Wait a minute! What's going on?"

"It would take too long to explain, kid. Maybe I'll see you again sometime."

"But you said I might be a target!"

"Yeah, well, that's the way it crumbles. Tell ya what.

Start running and maybe they won't find you until it's over."

My head was awhirl. Things were happening far too fast for clear thought. I still didn't know what or who the demon was or if I should trust him, but I did know one thing. He was the nearest thing to an ally I had in a situation where I was clearly outclassed.

"Couldn't you help me?"

"No time. I've got to move."

"Couldn't I come with you?"

"You'd just get in the way, maybe even get me killed."

"But without you, I'll be killed!"

I was getting desperate, but Aahz was unimpressed.

"Probably not. Tell ya what, kid. I've really got to get going, but just to show you I think you'll survive, I'll show you a little trick you might use sometime. You see all this crud Garkin used to bring me across the barrier? Well, it's not necessary. Watch close and I'll show you how we do it when our apprentices aren't watching."

I wanted to shout, to make him stop and listen to me, but he had already started. He spread his arms at shoulder height, looked heavenward, took a deep breath, then clapped his hands.

Nothing happened.

Chapter Three:

"The only thing more reliable than magik is one's friends!"

—MACBETH

AAHZ scowled and repeated the gesture, a bit quicker this time.

The scene remained unchanged.

I decided something was wrong.

"Is something wrong?" I asked politely.

"You'd better believe there's something wrong," Aahz snarled. "It's not working."

"Are you sure you're doing it right?"

"Yes, I'm sure I'm doing it right, just like I've been sure the last fifty times I did it!"

He was starting to sound annoyed.

"Can you. . . ."

"Look, kid. If I knew what was wrong, I'd have fixed it already. Now, just shut up and let me think!"

He sank down to sit cross-legged in the center of the pentagram where he began sketching vague patterns in the floor as he mumbled darkly to himself. I wasn't sure if he was trying some alternate incantation or was simply thinking hard, but decided it would be unwise to ask. Instead, I used the time to organize my scrambled thoughts.

I still wasn't sure if Aahz was a threat to me or if he was my only possible salvation from a greater threat. I mean, by this time I was pretty sure he was kidding about ripping my heart out, but that's the sort of thing one wants to be very sure of. One thing I had learned for certain, there was more to this magik stuff than floating feathers around.

"That's got to be it!"

Aahz was on his feet again, glaring at Garkin's body.

"That ill-begot son of a wombat!"

"What's a wombat?" I asked, then immediately wished I hadn't. The mental image that sprang into my mind was so horrifying I was sure I didn't want details. I needn't have worried. Aahz was not about to take time to answer me.

"Well, it's a pretty crummy joke. That's all I have to say."

"Um. . . . What are you talking about, Aahz?"

"I'm talking about Garkin! He did this to me. If I thought it would go this far, I would have turned him into a goat-fish when I had the chance."

"Aahz. . . . I still don't. . . ."

I stopped. He had ceased his ranting and was looking at me. I shrank back reflexively before I recognized the snarl as his smile. I liked it better when he was raving.

"I'm sorry, Skeeve," he purred. "I guess I haven't been very clear."

I was growing more uneasy by the minute. I wasn't used to having people, much less demons, being nice to me.

"Um. . . . That's okay. I was just wondering. . . ."

"You see, the situation is this. Garkin and I have been . . . playing little jokes on each other for some time now. It started one time when we were drinking and he stiffed me with the bill. Well, the next time I summoned him, I brought him in over a lake and he had to do his demon act armpit deep in water. He got even by . . . well, I won't bore you with details, but we've gotten in the habit of putting each other in awkward or embarrassing situations. It's really very childish, but quite harmless. But this time. . . ." Aahz's eyes started to narrow, "But this time the old frog-kisser's gone too . . . I mean, it seems to have gotten a little out of hand. Don't you agree?"

He bared his fangs at me again in a smile. I wanted very badly to agree with him, but I didn't have the foggiest idea what he was talking about.

"You still haven't told me what's wrong."

"What's wrong is that stinking slime-monger took away my powers!" he roared, forgetting his composure. "I'm blocked! I can't do a flaming thing unless he removes his stupid prankish spell and he can't 'cause he's dead! Now do you understand me, fly-bait?"

I made up my mind. Savior or not, I'd rather he went back where he came from.

"Well, if there was anything I could do. . . ."

"There is, Skeeve, my boy." Aahz was suddenly all purrs and teeth again. "All you have to do is fire up the old cauldron or whatever and remove this spell. Then we can each go our separate ways and. . . ."

"I can't do that."

"Okay, kid," his smile was a little more forced. "I'll stick around until you're on your feet. I mean, what are friends for?"

"That's not it."

"What do you want? Blood?" Aahz was no longer smiling. "If you're trying to hold me up, I'll. . . ."

"You don't understand!" I interrupted desperately. "I can't do it because I can't do it! I don't know how!"

That stopped him.

"Hmm. That could be a problem. Well, tell you what. Instead of pulling the spell here, what say you just pop me back to my own dimension and I'll get someone there to take it off."

"I can't do that either. Remember, I told you I'd never even heard of. . . ."

"Well, what *can* you do?!"

"I can levitate objects . . . well, small objects."

"And. . . ." he encouraged.

"And . . . um . . . I can light a candle."

"Light a candle?"

"Well . . . almost."

Aahz sank heavily into a chair and hid his face in his hands for several minutes. I waited for him to think of something.

"Kid, have you got anything in this dump to drink?" he asked finally.

"I'll get you some water."

"I said something to drink, not something to wash in!"

"Oh. Yessir!"

I hastened to bring him a goblet of wine from the small keg Garkin kept, hoping he wouldn't notice the vessel wasn't particularly clean.

"What will this do? Will it help you put your powers back?"

"No. But it might make me feel a little better." He tossed the wine down in one swallow, and studied the goblet disdainfully. "Is this the biggest container you've got?"

I cast about the room desperately, but Aahz was way ahead of me.

He rose, strode into the pentagram, and picked up the brazier. I knew from past experience it was deceptively heavy, but he carried it to the keg as if it were weightless. Not bothering to empty out Garkin's concoction, he filled it to the brim and took a deep draught.

"Aah! That's better." He sighed.

I felt a little queasy.

"Well, kid," he said, sweeping me with an appraising stare, "it looks like we're stuck with each other. The set-up isn't ideal, but it's what we've got. Time to bite the bullet and play the cards we're dealt. You do know what cards are, don't you?"

"Of course," I said, slightly wounded.

"Good."

"What's a bullet?"

Aahz closed his eyes as if struggling against some inner turmoil.

"Kid," he said at last, "there's a good chance this partnership is going to drive one of us crazy. I would guess it will be me unless you can knock off the dum-dum questions every other sentence."

"But I can't understand half of what you're saying."

"Hmm. Tell ya what. Try to save up the questions and ask me all at one time once a day. Okay?"

"I'll try."

"Right. Now here's the situation as I see it. If Isstvan is hiring Imps for assassins. . . ."

"What's an Imp?"

"Kid, will you give me a break?"

"I'm sorry, Aahz. Keep going."

"Right. Well . . . umm. . . . It's happening!" he made his appeal to the heavens. "I can't remember what I was saying!"

"Imps," I prompted.

"Oh! Right. Well, if he's hiring Imps and arming them with non-spec weapons, it can only mean he's up to his old tricks. Now since I don't have my powers, I can't get out of here to sound the alarm. That's where you come in, kid. . . . Kid?"

He was looking at me expectantly. I found I could contain my misery no longer.

"I'm sorry, Aahz," I said in a small, pitiful voice I hardly recognized as my own. "I don't understand a single thing you've said."

I suddenly realized I was about to cry, and turned away hurriedly so he wouldn't see. I sat there, with tears trickling down my cheeks, alternately fighting the urge to wipe them away and wondering why I was concerned over whether or not a demon saw me crying. I don't know how long I stayed that way, but I was brought back to reality by a gentle hand on my shoulder, a cold, gentle hand.

"Hey, kid. Don't beat on yourself," Aahz's voice was surprisingly sympathetic. "It's not your fault if Garkin was tight with his secrets. Nobody expects you to have learned something you were never taught, so there's no reason you should expect it either.''

''I just feel so stupid,'' I said, not turning. ''I'm not used to feeling stupid.''

''You aren't stupid, kid. That much I know. Garkin wouldn't have taken you for an apprentice if you were stupid. If anybody here's stupid, it's me. I got so carried away with the situation, I forgot myself and tried talking to an apprentice as if he were a full-blown magician. Now that's stupid.''

I still couldn't bring myself to respond.

''Heck, kid.'' He gave my shoulder a gentle shake. ''Right now you can do more magik than I can.''

''But you know more.''

''But I can't use it. You know, kid, that gives me an idea. With old Garkin dead there, you're kind of cut off. What say you sign on as my apprentice for a while. We'll take it from the top with me teaching you as if you were a new student who didn't know a thing. We'll take it step by step from the beginning. What da ya say?''

In spite of my gloom I felt my spirits lift. Like he said, I'm not stupid. I could recognize a golden opportunity when I saw one.

''Gee, that sounds great, Aahz.''

''Then it's a deal?''

''It's a deal,'' I answered and stuck out my hand.

''What's that?'' he snarled. ''Isn't my word good enough for you?''

''But you said. . . .''

''That's right. You're my apprentice now, and I don't go around shaking apprentices' hands.''

I withdrew my hand. It occurred to me this alliance might not be all roses and song.

''Now as I was saying, here's what we've got to do about the current situation. . . .''

''But I haven't had any lessons yet!''

''That's right. Here's your first lesson. When a crisis shapes up, you don't waste energy wishing for information or skills you haven't got. You dig in and handle it as best you can with what you've got. Now shut up while I fill you in on the situation . . . apprentice.''

I shut up and listened. He studied me for a moment, then gave a small satisfied nod, took another gulp from the brazier and began.

"Now, you have a vague idea about other dimensions because I told you about them earlier. You also have firsthand experience that magicians can open passages in the barriers between those dimensions. Well, different magicians use that power in different ways. Some of them, like Garkin, only use it to impress the yokels; summon a demon, visions of other worlds, that kind of schtick. But there are others whose motives are not so pure."

He paused to take another gulp of wine. Surprisingly, I felt no urge to interrupt with questions.

"Technology in different dimensions has progressed at different rates, as has magik. Some magicians use this to their own advantage. They aren't showmen, they're smugglers, buying and selling technology across the barriers for profit and power. Most of the inventors in any dimension are actually closet magicians."

I must have frowned without realizing it, but Aahz noted it and acknowledged it with a wink and a smirk.

"I know what you're thinking, Skeeve. It all sounds a little dishonest and unscrupulous. Actually, they're a fairly ethical bunch. There's a set of unwritten rules called the Smugglers Code they adhere to pretty closely."

"Smugglers Code?" I asked, forgetting myself for a moment. Aahz didn't seem to mind this time.

"It's like the Mercenaries Code, but less violent and more profitable. Anyway, as an example, one item in that code states you cannot bring an 'invention' into a dimension that is too far in advance of that dimension's technology, like bringing guided missiles into a longbow culture or lasers into a flint and powder era."

I kept my silence with great difficulty.

"As I've said, most magicians adhere to the code fairly closely, but once in a while a bad one crops up. That brings us to Isstvan."

I got a sudden chill at the sound of that name. Maybe

there *was* something different in the way Aahz pronounced it.

"Some say Isstvan isn't playing with a full deck. I think he's been playing with his wand too much. But whatever the reason, somewhere he's gotten it into his head he wants to rule the dimensions, all of them. He's tried it before, but we got wind of it in time and a bunch of us teamed up to teach him a lesson in manners. As a matter of fact, that's when I first met Garkin there."

He gestured with the brazier and slopped a bit of wine on the floor. I began to doubt his sobriety, but his voice seemed steady enough as he continued.

"I thought he had given the thing up after his last drubbing. We even gave him a few souvenirs to be sure he didn't forget. Then this thing pops up. If he's hiring cross-dimension help and arming them with advance technology weapons, he's probably trying to do it again."

"Do what?"

"I just told you. Take over the dimensions."

"I know, but how? I mean, how does what he does in this dimension help him rule the others?"

"Oh, that. Well, each dimension has a certain amount of power that can be channeled or converted into magik. Different dimensions have different amounts, and each dimension's power is divided up or shared by the magicians of that dimension. If he can succeed in controlling or killing the other magicians in this dimension, he can use its entire magical energy to attack another dimension. If he succeeds in winning there, he has the power from two dimensions to attack a third, and so on. As you can see, the longer he keeps his plot moving, the stronger he gets and the harder he'll be to stop."

"I understand now," I said, genuinely pleased and enthusiastic.

"Good. Then you understand why we've got to stop him."

I stopped being pleased and enthusiastic.

"We? You mean us? You and me?"

"I know it's not much of a force, kid, but like I said, it's all we've got."

"I think I'd like a little of that wine now."

"None of that, kid. You're in training now. You're going to need all the practice time you can get if we're going to stop Isstvan. Bonkers or not, he's no slouch when it comes to magik."

"Aahz," I said slowly, not looking up. "Tell me the truth. Do you think there's a chance you can teach me enough magik that we'll have a chance of stopping him?"

"Of course, kid. I wouldn't even try if we didn't have a chance. Trust me."

I wasn't convinced, and from the sound of his voice, neither was he.

Chapter Four:

"Careful planning is the key to safe and swift travel."

—ULYSSES

"HMMM . . . Well, it's not a tailored jump-suit, but it will have to do."

We had been trying to outfit Aahz in a set of clothes and he was surveying the results in a small dark mirror we had found, turning it this way and that to catch his reflection piecemeal.

"Maybe if we could find some other color than this terrible brown."

"That's all we've got."

"Are you sure?"

"Positive. I have two shirts, both brown. You're wearing one, and I'm wearing the other."

"Hmmm. . . ." he said, studying me carefully. "Maybe I would look better in the lighter brown. Oh, well, we can argue that out later."

I was curious as to his attention to his appearance. I mean, he couldn't be planning on meeting anyone. The sight of a green, scaly demon would upset most of the locals no matter what he was wearing. For the time being, however, I deemed it wisest to keep quiet and humor him in his efforts.

Actually, the clothes fit him fairly well. The shirt was a bit short in the sleeves due to the length of his arms, but not too because I was taller than him, which made up for most of the difference. We had had to cut off some of the trouser legs to cover for his shorter legs, but they, like the body of the shirt, were not too tight. I had made the clothes myself originally, and they tended to be a bit baggy, or at least they were on me. Tailoring is not my forte.

He was also wearing Garkin's boots, which fitted him surprisingly well. I had raised minor protest at this, until he pointed out Garkin had no further use for them but we did. Pragmatism, he called it. Situational ethics. He said it would come in handy if I was serious about becoming a magician.

"Hey, kid!" Aahz's voice interrupted my thoughts. He seemed to be occupied rummaging through the various chests and cupboards of the hut. "Don't you have anything here in the way of weapons?"

"Weapons?"

"Yeah, you know, the things that killed old Garkin there. Swords, knives, bows, stuff like that."

"I know what they are. I just wasn't expecting you to be interested in them, that's all."

"Why not?"

"Well . . . I thought you said you were a magician."

"We aren't going to go through *that* again, are we, kid? Besides, what's that got to do with weapons?"

"It's just that I've never known a magician who used weapons other than his powers."

"Really? How many magicians have you known?"

"One," I admitted.

"Terrific. Look, kid, if old Garkin didn't want to use weapons, that's his problem. Me, I want some. If you'll notice, Garkin is dead."

It was hard to argue with logic like that.

"Besides," he continued, "do you really want to take on Isstvan and his pack with nothing but your magik and my agility going for us?"

"I'll help you look."

We went to work rummaging for weapons, but aside from the crossbow that had killed Garkin, we didn't find much. One of the chests yielded a sword with a jewel-encrusted handle, and we discovered two knives, one white handled and one black handled, on Garkin's workbench. Aside from those, there was nothing even remotely resembling a fighting utensil in the hut. Aahz was not overjoyed.

"I don't believe this. A sword with a cruddy blade, bad balance, and phony jewels in the handle and two knives that haven't been sharpened since they were made. Anybody who keeps weapons like this should be skewered."

"He was."

"True enough. Well, if that's all we've got, that's what we'll have to use."

He slung the sword on his hip and tucked the white handled knife into his belt. I thought he would give me the other knife, but instead he stooped down and secured it in his boot.

"Don't I get one?"

"Can you use it?"

"Well. . . ."

He resumed his task. I had a small knife I used to skin small game tucked in my own belt inside my shirt. Even to my inexperienced eye it was of better quality than the two Aahz had just appropriated. I decided not to bring it to his attention.

"Okay, kid. Where did the old man keep his money?"

I showed him. One of the stones in the fireplace was loose and there was a small leather pouch hidden behind it. He peered at the coins suspiciously as they poured into his palm.

"Check me on this, kid. Copper and silver aren't worth much in this dimension, right?"

"Well, silver's sorta valuable, but it's not worth as much as gold."

"Then what's with this chicken-feed? Where's the real money?"

"We never really had much."

"Come off it . . . I haven't met a magician yet who didn't have a bundle socked away. Just because he never spent any of it doesn't mean he doesn't have it. Now think. Haven't you ever seen anything around that was gold or had gems?"

"Well, there are a few items, but they're protected by curses."

"Kid, think for a minute. If you were a doddering old wreck who couldn't fight your way out of a paper bag, how would you protect your treasures?"

"I don't know."

"Terrific. I'll explain while we gather it up."

In short order we had a modest heap of loot on the table, most of it items I had long held in awe. There was a gold statue of a man with the head of a lion, the Three Pearls of Kraul, a gold pendant in the shape of the sun with three of its rays missing, and a ring with a large jewel we took from Garkin's hand. Aahz held up the sun pendant.

"Now this is an example of what I mean. I suppose there's a story about what happened to the missing three rays?"

"Well," I began, "there was a lost tribe that worshipped a huge snake toad. . . ."

"Skip it. It's an old dodge. What you do is take your gold to a craftsman and have him fashion it into something with a lot of small out-juttings like fingers or arms or . . ." He held up the pendant. ". . . rays of sun. It gives you the best of two worlds.

"First, you have something mystical and supernatural, add a ghost story and no one will dare to touch it. Second, it has the advantage that if you need a little ready cash, you just break off a ray or an arm and sell it for the value of the gold. Instead of losing value, the price of the remaining item increases because of its mystical history, the strange circumstances under which it was torn asunder, purely fictional, of course."

Strangely enough, I was not surprised. I was beginning to wonder if anything Garkin had told me was true.

"Then none of these things have any real magical powers or curses?"

"Now, I didn't say that. Occasionally, you stumble across a real item, but they're usually few and far between."

"But how can you tell the real thing from a fake?"

"I take it that Garkin didn't teach you to see auras. Well, that figures. Probably was afraid you'd take his treasure and run. Okay, kid. Time for your first lesson. Have you ever daydreamed? You know, just stared at something and let your mind wander?"

I nodded.

"Okay, here's what I want you to do. Scoot down in your chair until your head is almost level with the table. That's right. Comfortable? Fine. Now I want you to look across the table at the wall. Don't focus on it, just stare at it and let your mind wander."

I did as he said. It was hard not focusing on a specific point, so I set my mind to wandering. What to think about? Well, what was I thinking about when the candle almost lit. Oh yes. I am Skeeve. I am powerful and my power is growing daily. I smiled to myself. With the demon's aid, I would soon become a knowledgeable sorcerer. And that would just be the start. After that. . . .

"Hey!" I said, sitting upright.

"What did you see?"

"It was . . . well, nothing, I guess."

"Don't give me a hard time, kid. What did you see?"

"Well, for a second there I thought I saw sort of a red glow around the ring, but when I looked at it squarely, it disappeared."

"The ring, eh? It figures. Well, that's it. The rest of the stuff should be okay."

He scraped the rest of the loot into a sack, leaving the ring on the table.

"What was it?"

"What? Oh, what you saw? That was an aura. Most people have them. Some places do, but it's a sure test to check if an item is truly magical. I'd be willing to bet that the ring is what old Garkin used to fry the assassin."

"Aren't we going to take it with us?"

"Do you know how to control it?"

"Well. . . .no."

"Neither do I. The last thing we need is to carry around a ring that shoots fire. Particularly if we don't know how to activate it. Leave it. Maybe the others will find it and turn it on themselves."

He tucked the sack into his waistband.

"What others?" I prompted.

"Hmmm? Oh, the other assassins."

"What other assassins?" I was trying to be calm, but I was slipping.

"That's right. This is the first time you've tangled with them, isn't it? I would have thought Garkin. . . ."

"Aahz, could you just tell me?"

"Oh! Sure, kid. Assassins never work alone. That's why they never miss. They work in groups of two to eight. There's probably a back-up team around somewhere. Realizing Isstvan's respect for Garkin, I'd guess he wouldn't send less than six out on an assignment like this, maybe even two teams."

"You mean all this time you've been fooling around with clothes and swords, there's been more assassins on the way?"

"Relax, kid. That's the back-up team. They'll be waiting a ways off and won't move until tomorrow at the earliest. It's professional courtesy. They want to give this bozo room to maneuver. Besides, it's tradition that the assassin who actually does the deed gets first pick of any random booty lying around before the others show up to take even shares. Everyone does it, but it's considered polite to not notice some of the loot has been pocketed before the official split."

"How do you know so much about assassins, Aahz?"

"Went with one for a while . . . lovely lass, but she couldn't keep her mouth shut, even in bed. Sometimes I wonder if any profession really guards its secrets as closely as they claim.''

"What happened?"

"With what?"

"With your assassin?"

"None of your business, kid." Aahz was suddenly brusque again. "We've got work to do."

"What are we going to do?"

"Well, first we bury the Imp. Maybe it will throw the others off our trail. With any luck, they'll think he grabbed all the loot and disappeared. It wouldn't be the first time."

"No, I mean after that. We're getting ready to travel, but where are we going?"

"Kid, sometimes you worry me. That isn't even magik. It's common sense military action. First, we find Isstvan. Second, we appraise his strength. Third, we make our plans, and fourth, we execute them, and hopefully him."

"Um . . . Aahz, could we back up to one for a minute? Where are we going to find Isstvan?"

That stopped him.

"Don't you know where he is?"

"I never even heard his name before today."

We sat in silence staring at each other for a long time.

Chapter Five:

"Only constant and conscientious practice in the Martial Arts will ensure a long and happy life."

—B. LEE

"I THINK I've got it figured out, kid."

As Aahz spoke, he paused in honing his sword to inspect the edge. Ever since our trek began he had seized every opportunity to work on his weapons. Even when we simply paused to rest by a stream he busied himself working their edges or adjusting their balance. I felt I had learned more about weapons in the last week just watching him tinker than I had in my entire previous life.

"Figured what out?"

"Why people in this world are trained in weapons or magik, but not both!"

"How's that?"

"Well, two reasons I can see just offhand. First off, it's a matter of conditioning. Reflexes. You'll react the way you're trained. If you've been trained with weapons, you'll react to crisis with a weapon. If you're trained in magik, you'll react with magik. The problem is, if you're trained both ways, you'll hesitate, trying to make up your mind which to use, and probably get clobbered in the process. So to keep things simple, Garkin

only trained you in magik. It's probably all he had been
trained in himself.''

I thought about it.

"That makes sense. What's the other reason?"

He grinned at me.

"Learning curve. If what you told me about life ex-
pectancy in this world is even vaguely accurate, and if
you're any example of how fast people in this world
learn, you only have time to learn one or the other.''

"I think I prefer the first explanation.''

He chortled to himself and went back to sharpening
his sword.

Once his needling would have bothered me, but now I
took it in stride. It seemed to be his habit to be critical of
everything in our world, and me in particular. After a
week of constant exposure to him, the only way I would
worry is if he stopped complaining.

Actually I was quite pleased with my progress in
magik. Under Aahz's tutelage, my powers were growing
daily. One of the most valuable lessons I had learned
was to draw strength directly from the earth. It was
a matter of envisioning energy as a tangible force, like
water, and drawing new energy up one leg and into my
mind while releasing exhausted energy down the other
leg and back into the earth. Already, I could completely
recharge myself even after a hard day's walking just by
standing motionless with my eyes closed for several
minutes and effecting this energy exchange. Aahz, as
always, was unimpressed. According to him, I should
have been able to do the energy exchange while we were
walking, but I didn't let his grumbling dampen my enthusiasm. I was learning, and at a faster pace than I had
dreamed possible.

"Hey, kid. Fetch me a piece of wood, will you?''

I smiled to myself and looked around. About ten feet
away was a small branch of deadwood about two feet
long. I leisurely stretched out a finger and it took flight,
floating gently across the clearing to hover in the air in
front of Aahz.

"Not bad, kid,'' he acknowledged. Then his sword

flashed out, cutting the branch into two pieces which dropped to the ground. He picked up one of the pieces and inspected the cut.

"Hmmm . . . there may be hope for this sword yet. Why did you let them fall?"

This last was directed at me.

"I don't know. I guess you startled me when you swung the sword."

"Oh, really?"

Suddenly he threw the stick at me. I yelped and tried to duck out of the way, but it bounced painfully off my shoulder.

"Hey! What was that for?"

"Call it an object lesson. You know you can control the stick because you just did it when you fetched it for me. So why did you duck out of the way? Why not just stop it with your magik?"

"I guess it never occurred to me. You didn't give me much time to think."

"Okay, so think! This time you know it's coming."

He picked up the second piece of wood and waited, grinning evilly, which with pointed teeth is easy. I ignored him, letting my mind settle; then I nodded that I was ready.

The stick struck me squarely in the chest.

"Ow!!" I commented.

"And there, my young friend, is the difference between classroom and field. Classroom is fine to let you know that things can be done and that you can do them, but in actual practice you will never be allowed the luxury of leisurely gathering your power, and seldom will you have a stationary target."

"Say, uh, Aahz. If you're really trying to build up my self-confidence, how come you always cut my legs out from under me every time I start thinking I'm getting someplace?"

He stood up, sheathing his sword.

"Self-confidence is a wonderful thing, kid, but not if it isn't justified. Someday we'll be staking one or both of our lives on your abilities, and it won't do us any good if you've been kidding yourself along. Now let's get down to work!''

"Um . . . have we got the time?"

"Relax, kid. Imps are tenacious, but they travel slow.''

Our strategy upon leaving the hut had been simple. Lacking a specific direction for our search, we would trace the force lines of the world until we either found Isstvan or located another magician who would be able to steer us to him.

One might ask what force lines are. I did. Force lines, as Aahz explained them, are those paths of a world along which its energies flow most freely. In many ways, they are not unlike magnetic lines.

One might ask what magnetic lines are. I did. I will not quote Aahz's answer to that, but it was not information.

Anyway, force lines are a magician's ally and enemy. Those who would tap the energies of those lines usually set up residence on or near one of those lines. This makes it easier for them to draw upon the energies. It also makes it easier for their enemies to find them.

It was Aahz's theory that searching the force lines was how Garkin was located. It was therefore logical that we should be able to find Isstvan the same way.

Of course, I knew nothing of force lines or how to follow them, at least until Aahz taught me. It was not a difficult technique, which was fortunate as I had my hands full trying to absorb all the other lessons Aahz was deluging me with.

One simply closes one's eyes and relaxes, trying to envision a two-pointed spear in glowing yellows and reds suspended in midair. The intensity of the glow indicates the nearness to a force line; the direction of the points shows the flow of energies. Rather like the needle of a compass, whatever that is.

Once we had determined that Garkin had set up shop directly on a force line, as Aahz had suspected, and established direction of the flow of energies, we had another problem. Which way did we follow it?

The decision was doubly important as, if Aahz was correct, there would be a team of Imp assassins waiting in one direction, very probably in the direction we wanted to go.

We solved the problem by traveling one day's journey perpendicular to the force line, then for two days parallel to the line in our chosen direction, then returning to the line before continuing our journey. We hoped this would bypass the assassins entirely.

It worked, and it didn't.

It worked in that we didn't walk into an ambush. It didn't work in that now it seemed they were on our trail, though whether they were actually tracking us or merely following the force line back to Isstvan was unknown.

"I keep telling you, kid," Aahz insisted, "it's a good sign. It means we've chosen the right direction, and that we'll reach Isstvan ahead of his assassins' report."

"What if we're heading in the wrong direction?" I argued. "What if they're really following us? How long do we travel in this direction before we give up and admit it?"

"How long do you figure it will take for you to learn enough magik to stand up to a pack of Imp assassins armed with off-dimension weapons?"

"Let's get to work," I said firmly.

He looked around, and pointed to a gnarled fruit tree strewn round with windfalls across the clearing.

"Okay. Here's what I want you to do. Stare at the sky or contemplate your navel or something. Then when I give the word, use your power to grab one of those fruits and toss it to me."

I don't know how many hours we spent on that drill. It's more difficult than it sounds, mustering one's powers from a standing start. Just when I thought I had it down pat, Aahz switched tactics. He would engage in a conversation, deliberately leading me on, then would interrupt me in mid-sentence with his signal. Needless to say, I failed miserably.

"Relax, kid. Look, try it this way. Instead of mustering your power from scratch each time, create a small space inside yourself and store up some energy there. Just habitually keep that reserve squirreled away and ready to cover for you while you get set to level your big guns.''

"What's a gun?''

"Never mind. Just build that reserve and we'll try it again.''

With this extra bit of advice at my disposal the drill went noticeably better. Finally Aahz broke off the practice session and put me to work helping him with his knife practice. Actually I rather enjoyed this task. It entailed my using my powers to levitate one of the fruits and send it flying around the clearing until Aahz pegged a knife into it. As an extra touch of finesse, I would then extract the knife and float it back to him for another try. The exercise was monotonous, but I never tired of it. It seemed almost supernatural the way the shimmering, somersaulting sliver of steel would dart out to intercept the fruit as Aahz practiced first overhand, then underhand, now backhand.

"Stop it, Skeeve!''

Aahz's shout jolted me out of my reverie. Without thinking, I reached out with my mind and . . . and the knife stopped in midair! I blinked, but held it there, floating a foot from the fruit which also hung suspended in place.

"Hel-lo! That's the stuff, Skeeve! Now there's something to have confidence in!''

"I did it!'' I said, disbelieving my own eyes.

"You sure did! That little piece of magik will save your life someday.''

Out of habit, I floated the knife back to him. He plucked it from the air and started to tuck it in his belt, then halted, cocking his head to one side.

"In the nick of time, too. Someone's coming.''

"How can you tell?''

"Nothing special. My hearing's a bit better than yours is all. Don't panic. It isn't the Imps. Hooved beast from the sound of it. No wild animal moves in that straight a line, or that obviously.''

"What did you mean, 'in the nick of time'? Aren't we going to hide?"

"Not this time." He grinned at me. "You're developing fast. It's about time you learned a new spell. We have a few days before whoever it is gets here."

"Days?"

Aahz was adapting rapidly to our dimension, but units of time still gave him trouble.

"Run through those time measurements again," he grumbled.

"In seconds, minutes, hours. . . ."

"Minutes! We've got a few minutes."

"Minutes! I can't learn a new spell in a few minutes!"

"Sure you can. This one's easy. All you've got to do is disguise my features to look like a man."

"How do I do that?"

"The same way you do everything else, with your mind. First, close your eyes . . . close 'em . . . okay, now picture another face. . . ."

All I could think of was Garkin, so I pictured the two faces side by side.

"Now move the new face over mine . . . and melt away or build up the necessary features. Like clay . . . just keep that in the back of your mind and open your eyes."

I looked, and was disappointed.

"It didn't work!"

"Sure it did."

He was looking in the dark mirror which he had fished from his belt pouch.

"But you haven't changed!"

"Yes I have. You can't see it because you cast the spell. It's an illusion, and since your mind knows the truth, it isn't fooled, but anyone else will be. Garkin, huh? Well, it'll do for now."

His identification of the new face took me aback.

"You can really see Garkin's face?"

"Sure, want to look?"

He offered the mirror and grinned. It was a bad joke. One of the first things we discovered about his dubious status in this world was that while he could see himself in mirrors, nobody from our world could. At least I couldn't.

I could now hear the sounds of the rider coming.

"Aahz, are you sure. . . ."

"Trust me, kid. There's nothing to worry about."

I was worried. The rider was in view now. He was a tall muscular man with the look of a warrior about him. This was reinforced by the massive war unicorn he was riding, laden with weapons and armor.

"Hey, Aahz. Shouldn't we. . . ."

"Relax, kid. Watch this."

He stepped forward, raising his arm.

"Hello, stranger! How far to the next town?"

The man veered his mount toward us. He half raised his arm in greeting, then suddenly stiffened. Heaving forward, he squinted at Aahz, then drew back in terror.

"By the Gods! A demon!"

Chapter Six:

"Attention to detail is the watchword for gleaning information from an unsuspecting witness."

—INSP. CLOUSEAU

THE warrior's terror did not immobilize him long. In fact, it didn't immobilize him at all! No sooner did he make his discovery than he took action. Strangely enough, the action was to lean back in his saddle and begin rummaging frantically through one of his saddle-bags, a precarious position at best.

Apparently I was not the only one to notice the instability of his pose. Aahz sprang forward with a yell, waving his arms in the unicorn's face. Being a reasonable creature, the unicorn reared and bolted, dumping the warrior on his head.

"By the Gods!" he bellowed, trying to untangle himself from the ungraceful heap of arms and weapons. "I've killed men for less!"

I decided that if his threat was to be avoided, I should take a personal hand in the matter. Reaching out with my mind, I seized a fist-sized rock and propelled it forcefully against his unhelmeted brow. The man went down like a pole-axed steer.

For a long moment Aahz and I considered the fallen man, catching our breath.

" 'Relax, Skeeve! This'll be easy, Skeeve! Trust me, Skeeve.' Boy, Aahz, when you miss a call you don't do it small, do you?"

"Shut up, kid!"

He was rummaging through his pouch again.

"I don't want to shut up, I want to know what happened to the 'foolproof' spell you taught me."

"I was kind of wondering that myself." He had produced the mirror again and was peering into it. "Tell you what, kid. Check his aura and watch for anything unusual."

" 'Shut up, kid! Check his aura, kid!' You'd think I was some kind of. . . . Hey!"

"What is it?"

"His aura! It's a sort of a reddish yellow except there's a blue patch on his chest."

"I thought so!!" Aahz was across the clearing in a bound, crouching at the fallen man like a beast of prey.

"Look at this!!"

On a thong around the man's neck was a crude silver charm depicting a salamander with one eye in the center of its forehead.

"What is it?"

"I'm not sure, but I've got a hunch. Now play along with me on this. I want you to remove the shape warp spell."

"What spell?"

"C'mon, kid, wake up! The spell that's changing my face."

"That's what I mean. What spell?"

"Now look, kid! Don't give me a lot of back talk. Just do it! He'll be waking up soon."

With a sigh I shut my eyes and set about the seemingly pointless task. It was easier this time, imagining Garkin's face, then melting away the features until Aahz's face was leering at me in my mind's eye. I opened my eyes and looked at Aahz. He looked like Aahz. Terrific.

"Now what?"

As if in answer, the warrior groaned and sat up. He shook his head as if to clear it and opened his eyes. His gaze fell on Aahz, whereupon he blinked, looked again, and reached for his sword, only to find it missing. Also missing were his dagger and hand-axe. Apparently Aahz had not been idle while I was removing the spell.

Aahz spoke first.

"Relax, stranger. Things are not as they seem."

The man sprang to his feet and struck a fighting stance, fists clenched.

"Beware, demon!" he intoned hollowly. "I am not without defenses."

"Oh yeah? Name three. But like I say, relax. First of all, I'm not a demon."

"Know you, demon, that this charm enables me to look through any spells and see you as you really are."

So that was it! My confidence in my powers came back with a rush.

"Friend, though you may not believe me, the sight of that talisman fills me with joy, for it enables me to prove what I am about to tell you."

"Do not waste your lies on me. Your disguise is penetrated! You are a demon!"

"Right. Could you do me one little favor?" Aahz leisurely sat cross-legged on the ground. "Could you take the charm off for a minute?"

"Take it off?" For a moment the man was puzzled, but he quickly rallied his forces. "Nay, demon. You seek to trick me into removing my charm that you might kill me!"

"Look, dummy. If we wanted to kill you we could have done it while you were knocked out cold!"

For the first time, the man seemed doubtful.

"That is, indeed, a fact."

"Then could you humor me for a moment and take the charm off?"

The warrior hesitated, then slowly removed the charm. He looked hard at Aahz and scowled.

"That's strange. You still look like a demon!"

"Correct, now let me ask you a question. Am I correct in assuming from your words you have some knowledge of demons?"

"I have been a demon hunter for over fifteen years now," he declared proudly.

"Oh, yeah?" For a minute I was afraid Aahz was going to blow the whole gambit, but he got himself back under control and continued.

"Then tell me, friend. In your long experience with demons, have you ever met one who looked like a demon?"

"Of course not! They always use their magik to disguise themselves."

Fat lot he knew about demons!

"Then that should prove my point!"

"What point?"

I thought for a moment Aahz was going to take him by the shoulders and shake him. It occurred to me that perhaps Aahz's subtleties were lost on this world.

"Let me try, Aahz. Look, sir. What he's trying to say is that if he were a demon he wouldn't look like a demon, but he does so he isn't."

"Oh!" said the man with sudden understanding.

"Now you've lost me," grumbled Aahz.

"But if you aren't a demon, why do you look like one?"

"Ahh . . .," Aahz sighed, "therein lies the story. You see, I'm accursed!"

"Accursed?"

"Yes. You see, I am a demon hunter like yourself. A rather successful one, actually. Established quite a name for myself in the field."

"I never heard of you," grumbled the man.

"Well, we've never heard of you either," I chimed in.

"You don't even know my name!"

"Oh, I'm sorry." I remembered my manners. "I'm Skeeve, and this . . . demon hunter is Aahz."

"Pleased to meet you. I am known as Quigley."

"If I could continue. . . ."

"Sorry, Aahz."

"As I was saying, I had achieved a certain renown among the demons due to my unprecedented success. At times it was rather bothersome, as when it was learned I was coming, most demons would either flee the territory or kill themselves."

"Does he always brag this much?"

"He's just getting started."

"Anyway . . . one day I was closing with a demon, a particularly ugly brute, when he startled me by addressing me by name. 'Aahz!' says he, 'Before you strike, you should know your career is at an end!' Of course I laughed at him, for I had slain demons more fierce than he, sometimes in pairs. 'Laugh if you will,' he boomed, 'but a conclave of demons empowered me to deal with you. Whether you kill me or not, you are doomed to suffer the same end you have visited on so many of us.' I killed him of course, assuming he was bluffing, but my life has not been the same ever since."

"Why not?"

"Because of the curse! When I returned to my horse, my faithful squire here took one look at me and fainted dead away."

"I did no such thing! I mean . . . it was the heat."

"Of course, Skeeve." Aahz winked slyly at Quigley.

"At any rate, I soon discovered to my horror that the demon had worked a spell on me before he expired, causing me to take on the appearance of a demon to all who beheld me."

"Fiendish. Clever, but fiendish."

"You see the subtlety of their plan! That I, fiercest of demon hunters, am now hunted in turn by my fellow humans. I am forced to hide like an animal with only my son here for companionship."

"I thought you said he was your squire."

"That, too. Oh, the irony of it all."

"Gee, that's tough. I wish I could do something to help."

"Maybe you can," Aahz smiled winningly.

Quigley recoiled. I found it reassuring that someone else shared my reaction to Aahz's smile.

"Um . . . how? I mean, I'm just a demon hunter."

"Precisely how you might be of assistance. You see, at the moment we happen to have several demons following us. It occurs to me we might be of mutual service to each other. We can provide you with targets, and you in turn can rid us of a bloody nuisance."

"They're bloody?" Quigley was horrified.

"Just an expression. Well, what do you say? Is it a deal?"

"I dunno. I'm already on a mission and I don't usually take on a new job until the last one's complete. The misinformed might think I was quitting or had been scared off or something. That sort of thing is bad for the reputation."

"It'd be no trouble at all," Aahz persisted. "It's not like you'll have to go out of your way. Just wait right here and they'll be along."

"Why are they following you, anyway?"

"A vile magician sent them after us after I was foolish enough to seek his aid. The curse, you know."

"Of course . . . wait a minute. Was that magician's name Garkin by any chance?"

"As a matter of fact it was. Why? Do you know him?"

"Why, he's my mission! That's the man I'm going to kill."

"Why?" I interrupted. "Garkin's no demon."

"But he consorts with demons, lad." Aahz scowled warningly at me. "That's enough for any demon hunter. Right, Quigley?"

"Right. Remember that, lad."

I nodded vigorously at him, feeling suddenly very nervous about this whole encounter.

"Where did you hear about Garkin anyway, Quigley?" Aahz asked casually.

"Strangely enough, from an innkeeper . . . Isstvan, I think he said his name was . . . a bit strange, but a sincere enough fellow. About three weeks ride back . . ., but we were talking about your problem. Why did he send demons after you?"

"Well, as I said, I sought him out to try to get him to

remove any curse. What I did not realize was that he was actually in league with demons himself. He had heard of me, and flatly refused me aid. What is more, after we left he set some of his demons on our trail.''

''I see. How many of them did you say there were?''

''Just two,'' Aahz assured him. ''We've caught glimpses of them occasionally.''

''Very well,'' concluded Quigley. ''I'll do it. I'll assist you in your battle.''

''That's fine except for one thing. We won't be here.''

''Why not? I should think that as a demon hunter you'd welcome the chance once the odds were even.''

''If I were here there would be no fight,'' Aahz stated grandly. ''As I have said, I have a certain reputation among demons. If they saw me here they would simply flee.''

''I frankly find that hard to believe,'' commented Quigley.

I was inclined to agree with him, but kept my silence.

''Well, I must admit their fear of my charmed sword has a bit to do with their reluctance to do battle.''

''Charmed sword?''

''Yes.'' Aahz patted the sword at his side. ''This weapon once belonged to the famous demon hunter Alfans De Clario.''

''Never heard of him.''

''Never heard of him? Are you sure you're a demon hunter? Why the man killed over two hundred demons with this sword. They say it is charmed such that whomever wields it cannot be killed by a demon.''

''How did he die?''

''Knifed by an exotic dancer. Terrible.''

''Yes, they're nasty that way. But about the sword, does it work?''

''It works as well as any sword, a little point-heavy, maybe, but. . . .''

''No. I mean the charm. Does it work?''

''I can testify that I haven't been killed by a demon since I started using it.''

"And demons actually recognize it and flee from its owner?"

"Exactly. Of course, I haven't had occasion to use it for years. Been too busy trying to get this curse removed. Sometimes I've thought about selling it, but if I ever get back into business it would be a big help in . . . um . . . reestablishing my reputation."

I suddenly realized what Aahz was up to. Quigley rose to the bait like a hungry pike-turtle.

"Hmm. . . ." he said. "Tell you what. Just to give a hand to a fellow demon hunter who's down on his luck, I'll take it off your hands for five gold pieces."

"Five gold pieces! You must be joking. I paid three hundred for it. I couldn't possibly let it go for less than two hundred."

"Oh, well, that counts me out. I only have about fifty gold pieces on me."

"Fifty?"

"Yes, I never travel with more than. . . ."

"But then again, times have been hard, and seeing as how you would be using it to do battle against the fiends who put the curse on me. . . . Yes, I think I could let you have it for fifty gold pieces."

"But that's all the money I have."

"Yes, but what good is a fat purse if you're torn asunder by a demon?"

"True enough. Let me see it."

He took the blade and hefted, giving it a few experimental swings.

"Crummy balance." He grimaced.

"You get used to it."

"Lousy steel," he declared, squinting at the blade.

"Nice edge on it, though."

"Well, my trainer always told me 'If you take care of your sword, it will take care of you!' "

"We must have had the same trainer."

The two of them smiled at each other. I felt slightly ill.

"Still, I dunno. Fifty pieces of gold is a lot."

"Just look at those stones in the handle."

"I did. They're fake."

"Aha! They're made to look fake. It hides their value."

"Sure did a nice job. What kind of stones are they?"

"Blarney stones."

"Blarney stones?"

"Yes. They're said to ensure your popularity with the ladies, if you know what I mean."

"But fifty gold pieces is all the money I have."

"Tell you what. Make it forty-five gold pieces and throw in your sword."

"My sword?"

"Of course. This beauty will take care of you, and your sword will keep my squire and I from being defenseless in this heathen land."

"Hmm. That seems fair enough. Yes, I believe you have made a deal, my friend."

They shook hands ceremoniously and began effecting the trade. I seized the opportunity to interrupt.

"Gee, it's a shame we have to part so soon."

"Why so soon?" The warrior was puzzled.

"No need to rush off," Aahz assured him, giving me a solid elbow in the ribs.

"But Aahz, we wanted to travel more before sundown and Quigley has to prepare for battle."

"What preparations?" asked Quigley.

"Your unicorn," I continued doggedly. "Don't you want to catch your unicorn?"

"My unicorn! All of my armor is on that animal!"

"Surely it won't wander far. . . ." Aahz growled.

"There are bandits about who would like nothing better than to get their hands on a good war unicorn." Quigley heaved himself to his feet. "And I want him at my side to help me fight the demons. Yes, I must be off. I thank you for your assistance, my friends. Safe journey until we meet again."

With a vague wave of his hand, he disappeared into the woods whistling for his mount.

"Now what was all that about?" Aahz exploded angrily.

"What, Aahz?"

"The big rush to get rid of him. As gullible as he was, I could have traded him out of his pants or anything else vaguely valuable he might have had on him. I specifically wanted to get my hands on that charm."

"Basically I wanted to see him on his way before he caught on to the flaw in your little tale."

"What, the son-nephew slip? He wouldn't have. . . ."

"No, the other thing."

"What other thing?"

I sighed.

"Look, he saw through your disguise because that pendant lets him see through spells, right?"

"Right, and I explained it away saying I was the victim of a demon's curse. . . ."

". . . that changed your appearance with a spell. But if he could see through spells, he should be able to see through that spell to see you as a normal man. Right?"

"Hmm. . . . Maybe we'd better be on our way now that we know where Isstvan is."

But I was unwilling to let my little triumph go so easily.

"Tell me, Aahz. What would you do if we encountered a demon hunter as smart as me?"

"That's easy." He smiled, patting the crossbow. "I'd kill him. Think about it."

I did.

Chapter Seven:

"Is there anything in the universe more beautiful and protective than the simple complexity of a spider's web?"

—CHARLOTTE

I CLOSED my eyes for concentration. This was more difficult than drawing energies from the force line directly into my body. I pointed a finger for focus, pointing at a spot some five yards distant from me.

The idea of drawing energies from a distant location and controlling them would have seemed impossible to me, until Aahz pointed out it was the same as the candle-lighting exercise I had already mastered. Now it did not seem impossible, merely difficult.

Confidently, I narrowed my concentration, and in my mind's eye saw a gleaming blue light appear at the designated point. Without breaking my concentration, I moved my finger overhead in a slow arc. The light followed the lead, etching a glowing blue trail in the air behind it. As it touched the ground again, or where I sensed the ground to be, I moved my finger again, moving the light into the second arc of the protective pentagram.

It occurred to me that what I was doing was not unlike forming the normal flat pentagram Garkin had used at the hut. The only difference being that instead of being inscribed on the floor, this was etched overhead with its points dipping downward to touch the earth. It was more an umbrella than a border.

The other major difference, I thought as I completed the task, was that I was doing it. Me. Skeeve. What I had once watched with awe, I was now performing as routine.

I touched the light down in its original place, completing the pentagram. Quietly pleased, I stood for a moment, eyes closed, studying the glowing blue lines etched in my mind's eye.

"Terrific, kid," came Aahz's voice. "Now what say you damp it down a bit before we draw every peasant and demon hunter in the country."

Surprised, I opened my eyes.

The pentagram was still there! Not imagined in my mind, but actually glowing overhead. Its cold blue light gave an eerie illumination to the scene that negated the warmth of our little campfire.

"Sorry, Aahz." I quickly eased my control on the energy and watched as the lines of the pentagram faded to invisibility. They were still there. I could feel their presence in the night air above me. Now, however, they could not be seen by normal vision.

More for the joy of it than out of any lack of confidence, I closed my eyes again and looked at them. They glowed there in shimmering beauty, a cooler, reassuring presence to counter the impatience of the red-gold glow of the force-line spear pointing doggedly toward tomorrow's path.

"Sit down, kid, and finish your lizard-bird."

We were out of the forest proper now, but despite the presence of the nearby road, game was still plentiful and fell ready victim to my snares. Aahz still refused to join me in the meals, insisting alcohol was the only thing in this dimension worth consuming, but I dined frequently and royally.

"You know, kid," he said, looking up from his endless sword-sharpening. "You're really coming along pretty well with your studies.''

"What do you mean?" I mumbled through a bone, hoping he would elaborate.

"You're a lot more confident with your magik. You'd better watch your controls, though. You had enough energy in that pentagram to fry anything that bumped against it.''

"I guess I'm still a bit worried about the assassins.''

"Relax, kid. It's been three days since we set 'em up in that ambush of Quigley's. Even if he didn't stop 'em, they'll never catch up with us now.''

"Did I really summon up that much power?" I urged, eager for praise.

"Unless you're actually engaged in magical battle, wards are used as a warning signal only. If you put too much energy into them it can have two potentially bad side effects. First, you can draw unnecessary attention to yourself by jarring or burning an innocent bystander who blunders into it. Second, if it actually reaches a magical opponent, it probably won't stop him; just alert him that he has a potentially dangerous foe in the area.''

"I thought it was a good thing if I could summon up lots of power.''

"Look, kid. This isn't a game. You're tapping into some very powerful forces here. The idea is to strengthen your control, not see how much you can liberate. If you get too careless with experimenting, you could end up helpless when the actual crunch comes.''

"Oh," I said, unconvinced.

"Really, kid. You've got to learn this. Let me try an example. Suppose for a minute you're a soldier assigned to guard a pass. Your superiors put you on the post and give you a stack of ten-pound rocks. All you have to do is watch to see if anyone comes, and if they do, drop a rock on their head. Are you with me so far?''

"I guess so.''

"Fine. Now it's a long, boring duty, and you have lots of time to think. You're very proud of your muscles, and decide it's a bit insulting that you were only given ten-pound rocks. Twenty-pound rocks would be more effective, and you think you could handle them as easily as the ten-pound variety. Logical?''

I nodded vaguely, still not sure what he was driving at.

''Just to prove the point to yourself, you heft a twenty-pound rock, and, sure enough, you can handle it. Then it occurs to you if you can handle a twenty-pounder, you should be able to handle a forty-pounder, or even a fifty-pounder. So you try. Then it happens.''

He was getting so worked up I felt no need to respond.

''You drop it on your foot, or you pull a muscle, or you keel over from heat exhaustion, or any one of a hundred other things. Then where are you?''

He leveled an accusing finger at me.

''The enemy strolls through the pass you're supposed to be guarding and you can't even lift the original ten-pound rock to stop them. All because you indulged in needless testing of idiotic muscle power!''

I was impressed, and gave the matter serious thought before replying.

''I see what you're saying, Aahz, but there's one flaw in your example. The keyword is 'needless.' Now in my case, it's not a matter of having a stack of ten-pound rocks that would do the job. I have a handful of gravel. I'm trying to scrounge around for a rock big enough to do some damage.''

''True enough,'' Aahz retorted, ''but the fact remains if you overextend yourself you won't be able to use what you already have. Even gravel can be effective if used at the right time. Don't underrate what you've got or what you're doing. Right now you're keeping the finder spear going, maintaining the wards, and keeping my disguise intact. That's a lot for someone of your abilities to be doing simultaneously. If something happened right now, which would you drop first?''

''Um. . . .''

''Too late! We're already dead. You won't have time to ponder energy problems. That's why you always have to hold some back to deal with immediate situations while you rally your energies from other activities. Now do you see?"

"I think so, Aahz," I said haltingly. "I'm a bit tired."

"Well, think about it. It's important. In the meantime get some sleep and try to store up your energies. Incidentally, let the finder spear go for now. You can summon it up again in the morning. Right now, it's just a needless drain."

"Okay, Aahz. How about your disguise?"

"Hmm . . . better keep that. It'll be good practice for you to maintain both that and the wards in your sleep. Speaking of which. . . ."

"Right, Aahz."

I drew my acquired assassin's cloak about me for warmth and curled up. Despite his gruff manner, Aahz was persistent that I get enough sleep as well as food.

Sleep did not come easily, however. I found I was still a bit wound up over casting the wards.

"Aahz?"

"Yeah, kid?"

"How would you say my powers right now stack up against the devils?"

"What devils?"

"The assassins that were following us."

"I keep telling you, kid. Those weren't Deveels, those were Imps."

"What's the difference?"

"I told you before. Imps are from Imper, and Deveels. . . ."

". . . are from Deva," I finished for him. "But what does that mean? I mean, are their powers different or something?"

"You'd better believe it, kid." Aahz snorted. "Deveels are some of the meanest characters you'd ever not want to tangle with. They're some of the most feared and respected characters in the dimensions."

"Are they warriors? Mercenaries?"

Aahz shook his head.

"Worse!" he answered. "They're merchants."

"Merchants?"

"Don't sneer, kid. Maybe merchants is too sedate a phrase to describe them. Traders Supreme is more like it."

"Tell me more, Aahz."

"Well, history was never my forte, but as near as I can tell, at one time the entire dimension Deva faced economic ruin. The lands suffered a plague that affected the elements. Fish could not live in its oceans, plants could not grow in the soil. Those plants that did grow were twisted and changed and poisoned the animals. The dimension was no longer able to support the life of its citizenry."

I lay, staring up at the stars as Aahz continued his tale.

"Dimension travel, once a frivolous pastime, now became the key to survival. Many left Deva, migrating singly or in groups to other dimensions. Their tales of their barren, miserable homeland served as a prototype for many religious groups' concept of an afterworld for evil souls.

"The ones who stayed, however, decided to use the power of dimension travel in a different way. They established themselves as traders, traveling the dimensions buying and selling wonders. What is common in one dimension is frequently rare in another. As the practice grew, they became rich and powerful . . . also the shrewdest hagglers in all the dimensions. Their techniques for driving a hard bargain have been passed down from generation to generation and polished until now they are without equal. They are scattered through the dimensions, returning to Deva only occasionally to visit the Bazaar."

"The Bazaar?" I prompted.

"No one can travel extensively in all the dimensions in one lifetime. The Bazaar on Deva is the place the Deveels meet to trade with each other. An off-dimension visitor there will be sore pressed to not lose o'er much, much less hold his own. It's said if you make a deal with a Deveel, you'd be wise to count your fingers afterward . . . then your arms and legs, then your relatives. . . ."

"I get the picture. Now how about the Imps?"

"The Imps." Aahz said the word as if it tasted bad. "The Imps are inferior to the Deveels in every way."

"How so?"

"They're cheap imitations. Their dimension, Imper, lies close to Deva, and the Deveels bargain with them so often they're almost bankrupt from the irresistible 'fair deals.' To hold their own, they've taken to aping the Deveels, attempting to peddle wonders through the dimensions. To the uneducated, they may seem clever and powerful; in fact, occasionally they try to pass themselves off as Deveels. Compared to the masters, however, they're bungling incompetents."

He trailed off into silence. I pondered his words, and they prompted another question.

"Say, Aahz?"

"Hmm? Yeah, kid?"

"What dimension do you come from?"

"Perv."

"Does that make you a Pervert?"

"No. That makes me a Pervect. Now shut up!"

I assumed he wanted me to go to sleep, and maintained silence for several minutes. There was just one more question I had to ask, however, if I was going to get any sleep at all.

"Aahz?"

"Keep it down, kid."

"What dimension is this?"

"Hmmm? This is Klah, kid. Now for the last time, shut up."

"What does that make me, Aahz?"

There was no answer.

"Aahz?"

I rolled over to look at him. He was staring out into the darkness and listening intently.

"What is it?"

"I think we've got company, kid."

As if in response to his words, I felt a tremor in the wards as something came through.

I bounded to my feet as two figures appeared at the edge of the firelight. The light was dimming, but was sufficient to reveal the fact that both figures were wearing the hooded cloaks of assassins, and the gold side was out!

Chapter Eight:

"In times of crisis, it is of utmost importance not to lose one's head."

—M. ANTOINETTE

THE four of us stood in frozen tableau for several minutes studying each other. My mind was racing, but could not focus on the definite course of action. I decided to follow Aahz's lead and simply stood regarding the two figures cooly, trying to ignore the two crossbows leveled steadily on us.

Finally, one of our visitors broke the silence.

"Well, Throckwoddle? Aren't you going to invite your friends to sit down?"

Surprisingly, this was addressed to me!

"Ummm. . . ." I said.

"Yes, Throckwoddle," Aahz drawled, turning to me. "And aren't you going to introduce me to your colleagues?"

"Um. . . ." I repeated.

"Perhaps he doesn't remember us," the second figure injected sarcastically.

"Nonsense," responded the first with equal sarcasm. "His two oldest friends? Brockhurst and Higgens? How could he possibly not remember our names? Just because he forgot to share the loot doesn't mean he'd forget our names. Be fair, Higgens.''

"Frankly, Brockhurst,'' responded the other. ''I'd rather he remembered the loot and forgot our names.''

Their words were stuffy and casual, but the crossbows never wavered.

I was beginning to get the picture. Apparently these were the two Imps Aahz had assured me couldn't overtake us. Fortunately, it seemed they thought I was the Imp who had killed Garkin . . . at least I thought it was fortunate.

"Gentlemen,'' Aahz exclaimed, stepping forward. "Let me say what a great pleasure it is to. . . .''

He stopped as Brockhurst's crossbow leapt to his shoulder in one smooth move.

"I'm not sure who you are,'' he intoned. ''But I'd advise you to stay out of this. This is a private matter between the three of us.''

"Brockhurst,'' interrupted Higgens. "It occurs to me we may be being a bit hasty in our actions.''

"Thank you, Higgens,'' I said, greatly relieved.

"Now that we've established contact,'' he continued, favoring me with an icy glare, ''I feel we should perhaps secure our traveling companion before we continue this . . . discussion.''

"I suppose you're right, Higgens,'' Brockhurst admitted grudgingly. "Be a good fellow and fetch him along while I watch these two.''

"I feel that would be ill-advised on two counts. First, I refuse to approach that beast alone, and second, that would leave you alone facing two to one odds, if you get my point.''

"Quite. Well, what do you suggest?''

"That we both fetch our traveling companion and return without delay.''

"And what is to keep these two from making a hasty departure?''

"The fact that we'll be watching them from somewhere in the darkness with crossbows. I believe that should be sufficient to discourage them from making . . . ah . . . any movements which might be subject to misinterpretation.''

"Very well," Brockhurst yielded grudgingly. "Throckwoddle, I would strongly suggest you not attempt to avoid us further. While I don't believe we could be any more upset with you than we already are, that might actually succeed in provoking us further.''

With that, the two figures faded back into darkness.

"What are we going to do, Aahz?" I whispered frantically.

He seemed not to hear me.

"Imps!" he chortled, rubbing his hands together gleefully. "What a stroke of luck!''

"Aahz! They're going to kill me!''

"Hm? Relax, kid. Like I said, Imps are gullible. If they were really thinking, they would have shot us down without talking. I haven't met an Imp yet I couldn't talk circles around.''

He cocked his head, listening.

"They're coming back now. Just follow my lead. Oh yes . . . I almost forgot. Drop the disguise on my features when I give you the cue.''

"But you said they couldn't catch. . . .''

I broke off as the two Imps reappeared. They were leading a war unicorn between them. The hoods of the cloaks were back now, revealing their features. I was moderately surprised to see they looked human, seedy perhaps, but human nonetheless. Then I saw Quigley.

He was sitting woodenly astride the unicorn, lurching back and forth with the beast's stride. His eyes were staring fixedly straight ahead and his right arm was raised as if in salutation. The light of the fire reflected off his face as if it were glass, and I realized with horror he was no longer alive, but a statue of some unidentified substance.

Any confidence I might have gained from Aahz's assurances left me in a rush. Gullible or not, the Imps played for keeps, and any mistake we made would in all likelihood be our last.

"Who's that?" Aahz asked, interrupting my thoughts.

I realized I had been dangerously close to showing a betraying sign of recognition of the statue.

"There will be time for that later, if indeed there is a later," said Higgens, grimly dropping the unicorn's reins and raising his crossbow.

"Yes," echoed Brockhurst, imitating Higgens's move with his own weapon. "First there is a matter of an explanation to be settled. Throckwoddle?"

"Gentlemen, gentlemen," said Aahz soothingly, stepping between me and the crossbows. "Before you proceed I must insist on introducing myself properly. If you will but allow me a moment while I remove my disguise."

The sight of the two weapons had rattled me so badly I almost missed my cue. Fortunately, I managed to gather my scattered senses and closed my eyes, shakily executing the change features spell to convert Aahz back to his normal dubious appearance.

I'm not sure what reaction I had expected from the Imps at the transformation, but the one I got surpassed any possible expectations.

"By the Gods below!" gasped Brockhurst.

"A Pervert!" gasped Higgens.

"That's Pervect!" smiled Aahz, showing all his pointed teeth. "And don't ever forget it, friend Imps."

"Yessir!" they chorused in unison.

They were both standing in slack-jawed amazement, crossbows dangling forgotten in their hands. From their terrified reactions, I began to suspect that despite all his bragging, Aahz had perhaps not told me everything about his dimension or the reputation of its inhabitants.

Aahz ignored their stares and plopped down again at his place by the fire.

"Now that that's established, why don't you put away those silly crossbows and sit down so we can chat like civilized folk, eh?"

He gestured impatiently and they hastened to comply.

I also resumed a sitting position, not wishing to be the only one left standing.

"But . . . what are . . . why are you here . . . sir . . . if you don't mind my asking?" Brockhurst finally managed to get the whole question out.

However incompetent he might be as a demon, he sure knew how to grovel.

"Ah!" smiled Aahz. "Therein lies the story."

I settled back. This could take a while.

"I was summoned across the dimensions barrier by one Garkin, a magician I have never cared much for. It seems he was expecting some trouble from a rival and was eager to enlist my aid for the upcoming fracas. Now, as I said before, I had never been fond of Garkin and was not particularly wild about joining him. He began growing unpleasant in his insistence to the point that I considered swaying from my normal easygoing nature to take action against him, when who should appear but Throckwoddle here who did me the favor of putting a quarrel into the old slime-stirrer."

Aahz acknowledged me with an airy wave. I tried to look modest.

"Naturally we fell to chatting afterward, and he mentioned he was in the employment of one Isstvan and that his action against Garkin had been part of an assignment."

"You answered questions about an assignment?" Higgens turned to me aghast.

"Yes I did," I snarled at him. "Wouldn't you, considering the circumstances?"

"Oh, yes . . . of course. . . ." He darted a nervous glance at Aahz and lapsed into respectful silence again.

"Anyway," Aahz continued, "it occurred to me I owed this fellow Isstvan a favor for ridding me of a nagging nuisance, so I suggested I accompany Throckwoddle back to his employer that I might offer him my services, on a limited basis, of course."

"You could have waited for us." Brockhurst glowered at me.

"Well . . . I wanted . . . you see . . . I. . . ."

"I insisted," Aahz smiled. "You see, my time is quite valuable and I had no desire to waste it waiting around."

"Oh," said Brockhurst.

Higgens was not so easily swayed.

"You could have left us a message," he muttered.

"We did," Aahz replied. "My ring, in full view on the table. I see you found it."

He pointed an accusing finger at Brockhurst. I noticed for the first time the Imp was wearing Garkin's ring.

"This ring?" Brockhurst started. "Is it yours? I thought it was part of Garkin's loot that had been overlooked."

"Yes, it's mine." Aahz bared his teeth. "I'm surprised you didn't recognize it. But now that we're united, you will, of course, return it."

"Certainly!" the Imp fumbled in his haste to remove the ring.

"Careful there," Aahz cautioned. "You know how to operate it, don't you? It can be dangerous in ignorant hands."

"Of course I know how to operate it," Brockhurst replied in an injured tone. "You press against the ring with the fingers on either side of it. I saw one like it at the Bazaar on Deva once."

He tossed the ring to Aahz who caught it neatly and slipped it on his finger. Fortunately it fit. I made a mental note to ask Aahz to let me try using the ring sometime, now that we knew how it worked.

"Now that I've explained about me, how about answering my question," Aahz said, leveling a finger at the Quigley statue. "Who is that?"

"We aren't sure ourselves," Higgens admitted.

"It's all quite puzzling, really," Brockhurst added.

"Would you care to elaborate on that?" Aahz prompted.

"Well, it happened about three days back. We were following your trail to . . . um . . . with hopes of reuniting our group. Suddenly this warrior gallops out of the brush ahead of us and bars our path. It was as if he knew we were coming and was waiting for us. 'Isstvan was right!' he shouts, 'This region *does* abound with demons!' "

"Isstvan?" I said, doing my best to look puzzled.

"That's what he said. It surprised us, too. I mean, here we are working for Isstvan, and were set upon by a man claiming to be sent by the same employer. Anyway, then he says, 'Behold the weapon of your doom!' and draws a sword."

"What kind of sword was it?" Aahz asked innocently.

"Nothing special. Actually a little substandard from all we could see. Well, it put us in a predicament. We had to defend ourselves, but were afraid to harm him on the off-chance he really was working for Isstvan."

"What did you do?" I asked.

"Frankly, we said 'to heck with it' and took the easy way out. Higgens here bounced one of his stone balls off the guy's forehead and froze him in place. We've been dragging him along ever since. We figure we'll dump him in Isstvan's lap and let him sort it out."

"A wise solution," commented Aahz.

They inclined their heads graciously at the compliment.

"One question I'd like to ask," I interjected. "How were you able to overtake us, encumbered as you were?"

"Well, it was no small problem. We had little hope of overtaking you as it was, and with our new burden, it appeared it would be impossible," Brockhurst began.

"We were naturally quite eager to . . . ah . . . join you, so we resorted to desperate measures," Higgens continued. "We took a side trip to Twixt and sought the aid of the Deveel there. It cost us a pretty penny, but he finally agreed to teleport our group to the trail ahead of you, allowing us to make our desired contact."

"Deveel? What Deveel?" Aahz interrupted.

"Frumple. The Deveel at Twixt. The one who. . . ."

Brockhurst broke off suddenly, his eyes narrowing suspiciously. He shot a dark glance at Higgens, who was casually reaching for his crossbow.

"I'm surprised Throckwoddle hasn't mentioned Frumple to you," Higgens purred. "After all, he's the one who told us about him."

Chapter Nine:

"To function efficiently, any group of people or employees must have faith in their leader."

—CAPT. BLIGH (ret.)

"YES, Throckwoddle." If anything, Aahz's voice was even more menacing than the Imp's. "Why didn't you tell me about the Deveel?"

"It . . . ah . . . must have slipped my mind," I mumbled.

With a massive exertion of self-control, I shot my most withering glare at the Imps, forcing myself to ignore the menace of the crossbows. I was rewarded by seeing them actually look guilty and avoid my gaze.

"Slipped your mind! More likely you were trying to hold back a bit of information from me," Aahz said accusingly. "Well, now that it's out, let's have the rest of it. What about this Deveel?"

"Ask Brockhurst," I grumbled. "He seems to be eager to talk about it."

"Well, Brockhurst?" Aahz turned to him.

The Imp gave me an apologetic shrug as he started.

"Well, I guess I've already told you most of it. There's a Deveel, Frumple, in residence in Twixt. He goes under the cover of Abdul the Rug Merchant, but he actually maintains a thriving trade in the usual Deva

71

manner, buying and selling across the dimensions."

"What's he doing in Klah?" Aahz interrupted. "I mean there's not much business here. Isn't it a little slow for a Deveel's taste?"

"Well, Throckwoddle said. . . ." Brockhurst broke off and shot me a look.

"Go on, tell him." I tried to sound resigned.

"Well," the Imp continued, "rumor has it that he was exiled from Deva and is in hiding here, ashamed to show his face in a major dimension."

"Barred from Deva? Why? What did he do?"

I was glad Aahz asked. It would have sounded strange coming from me.

"Throckwoddle wouldn't tell us. Said Frumple was sensitive on the subject and we shouldn't bring it up."

"Well, Throckwoddle?" Aahz turned to me.

I was so caught up in the story it took me a few beats before I remembered that I really didn't know.

"Um . . . I can't tell you," I said.

"What?" Aahz scowled.

I began to wonder how much he was caught up in the story and had lost track of the realities of the situation.

"I learned his secret by accident and hold it as a personal confidence," I said haughtily. "During our travels these last few days, I've learned some rather interesting items about you and hold them in the same esteem. I trust you will respect my silence on the matter of Frumple as I expect others to respect my silence about those matters pertaining to you."

"Okay, okay. You've made your point," Aahz conceded.

"Say . . . um . . . Throckwoddle," Higgens interrupted. "I would suggest we all shed our disguises like our friend Perver . . . um, Pervect here has. No sense in using up our energies keeping up false faces among friends."

His tone was casual, but he sounded suspicious. I noticed he had not taken his hand off his crossbow.

"Why?" argued Brockhurst. "I prefer to keep my disguise on at all times when in another dimension.

Lessens the chance of forgetting to put it on at a crucial moment.''

"I think Higgens is right," Aahz stated before I could support Brockhurst. "I for one like to see the true faces of the people I'm talking to."

"Well," grumbled Brockhurst, "if everyone is going to insist."

He closed his eyes in concentration, and his features began to shimmer and melt.

I didn't watch the whole process. My mind was racing desperately back to Garkin's hut, when Aahz held up the charred face of the assassin. I hastily envisioned my own face next to it and began working, making certain obvious modifications to its appearance to repair the fire damage.

When I was done, I snuck a peek out of one eye. The other two had changed already. My attention was immediately drawn to their complexion. Theirs was a pinkish red, while mine wasn't. I hastily re-closed my eye and made the adjustment.

Satisfied now, I opened my eyes and looked about me. The other two Imps now showed the apparently characteristic pointed ears and chins. Aahz looked like Aahz. The situation had completely reversed since the Imps had arrived. Instead of being normal surrounded by three disguised demons, I was now surrounded by three demons while I was disguised. Terrific.

"Ahh. That's better," chortled Aahz.

"You know, Throckwoddle," Higgens said, cocking a head at me. "For a moment there in the firelight you looked different. In fact. . . ."

"Come, come, gentlemen," Aahz interrupted. "We have serious matters to discuss. Does Isstvan know about Frumple's existence?"

"I don't believe so," answered Brockhurst. "If he did, he would have either enlisted him or had him assassinated."

"Good," exclaimed Aahz. "He could very well be the key to our plot."

"What plot?" I asked.

"Our plot against Isstvan, of course."

"What?" exclaimed Higgens, completely distracted from me now. "Are you insane?"

"No," retorted Aahz. "But Isstvan is. I mean, think! Has he been acting particularly stable?"

"No," admitted Brockhurst. "But then neither has any other magician I've met, present company included."

"Besides," Higgens interrupted, "I thought you were on your way to help him."

"That's before I heard your story," Aahz pointed out. "I'm not particularly eager to work for a magician who pits his own employees against each other."

"When did he do that?" Higgens asked.

Aahz made an exasperated gesture.

"Think, gentlemen! Have you forgotten our stony-faced friend there?" He jerked a thumb at the figure on the unicorn. "If you recall your tale correctly, his words seemed to imply he had been sent by Isstvan to intercept you."

"That's right," said Brockhurst. "So?"

"What do you mean, 'So?'" Aahz exploded. "That's it! Isstvan sent him to kill you. Either he was trying to cut his overhead by assassinating his assassins before payday, or he's so unstable mentally he's lashing out blindly at everyone, including his own allies. Either way he doesn't sound like the most benevolent of employers."

"You know, I believe he has a point there," I observed, determined to be of some assistance in this deception.

"But if that's true, what are we to do?" asked Higgens.

"Well, I don't have a firm plan of action," Aahz admitted. "But I have some general ideas that might help."

"Such as?" prompted Brockhurst.

"You go back to Isstvan. Say nothing at all of your suspicions. If you do, he might consider you dangerous and move against you immediately. What's more, refuse any new assignments. Find some pretext to stay as close to him as possible. Learn all about his habits and weaknesses, but don't do anything until we get there.''

"Where are you going?'' asked Higgens.

"We are going to have a little chat with Frumple. If we're going to move against Isstvan, the support of a Deveel could be invaluable.''

"And probably unobtainable,'' grumpled Brockhurst. "I've never known a Deveel yet to take sides in a fight. They prefer being in a position to sell to both sides.''

"What do you mean 'we'?'' asked Higgens. "Isn't Throckwoddle coming with us?''

"No. I've developed a fondness for his company. Besides, if he doesn't agree to help us, it would come in handy to have an assassin close by. Frumple's too powerful to run the risk of leaving him unallied to help Isstvan.''

As Aahz was speaking, Brockhurst casually leaned back out of his line of vision and silently mouthed the word "Pervert" at Higgens. Higgens quietly nodded his agreement, and they both shot me sympathetic glances.

"Well, what do you think?'' Aahz asked in conclusion.

"Hmm . . . what do we do with him?'' Higgens indicated the Quigley statue with a jerk of his head.

"We'll take him with us,'' I chimed in hastily.

"Of course!'' agreed Aahz, shooting me a black look. "If you two took him back to Isstvan, he might guess you suspected his treachery.''

"Besides,'' I added, "maybe we can revive him and convince him to join us in our battle.''

"I suppose you'll be wanting the antidote then.'' Higgens sighed, fishing a small vial from inside his cloak and tossing it to me. "Just sprinkle a little on him and he'll return to normal in a few minutes. Watch yourself, though. There's something strange about him. He seemed to be able to see right through our disguises.''

"Where's the sword you were talking about?'' Aahz asked.

"It's in his pack. Believe me, it's junk. The only reason we brought it along was that he seemed to put so much stock in it. It'll be curious to find out what he thought it was when we revive him."

"Well, I believe that just about covers everything," Brockhurst sighed. "I suggest we get some sleep and start on our respective journeys first thing in the morning."

"I suggest you start on your journey now," Aahz said pointedly.

"Now?" Brockhurst exclaimed.

"But it's the middle of the night," Higgens pointed out.

"Might I remind you gentlemen that the longer you are away from Isstvan, the greater the chances are he'll send another assassin after you."

"He's right, you know," I said thoughtfully.

"I suppose so," grumbled Higgens.

"Well," said Brockhurst, rising to his feet, "I guess we'll be on our way then as soon as we divide Garkin's loot."

"On the contrary," stated Aahz. "Not only do we not divide the loot, I would suggest you give us whatever funds you have at your disposal."

"What?" they chorused, their crossbows instantly in their hands again.

"Think, gentlemen," Aahz said soothingly. "We'd be trying to bargain with a Deveel for his support. As you yourselves have pointed out, they are notoriously unreasonable in their prices. I would hate to think we might fail in our negotiations for a lack of funds."

There was a pregnant silence as the Imps sought to find a hole in his logic.

"Oh, very well," Brockhurst conceded at last, lowering his crossbow and reaching for his purse.

"I still don't think it will do any good," Higgens grumbled, imitating Brockhurst's move. "You probably couldn't buy off a Deveel if you had the Gnomes themselves backing you."

They passed the purses over to Aahz, who hefted

them judiciously before tucking them into his own waistband.

"Trust me, gentlemen." Aahz smiled. "We Pervects have methods of persuasion that are effective even on Deveels."

The Imps shuddered at this and began edging away.

"Well . . . umm . . . I guess we'll see you later," Higgens mumbled. "Watch yourself, Throckwoddle."

"Yes," added Brockhurst. "And be sure when you're done, the Deveel is either with us or dead."

I tried to think of something to say in return, but before anything occurred to me they were gone.

Aahz cocked an eyebrow at me and I held up a restraining hand until I felt them pass through the wards. I signaled him with a nod.

"They've gone," I said.

"Beautiful!" exclaimed Aahz gleefully. "Didn't I tell you they were gullible?"

For once I had to admit he was right.

"Well, get some sleep now, kid. Like I said before, tomorrow's going to be a busy day, and all of a sudden it looks like it's going to be even busier."

I complied, but one question kept nagging at me.

"Aahz?"

"Yeah, kid."

"What dimension do the Gnomes come from?"

"Zoorik," he answered.

On that note, I went to sleep.

Chapter Ten:

"Man shall never reach his full capacity while chained to the earth. We must take wing and conquer the heavens."

—ICARUS

"ARE you sure we're up to handling a Deveel, Aahz?" I was aware I had asked the question countless times in the last few days, but I still needed reassurance.

"Will you relax, kid?" Aahz growled. "I was right about the Imps, wasn't I?"

"I suppose so," I admitted hesitantly.

I didn't want to tell Aahz, but I wasn't that happy with the Imp incident. It had been a little too close for my peace of mind. Since the meeting, I had been having recurring nightmares involving Imps and crossbows.

"Look at it this way, kid. With any luck this Frumple character will be able to restore my powers. That'd take you off the hotseat."

"I guess so," I said without enthusiasm.

He had raised this point several times since learning about Frumple. Each time he did, it gave me the same feeling of discomfort.

"Something bothering you, kid?" Aahz asked, cocking his head at me.

"Well . . . it's . . . Aahz, if you do get your powers back, will you still want me as an apprentice?"

"Is that what's been eating at you?" he seemed genuinely surprised. "Of course I'll still want you. What kind of a magician do you think I am? I don't choose my apprentices lightly."

"You wouldn't feel I was a burden?"

"Maybe at first, but not now. You were in at the start of this Isstvan thing; you earned the right to be in on the end of it."

Truth to tell, I wasn't all that eager to be there when Aahz confronted Isstvan, but that seemed to be the price I would have to pay if I was going to continue my association with Aahz.

"Um . . . Aahz?"

"Yeah, kid?"

"Just one more question?"

"Promise?"

"How's that?"

"Nothing. What's the question, kid."

"If you get your powers back, and I'm still your apprentice, which dimension will we live in?"

"Hmm. To be honest, kid, I hadn't really given it much thought. Tell ya what, we'll burn that bridge when we come to it, okay?"

"Okay, Aahz."

I tried to get my mind off the question. Maybe Aahz was right. No sense worrying about the problem until we knew for sure it existed. Maybe he wouldn't get his powers back. Maybe I'd get to be the one to fight Isstvan after all. Terrific.

"Hey! Watch the beast, kid!"

Aahz's voice broke my train of thought. We were leading the war unicorn between us, and the beast chose this moment to act up.

It nickered and half-reared, then planted its feet and tossed its head.

"Steady . . . ow!"

Aahz extended a hand trying to seize its bridle and received a solid rap on the forearm from the unicorn's horn for his trouble.

"Easy, Buttercup," I said soothingly. "There's a good boy."

The beast responded to my coaxings, first by settling down, pawing the ground nervously, then finally by rubbing his muzzle against me.

Though definitely a friendly gesture, this is not the safest thing to have a unicorn do to you. I ducked nimbly under his swinging horn and cast about me quickly. Snatching an orange flower from a nearby bush, I fed it to him at an arm's length. He accepted the offering and began to munch it contentedly.

"I don't think that beast likes demons," Aahz grumbled sullenly, rubbing his bruised arm.

"It stands to reason," I retorted. "I mean, he *was* a demon hunter's mount, you know."

"Seems to take readily enough to you, though," Aahz observed. "Are you sure you're not a virgin?"

"Certainly not," I replied in my most injured tones.

Actually I was, but I would have rather been fed to vampire-slugs than admit it to Aahz.

"Speaking of demon hunters, you'd better check on our friend there," Aahz suggested. "It could get a bit grisly if an arm or something broke off before we got around to restoring him."

I hastened to comply. We had rigged a drag-litter for the Quigley-statue to avoid having to load and unload him each night, not to mention escaping the chore of saddling and unsaddling the war unicorn. The bulk of the gear and armor was sharing the drag-litter with the Quigley-statue, a fact which seemed to make the unicorn immensely happy. Apparently it was far easier to drag all that weight than to carry it on one's back.

"He seems to be okay, Aahz," I reported.

"Good," he sneered. "I'd hate to think of anything happening to him, accidental-like."

Aahz was still not happy with our traveling companions. He had only grudgingly given in to my logic for bringing them along as opposed to leaving them behind. I had argued that they could be of potential assistance in dealing with the Deveel, or at least when we had our final showdown with Isstvan.

In actuality, that wasn't my reasoning at all. I felt a bit guilty about having set Quigley up to get clobbered by the Imps and didn't want to see any harm befall him because of it.

"It would make traveling a lot easier if we restored him," I suggested hopefully.

"Forget it, kid."

"But Aahz. . . ."

"I said forget it! In case you've forgotten, that particular gentleman's major pastime seems to consist of seeking out and killing demons. Now I'm aware my winning personality may have duped you into overlooking the fact, but I am a demon. As such, I am not about to accept a living, breathing, and most importantly, functioning demon hunter as a traveling companion."

"We fooled him before!" I argued.

"Not on a permanent basis. Besides, when would you practice your magik if he was restored? Until we meet with the Deveel, you're still our best bet against Isstvan."

I wished he would stop mentioning that. It made me incredibly uncomfortable when he did. Besides, I couldn't think of a good argument to it.

"I guess you're right, Aahz," I admitted.

"You'd better believe I'm right. Incidentally, since we seem to be stopped anyway, this is as good a time as any for your next lesson."

My spirits lifted. Besides my natural eagerness to extend my magical abilities, Aahz's offer contained an implied statement that he was pleased with my progress so far in earlier lessons.

"Okay, Aahz," I said, looping the unicorn's reins around a nearby bush. "I'm ready."

"Good," smiled Aahz, rubbing his hands together. "Today we're going to teach you to fly."

My spirits fell again.

"Fly?" I asked.

"That's what I said, kid. Fly. Exciting, isn't it?"

"Why?"

"Whadya mean, why? Ever since we first cast jealous eyes on the creatures of the air we've wanted to fly. Now you're getting a chance to learn. That's why it's exciting!"

"I meant, why should I want to learn to fly?"

"Well . . . because everybody wants to fly."

"I don't," I said emphatically.

"Why not?"

"I'm afraid of heights, for one thing," I answered.

"That isn't enough reason to not learn," Aahz scowled.

"Well, I haven't heard any reasons yet as to why I should." I scowled back at him.

"Look, kid," Aahz began coaxingly, "It isn't so much flying as floating on air."

"The distinction escapes me," I said dryly.

"Okay, kid. Let me put it to you this way. You're my apprentice, right?"

"Right," I agreed suspiciously.

"Well, I'm not going to have an apprentice that can't fly! Get me!?" he roared.

"All right, Aahz. How does it work?" I knew when I was beaten.

"That's better. Actually it doesn't involve anything you don't already know. You know how to levitate objects, right?"

I nodded slowly, puzzled.

"Well, all flying is is levitating yourself."

"How's that again?"

"Instead of standing firm on the ground and lifting an object, you push against the ground with your will and lift yourself."

"But if I'm not touching the ground, where do I draw my power from?"

"From the air! C'mon, kid, you're a magician, not an elemental."

"What's an elemental?"

"Forget it. What I meant was you aren't bound to any of the four elements, you're a magician. You con-

trol them, or at least influence them and draw your
power from them. When you're flying, all you have to
do is draw your power from the air instead of the
ground.''

"If you say so, Aahz," I said doubtfully.

"Okay, first locate a force line."

"But we left it when we started off to see the Deveel,"
I argued.

"Kid, there are lots of force lines. Just because we left
one of the ground force lines doesn't mean we're completely out of touch. Check for a force line in the air."

"In the air?"

"Believe me, kid. Check."

I sighed and closed my eyes. Turning my face sky-
ward, I tried to picture the two-headed spear. At first I
couldn't do it, then realized with a start I was seeing a
spear, but a different spear. It wasn't as bright as the
last spear had been, but glowed softly with icy blues and
whites.

"I think I've got one, Aahz!" I gasped.

"It's blue and white, right?" Aahz sneered sarcastically.

"Yes, but it's not as bright as the last one."

"It's probably further away. Oh well, it's close
enough for you to draw energy from. Well, give it a try,
kid. Hook into that force line and push the ground
away. Slowly now."

I did as I was instructed, reaching out with my mind
to tap the energies of that icy vision. The surge of power
I felt was unlike any I had experienced before. Whereas
before when I summoned the power I felt warm and
swollen with power, this time I felt cool and relaxed.
The power flow actually made me feel lighter.

"Push away, kid," came Aahz's voice. "Gently!"

Lazily I touched the ground with my mind, only
casually aware of the curious sensation of not physically
feeling anything with my feet.

"Open your eyes, kid! Adjust your trim."

Aahz's voice came to me from a strange location this
time. Surprised, my eyes popped open.

I was floating some ten feet above the ground at an angle that was rapidly drifting toward a horizontal position. I was flying!

The ground came at me in a rush. I had one moment of dazed puzzlement before it slammed into me with jarring reality.

I lay there for a moment forcing air back into my lungs and wondering if I had broken anything.

"Are you okay, kid?" Aahz was suddenly looming over me. "What happened anyway?"

"I . . . I was flying!" I forced the words at last.

"Yeah, so? Oh, I get it. You were so surprised you forgot to maintain the energy flow, right?"

I nodded, unable to speak.

"Of all the dumb . . . look, kid, when I tell you you're going to fly, believe it!"

"But. . . ."

"Don't 'but' me! Either you believe in me as a teacher or you don't! There's no buts about it!"

"I'm sorry, Aahz." I was getting my breath back again.

"Ahh . . . didn't mean to jump on you like that, kid, but you half scared me to death with that fall. You've got to understand we're starting to get into some pretty powerful magik now. You've got to expect them to work. A surprise-break like that last one with the wrong thing could get you killed, or me for that matter."

"I'll try to remember, Aahz. Shall I try it again?"

"Just take it easy for a few minutes, kid. Flying can take a lot out of you, even without the fall."

I closed my eyes and waited for my head to stop whirling.

"Aahz?" I said finally.

"Yeah, kid?"

"Tell me about Perv."

"What about it?"

"It just occurred to me, those Imps seemed scared to death when they realized you were a Pervect. What kind of a reputation does your dimension have?"

"Well," he began, "Perv is a self-sufficient, standoffish dimension. We may not have the best fighters, but they're close enough that other dimension travelers give them lots of room. Technology and magik exist side by side and are intertwined with each other. All in all it makes a pretty powerful little package."

"But why should anyone be afraid of that?"

"As I said, Perv has a lot going for it. One of the side effects of success is an abundance of hangers-on. There was a time when we were close to being swamped with refugees and immigrants from other dimensions. When they got to be too much of a nuisance, we put a stop to it."

"How?" I pushed.

"First, we took the non-contributing outsiders and ran 'em out. Then, for an added measure of insurance, we encouraged the circulation of rumors of certain anti-social attitudes of Pervects toward those from other dimensions."

"What kind of rumors?"

"Oh, the usual. That we eat our enemies, torture folks for amusement and have sexual practices that are considered dubious by any dimension's standards. Folks aren't sure how much is truth and how much is exaggeration, but they're none too eager to find out firsthand."

"How much of it is true, Aahz?" I asked propping myself up on one elbow.

He grinned evilly at me.

"Enough to keep 'em honest."

I was going to ask what it took to be considered a contributing immigrant, but decided to let it pass for a while.

Chapter Eleven:

*"One of the joys of travel is visiting new
towns and meeting new people."*

—G. KHAN

"AH! What a shining example of civilization!" chortled
Aahz exuberantly as he peered about him, delighted as a
child on his first outing.

We were sauntering casually down one of the lesser
used streets of Twixt. Garbage and beggars were strewn
casually about while beady rodent eyes, human and in-
human, studied us from the darkened doors and windows. It was a cluster of buildings crouched around an
army outpost which was manned more from habit than
necessity. The soldiers we occasionally encountered had
degenerated enough from the crisp recruiting poster
model that it was frequently difficult to tell which
seemed more menacing and unsavory, the guards or the
obviously criminal types they were watching.

"If you ask me, it looks more like mankind at its
worst!" I mumbled darkly.

"That's what I said, a shining example of civilization!"

There wasn't much I could say to that, not feeling like
getting baited into another one of Aahz's philosophical
lectures.

"Aahz, is it my imagination or are people staring at us?"

"Relax, kid. In a town like this the citizens will always instinctively size up a stranger. They're trying to guess if we're victims or victimizers. Our job is to make sure they think we're in the second category."

To illustrate his point he suddenly whirled and crouched like a cat, glaring back down the street with a hand on his sword hilt.

There was sudden movement at the windows and doorways as roughly a dozen half-seen forms melted back into the darkness.

One figure didn't move. A trollop leaning on a windowsill, her arms folded to display her ill-covered breasts, smiled invitingly at him. He smiled and waved. She ran an insolent tongue tip slowly around her lip and winked broadly.

"Um . . . Aahz?"

"Yeah, kid?" he replied, without taking his eyes from the girl.

"I hate to interrupt, but you're supposed to be a doddering old man, remember?"

Aahz was still disguised as Garkin, a fact which seemed to have momentarily slipped his mind.

"Hmm? Oh, yeah. I guess you're right, kid. It doesn't seem to bother anybody else though. Maybe they're used to feisty old men in this town."

"Well, could you at least stop going for your sword? That's supposed to be our surprise weapon."

Aahz was wearing the assassin's cloak now, which he quickly pulled forward again to hide his sword.

"Will you get off my back, kid? Like I said, nobody seems to be paying any attention."

"Nobody?" I jerked my head pointedly toward the girl in the window.

"Her? She's not paying any more attention to us than she is anyone else on the street."

"Really?"

"Well, if she is, it's more because of you than because of me."

"Me? C'mon, Aahz."

"Don't forget, kid, you're a pretty impressive person now."

I blinked. That hadn't occurred to me. I had forgotten I was disguised as Quigley now.

We had hidden the demon hunter just outside of town . . . well, actually we buried him. I had been shocked by the suggestion at first, but as Aahz pointed out, the statue didn't need any air and it was the only surefire way we had of ensuring he wouldn't be found by anyone else.

Even the war unicorn following us, now fully saddled and armored, did not help me keep my new identity in mind. We had been traveling together too long now.

I suppose I should have gotten some satisfaction from the fact I could now maintain not only one, but two disguises without consciously thinking about it. I didn't. I found it unnerving that I had to remember other people were seeing me differently than I was seeing myself.

I shot a glance at the trollop. As our eyes met, her smile broadened noticeably. She displayed her increased enthusiasm by leaning further out of the window until I began to worry about her falling out . . . of the window or her dress.

"What did I tell you, kid!" Aahz slapped me enthusiastically on the shoulder and winked lewdly.

"I'd rather she was attracted to me for me as I really am," I grumbled darkly.

"The price of success, kid," Aahz responded philosophically. "Well, no matter. We're here on business, remember?"

"Right," I said firmly.

I turned to continue our progress, and succeeded only in whacking Aahz soundly in the leg with my sword.

"Hey! Watch it, kid!"

It seemed there was more to this sword-carrying than met the casual eye.

"Sorry, Aahz," I apologized. "This thing's a bit point-heavy."

"Yeah? How would you know?" my comrade retorted.

"Well . . . you said. . . ."

"I said? That won't do it, kid. What's point-heavy for me may not be point-heavy for you. Weapon balance is a personal thing."

"Well . . . I guess I'm just not used to wearing a sword," I admitted.

"It's easy. Just forget you're wearing it. Think of it as part of you."

"I did. That's when I hit you."

"Hmm . . . we'll go into it more later."

Out of the corner of my eye, I could still see the trollop. She clapped her hands in silent applause and blew me a kiss. I suddenly realized she thought I had deliberately hit Aahz, a premeditated act to quell a rival. What's more, she approved of the gesture.

I looked at her again, more closely this time. Maybe later I would give Aahz the slip for a while and. . . .

"We've got to find Frumple." Aahz's voice interrupted my wandering thoughts.

"Hmm . . . ? Oh. How, Aahz?"

"Through guile and cunning. Watch this, kid."

So saying, he shot a quick glance up and down the street. A pack of three urchins had just rounded the corner, busily engaged in a game of keep-away with one of the group's hat.

"Hey!" Aahz hailed them. "Where can I find the shop of Abdul the Rug Dealer?"

"Two streets up and five to the left," they called back, pointing the direction.

"See, kid? That wasn't hard."

"Terrific," I responded, unimpressed.

"Now what's wrong, kid?"

"I thought we were trying to avoid unnecessary attention."

"Don't worry, kid."

"Don't worry!? We're on our way to meet a Deveel on a supposedly secret mission, and you seem to be determined to make sure everybody we see notices us and knows where we're going."

"Look, kid, how does a person normally act when they come into a new town?"

"I don't know," I admitted. "I haven't been in that many towns."

"Well, let me sketch it out for you. They want to be noticed. They carry on and make lots of noise. They stare at the women and wave at people they've never seen before."

"But that's what we've been doing."

"Right! Now do you understand?"

"No."

Aahz heaved an exasperated sigh.

"C'mon, kid. Think a minute, even if it hurts. We're acting like anyone else would walking into a strange town, so nobody will look at us twice. They won't pay any more attention to us than they would any other newcomer. Now if we followed your suggestion and came skulking into town, not talking to anyone or looking at anything, and tried real hard not to be noticed, then everyone and his kid brother would zero in on us trying to figure out what we were up to. Now do you understand?"

"I . . . I think so."

"Good . . . cause there's our target."

I blinked and looked in the direction of his pointing finger. There squatting between a blacksmith's forge and a leatherworker's displays was the shop. As I said, I was new to city life, but I would have recognized it as a rug merchant's shop even if it was not adorned with a large sign proclaiming it such. The entire front of the shop was lavishly decorated with colorful geometric patterns apparently meant to emulate the patterns of the rugs inside. I guess it was intended to look rich and prosperous. I found it unforgivably gaudy.

I had been so engrossed in our conversation, I had momentarily forgotten our mission. With the shop now confronting us at close range, however, my nervousness came back in a rush.

"What are we going to do, Aahz?"

"Well, first of all I think I'm going to get a drink."

"A drink?"

"Right. If you think I'm going to match wits with a Deveel on an empty stomach, you've got another think coming."

"A drink?" I repeated, but Aahz was gone, striding purposefully toward a nearby tavern. There was little for me to do but follow, leading the unicorn.

The tavern was a dingy affair, even to my rustic eye. A faded awning sullenly provided shade for a small cluster of scarred wooden tables. Flies buzzed around a cat sleeping on one of the tables . . . at least I like to assume it was asleep.

As I tied the unicorn to one of the awning supports, I could hear Aahz bellowing at the innkeep for two of his largest flagons of wine. I sighed, beginning to despair that Aahz would never fully adapt to his old-man disguise. The innkeep did not seem to notice any irregularity between Aahz's appearance and his drinking habits, however. It occurred to me that Aahz might be right in his theories of how to go unnoticed. City people seemed to be accustomed to loud rude individuals of any age.

"Sit down, kid," Aahz commanded. "You're making me nervous hovering around like that."

"I thought we were going to talk with the Deveel," I grumbled, sinking into a chair.

"Relax, kid. A few minutes one way or the other won't make that much difference. Besides, look!"

A young, well-dressed couple was entering the rug shop.

"See? We couldn't have done any business anyway. At least not until they left. The kind of talk we're going to have can't be done in front of witnesses. Ahh!"

The innkeeper had arrived, clinking the two flagons of wine down on the table in a lackluster manner.

"About time!" Aahz commented, seizing a flagon in each hand and immediately draining one. "Aren't you going to have anything, kid?"

A toss of his head and the second flagon was gone.

"While my friend here makes up his mind, bring me

two more . . . and make them decent sizes this time if you have to use a bucket!''

The innkeep retreated, visibly shaken. I wasn't. I had already witnessed Aahz's capacity for alcohol, astounding in an era noted for heavy drinkers. What did vex me a bit was that the man had departed without taking my order.

I did eventually get my flagon of wine, only to find my stomach was too nervous to readily accept it. As a result, I wound up sipping it slowly. Not so Aahz. He continued to belt them down at an alarming rate. For quite some time he drank. In fact, we sat for nearly an hour, and there was still no sign of the couple who had entered the shop.

Finally, even Aahz began to grow impatient.

"I wonder what's taking them so long," he grumbled.

"Maybe they're having trouble making up their mind," I suggested.

"C'mon, kid. The shop's not that big. He can't have too large a selection."

He downed the last of his wine and stood up.

"We've waited long enough," he declared. "Let's get this show on the road."

"But what about the couple?" I reminded him.

"We'll just have to inspire them to conclude their business with a bit more speed."

That had a vaguely ominous ring to it, and Aahz's toothy grin was additional evidence that something unpleasant was about to happen.

I was about to try to dissuade him, but he started across the street with a purposeful stride that left me standing alone.

I hurried to catch up with him, leaving the unicorn behind in my haste. Even so, I was unable to overtake him before he had entered the shop.

I plunged after him, fearing the worst. I needn't have worried. Except for the proprietor, the shop was empty. There was no sign of the couple anywhere.

Chapter Twelve:

"First impressions are of major importance in business matters."

—J. PIERPONT FINCH

"MAY I help you, gentlemen?"

The proprietor's rich robes did not successfully hide his thinness. I am not particularly muscular . . . as Skeeve, that is . . . but I had the impression that if I struck this man, he wouldn't bruise, he'd shatter. I mean, I've seen skinny men before, but he seemed to be a skeleton with a too-small skin stretched over the bones.

"We'd like to talk with Abdul," Aahz said loftily.

"I am he, and he is I," recited the proprietor. "You see before you Abdul, a mere shadow of a man, pushed to the brink of starvation by his clever customers."

"You seem to be doing all right for yourself," I murmured, looking about me.

The shop was well stocked, and even my untraveled eye could readily detect the undeniable signs of wealth about. The rugs were delicately woven in soft fabrics unfamiliar to me, and gold and silver shone from the depths of their designs. Obviously these rugs were intended for the wealthy, and it seemed doubtful their current owner would be suffering from a lack of comfort.

"Ahh. Therein lies the tale of my foolishness," cried the proprietor wringing his hands. "In my blind confidence, I sank my entire holdings into my inventory. As a result, I starve in the midst of plenty. My customers know this and rob me in my vulnerable times. I lose money on every sale, but a man must eat."

"Actually," Aahz interrupted, "we're looking for something in a deep shag wall-to-wall carpet."

"What's that? . . . I mean, do not confuse poor Abdul so, my humble business. . . ."

"Come off it, Abdul . . . or should I say Frumple." Aahz grinned his widest grin. "We know who you are and what you are. We're here to do a little business."

At his words, the proprietor moved with a swiftness I would not have suspected him capable of. He was at the door in a bound, throwing a bolt and lowering a curtain which seemed to be of a substance even more strange than that of his rugs.

"Where'd you learn your manners!" he snarled back over his shoulder in a voice quite unlike the one used by the whiney proprietor. "I've got to live in this town, you know."

"Sorry," Aahz said, but he didn't sound at all apologetic.

"Well, watch it next time you come barging in and start throwing my name around. People here are not particularly tolerant of strange beings or happenings."

He seemed to be merely grumbling to himself, so I seized the opportunity to whisper to Aahz.

"Psst. Aahz. What's a wall-to-wall. . . ."

"Later, kid."

"You!" The proprietor seemed to see me for the first time. "You're the statue! I didn't recognize you moving."

"Well . . . I. . . ."

"I should have known," he raved on. "Deal with Imps and you invite trouble. Next thing you know every. . . ."

He broke off suddenly and eyed us suspiciously. His hand disappeared into the folds and emerged with a clear crystal. He held it up and looked through it like an eye glass, scrutinizing us each in turn.

"I should have known," he spat. "Would you be so kind as to remove your disguises? I like to know who I'm doing business with."

I glanced at Aahz who nodded in agreement.

Closing my eyes, I began to effect the change to our normal appearance. I had enough time to wonder if Frumple would wonder about my transformation, if he realized I was actually a different person than the statue he had seen earlier. I needn't have worried.

"A Pervert!" Frumple managed to make the word sound slimy.

"That's Pervect if you want to do business with us." Aahz corrected.

"It's Pervert until I see the color of your money," Frumple sneered back.

I was suddenly aware he was studying me carefully.

"Say, you wouldn't by any chance be an Imp named Throckwoddle, would you?"

"Me? No! I . . . I'm. . . ."

But he was already squinting at me through the crystal again.

"Hmph," he grunted, tucking his viewer back in his robe. "I guess you're okay. I'd love to get my hands on that Throckwoddle, though. He's been awfully free spreading my name around lately."

"Say, Frumple," Aahz interjected. "You aren't the only one who likes to see who he's doing business with, you know."

"Hm? Oh! Very well, if you insist."

I expected him to close his eyes and go to work, but instead he dipped a hand into his robe again. This time he produced what looked like a small hand mirror with some sort of a dial on the back. Peering into the mirror, he began to gently turn the dial with his fingers.

The result was immediate and startling. Not merely his face, but his whole body began to change, filling out, and taking on a definite reddish hue. As I watched, his brows thickened and grew closer together, his beard line crept up his face as if it were alive, and his eyes narrowed cruelly. Almost as an afterthought, I noted that his feet were now shiny cloven hooves and the tip of a pointed tail appeared at the bottom hem of his robe.

In an impressively short period of time, he had transformed into a . . . well, a devil!

Despite all my preparations, I felt the prickle of superstitious fear as he put away the mirror and turned to us again.

"Are you happy now?" he grumbled at Aahz.

"It's a start," Aahz conceded.

"Enough banter," Frumple was suddenly animated again. "What brings a Pervert to Klah? Slumming? And where does the kid fit in?"

"He's my apprentice," Aahz informed him.

"Really?" Frumple swept me with a sympathetic gaze. "Are things really that tough, kid? Maybe we could work something out."

"He's quite happy with the situation," interrupted Aahz. "Now let's get to our problem."

"You want me to cure the kid's insanity?"

"Huh? No. C'mon, Frumple. We came here on business. Let's declare a truce for a while, okay?"

"If you insist. It'll seem strange, though; Perverts and Deveels have never really gotten along."

"That's Pervects!"

"See what I mean?"

"Aahz!" I interrupted. "Could you just tell him?"

"Hmm? Oh. Right, kid. Look, Frumple. We've got a problem we were hoping you could help us with. You see, I've lost my powers."

"What!?" exploded Frumple. "You came here without the magical ability to protect yourself against being followed? That tears it. I spend seven years building a comfortable front here, and some idiot comes along and. . . ."

"Look, Frumple. We told you the kid here's my apprentice. He knows more than enough to cover us."

"A half-trained apprentice! He's trusting my life and security to a half-trained apprentice!"

"You seem to be overlooking the fact we're already here. If anything was going to happen it would have happened already."

"Every minute you two are here you're threatening my existence."

". . . which is all the more reason for you to deal with our problem immediately and stop this pointless breast-beating!"

The two of them glared at each other for a few moments, while I tried to be very quiet and unnoticeable. Frumple did not seem to be the right choice for someone to pin our hopes on.

"Oh, all right!" Frumple grumbled at last. "Since I probably won't be rid of you any other way."

He strode to the wall and produced what looked like a length of rope from behind one of the rugs.

"That's more like it," Aahz said triumphantly.

"Sid down and shut up," ordered our host.

Aahz did as he was bid, and Frumple proceeded to circle him. As he moved, the Deveel held the rope first this way, then that, sometimes looped in a circle, other times hanging limp. All the while he stared intently at the ceiling as if reading a message written there in fine print.

I didn't have the faintest idea what he was doing, but it was strangely enjoyable to watch someone order Aahz about and get away with it.

"Hmm. . . ." the Deveel said at last. "Yes, I think we can say that your powers are definitely gone."

"Terrific!" Aahz growled. "Look, Frumple. We didn't come all this way to be told something we already knew. You Deveels are supposed to be able to do anything. Well, do something!"

"It's not that easy, Pervert!" Frumple snapped back. "I need information. How did you lose your powers, anyway?"

"I don't know for sure," Aahz admitted. "I was summoned to Klah by a magician and when I arrived they were gone."

"A magician? Which one?"

"Garkin."

"Garkin? He's a mean one to cross. Why don't you just get him to restore your powers instead of getting me involved?"

"Because he's dead. Is that reason enough for you?"

"Hmm . . . that makes it difficult."

"Are you saying you can't do anything?" Aahz sneered. "I should have known. I always thought the reputation of the Deveels was overrated."

"Look, Pervert! Do you want my help or not? I didn't say I couldn't do anything, just that it would be difficult."

"That's more like it," Aahz chortled. "Let's get started."

"Not so fast," interrupted Frumple. "I didn't say I would help you, just that I could."

"I see," sneered Aahz. "Here it comes, kid. The price tag. I told you they were shake-down artists."

"Actually," the Deveel said dryly, "I was thinking of the time factor. It would take a while for me to make my preparations, and I believe I've made my feelings quite clear about you staying here longer than is absolutely necessary."

"In that case," smiled Aahz, "I suggest you get started. I believe I've made *my* feelings quite clear that we intend to stay here until the cure is effected."

"In that case," the Deveel smiled back at him, "I believe *you* raised the matter of cost. How much do you have with you?"

"Well, we have. . . ." I began.

"*That* strikes me as being unimportant," Aahz glared warningly at me. "Suppose you tell us how much you feel is a fair price for your services."

Frumple graced him with one withering glare before sinking thoughtfully into his calculations.

"Hmm . . . material cost is up . . . and of course,

there's my time . . . and you did call without an appointment . . . let's say it would cost you, just as a rough estimate, mind you, oh, in the neighborhood of . . . Say!''

He suddenly brightened and smiled at us.

''Maybe you'd be willing to work this as a trade. I cure you, and you do me a little favor.''

''What kind of a favor?'' Aahz asked suspiciously.

For once I was in complete agreement with him. Something in Frumple's voice did not inspire confidence.

''A small thing, really,'' the Deveel purred. ''Sort of a decoy mission.''

''We'd rather pay cash,'' I asserted firmly.

''Shut up, kid,'' Aahz advised. ''What kind of a decoy mission, Frumple?''

''You may have noticed the young couple who entered my shop ahead of you. You did! Good. Then you have doubtless noticed they are not on the premises currently.''

''How did they leave?'' I asked curiously.

''I'll get to that in a moment,'' Frumple smiled. ''Anyway, theirs is an interesting if common story. I'll spare you the details, but in short, they're young lovers kept apart by their families. In their desperation, they turned to me for assistance. I obliged them by sending them to another dimension where they can be happy free of their respective family's intervention.''

''For a fee, of course,'' Aahz commented dryly.

''Of course,'' Frumple smiled.

''C'mon, Aahz,'' I chided. ''It sounds like a decent thing to do, even if he was paid for it.''

''Quite so!'' beamed the Deveel. ''You're quite perceptive for one so young. Anyway, my generosity has left me in a rather precarious position. As you have no doubt noticed, I am quite concerned with my image in this town. There is a chance that image may be threatened if the couple's relatives succeed in tracking them to my shop and no farther.''

''That must have been some fee,'' Aahz mumbled.

''Now my proposition is this: in exchange for my assistance, I would ask that you two disguise yourselves as that couple and lay a false trail away from my shop."

"How much of a false trail?" I asked.

"Oh, it needn't be anything elaborate. Just be seen leaving town by enough townspeople to ensure that attention will be drawn away from my shop. Once out of sight of town, you can change to any disguise you like and return here. By that time, my preparations for your cure should be complete. Well, what do you say? Is it a deal?"

Chapter Thirteen:

"The secret to winning the support of large groups of people is positive thinking."

—N. BONAPARTE

"PEOPLE are staring at us, Aahz."

"Relax, kid. They're supposed to be staring at us."

To illustrate his point, he nodded and waved to a knot of glowering locals. They didn't wave back.

"I don't see why I have to be the girl," I grumbled.

"We went through that before, kid. You walk more like a girl than I do."

"That's what you and Frumple decided. I don't think I walk like a girl at all!"

"Well, let's say I walk less like a girl than you do."

It was hard to argue with logic like that, so I changed subjects.

"Couldn't we at least travel by less populated streets?" I asked.

"Why?" countered Aahz.

"Well, I'm not too wild about having a lot of people seeing me when I'm masquerading as a girl."

"C'mon, kid. The whole idea is that no one would recognize you. Besides, you don't know anybody in this town. Why should you care what they think of you?"

"I just don't like it, that's all," I grumbled.

"Not good enough," Aahz asserted firmly. "Being seen is part of our deal with Frumple. If you had any objections you should have said so before we closed the negotiations."

"I never got a chance," I pointed out. "But since the subject's come up, I do have a few questions."

"Such as?"

"Such as what are we doing?"

"Weren't you paying attention, kid? We're laying a false trail for. . . ."

"I know that," I interrupted. "What I mean is, why arc we doing what we're doing? Why are we doing Frumple a favor instead of just paying his price?"

"You wouldn't ask that if you'd ever dealt with a Deveel before," Aahz snorted. "Their prices are sky-high, especially in a case like ours when they know the customer is desperate. Just be thankful we got such a good deal."

"That's what I mean, Aahz. Are we *sure* we've gotten a good deal?"

"What do you mean?"

"Well, from what I've been told, if you think you've gotten a good deal from a Deveel, it usually means you've overlooked something."

"Of course you speak from a wide range of experience," Aahz sneered sarcastically. "Who told you so much about dealing with Deveels?"

"You did," I said pointedly.

"Hmmm. You're right, kid. Maybe I have been a little hasty."

Normally I would have been ecstatic over having Aahz admit I was right. Somehow, however, in the current situation, it only made me feel that much more uncomfortable.

"So what are we going to do?" I asked.

"Well, normally I deal honestly unless I think I'm being double-crossed. This time, however, you've raised sufficient doubt in my mind that I think we should bend the rules a little."

"Situational ethics again?"

"Right!"

"So what do we do?"

"Start looking for a relatively private place where we can dump these disguises without being noticed."

I began scanning the streets and alleys ahead of us. My uneasiness was growing into panic, and it lent intensity to my search.

"I wish we had our weapons along," I muttered.

"Listen to him," Aahz jeered. "It wasn't that long ago you were telling me all about how magicians don't need weapons. C'mon, kid. What would you do with a weapon if you had one?"

"If you want to get specific," I said dryly, "I was wishing *you* had a weapon."

"Oh! Good point. Say . . . ah . . . kid? Are you still looking for a private place?"

"Yeah, I've got a couple possibles spotted."

"Well forget it. Start looking for something wide open with a lot of exits."

"Why the change in strategy," I asked.

"Take a look over your shoulder . . . casual like."

I did as I was bid, though it was not as casual as it might have been. It turned out my acting ability was the least of our worries.

There was a crowd of people following us. They glared at us darkly and muttered to themselves. I wanted very badly to believe we were not the focus of their attention, but it was obvious that was not the case. They were clearly following us, and gathering members as they went.

"We're being followed, Aahz!" I whispered.

"Hey, kid. I pointed them out to you, remember?"

"But why are they following us? What do they want?"

"Well, I don't know for sure, of course, but I'd guess it has something to do with our disguises."

I snuck another glance at the crowd. The interest in us did not seem to be lessening at all. If anything, the crowd was even bigger and looked even angrier. Terrific.

"Say, Aahz?" I whispered.

"Yeah, kid?"

"If they're after us because of our disguises, why don't we just change back?"

"Bad plan, kid. I'd rather run the risk of them having some kind of grudge against the people we're impersonating than facing up to the consequences if they found out we were magicians."

"So what do we do?"

"We keep walking and hope we run into a patrol of soldiers that can offer us some protection."

A fist-sized rock thudded into the street ahead of us, presumably thrown by one of the people following us.

". . . or. . . ." Aahz revised hastily, "we can stop right now and find out what this is all about."

"We could run," I suggested hopefully, but Aahz was already acting on his earlier suggestion.

He stopped abruptly and spun on his heel to face the crowd.

"What is the meaning of this?" he roared at the advancing multitude.

The crowd lurched to a halt before the direct address, those in the rear colliding with those in front who had already stopped. They seemed a bit taken aback by Aahz's action and milled about without direction.

I was pleasantly surprised at the success of my companion's maneuver, but Aahz was never one to leave well enough alone.

"Well?" he demanded, advancing on them. "I'm waiting for an explanation."

For a moment the crowd gave ground before his approach. Then an angry voice rang out from somewhere in the back.

"We want to know about our money!"

That opened the door.

"Yeah! What about our money?!"

The cry was taken up by several other voices, and the crowd began to growl and move forward again.

Aahz stood his ground and held up a hand commanding silence.

"What about your money?" he demanded haughtily.

"Oh, no, you don't," came a particularly menacing voice. "You aren't going to talk your way out of it this time!"

A massive bald man brandishing a butcher's cleaver shouldered his way through the crowd to confront Aahz.

"My good man," Aahz sniffed. "If you're implying. . . ."

"I'm implying nothing!" The man growled. "I'm saying it flat out. You and that trollop of yours are crooks!"

"Now, aren't you being just a bit hasty in. . . ."

"Hasty!" the man bellowed. "Hasty! Mister, we've already been too patient with you. We should have run you out of town when you first showed up with your phoney anti-demon charms. That's right, I said phoney! Some of us knew it from the start. Anyone with a little education knows there's no such things as demons."

For a moment I was tempted to let Aahz's disguise drop. Then I looked at the crowd again and decided against it. It wasn't a group to joke with.

"Now, some folks bought the charms because they were gullible, some as a gag, some of us because . . . well, because everyone else was buying them. But we all bought them, just like we bought your story that they had to be individually made and you needed the money in advance."

"That was all explained at the time," Aahz protested.

"Sure it was. You're great at explanations. You explained it just like you explained away those two times we caught you trying to leave town."

"Well . . . we . . . uh," Aahz began.

"Actually," I interrupted, "we were only. . . ."

"Well, we've had enough of your explanations. That's what we told you three days ago when we gave you two days to either come up with the charms or give us our money back."

"But these things take time. . . ."

"You've used up that excuse. Your time was up yesterday. Now do we get our money, or. . . ."

"Certainly, certainly," Aahz raised his hands soothingly.

"Just give me a moment to speak with my colleague."

He smiled at the crowd as he took me by the arm and drew me away.

"What are we going to do, Aahz?"

"*Now* we run," he said calmly.

"Huh?" I asked intelligently.

I was talking to thin air. Aahz was already legging it speedily down the street.

I may be slow at times, but I'm not *that* slow. In a flash I was hot on his heels.

Unfortunately, the crowd figured out what Aahz was up to about the same time I did. With a howl they were after us.

Surprisingly, I overtook Aahz. Either he was holding back so I could catch up, or I was more scared than I thought, which is impossible.

"Now what?" I panted.

"Shut up and keep running, kid," Aahz barked, ducking around a knot of people.

"They're gaining on us," I pointed out.

Actually, the group we had just passed had joined the pursuit, but it had the same effect as if the crowd was gaining.

"Will you knock it off and help me look?" Aahz growled.

"Sure. What are we looking for?"

"A couple dressed roughly like us," he replied.

"What do we do if we see them?"

"Simple," Aahz replied. "We plow into them full tilt, you swap our features for theirs, and we let the mob tear *them* apart."

"That doesn't sound right somehow," I said doubtfully.

"Kid, remember what I told you about situational ethics?"

"Yeah."

"Well, this is one of those situations."

I was convinced, though not so much by Aahz's logic as by the rock that narrowly missed my head. I don't know how the crowd managed to keep its speed and still pick up things to throw, but it did.

I began watching for a couple dressed like us. It's harder than it sounds when you're at a dead run with a mob at your heels.

Unfortunately, there was no one in sight who came close to fitting the bill. Whomever it was we were impersonating seemed to be fairly unique in their dress.

"I wish I had a weapon with me," Aahz complained.

"We've already gone through that," I called back. "And besides, what would you do if you had one? The only thing we've got that might stop them is the fire ring."

"Hey! I'd forgotten about that," Aahz gasped. "I've still got it on."

"So what?" I asked. "We can't use it."

"Oh, yeah? Why not?"

"Because then they'd know we're magicians."

"That won't make any difference if they're dead."

Situational ethics or not, my stomach turned at the thought of killing that many people.

"Wait, Aahz!" I shouted.

"Watch this, kid." He grinned and pointed his hand at them.

Nothing happened.

Chapter Fourteen:

"A little help at the right time is better than a lot of help at the wrong time."

—Tevye

"C'MON, Aahz!" I shouted desperately, overturning a fruit stand in the path of the crowd.

Now that it seemed my fellow-humans were safe from Aahz, my concern returned to making sure he was safe from them.

"I don't believe it!" Aahz shouted, as he darted past.

"What?" I called, sprinting after him.

"In one day I believed both a Deveel and an Imp. Tell you what, kid. If we get out of this, I give you my permission to kick me hard. Right in the rump, twice."

"It's a deal!" I panted.

This running was starting to tax my stamina. Unfortunately, the crowd didn't seem tired at all. That was enough to keep me running.

"Look, kid!" Aahz was pointing excitedly. "We're saved."

I followed his finger. A uniformed patrol was marching . . . well, sauntering down the street ahead of us.

"It's about time," I grumbled, but I was relieved nonetheless.

The crowd saw the soldiers, too. Their cries increased

111

in volume as they redoubled their efforts to reach us.

"C'mon, kid! Step on it!" Aahz called. "We're not safe yet."

"Step on what?" I asked, passing him.

Our approach to the patrol was noisy enough that by the time we got there, the soldiers had all stopped moving and were watching the chase. One of them, a bit less unkempt than the others, had shouldered his way to the front of the group and stood sneering at us with folded arms. From his manners, I guessed he was an officer. There was no other explanation for the others allowing him to act the way he was.

I skidded to a stop in front of him.

"We're being chased!" I panted.

"Really?" he smiled.

"Let me handle this, kid," Aahz mumbled, brushing me aside. "Are you the officer in charge, sir?"

"I am," the man replied.

"Well, it seems that these . . . citizens," he pointed disdainfully at our pursuers, "intend us bodily harm. A blatant disregard for your authority . . . sir!"

The mob was some ten feet distant and stood glaring alternately at us and the soldiers. I was gratified to observe that at least some of them were breathing hard.

"I suppose you're right," the officer yawned. "We should take a hand in this."

"Watch this, kid," Aahz whispered, nudging me in the ribs as the officer stepped forward to address the crowd.

"All right. You all know it is against the law for citizens to inflict injuries on each other," he began.

The crowd began to grumble darkly, but the officer waved them into silence as he continued.

"I know, I know. We don't like it either. If it were up to us we'd let you settle your own differences and spend our time drinking. But it's not up to us. We have to follow the laws the same way you do, and the laws say only the military can judge and punish the citizenry."

"See?" I whispered. "There are some advantages to civilization."

"Shut up, kid," Aahz hissed back.

"So even though I know you'd love to beat these two to a bloody pulp, we can't let you do it. They must be hanged in accordance with the law!"

"What?"

I'm not sure if I said it, or Aahz, or if we cried out in unison. Whichever it was, it was nearly drowned out in the enthusiastic roar of the crowd.

A soldier seized my wrists and twisted them painfully behind my back. Looking about, I saw the same thing had happened to Aahz. Needless to say, this was not the support we had been hoping for.

"What did you expect?" the officer sneered at us. "If you wanted help from the military, you shouldn't have included us on your list of customers. If we had had our way, we would have strung you up a week ago. The only reason we held back was these yokels had given you extra time and we were afraid of a riot if we tried anything."

Our wrists were secured by thongs now. We were slowly being herded toward a lone tree in front of one of the open-air restaurants.

"Has anyone got some rope?" the officer called to the crowd.

Just our luck, somebody did. It was passed rapidly to the officer, who began ceremoniously tying nooses.

"Psst! kid!" Aahz whispered.

"What now?" I mumbled bitterly.

My faith in Aahz's advice was at an all-time low.

"When they go to hang you, fly!"

"What?"

Despite myself, I was seized with new hope.

"C'mon, kid. Wake up! Fly. Like I taught you on the trail."

"They'd just shoot me down."

"Not fly away, dummy. Just fly. Hover at the end of the rope and twitch. They'll think you're hanging."

I thought about it . . . hard. It might work, but . . . I noticed they were tossing the nooses over a lower limb of the tree.

"Aahz! I can't do it. I can't levitate us both. I'm not that good yet."

"Not both of us, kid. Just you. Don't worry about me."

"But . . . Aahz. . . ."

"Keep my disguise up, though. If they figure out I'm a demon they'll burn the bodies . . . both of them."

"But Aahz. . . ."

We were out of time. Rough hands shoved us forward and started fitting the nooses over our heads.

I realized with a start I had no time to think about Aahz. I'd need all my concentration to save myself, if there was even time for that!

I closed my eyes and sought desperately for a force line in the air. There was one there . . . faint, but there. I began to focus on it.

The noose tightened around my neck and I felt my feet leave the ground. I felt panic rising in me and forced it down.

Actually it was better this way. They should feel weight on the rope as they raised me. I concentrated on the force line again . . . focus . . . draw the energies . . . redirect them.

I felt a slight loosening of the noose. Remembering Aahz's lectures on control, I held the energies right there and tried an experimental breath. I could get air! Not much, it was true, but enough to survive.

What else did I have to do? Oh yes, I had to twitch. I thought back to how a squirrel-badger acted when caught in a snare.

I kicked my legs slightly and tried an experimental tremor. It had the overall effect of tightening the noose. I decided to try another tactic. I let my head loll to one side and extended my tongue out of the corner of my mouth.

It worked. There was a sudden increase in the volume of the catcalls from the crowd to reward my efforts.

I held that pose.

My tongue was rapidly drying out, but I forced my mind away from it. To avoid involuntarily swallowing, I tried to think of other things.

Poor Aahz. For all his gruff criticism and claims of not caring for anyone else but himself, his last act had been to think of my welfare. I promised myself that when I got down from here. . . .

What would happen when I got down from here? What do they do with bodies in this town? Do they bury them? It occurred to me it might be better to hang than be buried alive.

"The law says they're supposed to hang there until they rot!"

The officer's voice seemed to answer my thoughts and brought my mind back to the present.

"Well, they aren't hanging in front of the law's restaurant!" came an angry voice in response.

"Tell you what. We'll come back at sundown and cut them down."

"Sundown? Do you realize how much money I could lose before sundown? Nobody wants to eat at a place where a corpse dangles its toes in his soup. I've already lost most of the lunch rush!"

"Hmm . . . It occurs to me that if the day's business means that much to you, you should be willing to share a little of the profit."

"So that's the way it is, is it? Oh, very well. Here . . . for your troubles."

There was the sound of coins being counted out.

"That isn't very much. I have to share with my men, you know."

"You drive a hard bargain! I didn't know bandits had officers."

More coins were counted, accompanied by the officer's chuckle. It occurred to me that instead of studying magik, I should be devoting my time to bribes and graft. It seemed to work better.

"Men!" the officer called. "Cut this carrion down and haul it out of town. Leave it at the city limits as a warning to anyone else who would seek to cheat the citizens of Twixt."

"You're too considerate." The restaurant owner's voice was edged with sarcasm.

"Think nothing of it, citizen," the officer sneered.

I barely remembered to stop flying before they cut the rope. I bit my tongue as I started into the ground, and risked sneaking it back into my mouth. No one noticed.

Unseen hands grabbed me under the armpits and by the ankles, and the journey began to the city limits.

Now that I knew I wasn't going to be buried, my thoughts returned to my future.

First, I would have to do something to Frumple. What, I wasn't sure, but something. I owed Aahz that much. Maybe I could restore Quigley and enlist his aid. He was supposed to be a demon hunter. He was probably better equipped to handle a Deveel than I was. Then again, remembering Quigley, that might not be a valid assumption.

Then there was Isstvan. What was I going to do about him? I wasn't sure I could beat him with Aahz's help. Without it, I wouldn't stand a chance.

"This should be far enough. Shall we hang them again?"

I froze at the suggestion. Fortunately the voice at my feet had different ideas.

"Why bother? I haven't seen an officer yet who'd move a hundred paces from a bar. Let's just dump 'em here."

There was a general chorus of assent, and the next minute I was flying through the air again. I tried to relax for the impact, but the ground knocked the wind out of me again.

If I was going to continue my efforts to master flying, I'd have to devote more time to the art of forced landings.

I lay there motionless. I couldn't hear the soldiers any more, but I didn't want to run the risk of sitting up and betraying the fact I wasn't dead.

"Are you going to lay there all day or are you going to help me get untied?"

My eyes flew open involuntarily. Aahz was sitting there grinning down at me.

There was only one sensible thing to do, and I did it. I fainted.

Chapter Fifteen:

"Anyone who uses the phrase 'easy as taking candy from a baby' has never tried taking candy from a baby."

—R. HOOD

"CAN we move now?" I asked.

"Not yet, kid. Wait until the lights have been out for a full day."

"You mean a full hour."

"Whatever. Now shut up and keep watching."

We were waiting in the dead-end alley across the street from Frumple's shop. Even though we were supposedly secure in our new disguises, I was uneasy being back in the same town where I had been hung. It's a hard feeling to describe to someone who hasn't experienced it. Then too, it was strange being with Aahz after I had gotten used to the idea of him being dead.

Apparently the neck muscles of a Pervect are considerably stronger than those of a human. Aahz had simply tensed those muscles and they provided sufficient support to keep the noose from cutting off his air supply.

As a point of information, Aahz had further informed me that his scales provided better armor than most chain-mail or plate armor available in this dimension. I had heard once that demons could only be

117

destroyed by specially constructed weapons or by burning. It seemed the old legends may have actually had some root in fact.

"Okay, kid," Aahz whispered. "I guess we've waited long enough."

He eased himself out of the alley and led me in a long circle around the shop, stopping again only when we had returned to our original spot by the alley.

"Well, what do you think, kid?"

"Don't know. What were we looking for?"

"Tell me again about how you planned to be a thief," Aahz sighed. "Look, kid. We're looking over a target. Right?"

"Right," I replied, glad to be able to agree with something.

"Okay, how many ways in and out of that shop did you see?"

"Just one. The one across the street there."

"Right. Now how do you figure we're going to get into the shop?"

"I don't know," I said honestly.

"C'mon, kid. If there's only one way in. . . ."

"You mean we're just going to walk in the front door?"

"Why not? We can see from here the door's open."

"Well . . . if you say so, Aahz. I just thought it would be harder than that."

"Whoa! Nobody said it was going to be easy. Just because the door's open doesn't mean the door's open."

"I didn't quite get that, Aahz."

"Think, kid. We're after a Deveel, right? He's got access to all kinds of magic and gimmicks. Now what say you close your eyes and take another look at that door."

I did as I was told. Immediately the image of a glowing cage sprang into my mind, a cage that completely enclosed the shop.

"He's got some kind of ward up, Aahz," I informed my partner.

It occurred to me that a few short weeks ago I would have held such a structure in awe. Now, I accepted it as relatively normal, just another obstacle to be overcome.

"Describe it to me," Aahz hissed.

"Well . . . it's bright . . . whitish purple . . . there's a series of bars and crossbars forming squares about a hand-span across. . . ."

"Is it just over the door, or all over the shop?"

"All over the shop. The top's covered, and the bars run right into the ground."

"Hmm, well, we'll just have to go through it. Listen up, kid. Time for a quick lesson."

I opened my eyes and looked at the shop again. The building looked as innocent as it had when we first circled it. It bothered me that I couldn't sense the cage's presence the way I could our own wards.

"What is it, Aahz?" I asked uneasily.

"Hmm? Oh, it's a ward, kind of like the ones we use, but a lot nastier."

"Nastier, how?"

"Well, the kind of wards I taught you to build are an early warning system and not much else. From the sounds of it, the stuff Frumple is using will do considerably more. Not only will it kill you, it'll knock you into pieces smaller than dust. It's called disintegration."

"And we're going to go through it?" I asked, incredulously.

"*After* you've had a quick lesson. Now, remember your feather drills? How you'd wrap your mind around the feather for control?"

"Yeah," I said, puzzled.

"Well, I want you to do the same thing, but without the feather. Pretend you're holding something that isn't there. Form the energies into a tube."

"Then what?"

"Then you insert the tube into one of the squares in the cage and expand it."

"That's all?"

"That's it. C'mon now. Give it a try."

I closed my eyes and reached out with my mind.

Choosing a square in the center of the open doorway, I
inserted my mental tube and began to expand it. As it
touched the bars forming the square, I experienced a
tingle and a physical pressure as if I had encountered a
tangible object.

"Easy, kid," Aahz said softly. "We just want to
bend the bars a bit, not break them."

I expanded the tube. The bars gave way slowly, until
they met with the next set. Then I experienced another
tingle and additional pressure.

"Remember, kid. Once we're inside, take your time.
Wait for your eyes to adjust to the dark. We don't want
to tip Frumple off by stumbling around and knocking
things over."

I was having to strain now. The tube had reached
another set of bars now, making it a total of twelve bars
I was forcing outward.

"Have you got it yet?" Aahz's whisper sounded anxious.

"Just a second . . . Yes!"

The tube was now big enough for us to crawl through.

"Are you sure?"

"Yes."

"Okay. Lead the way, kid. I'll be right behind you."

Strangely enough, I felt none of my usual doubts as I
strode boldly across the street to the shop. Apparently
my confidence in my abilities was growing, for I didn't
even hesitate as I began to crawl through the tube. The
only bad moment I had was when I suddenly realized I
was crawling on thin air about a foot off the ground.
Apparently I had set the tube a little too high, but no
matter. It held! Next time I would know better.

I eased myself out of the end of the tube and stood in
the shop's interior. I could hear the soft sounds of
Aahz's passage behind me as I waited for my eyes to adjust to the dark.

"Ease away from the door, kid," came Aahz's whispered advice in my ear as he stood behind me. "You're
standing in a patch of moonlight. And you can collapse
the tube now."

Properly notified, I shifted away from the moonlight. I was pleased to note, however, that releasing the tube did not make a significant difference in my mental energies. I was progressing to where I could do more difficult feats with less energy than when I started. I was actually starting to feel like a magician.

I heard a slight noise behind me and craned my neck to look. Aahz was quietly drawing the curtains over the door.

I smiled grimly to myself. Good! We don't want witnesses.

My eyes were nearly adjusted now. I could make out shapes and shadows in the darkness. There was a dark lump in the corner that breathed heavily. Frumple!

I felt a hand on my shoulder. Aahz pointed out a lamp on a table and held up four fingers.

I nodded and started counting slowly to four. As I reached the final number, I focused a quick flash of energy at the lamp, and its wick burst into flame, lighting the shop's interior.

Aahz was kneeling beside Frumple, knife in hand. Apparently he had succeeded in finding at least some of our weapons in the dark.

Frumple sat up blinking, then froze in place. Aahz had the point of his knife hovering a hairsbreadth from the Deveel's throat.

"Hello, Frumple," he smiled. "Remember us?"

"You!" gasped the Deveel. "You're supposed to be dead!"

"Dead?" Aahz purred. "How could any harm befall us with our old pal Frumple helping us blend with the citizenry?"

"Gentlemen!" our victim squealed. "There seems to have been a mistake!"

"That's right," I commented. "And you made it."

"You don't understand!" Frumple persisted, "I was surprised and horrified when I heard about your deaths."

"Yeah, we weren't too happy about it ourselves."

"Later, kid. Look, Frumple. Right now we have both

the ability and the motive to kill you. Right?''

"But I. . . .''

"Right?''

Aahz moved the knife until the point was indenting the skin on Frumple's throat.

"Right!'' the Deveel whispered.

"Okay, then.'' Aahz withdrew the knife and tucked it back in his waistband. "Now let's talk business.''

"I . . . I don't understand,'' Frumple stammered, rubbing his throat with one hand as if to assure himself that it was still there.

"What it means,'' Aahz explained, "is that we want your help more than we want revenge. Don't relax too much, though. The choice wasn't that easy.''

"I . . . I see. Well, what can I do for you?''

"C'mon, Frumple. You can honor our original deal. You've got to admit we've laid one heck of a false trail for your two fugitives. Now it's your turn. Just restore my powers and we'll be on our way.''

The Deveel blanched, or at least he turned from red to pink.

"I can't do that!'' he exclaimed.

"What?''

The knife appeared in Aahz's hand again as if by magik.

"Now look, you double-dealing refugee. Either you restore my powers or. . . .''

"You don't understand,'' Frumple pleaded. "I don't mean I won't restore your powers. I mean I can't. I don't know what's wrong with you or how to counter it. That's why I set you up with the mob. I was afraid if I told you before, you wouldn't believe me. I've spent too much time establishing myself here to risk being exposed by an unsatisfied customer. I'm sorry, I really am, and I know you'll probably kill me, but I can't help you!''

Chapter Sixteen:

"Just because something doesn't do what you planned it to do doesn't mean it's useless."

—T. EDISON

"HMMM," Aahz said thoughtfully. "So you're powerless to restore my powers?"

"Does that mean we can kill him after all?" I asked eagerly. I had been hopeful of having Aahz's powers restored, but in lieu of that, I was still a bit upset over having been hung.

"You're a rather vicious child," Frumple looked at me speculatively. "What's a Pervect doing traveling with a Klahd, anyway?"

"Who's a clod?" I bristled.

"Easy, kid," Aahz said soothingly. "Nothing personal. Everyone who's native to this dimension is a Klahd. Klah . . . Klahds . . . get it?"

"Well, I don't like the sound of it," I grumbled.

"Relax, kid. What's in a name, anyway?"

"Then it doesn't really matter to you if people call you a Pervect or a Pervert?"

"Watch your mouth, kid. Things are going bad enough without you getting cheeky."

"Gentlemen, gentlemen," Frumple interrupted. "If you're going to fight would you mind going outside? I mean, this *is* my shop."

"Can we kill him now, Aahz?"

"Ease up, kid. Just because he can't restore my powers doesn't mean he's totally useless. I'm sure that he'll be more than happy to help us, particularly after he failed to pay up on our last deal. Right, Frumple?"

"Oh, definitely. Anything I can do to make up for the inconvenience I've caused you."

"Inconvenience?" I asked incredulously.

"Steady, kid. Well, Frumple, you could start by returning the stuff we left here when we went off on your little mission."

"Of course. I'll get it for you." .

The Deveel started to rise, only to find Aahz's knife threatening him again.

"Don't trouble yourself, Frumple, old boy," Aahz smiled. "Just point out where they are and we'll fetch them ourselves . . . and keep your hands where I can see them."

"The . . . your things are over there . . . in the big chest against the wall," Frumple's eyes never left the knife as he spoke.

"Check it out, kid."

I did and, surprisingly, the items were exactly where the Deveel said they would be. There was, however, an intriguing collection of other strange items in the chest also.

"Hey, Aahz!" I called. "Take a look at this!"

"Sure, kid."

He backed across the shop to join me. As he did, he flipped the knife into what I now recognized as a throwing grip. Apparently Frumple recognized it too, because he stayed frozen in position.

"Well, what have we here?" Aahz chortled.

"Gentlemen," the Deveel called plaintively. "I could probably help you better if I knew what you needed."

"True enough," Aahz responded, reclaiming his weapons.

"Frumple, it occurs to me we haven't been completely open with you. That will have to be corrected if we're going to be allies."

"Wait a minute, Aahz," I interrupted. "What makes you think we can trust him after he's tried so hard to get us killed?"

"Simple, kid. He tried to get us killed to protect himself, right?"

"Well. . . ."

"So once we explain it's in his own self-interest to help us, he should be completely trustworthy."

"Really?" I sneered.

"Well, as trustworthy as any Deveel can be," Aahz admitted.

"I resent the implications of that, Pervert!" Frumple exclaimed. "If you want any help, you'd better. . . ." Aahz's knife flashed through the air and thunked into the wall scant inches from the Deveel's head.

"Shut up and listen, Frumple!" he snarled. "And that's Pervect!"

"What's in a name, Aahz?" I asked innocently.

"Shut up, kid. Okay, Frumple, does the name Isstvan mean anything to you?"

"No. Should it?"

"It should if you want to stay alive. He's a madman magician who's trying to take over the dimensions, starting with this one."

"Why should that concern me?" Frumple frowned. "We Deveels trade with anyone who can pay the price. We don't concern ourselves with analyzing politics or mental stability. If we only dealt with sane beings, it would cut our business by a third . . . maybe more."

"Well, you'd better concern yourself this time. Maybe you didn't hear me. Isstvan is starting with this dimension. He's out to get a monopoly on Klah's energies to use on other dimensions. To do that, he's out to kill anyone else in this dimension who knows how to tap those energies. He's not big on sharing."

"Hmmm. Interesting theory, but where's the proof —I mean, who's he supposed to have killed?"

"Garkin, for one," I said, dryly.

"That's right," Aahz snarled. "You're so eager to know why the two of us are traveling together. Well, Skeeve here was Garkin's apprentice until Isstvan sent his assassins to wipe out the competition."

"Assassins?"

"That's right. You saw two of them, those Imps you teleported about a week back." Aahz flourished the assassin's cloak we had acquired.

"Where did you think we got this? In a rummage sale?"

"Hmmm," Frumple commented thoughtfully.

"And he's arming them with tech weapons. Take a look at this crossbow quarrel."

Aahz lobbed one of the missiles to the Deveel who caught it deftly and examined it closely.

"Hmmm. I didn't notice that before. It's a good camouflage job, but totally unethical."

"Now do you see why enlisting your aid takes priority over the pleasure of slitting your lying throat?"

"I see what you mean," Frumple replied without rancor. "It's most convincing. But what can I do?"

"You tell us. You Deveels are supposed to have wonders for every occasion. What have you got that would give us an edge over a madman who knows his magik?"

Frumple thought for several minutes. Then shrugged. "I can't think of a thing just offhand. I haven't been stocking weapons lately. Not much call for them in this dimension."

"Terrific," I said. "Can we kill him now, Aahz?"

"Say, could you put a muzzle on him?" Frumple said. "What's your gripe anyway, Skeeve?"

"I don't take well to being hung," I snarled.

"Really? Well, you'll get used to it if you keep practicing magik. It's being burned that's really a pain."

"Wait a minute, Frumple," Aahz interrupted. "You're acting awfully casual about hanging for someone who was so surprised to see us alive."

"I was. I underestimated your apprentice's mastery of the energies. If I had thought you could escape, I would have thought of something else. I *was* trying to get you killed, after all."

"He doesn't sound particularly trustworthy," I observed.

"You will notice, my young friend, that I stated my intentions in the past tense. Now that we share a common goal, you'll find me much easier to deal with."

"Which brings us back to our original question," Aahz asserted. "What can you do for us, Frumple?"

"I really don't know," the Deveel admitted. "Unless . . . I know! I can send you to the Bazaar!"

"The Bazaar?" I asked.

"The Bazaar on Deva! If you can't find what you need there, it doesn't exist. Why didn't I think of that before? That's the answer!"

He was on his feet now, moving toward us.

"I know you're in a hurry, so I'll get you started. . . ."

"Not so fast, Frumple."

Aahz had his sword out menacing the Deveel.

"We want a guarantee this is a round trip you're sending us on."

"I . . . I don't understand."

"Simple. You tried to get rid of us once. It occurs to me you might be tempted to send us off to some backwater dimension with no way to get back."

"But I give you my word that. . . ."

"We don't want your word," Aahz grinned. "We want your presence."

"What?"

"Where we go, you go. You're coming with us, just to be extra sure we get back."

"I can't do that!" Frumple seemed honestly terrified. "I've been banned from Deva! You don't know what they'd do to me if I went back."

"That's too bad. We want a guaranteed return before we budge, and that's you!"

"Wait a minute! I think I've got the answer!"

The Deveel began frantically rummaging through chests. I watched, fascinated, as an astounding array of strange objects emerged as he searched.

"Here it is!" he cried at last, holding his prize aloft.

It appeared to be a metal rod, about eight inches long and two inches in diameter. It had strange markings on its sides, and a button on the end.

"A D-Hopper!" Aahz exclaimed. "I haven't seen one of those in years."

Frumple tossed it to him.

"There you go. Is that guarantee enough?"

"What is it, Aahz?" I asked, craning my neck to see.

He seized the ends of the rod and twisted in opposite directions. Apparently it was constructed of at least two parts, because the symbols began to slide around the rod in opposite directions.

"Depending on where you want to go, you align different symbols. Then you just push the button and. . . ."

"Wait a minute!" Frumple cried. "We haven't settled on a price for that yet!"

"Price?" I asked.

"Yeah, price! Those things don't grow on trees, you know."

"If you will recall," Aahz murmured, "you still owe us from our last deal."

"True enough," Frumple agreed. "But as you yourself pointed out, those D-Hoppers are rare. A real collector's item. It's only fair that our contract be renegotiated at a slightly higher fee."

"Frumple, we're in too much of a hurry to argue," Aahz announced. "I'll say once what we're willing to relinquish over and above our original deal and you can take it or leave it. Fair enough?"

"What did you have in mind?" Frumple asked, rubbing his hands together eagerly.

"Your life."

"My . . . Oh! I see. Yes, that . . . um . . . should be an acceptable price."

"I'm surprised at you, Frumple," I chimed in. "Letting a collector's item go that cheap."

"C'mon, kid." Aahz was adjusting the settings on the D-Hopper. "Let's get moving."

"Just a second, Aahz. I want to get my sword."

"Leave it. We can pick it up on the way back."

"Say, Aahz, how long does it take to travel between dimensions any. . . ."

The walls of Frumple's hut suddenly dissolved in a kaleidoscope of color.

"Not long, kid. In fact, we're there."

And we were.

Chapter Seventeen:

"The wonders of the ages assembled for your edification, education, and enjoyment—for a price."

—P. T. BARNUM

WHILE I knew my home dimension wasn't particularly colorful, I never really considered it drab . . . until I first set eyes on the Bazaar at Deva.

Even though both Aahz and Frumple, and even the Imps, had referred to this phenomenon, I had never actually sat back and tried to envision it. It was just as well. Anything I could have fantasized would have been dwarfed by the real thing.

The Bazaar seemed to stretch endlessly in all directions as far as the eye could see. Tents and lean-tos of all designs and colors were gathered in irregular clumps that shoved against each other for more room.

There were thousands of Deveels everywhere of every age and description. Tall Deveels, fat Deveels, lame Deveels, bald Deveels, all moved about until the populace gave the appearance of being one seething mass with multiple heads and tails. There were other beings scattered through the crowd. Some of them looked like nightmares come to life; others I didn't recognize as being alive until they moved, but they all made noise.

The noise! Twixt had seemed noisy to me after my

secluded life with Garkin, but the clamor that assailed my ears now defied all description. There were shrieks and dull explosions and strange burbling noises emanating from the depths of the booths around us, competing with the constant din of barter. It seemed no one spoke below a shout. Whether weeping piteously, barking in anger, or displaying bored indifference, all bartering was to be done at the top of your lungs.

"Welcome to Deva, kid," Aahz gestured expansively. "What do you think?"

"It's loud," I observed.

"What?"

"I said, 'it's loud!' " I shouted.

"Oh, well. It's a bit livelier than your average Farmer's Market or Fisherman's Wharf, but there are noisier places to be."

I was about to respond when a passerby careened into me. He, or she, had eyes spaced all around his head and fur-covered tentacles instead of arms.

"Wzklp!" it said, waving a tentacle as it continued on its way.

"Aahz!"

"Yeah, kid?"

"It just occurred to me. What language do they speak on Deva?"

"Hmm? Oh! Don't worry about it, kid. They speak all languages here. No Deveel that's been hatched would let a sale get away just because they couldn't speak the right tongue. Just drop a few sentences on 'em in Klahdish and they'll adapt fast enough."

"Okay, Aahz. Now that we're here, where do we go first?"

There was no answer. I tore my eyes away from the Bazaar and glanced at my partner. He was standing motionless, sniffing the air.

"Aahz?"

"Hey kid, do you smell that?" he asked eagerly.

I sniffed the air.

"Yeah!" I gagged. "What died?"

"C'mon, kid. Follow me."

He plunged off into the crowd, leaving me little choice but to trail after him. Hands plucked at our sleeves as we passed, and various Deveels leaned out of their stalls and tents to call to us as we passed, but Aahz didn't slacken his pace. I couldn't get a clear look at any of the displays as we passed. Keeping up with Aahz demanded most of my concentration. One tent, however, did catch my eye.

"Look, Aahz!" I cried.

"What?"

"It's raining in that tent!"

As if in answer to my words, a boom of thunder and a crackle of lightning erupted from the display.

"Yeah. So?" Aahz dismissed it with a glance.

"What are they selling, rain?"

"Naw. Weather-control devices. They're scattered through the whole Bazaar instead of hanging together in one section. Something about the devices interfering with each other."

"Are all the displays that spectacular?"

"That isn't spectacular, kid. They used to do tornados until the other booths complained and they had to limit their demonstrations to the tame stuff. Now hurry up!"

"Where are we going anyway, Aahz? And what *is* that smell?"

The repulsive aroma was growing noticeably stronger.

"That," proclaimed Aahz, coming to a halt in front of a dome-shaped tent, "is the smell of Pervish cooking!"

"Food? We came all this way so you could have a meal?"

"First things first, kid. I haven't had a decent meal since Garkin called me out of the middle of a party and stranded me in your idiot dimension."

"But we're supposed to be looking for something to use against Isstvan."

"Relax, kid. I haggle better on a full stomach. Just wait here. I won't be long."

"Wait here? Can't I go in with you?"

"I don't think you'd like it, kid. To anyone who wasn't born on Perv, the food looks even worse than it smells."

I found that hard to believe, but pursued the argument gamely.

"I'm not all that weak-stomached, you know. When I was living in the woods, I ate some pretty weird things myself."

"I'll tell ya, kid, the main problem with Pervish food is keeping the goo from crawling out of the bowl while you're eating it."

"I'll wait here," I decided.

"Good. Like I say, I won't be long. You can watch the dragons until I get back."

"Dragons?" I said, but he had already disappeared through the tent flap.

I turned slowly and looked at the display behind me.

Dragons!

There was an enormous stall stocked with dragons not fifteen feet from where I was standing. Most of the beasts were tethered at the back wall which kept me from seeing them as we approached, but upon direct viewing there was no doubt they were dragons.

Curiosity made me drift over to join the small crowd in front of the stall. The stench was overwhelming, but after a whiff of Pervish cooking, it seemed almost pleasant.

I had never seen a dragon before, but the specimens in the stall lived up to the expectations of my daydreams. They were huge, easily ten or fifteen feet high at the shoulder and a full thirty feet long. Their necks were long and serpentine, and their clawed feet dug great gouges in the ground as they shifted their weight nervously.

I was surprised to see how many varieties there were. It had never occurred to me that there might be more than one type of dragon, but here was living proof to the contrary. Besides the green dragons I had always envisioned, there were red, black, gold and blue dragons. There was even one that was mauve. Some were winged and some weren't. Some had wide, massive jaws and others had narrow snouts. Some had eyes that were squinting and slanted, while others had huge moonlike eyes that never seemed to blink. They had two things in common, however: they were all big and they all looked thoroughly nasty.

My attention was drawn to the Deveel running the operation. He was the biggest Deveel I had ever seen, fully eight feet tall with arms like trees. It was difficult to say which was more fearsome in appearance, the dragons or their keeper.

He brought one of the red dragons to the center of the stall and released it with a flourish. The beast raised its head and surveyed the crowd with seething yellow eyes. The crowd fell back a few steps before that gaze. I seriously considered leaving.

The Deveel shouted a few words at the crowd in gibberish I couldn't understand, then picked up a sword from the rack by the wall.

Fast as a cat, the dragon arched his neck and spat a stream of fire at its keeper. By some miracle, the flame parted as it hit the Deveel and passed harmlessly on either side of him.

The keeper smiled and turned to shout a few more words at his audience. As he did, the dragon leapt at him with murderous intent. The Deveel dove to the ground and rolled out from under the attack as the beast landed with an impact that shook the tent. The dragon whirled, but the keeper was on his feet again, holding aloft a pendant before the beast's eyes.

I didn't understand his move, but apparently the dragon did, for it cowered back on its haunches. The Deveel pointed forcefully and it slunk back to its place at the back of the stall.

A small ripple of applause rippled through the crowd. Apparently they were impressed with the ferocity of the dragon's attack. Me, I was impressed by the pendant.

The keeper acknowledged the applause and launched into another spiel of gibberish, this time punctuated by gestures and exclamations.

I decided it was about time for me to go.

"Gleep!"

There was a tug at my sleeve.

I looked around. There, behind me, was a small dragon! Well, he was about four feet high and ten feet long, but after looking at the other dragons, he seemed small. He was green with big blue eyes and what appeared to be a drooping white mustache.

For a split second I was panicky, but that rapidly gave way to curiosity. He didn't look dangerous. He seemed quite content just standing there chewing on. . . .

My sleeve! The beast was eating a piece of my sleeve! I looked down and confirmed that part of my shirt was indeed missing.

"Gleep," said the dragon again, stretching his neck out for another mouthful.

"Go away!" I said, and cuffed him before I realized what I was doing.

"Gleep?" it said, puzzled.

I started to edge away. I was unsure of what to do if he cut loose with a blast of fire and therefore eager to avoid it.

"Gleep," it said, shuffling after me.

"Gazabkp!" roared a voice behind me.

I spun and found myself looking at a hairy stomach. I followed it up, way up, and saw the dragon keeper's face looming over me.

"I'm sorry," I apologized readily. "I don't speak your language."

"Oh. A Klahd!" The Deveel boomed. "Well, the statement still stands. Pay up!"

"Pay up for what?"

"For the dragon! What do you think, we're giving away samples?"

"Gleep!" said the dragon, pressing his head against my leg.

"There seems to be some mistake," I said hastily.

"I'll say there is," the Deveel scowled. "And you're making it. We don't take kindly to shoplifters on Deva!"

"Gleep!" said the dragon.

Things were rapidly getting out of hand. If I ever needed Aahz's help or advice, it was now. I shot a desperate glance toward the tent he was in, hoping beyond hope to see him emerge.

He wasn't there. In fact, the tent wasn't there! It was gone, vanished into thin air, and so had Aahz!

Chapter Eighteen:

"No matter what the product or service might be, you can find it somewhere else cheaper!"

—E. SCROOGE

"WHERE did that tent go?" I demanded desperately.

"What tent?" The keeper blinked, looming behind me.

"That tent," I exclaimed, pointing at the now vacant space.

The Deveel frowned, craning his neck, which at his height, gave him considerable visibility.

"There isn't any tent there," he announced with finality.

"I know! That's the point!"

"Hey! Quit trying to change the subject!" The keeper growled, poking me in the chest with an unbelievably large finger. "Are you going to pay for the dragon or not?"

I looked around for support, but no one was watching. Apparently disputes such as this were common on Deva.

"I told you there's been a mistake! I don't want your dragon."

"Gleep!" said the dragon, cocking his head at me.

"Don't give me that!" the keeper boomed. "If you didn't want him, why did you feed him?"

"I didn't feed him! He ate a piece of my sleeve!"

"Gleep!" said the dragon, making another unsuccessful pass at my shirt.

"So you admit he got food from you?"

"Well . . . in a manner of speaking . . . Yeah! So what?" I was getting tired of being shouted at.

"So pay up! He's no good to me anymore."

I surveyed the dragon. He didn't seem to be any the worse for having eaten the shirt.

"What's wrong with him? He looks all right to me."

"Gleep!" said the dragon, and sidled up to me again.

"Oh! He's fine," the keeper sneered. "Except now he's attached. An attached dragon isn't any good except to the person or thing he's attached to."

"Well, who's he attached to?"

"Don't get smart with me! He's attached to you! Has been ever since you fed him."

"Well, feed him again and unattach him! I have pressing matters elsewhere."

"Just like that, huh?" the Deveel said skeptically, towering to new heights. "You know very well it doesn't work that way. Once a dragon's attached, it's attached forever. That's why they're so valuable."

"Forever?" I asked.

"Well . . . until one of you dies. But any fool knows not to feed a dragon unless they want it attached to them. The idiot beasts are too impressionable, especially the young ones like this."

I looked at the dragon again. He was very young. His wings were just beginning to bud, which I took as a sign of immaturity, and his fangs were needle-sharp instead of worn to rounded points like his brethren in the stall. Still, there was strength in the muscles rippling beneath those scales . . . yes, I decided, I'd back my dragon in a fight against any. . . .

"Gleep!" said the dragon, licking both ends of his

mustache simultaneously with his forked tongue.

That brought me to my senses. A dragon? What did I want with a dragon?

"Well," I said haughtily, "I guess I'm not just any fool, then. If I had known the consequences of allowing him to eat my sleeve, I would have . . ."

"Look, sonny!" The Deveel snarled, poking my chest again. "If you think you're going to. . . ."

Something inside me snapped. I knocked his hand away with a fury that surprised me.

"The name isn't 'Sonny,' " I hissed in a low voice I didn't recognize as my own. "It's Skeeve! Now lower your voice when you're talking to me and keep your dirty finger to yourself!"

I was shaking, though whether from rage or from fear I couldn't tell. I had spent my entire burst of emotion in that tirade and now found myself wondering if I would survive the aftermath.

Surprisingly, the keeper gave ground a few steps at my tirade, and was now studying me with new puzzlement. I felt a pressure at the back of my legs and risked a glance. The dragon was now crouched behind me, craning his neck to peer around my waist at the keeper.

"I'm sorry." The keeper was suddenly humble and fawning. "I didn't recognize you at first. You said your name was . . . ?"

"Skeeve." I prompted haughtily.

"Skeeve." He frowned thoughtfully. "Strange. I don't remember that name."

I wasn't sure who or what he thought I was, but if I had learned one thing traveling with Aahz, it was to recognize and seize an advantage when I saw one.

"The secrecy surrounding my identity should be a clue in itself, if you know what I mean," I murmured, giving him my best conspiratorial wink.

"Of course," he responded. "I should have realized immediately. . . ."

"No matter," I yawned. "Now then, about the dragon. . . ."

"Yes. Forgive me for losing my temper, but you can see my predicament."

It seemed strange having someone that immense simpering at me, but I rose to the occasion.

"Well, I'm sure we can work something out," I smiled.

As I spoke, a thought flashed through my head. Aahz had all our money! I didn't have a single item of any value on me except. . . .

I reached into my pocket, forcing myself to make the move casual. It was still there! The charm I had taken from Quigley's statue-body that allowed the wearer to see through spells. I had taken it when Aahz wasn't looking and had kept it hidden in case it might be useful in some crisis. Well, this definitely looked like a crisis!

"Here!" I said, tossing the charm to him. "I believe this should settle our accounts."

He caught it deftly and gave it a fast, squinting appraisal.

"This?" he said. "You want to purchase a hatchling dragon for this?"

I had no idea of the charm's relative worth, but bluffing had gotten me this far.

"I do not haggle," I said coldly. "That is my first and final offer. If it is not satisfactory, then return the charm and see if you can get a better price for an attached dragon."

"You drive a hard bargain, Skeeve." The Deveel was still polite, but his smile looked like it hurt. "Very well, it's a deal. Shake on it."

He extended his hand.

There was a sudden hissing noise and my vision was obscured. The dragon had arched his neck forward over my head and was confronting the Deveel eye-to-eye. His attitude was suddenly a miniature version of the ferocity I had seen displayed earlier by his larger brethren. I realized with a start that he was defending me!

Apparently the keeper realized it too, for he jerked back his hand as if he had just stuck it in an open fire.

". . . if you could call off your dragon long enough for us to close the deal?" he suggested with forced politeness.

I wasn't sure just how I was supposed to do this, but I was willing to give it a try.

"He's okay!" I shouted, thumping the dragon on the side of the neck to get his attention.

"Gleep?" said the dragon, turning his head to peer into my face.

I noticed his breath was bad enough to kill an insect in flight.

"It's okay," I repeated, edging out from under his neck.

Since I was already moving, I stepped forward and shook the keeper's hand. He responded absently, never taking his eyes from the dragon.

"Say," I said. "Confidentially, I'm rather new to the dragon game. What does he eat . . . besides shirts. I mean."

"Oh, a little of this and a little of that. They're omnivorous, so they can eat anything, but they're picky eaters. Just let him alone and he'll choose his own diet . . . old clothes, selected leaves, house pets."

"Terrific!" I mumbled.

"Well, if you'll excuse me I've got other customers to talk to."

"Just a minute! Don't I get one of those pendants like you used to control the big dragons?"

"Hmm? What for?"

"Well . . . to control my dragon."

"Those are to control unattached dragons. You don't need one for one that's attached to you and it wouldn't work on a dragon that's attached to someone else."

"Oh," I said, with a wisdom I didn't feel.

"If you want one, though, I have a cousin who has a stall that sells them. It's about three rows up and two rows over. It might be a good investment for you. Could save wear and tear on your dragon if you come up against an unattached dragon. It'd give junior there a better chance of growing up."

"That brings up another question," I said. "How long does it take?"

"Not long. It's just three rows up and. . . ."

"No. I mean how long until my dragon reaches maturity?"

"Oh, not more than four or five centuries."

"Gleep!"

I'm not sure if the dragon said that or I did.

Chapter Nineteen:

"By persevering over all obstacles and distractions, one may unfailingly arrive at his chosen goal or destination."

—C. COLUMBUS

"C'MON, Gleep," I said.

"Gleep," my dragon responded, falling in behind me.

Now that I was the not-so-proud owner of a permanently immature dragon, I was more eager than ever to find Aahz. At the moment, I was alone in a strange dimension, penniless, and now I had a dragon tagging after me. The only way things could be worse would be if the situation became permanent, which could happen if Aahz decided to return to Klah without me.

The place previously occupied by the Pervish restaurant tent was definitely empty, even at close examination, so I decided to ask the Deveel running the neighboring booth.

"Um . . . excuse me, sir."

I decided I was going to be polite as possible for the duration of my stay on Deva. The last thing I needed was another dispute with a Deveel. It seemed, however, in this situation I needn't have worried.

"No excuses are necessary, young sahr." The proprietor smiled eagerly, displaying an impressive number of teeth.

"You are interested in purchasing a stick?"

"A stick?"

"Of course!" the Deveel gestured grandly around his stall. "The finest sticks in all the dimensions."

"Aah . . . thanks, but we have plenty of sticks in my home dimension."

"Not like these sticks, young sahr. You are from Klah, are you not?"

"Yes, why?"

"I can guarantee you, there are no such sticks as these in all of Klah. They come from a dimension only I have access to and I have not sold them in Klah or to anyone who was going there."

Despite myself, my curiosity was piqued. I looked again at the sticks lining the walls of the stall. They looked like ordinary sticks such as could be found anywhere.

"What do they do?" I asked cautiously.

"Aah! Different ones do different things. Some control animals, others control plants. A few very rare ones allow you to summon an army of warriors from the stones themselves. Some of the most powerful magicians of any dimension wield staffs of the same wood as these sticks, but for most people's purposes the smaller model will suffice."

"Gleep!" said the dragon, sniffing at one of the sticks.

"Leave it alone!" I barked, shoving his head away from the display.

All I needed was to have my dragon eat up the entire stock of one of these super-merchants.

"May I inquire, is that your dragon, young sahr?"

"Well . . . sort of."

"In that case, you might find a particular use for a stick most magicians wouldn't."

"What's that?"

"You could use it to beat your dragon."

"Gleep!" said the dragon, looking at me with his big blue eyes.

"Actually, I'm not really interested in a stick."

I thought I'd better get to my original purpose before this conversation got out of hand.

"Ridiculous, young sahr. Everybody should have a stick."

"The reason I stopped here in the first place is I wondered if you knew what happened to that tent."

"What tent, young sahr?"

I had a vague feeling of having had this conversation before.

"The tent that was right there next to your stall."

"The Pervish restaurant?" The Deveel's voice was tinged with horror.

"Gleep," said the dragon.

"Why would you seek such place, young sahr? You seem well-bred and educated."

"I had a friend who was inside the tent when it vanished."

"You have a Pervert for a friend?" His voice had lost its friendly tone.

"Well actually . . . um . . . it's a long story."

"I can tell you this much, punk. It didn't disappear, it moved on," the Deveel snarled, without the accent or politeness he had displayed earlier.

"Moved on?"

"Yeah. It's a new ordinance we passed. All places serving Pervish food have to migrate. They cannot be established permanently, or even temporarily at any point in the Bazaar."

"Why?" I asked.

"Have you ever smelled Pervish food? It's enough to make a scavenger nauseous. Would you want to man a stall downwind of that for a whole day? In this heat?"

"I see what you mean," I admitted.

"Either they moved or the Bazaar did, and we have them outnumbered."

"But what exactly do you mean, move?"

"The tents! All that's involved is a simple spell or two. Either they constantly move at a slow pace, or they stay in one place for a short period and then scuttle off to a new location, but they all move."

"How does anyone find one, then, if they keep moving around?"

"That's easy, just follow your nose."

I sniffed the air experimentally. Sure enough, the unmistakable odor was still lingering in the air.

"Gleep!" the dragon had imitated my action and was now rubbing his nose with one paw.

"Well, thank you . . . for . . . your. . . ."

I was talking to thin air. The Deveel was at the other end of the stall, baring his teeth at another customer. It occurred to me that the citizens of Deva were not particularly concerned with social pleasantries beyond those necessary to transact a sale.

I set out to follow the smell of the Pervish restaurant with the dragon faithfully trailing along behind. Despite my growing desire to reunite with Aahz, my pace was considerably slower than that Aahz had set when we first arrived. I was completely mesmerized by this strange Bazaar and wanted to see as much of it as I could.

Upon more leisurely examination, there did seem to be a vague order to the Bazaar. The various stalls and booths were generally grouped by type of merchandise. This appeared to be more from circumstance than by plan. Apparently, if one Deveel set up a display, say, of invisible cloaks, in no time at all he had a pack of competitors in residence around him, each vying to top the other for quality of goods or prices. Most of the confused babble of voices were disputes between the merchants over the location of their respective stalls or the space occupied by the same.

The smell grew stronger as I wandered through an area specializing in exotic and magical jewelry, which I resisted the temptation to examine more closely. The temptation was even stronger as I traversed an area which featured weaponry. It occurred to me that I might find a weapon here we could use against Isstvan, but the smell of the Pervish food was even stronger now, and I steeled myself to finish my search. We could look for a weapon after I found Aahz. From the intensity of the stench, I was sure we would find our objective soon.

"C'mon, Gleep," I encouraged.

The dragon was hanging back now and didn't respond except to speed his pace a bit.

I expectantly rounded one last corner and came to an abrupt halt. I had found the source of the odor.

I was looking at the back of a large display of some alien livestock. There was a large pile of some moist green and yellow substance in front of me. As I watched, a young Deveel emerged from the display holding a shovel filled with the same substance. He glanced at me quizzically as he heaved the load onto the pile and returned to the display.

A dung heap! I had been following the smell of a dung heap!

"Gleep!" said the dragon, looking at me quizzically.

He seemed to be asking me what we were going to do next. That was a good question.

I stood contemplating my next move. Probably the best chance would be to retrace our steps back to the stick seller and try again.

"Spare a girl a little time, handsome?"

I whirled around. A girl was standing there, a girl unlike any I had ever seen before. She was Klahdish in appearance and could have passed for another of my dimension except for her complexion and hair. Her skin was a marvelous golden-olive hue, and her head was crowned with a mane of light green hair that shimmered in the sun. She was a little taller than me and incredibly curvaceous, her generous figure straining against the confines of her clothes.

". . . or have you really got a thing about dung heaps?" she concluded.

She had almond cat-eyes that danced with mischief as she talked.

"Um . . . are you talking to me?" I stammered.

"Of course I'm talking to you," she purred, coming close to me and twining her arms around my neck. "I'm certainly not talking to your dragon. I mean, he's cute and all, but my tastes don't run in those directions."

"Gleep!" said the dragon.

I felt my body temperature soar. The touch of her arms caused a tingling sensation which seemed to wreak havoc on my metabolism.

"Um . . . actually I'm looking for a friend," I blurted.

"Well, you've found one," she murmured, moving her body against me.

"Aah . . . I . . . um." Suddenly I was having trouble concentrating. "What is it you want?"

"Hmm," she said thoughtfully, "Even though it's not my normal line, I think I'd like to tell your fortune . . . free."

"Oh?" I said, surprised.

This was the first time since I reached the Bazaar that anyone had offered me anything for free. I didn't know if I should be happy or suspicious.

"You're going to have a fight," she whispered in my ear. "A big one."

"What?" I exclaimed. "When? With who?"

"Easy, handsome," she warned, tightening her grip around my neck. "When is in a very few minutes. With who is the rat pack over my shoulder . . . don't look right at them!"

Her final sharp warning checked my reflexive glance. Moving more cautiously, I snuck a peek out of the corner of my eye.

Lounging against a shop wall, watching us closely, were a dozen or so of the ugliest, nastiest looking characters I have ever seen.

"Them? I mean, all of them?" I asked.

"Uh-huh!" she confirmed, snuggling into my chest.

"Why?" I demanded.

"I probably shouldn't tell you this," she smiled, "but because of me."

Only her firm grip on me kept me from dislodging her with a shove.

"You? What about you?"

"Well, they're an awfully greedy bunch. One way or another, they're going to make some money from this encounter. Normally, you'd give the money to me and I'd cut them in for a share. In the unlikely event that doesn't work, they'll pretend to be defending my honor and beat it out of you."

"But you don't understand! I don't have any money."

"I know that. That's why you're going to get into a fight, see?"

"If you knew I didn't have any money, why did you. . . ."

"Oh, I didn't know when I first stopped you. I found out just now when I searched you."

"Searched me?"

"Oh, come on, handsome. There's more ways to search a person than with your hands," she winked knowingly at me.

"Well, can't you tell them I don't have any money?"

"They wouldn't believe me. The only way they'd be convinced is searching you themselves."

"I'd be willing to let them if that's what it takes to convince them."

"I don't think you would," she smiled, stroking my face with her hand. "One of the things they'll look for is if you swallowed your money."

"Oh!" I said, "I see what you mean. But I can't fight them. I don't have any weapons."

"You have that little knife under your shirt at the small of your back," she pointed out.

I had forgotten about my skinning knife. I started to believe in her no-hands frisking technique.

"But I've never been in a fight before."

"Well, I think you're about to learn."

"Say, why are you telling me all this, anyway?" I asked.

"I don't know," she shrugged. "I like your act. That's why I singled you out in the first place. Then again, I feel a little guilty about having gotten you into this."

"Will you help me?"

"I don't feel *that* guilty, handsome," she smiled. "But there is one more thing I can do for you."

She started to pull me toward her.

"Wait a minute," I protested. "Won't that. . . ."

"Relax, handsome," she purred. "You're about to get pounded for offending my honor. You might as well get a little of the sweet along with the bitter."

Before I could protest further, she kissed me. Long and warm and sweet, she kissed me.

I had never been kissed by anyone except my mother. This was different! The fight, the dragon, Aahz, everything faded from my mind. I was lost in the wonder of that moment.

"Hey!"

A rough hand fell on my shoulder and pulled us apart.

"Is this shrimp bothering you, lady?"

The person on the other end of that hand was no taller than I was, but he was twice as broad and had short, twisted tusks protruding from his mouth. His cronies had fanned out behind him, effectively boxing me in against the dung heap.

I looked at the girl. She shrugged and backed away.

It looked like I was going to have to fight all of them. Me and the dragon. Terrific.

I remembered my skinning knife. It wasn't much, but it was all I had. As casually as I could, I reached behind me and tugged at my shirt, trying to pull it up so I could get at the knife. The knife promptly fell down inside my pants.

The wrecking crew started forward.

Chapter Twenty:

"With the proper consideration in choice of allies, victory may be guaranteed in any conflict."

—B. ARNOLD

"GET 'em, Gleep!" I barked.

The dragon bounded into action, a move which I think surprised me more than it did my assailants.

It leaped between me and the advancing rat pack and crouched there, hissing menacingly. His tail gave a mighty lash which neatly swept the legs out from under two of the flanking members of the party. Somehow, he seemed much bigger when he was mad.

"Watch out! He's got a dragon!" the leader called.

"Thanks for the warning!" one of the fallen men growled, struggling to regain his feet.

"I've got him!" came a voice from my left.

I turned just in time to see a foot-long dagger flashing through the air at the dragon's neck. My dragon!

Suddenly I was back at the practice sessions. My mind darted out and grabbed at the knife. It jerked to a halt in midair and hovered there.

"Nice move, handsome!" the girl called.

"Hey! The shrimp's a magician!"

The pack fell back a few steps.

"That's right!" I barked. "Skeeve's the name,

151

magik's the game. What kind of clod did you think you were dealing with?''

With that, I brought the dagger down, swooping it back and forth through their formation. I was mad now. One of these louts had tried to kill my dragon!

"A dozen of you isn't enough!" I shouted. "Go back and get some friends . . . if you have any!"

I cast about desperately for something else to throw. My eyes fell on the dung heap. I smiled to myself despite my anger. Why not?

In a moment I had great gobs of dung hurtling through the air at my assailants. My accuracy wasn't the best, but it was good enough as the outraged howls testified.

"Levitation!" the leader bawled. "Quanto! Stop him!"

"Right, boss!"

One of the plug-uglies waved in affirmation and started rummaging through his belt pouch.

He had made a mistake identifying himself. I didn't know what he was about to come up with, but I was sure I didn't want to wait and find out.

"Stop him, Gleep!" I ordered, pointing to the victim.

The dragon raised his head and fixed his gaze on the fumbling brigand. With a sound that might have been a roar if he were older, he shot a stream of flame and charged.

It wasn't much of a stream of flame, and it missed to boot, but it was enough to get the brigand's attention. He looked up to see a mountain of dragon flesh bearing down on him and panicked. Without pausing to call to his comrades, he spun and ran off screaming with the dragon in hot pursuit.

"Okay, shrimp! Let's see you stop this!"

I jerked my attention back to the leader. He was standing now, confidently holding aloft a stick. Yesterday it wouldn't have fazed me, but knowing what I did now, I froze. I didn't know what model it was, but apparently the leader was confident its powers would surpass my own.

He grinned evilly and slowly began to level the stick at me.

I tried desperately to think of a defense, but couldn't. I didn't even know what I was supposed to be defending against!

Suddenly, something flashed across my line of vision and the stick was gone.

I blinked and looked again. The stick was lying on the ground, split by a throwing knife, a black-handled throwing knife.

"Any trouble here, Master Skeeve?" a voice boomed.

I spun toward the source of the voice. Aahz was standing there, cocked crossbow leveled at the pack. He was grinning broadly, which I have mentioned before is not that comforting to anyone who doesn't know him.

"A Pervert!" the leader gasped.

"What?" Aahz swung the crossbow toward him.

"I mean a Pervect!" the leader amended hastily.

"That's better. How about it, Skeeve? You want 'em dead or running?"

I looked at the rat pack. Without breaking their frozen tableau, they pleaded with me with their eyes.

"Um . . . running, I think," I said thoughtfully. "They smell bad enough alive. Dead they might give the Bazaar a bad name."

"You heard him," Aahz growled. "Move!"

They disappeared like they had melted into the ground.

"Aahz!"

The girl came flying forward to throw her arms around him.

"Tanda!" Aahz exclaimed, lowering the crossbow. "Are you mixed up with that pack?"

"Are you kidding? I'm the bait!" she winked bawdily.

"Little low class for you, isn't it?"

"Aah . . . it's a living."

"Why'd you leave the Assassins?"

"Got tired of paying union dues."

"Um . . . harrumph. . . ." I interrupted.

"Hmm?" Aahz looked around. "Oh! Sorry, kid. Say, have you two met?"

"Sort of," the girl acknowledged. "We . . . say, is this the friend you were looking for, handsome?"

"Handsome?" Aahz wrinkled his nose.

"Well, yes," I admitted. "We got separated back by the. . . ."

"Handsome?" Aahz repeated.

"Oh, hush!" the girl commanded, slapping his stomach playfully. "I like him. He's got style."

"Actually, I don't believe we've met formally," I said, giving my most winning smile. "My name is Skeeve."

"Well, la-de-dah!" Aahz grumbled.

"Ignore him. I'm Tananda, but call me Tanda."

"Love to," I leered.

"If you two are quite through. . . ." Aahz interrupted, "I have a couple questions. . . ."

"Gleep!" said the dragon, prancing up to our assemblage.

"What's that?" Aahz demanded.

"It's a dragon," I said helpfully.

Tanda giggled rudely.

"I know that," Aahz barked. "I mean what is he doing here?"

Suddenly I was hesitant to supply the whole story.

"There are lots of dragons at the Bazaar, Aahz," I mumbled, not looking at him. "In fact, there's a stall just down the way that. . . ."

"What is *that* dragon doing *here*?"

"Gleep!" said the dragon, rubbing his head against my chest.

"Um . . . he's mine," I admitted.

"Yours?" Aahz bellowed. "I told you to look at the dragons, not buy one!"

"But Aahz. . . ."

"What are we going to do with a dragon?"

"I got a good deal on him," I chimed hopefully.

"What did you say, kid?"

"I said I got a good deal. . . ."

"From a Deveel?"

"Oh. I see what you mean."

"C'mon. Let's have it. What were the terms of this fantastic deal?"

"Well . . . I . . . that is. . . ."

"Out with it!"

"I traded Quigley's pendant for him."

"Quigley's pendant? The one that sees through spells? You traded a good magical pendant for a half-grown dragon?"

"Oh, give him a break, Aahz," Tanda interrupted. "What do you expect letting him wander off alone that way? You're lucky he didn't get stuck with half the tourist crud on Deva! Where were you all this time, anyway?"

"Well . . . I was . . . um. . . ."

"Don't tell me," she said, holding up a hand. "If I know you, you were either chasing a girl or stuffing your face, right?"

"She's got you there, Aahz," I commented.

"Shut up, kid."

". . . so don't get down on Skeeve here. Compared to what could have happened to him, he didn't do half bad. How did you find us, anyway?"

"I listened for the sounds of a fight and followed it," Aahz admitted.

"See! You were expecting him to get into trouble. Might I point out he was doing just fine before you barged in. He and his dragon had those thugs treed all by themselves. He's pretty handy with that magik, you know."

"I know," Aahz responded proudly. "I taught him."

"Gee, thanks, Aahz."

"Shut up, kid."

"Gleep," said the dragon, craning his neck around to look at Aahz upside down.

"A dragon, huh?" Aahz said, studying the dragon more thoughtfully.

"He might help us against Isstvan," I suggested hopefully.

"Isstvan?" Tanda asked quizzically.

"Yeah," Aahz replied. "You remember him, don't you? Well, he's up to his old tricks, this time on Klah."

"So that's what's going on, huh? Well, what are we going to do about it?"

"We?" I asked, surprised.

"Sure," she smiled. "This racket is a bit low class, like Aahz says. I might as well tag along with you two for a while . . . if you don't mind, that is."

"Terrific!" I said, and meant it for a change.

"Not so fast, Tanda," Aahz cautioned. "There are a few details you haven't been filled in on yet."

"Such as?"

"Such as I've lost my powers."

"No fooling? Gee, that's tough."

"That means we'll be relying on the kid here to give us cover in the magik department."

"All the more reason for me to come along. I've picked up a few tricks myself."

"I know," Aahz leered.

"Not like that," she said, punching him in the side. "I mean magik tricks."

"Even so, it's not going to be easy."

"C'mon, Aahz," Tanda chided. "Are you trying to say it wouldn't be helpful having a trained Assassin on your side?"

"Well . . . it could give us a bit of an advantage," Aahz admitted.

"Good! Then it's settled. What do we do first?"

"There're some stalls just around the corner that carry weapons," I suggested. "We could. . . ."

"Relax, kid. I've already taken care of that."

"You have?" I asked, surprised.

"Yeah. I found just what we need over in the practical jokes section. I was just looking for you before we headed back."

"Then we're ready to go?" Tanda asked.

"Yep," Aahz nodded, fishing the D-Hopper out of his shirt.

"What about my dragon?"

"What about him?"

"Are we going to take him with us?"

"Of course we're going to take him with us. We don't leave anything of value behind."

"Gleep!" said the dragon.

". . . and he must be valuable to someone!" Aahz finished, glaring at the dragon.

He pressed the button on the D-Hopper. The Bazaar wavered and faded . . . and we were back in Frumple's shop . . . sort of.

"Interesting place you've got here," Tanda commented dryly. "Did you do the decor?"

All that was left of Frumple's shop was a burnt-out shell.

Chapter Twenty-One:

"One must deal openly and fairly with one's forces if maximum effectiveness is to be achieved."

—D. VADER

"WHAT happened?" I demanded of Aahz.

"Hey, kid. I was on Deva, too. Remember?"

"Um . . . hey, guys. I hate to interrupt," Tanda interrupted, "but shouldn't something be done about disguises?"

She was right. Being on Deva had made me forget the mundane necessities of our existence. I ignored Aahz's sarcastic reply and set to work.

Aahz returned to his now traditional Garkin disguise. Tanda was fine once I changed her complexion and the color of her hair. After a bit of thought, I disguised Gleep as the war unicorn. It was a bit risky, but it would do as long as he kept his mouth shut. Me, I left as myself. I mean, what the heck. Tanda liked my looks the way they were.

Fortunately the sun wasn't up yet, so there weren't any people about to witness the transformation.

"Say, handsome," Tanda commented, observing the results of my work, "you're a pretty handy guy to have around."

"His name's Skeeve," Aahz grumbled.

"Whatever," Tanda murmured. "He's got style."

She snuggled up to me.

"Gleep!" said the dragon, pressing his head against my other side.

I was starting to feel awfully popular.

"If you can spare a few minutes, kid," Aahz commented dryly, "we do have a mission, remember?"

"That's right," I said, forcing my attention away from Tanda's advances. "What do you think happened to Frumple?"

"Either the citizens of Twixt got wise to him, or he's off to tell Isstvan we're coming, would be my two guesses."

"Who's Frumple?" Tanda asked.

"Hmm? Oh, he's the resident Deveel," Aahz said. "He's the one who helped us get to the Bazaar."

". . . at sword point," I added sarcastically.

"What's a Deveel doing here?"

"All we know is that rumor has it he was barred from Deva," I told her.

"Hmm . . . sounds like a bit of a nasty character."

"Well, he won't win any popularity contests."

"It occurs to me," Aahz interrupted, "that if either of my two guesses are correct, we'd best be on our way. Time seems to be running out."

"Right," agreed Tanda. "Which way is Isstvan?"

"First, we've got to pick up Quigley," I inserted.

"Why?" asked Aahz. "Oh, I suppose you're right, kid. We're going to need all the help we can muster."

"Who's Quigley?" Tanda asked.

"Later, Tanda," Aahz insisted. "First help us see if there's anything here worth salvaging."

Unfortunately, there wasn't. In fact, there weren't even the charred remains of anything left for our discovery. Even the garish sword I had left behind seemed to have vanished.

"That settles it," Aahz commented grimly as we completed our search. "He's on his way to Isstvan."

"The natives might have taken the sword after they burned the place," I suggested hopefully.

"No way, kid. Even yokels like these wouldn't bother with a crummy sword like that."

"It was that bad?" Tanda asked.

"It was that bad," Aahz assured her firmly.

"If it was that worthless, why would Frumple take it with him?" I asked.

"For the same reason we've been lugging it around," Aahz said pointedly. "There's always some sucker to unload it on for a profit. Remember Quigley?"

"Who's Quigley?" Tanda insisted.

"Well," sighed Aahz, "at the moment he's a statue, but in duller times he's a demon hunter."

"Swell," she commented sarcastically. "Just what we need."

"Wait until you meet him," Aahz rolled his eyes and sighed. "Oh well, let's go."

Our departure from Twixt was blissfully uneventful. On the road, we rehearsed our story until, by the time we finally dug up Quigley and sprinkled him with the restoring power, we were ready to present a united front.

"Really? Turned to stone, you say?" he said, brushing the dirt from his clothes.

"Yes," Aahz assured him. "They were looting your body when we launched our counterattack. It's lucky for you we decided to come back and fight at your side."

"And they took my magik sword and my amulet?"

I felt a little uneasy on those subjects, but Aahz never batted an eye.

"That's right, the blackguards!" he snarled. "We tried to stop them, but they eluded us."

"Well, at least they didn't get my war unicorn," muttered the demon hunter.

"Um. . . ." I said, bracing myself for my part in this charade. "We've got some bad news about that, too."

"Bad news?" Quigley frowned, "I don't understand. I can see the beast with my own eyes and he seems fit enough."

"Oh, he's fine physically," Aahz reassured him, "but before they disappeared, the demons put a spell on him."

"A spell?"

"Yes," I said. "Now he . . . um . . . well . . . he thinks he's a dragon."

"A dragon?" Quigley exclaimed.

"Gleep!" said the dragon.

"And that's not all," Aahz continued. "The beast was so wild at first that only through the continued efforts of my squire here were we able to gentle him at all. Frankly, I was for putting the poor animal out of its misery, but he insisted he could tame it and you see before you the results of his patient teachings."

"That's wonderful!" exclaimed Quigley.

"No. That's terrible," corrected Aahz. "You see, in the process, your animal has formed a strong attachment for my squire . . . stronger, I fear, than his attachment for you."

"Hah! Ridiculous," Quigley proclaimed. "But I do feel I owe you an additional debt of gratitude, lad. If there's ever anything I can . . ."

He began to advance on me with his hand extended. In a flash, Gleep was between us, head down and hissing.

Quigley froze, his eyes bulging with surprise.

"Stop that!" I ordered, cuffing the dragon.

"Gleep!" said the dragon, slinking back to his place behind me.

"See what I mean?" Aahz said pointedly.

"Hmm. . . ." Quigley mumbled thoughtfully. "That's strange, he never defended me that way."

"I guess we'll just have to buy him from you," I said eagerly.

"Buy him?" Quigley turned his attention to me again.

Aahz tried to catch my eye, shaking his head emphatically, but I ignored him.

"That's right," I continued. "He's no good to you this way, and since we're sort of to blame for what happened to him. . . ."

"Think nothing of it, lad." Quigley drew himself up proudly. "I give him to you as a gift. After all, if it weren't for you he'd be dead anyway, and so would I, for that matter."

"But I. . . ."

"No! I will hear nothing more." The demon hunter

held up a restraining hand. "The matter is closed. Treat him well, lad. He's a good animal."

"Terrific," muttered Aahz.

"Gleep," said the dragon.

I felt miserable. It had occurred to me that our plans involved taking shameless advantage of Quigley's gullibility. As he was my only fellow Klahd in this adventure, I had wanted to force Aahz into giving him some money under the guise of buying the "war unicorn." It would have salved my conscience a bit, but Quigley's generosity and sense of fair play had ruined my plan. Now I felt worse than before.

"Actually, Quigley," Aahz smiled, "If there's anyone you should thank, it should be Tananda here. If it were not for her, we would be in dire straits indeed."

"It's about time," mumbled Tanda, obviously unimpressed with Aahz's rhetoric.

"Charmed, milady," Quigley smiled, taking her hand to kiss.

"She's a witch," added Aahz casually.

"A witch?" Quigley dropped her hand as if it had bitten him.

"That's right, sugar," Tanda smiled, batting her eyes at him.

"Perhaps I should explain," Aahz interrupted mercifully. "Tananda here has certain powers she has consented to use in support of our war on demons. You already noticed I have regained my normal appearance?"

Another blatant lie. Aahz was currently disguised as Garkin.

"Yes," the demon hunter admitted hesitantly.

"Tananda's work," Aahz confided. "Just as it was her powers that restored you after you had been turned to stone."

"Hmmm. . . ." Quigley said, looking at Tanda again.

"Really, you must realize, Quigley, that when one fights demons, sometimes it is helpful to employ a demon's weapons," Aahz admonished gently.

"Tananda here can be a powerful ally . . . and frankly, I find your attitude toward her deplorable and ungrateful."

"Forgive me, milady," Quigley sighed, stepping up to her again. "I did not mean to offend you. It's just that . . . well . . . I've had some bad experiences with those who associate with demons."

"Think nothing of it, sugar," said Tanda the demon, taking his hand, "And call me Tanda."

While they were occupied with each other, I seized the opportunity and snagged Aahz's arm.

"Hm? What is it, kid?"

"Give him back his sword!" I hissed.

"What? No way, kid. By my count he's still got five pieces of gold left. I'll sell it to him."

"But he gave us his unicorn."

"He gave us a dragon . . . your dragon! I fail to see anything benevolent in that."

"Look, Aahz. Either you give him that sword or you can work your own magik! Get me?"

"Talk about ingratitude! Look kid, if you. . . ."

"Aahz!" Tanda's voice interrupted our dispute. "Come help me convince Quigley to join our mission."

"Would that I could, milady," Quigley sighed, "but I would be of little help. This late misfortune has left me afoot, weaponless, and penniless."

"Actually," Aahz chimed, "you still have five. . . ."

I interrupted him with an elbow in his ribs.

"What was that, Aahz?" Quigley asked.

"Aah . . . my . . . um . . . squire and I were just discussing that and we have reached a decision. So . . . um . . . so fine a warrior should not be left so destitute, so . . . um . . . we. . . ."

"We've decided to give you back your sword," I announced proudly.

"Really?" Quigley's face lit up.

"I didn't know you had it in you, Aahz," Tanda smiled sweetly.

"I say, this is comradeship indeed." Quigley was obviously beside himself with joy. "How can I ever repay you?"

"By never mentioning this to anyone," Aahz growled.

"How's that again?"

"I said don't mention it," Aahz amended. "It's the least we can do."

"Believe him," I smiled.

"Now I will gladly assist you on your mission," Quigley answered. "Why, with a weapon and good comrades, what more could a warrior ask for?"

"Money," Aahz said bluntly.

"Oh Aahz." Tanda punched him a little too hard for it to be playful. "You're such a kidder."

"Don't you want to know what the mission is?" I asked Quigley.

"Oh, yes, I suppose you're right, lad. Forgive me. I was carried away by my enthusiasm."

"Tell him, Skeeve," prompted Tanda.

"Actually," I said, with a sudden flash of diplomacy, "Aahz explains it much better than I do."

"It's really quite simple," mumbled Aahz, still sulking a bit. "We're going after Isstvan."

"Isstvan?" Quigley looked puzzled. "The harmless old innkeeper?"

"Harmless? Harmless, did you say?" Aahz took the bait. "Quigley, as one demon hunter to another, you've got a lot to learn."

"I do all right for myself."

"Sure you do. That's why you got turned to stone, remember?"

"I got turned to stone because I put my faith in a magik sword that. . . ."

Things were back to normal.

"Gentlemen, gentlemen," I interrupted. "We were talking about the upcoming mission."

"Right, kid. As I was saying, Quigley, that harmless old innkeeper is working so closely with demons I wouldn't be surprised to learn he was one himself."

"Impossible!" scoffed Quigley. "Why, the man sent me out hunting for demons."

"Ahh!" smiled Aahz. "Therein lies the story."

I caught Tanda's eyes and winked. She smiled back at me and nodded. This might take a while, but as of now Quigley was in the bag!

Chapter Twenty-Two:

"This is another fine myth you've gotten me into!"

—LOR L. AND HAR D.

THERE was something there in the shadows. I could sense its presence more than see it. It was dark and serpentine . . . and it was watching me.

I was alone. I didn't know where the others had gone, but I knew they were counting on me.

"Who's there?" I called.

The voice that came back to me out of the darkness echoed hollowly.

"I am Isstvan, Skeeve. I've been waiting for you."

"You know who I am?" I asked, surprised.

"I know all about you and your friends. I've known all along what you're trying to do."

I tried to set wards about me, but I couldn't find a force line. I tried to run, but I was rooted to the spot.

"See how my powers dwarf yours? And you expected to challenge me."

I tried to fight back a wave of despair.

"Wait until the others come," I cried defiantly.

"They already have," the voice boomed. "Look!"

Two objects came rolling at me out of the darkness. I

saw with horror that they were heads! Tanda's and Quigley's!

I felt ill, but clung to a shred of hope. There was still no sign of Aahz. If he was still at large, we might. . . .

"Don't look to your Pervert for help," the voice answered my thoughts. "I've dealt with him too."

Aahz appeared, sheathed in fire. He staggered and fell, writhing on the ground as the flames consumed his body.

"Now it's just you and me, Skeeve!" the voice echoed. "You and me."

"I'll go!" I shouted desperately. "You've won. Just let me go."

The darkness was moving closer.

"It's too late. I'm coming for you Skeeve . . . Skeeve. . . ."

"Skeeve!"

Something was shaking my shoulder. I bolted upright, blinking my eyes as the world swam back into focus.

The camp was asleep. Aahz was kneeling beside me, the glow from the campfire's dying embers revealing the concerned expression on his face.

"Wake up, kid! If you keep thrashing around, you'll end up in the fire."

"It's Isstvan!" I explained desperately. "He knows all about us."

"What?"

"I was talking to him. He came into my dream!"

"Hmmm . . . sounds more like a plain old nightmare," Aahz proclaimed. "I warned you not to let Tanda season the food."

"Are you sure?" I said doubtfully.

"Positive," Aahz insisted. "If Isstvan knew we were coming, he'd hit us with something a lot more powerful than making faces at you in a dream."

I guess that was supposed to reassure me. It didn't. All it did was remind me I was thoroughly outclassed in the upcoming campaign.

"Aahz, can't you tell me anything about Isstvan?

What he looks like, for instance."

"Not a chance, kid," Aahz grinned at me.

"Why not?"

"Because we won't both see him the same way, or at least we wouldn't describe him the same way. If I describe him to you, one of two things will happen when you first see him. If he looks scarier to you than I've described him, you'll freeze. If he looks more harmless than I've described him, you'll relax. Either way, it'll slow your reactions and give him the first move. There's no point in gaining the element of surprise if we aren't going to use it."

"Well," I persisted. "Couldn't you at least tell me about his powers? What can he do?"

"For one thing, it would take too long. Just assume that if you can imagine it, he can do it."

"What's the other?" I asked.

"The other what?"

"You said 'for one thing.' That implies you have at least one other reason."

"Hmm," Aahz pondered. "Well, I'm not sure you'll understand, but to a certain degree what he can do, I mean the whole list, is irrelevant."

"Why?"

"Because we're taking the initiative. That puts him in a reactive instead of an active role."

"You're right," I said thoughtfully. "I don't understand."

"Look kid, if we just sat here and waited for him, he could take his time and choose exactly what he wanted to do and when he wanted to do it. That's an active role and lets him play with his entire list of powers. Right?"

"I guess so."

"But we aren't doing that. We're carrying the attack to him. That should limit him as to what he can do. There are only a certain number of responses he can successfully use to each of our gambits, and he'll have to use them because he can't afford to ignore the attack. Most of all, we'll rob him of time. Instead of leisurely choosing what he's going to do next, he'll have to choose fast. That means he'll go with the option he's surest of, the one he does best.''

I considered this for a few moments. It sort of made sense.

"Just one question, Aahz," I asked finally.

"What's that, kid?"

"What if you've guessed wrong?"

"Then we drop back ten and punt," he answered lightly.

"What's a. . . ."

"Then we try something else," he amended hastily.

"Like what?"

"Can't tell yet," Aahz shrugged. "Too many variables. We're going with my best guess right now. Beyond that we'll just have to wait and see."

We sat staring into the dying fire for a few minutes, each lost in our own thoughts.

"Say, Aahz?" I said at last.

"Yea, kid?"

"Do you think we'll reach Isstvan before Frumple does?"

"Relax, kid. Frumple's probably drinking wine and pinching bottoms in some other dimension by now."

"But you said. . . ."

"I've had time to think about it since then. The only reason a Deveel does anything is for a profit or out of fear. As far as his sticking his head into this brawl goes, I figure the fear will outweigh the profit. Trying to sell information to a madman is risky at best. My bet is he's lying low until the dust settles."

I reminded myself again of my faith in Aahz's expertise in such matters. It occurred to me, however, there was an awful lot of guesswork in our planning.

"Um, Aahz? Wouldn't it be a little safer if we had invested in a couple of those jazzy weapons back in Deva?"

"We don't need them," he replied firmly. "Besides, they're susceptible to Gremlins. I'd rather go into a fight with a crude but reliable weapon than pin my hopes on a contraption that's liable to malfunction when you need it most."

"Where are Gremlins from?" I asked.

"What?"

"Gremlins. You said. . . ."

"Oh, that. It's just a figure of speech. There are no such things as Gremlins."

I was only listening with half an ear. I suddenly realized that while I could see Quigley's sleeping form, there was no sign of Tanda or Gleep.

"Where's . . . um . . . where's Gleep?" I asked abruptly.

Aahz grinned at me.

"Gleep is standing watch . . . and just in case you're interested, so's Tanda."

I was vaguely annoyed he had seen through me so easily, but was determined not to show it.

"When is . . . um . . . are they coming back?"

"Relax, kid. I told Tanda to leave you alone tonight. You need the sleep for tomorrow."

He jerked his head pointedly toward the assassin's robe I had been using for a pillow. I grudgingly resumed my horizontal position.

"Did I wake you up, Aahz?" I asked apologetically. "With the nightmare, I mean."

"Naw. I was still up. Just making a few last-minute preparations for tomorrow."

"Oh," I said drowsily.

"Say, uh, kid?"

"Yes, Aahz?"

"We probably won't have much time to talk tomorrow when Quigley's awake, so while we've got a few minutes alone I want to say however it goes tomorrow . . . well . . . it's been nice working with you, kid."

"Gee, Aahz. . . ." I said starting to sit up.

A rough hand interrupted me and pushed me back down.

"Sleep!" Aahz commanded, but there was a gentle note lurking in his gruff tone.

Chapter Twenty-Three:

"Since prehistoric man, no battle has ever gone as planned."

—D. GRAEME

WE crouched in a grove of small trees on a knoll overlooking the inn, studying our target. The inn was as Quigley had described it, an isolated two-story building with an attached stable squatting by a road overgrown with weeds. If Isstvan was relying on transients to support his business, he was in trouble, except we knew he was doing no such thing. He was mustering his strength to take over the dimensions, and the isolated inn was a perfect base for him to work from.

"Are you sure there are no wards?" Aahz whispered.

He addressed his question to Tanda. She in turn shot me a glance. I gave a small nod of my head.

"Positive," she whispered back.

It was all part of our plan. As far as Quigley was concerned, Tanda was the only one of our group that had any supernatural powers.

"Good," said the demon hunter. "Demon powers make me uneasy. The less we have to deal with, the better I like it."

"Don't get your hopes up," Aahz commented, not taking his eyes from the inn. "They're there all right.

The easier it is to get in, the harder it'll be to get out . . . and they're making it awfully easy for us to get in.''

"I don't like it," said Tanda firmly.

"Neither do I," admitted Aahz. "But things aren't going to get any better, so let's get started. You might as well get into disguise now."

"Right, Aahz," she said.

Neither of them looked at me. In fact Aahz stared directly at Tanda. This kept Quigley's attention on her also, though I must admit it helped that she began to writhe and gyrate wildly. Unobserved, I shut my eyes and got to work.

I was getting pretty good at this disguise game, which was fortunate because I was going to be sorely tested today. With a few masterful strokes, I converted Tanda's lovely features into the dubious face of the Imp Higgens . . . or rather Higgens's human disguise. This done, I opened my eyes again.

Tanda was still gyrating. It was a pleasant enough sight that I was tempted to prolong it, but we had work to do. I cleared my throat and Tanda acknowledged the signal by stopping.

"How do I look?" she asked proudly.

"Terrific!" I exclaimed with no trace of modesty.

Aahz shot me a dirty look.

"It's uncanny!" Quigley marveled. "How do you do that?"

"Professional secret." Tanda winked at him.

"Off with you!" Aahz commanded. "And you too, Skeeve."

"But Aahz, couldn't I. . . ."

"No you can't. We've discussed it before. This mission's far too dangerous for a lad of your inexperience."

"Oh, all right, Aahz," I said, crestfallen.

"Cheer up, lad," Quigley told me. "Your day will come. If we fail, the mission falls to you."

"I suppose so. Well, good luck. . . ."

I turned to Tanda, but she was already gone, vanished

as if the ground had swallowed her up.

"I say!" exclaimed Quigley. "She does move quietly, doesn't she?"

"I told you she could handle herself," Aahz said proudly. "Now it's your turn, Skeeve."

"Right, Aahz!"

I turned to the dragon.

"Stay here, Gleep. I'll be back soon, and until then you do what Aahz says. Understand?"

"Gleep?" said the dragon, cocking his head.

For a minute I thought he was going to ruin everything, but then he turned and slunk to Aahz's side and stood there regarding me with mournful blue eyes.

Everything was ready.

"Well, good-bye. Good luck!" I called, and trudged slowly back over the knoll, hopefully a picture of abject misery.

Once out of sight, however, I turned and began to sprint as fast as I could in a wide circle around the inn.

On the surface, our plan was quite simple. Aahz and Quigley were to give Tanda enough time to circle around the inn and enter it over the stable roof. Then they were to boldly enter the front door. Supposedly this would create a diversion, allowing Tanda to attack Isstvan magically from the rear. I was to wait safely on the knoll until the affair was settled.

In actuality, our plan was a bit more complex. Unbeknownst to Quigley, I was also supposed to circle the inn and find a covert entrance. Then, at the appropriate moment, Tanda and I were to create a magical diversion, allowing Aahz to use the secret weapon he had acquired on Deva.

A gully blocked my path. I took to the air without hesitation and flew over it. I had to be in position in time, or Aahz would have no magical support at all.

Actually magik was quite easy here. The inn was sitting squarely on an intersection of two ground force lines, while a force line in the air passed directly overhead. Whatever happened in the upcoming battle of magik, we wouldn't suffer for a lack of energy.

I wished I knew more about Aahz's secret weapon. He had been doggedly mysterious about it, and neither Tanda nor I had been able to pry any information out of him. He had said it had to be used at close range. He had said it couldn't be used while Isstvan was watching him. He had said it was our only hope to beat Isstvan. He had said it was supposed to be a surprise.

Terrific!

Maybe when all this was over I would find a mentor who didn't have a sense of humor.

I slowed my pace. I was coming to the back of the inn now. The brush had grown right up to the wall, which made my approach easy.

I paused and checked for wards again.

Nothing.

Trying to force Aahz's "easy in, hard out" prophecy from my mind, I scanned the upper windows. None of them were open, so I chose the nearest one and levitated to it. Hovering there, I cautiously pushed, then pulled at the frame.

Locked!

Hurriedly, I pulled myself along the wall with my hands to the next window.

Also locked.

It occurred to me it would be ironic if, after all our magical preparations, we were stopped by something as mundane as a locked window.

To my relief, the next window yielded to my pressure, and in a moment I was standing inside the inn, trying to get my heartbeat under control.

The room I was in was furnished, but vacant. Judging from the dust on the bed, it had been vacant for some time.

I wondered for a moment where demons slept, if they slept at all, then forced the question from my mind. Time was running out and I wasn't in position yet.

I darted silently across the room and tried the door. Unlocked!

Getting down on my hands and knees, I eased the

door open and crawled through, pushing it shut behind me.

After studying the inn's interior so often in Quigley's dirt sketches, it seemed strange to actually be here. I was on the long side of an L-shaped mezzanine which gave access to the upper-story rooms. Peering through the bars of the railing that lined the mezzanine, I could look down into the inn proper.

There were three people currently occupying a table below. I recognized the disguised features of Higgens and Brockhurst as two of them. The third was sitting hunched with his back to me and I couldn't make out his face.

I was debating shifting to another position to get a better view, when a fourth figure entered bearing an enormous tray with a huge jug of wine on it as well as an assortment of dirty flagons.

"This round's on the house, boys!" the figure chortled merrily. "Have one on old Isstvan."

Isstvan! That was Isstvan?

The waddling figure below did not seem to display any of the menacing features I had expected in a would-be ruler of the dimensions.

Quickly I checked him for a magical aura. There was none. It wasn't a disguise. He really looked like that. I studied him carefully.

He was tall, but his stoutness kept his height from being imposing. He had long white hair and a longer white beard which nearly covered his chest with its fullness. His bright eyes were set in a face that seemed to be permanently smiling, and his nose and cheeks were flushed, though whether from drink or laughter I couldn't tell.

This was the dark figure of evil I had been dreading all these weeks? He looked to be exactly what Quigley said he was . . . a harmless old innkeeper.

A movement at the far end of the mezzanine caught my eye. Tanda! She was crouched behind the railing as I was on the other side of the stairs, and at first I thought I had just seen the movement of her easing into position. Then she looked my way and cautiously waved her hand again, and I realized she was signaling for my attention.

I waved an acknowledgment, which she must have seen, for she stopped signaling and changed to another set of actions. Glancing furtively at the figures below to be sure she wasn't observed, she began a strange pantomime.

First she made several repeated gestures around her forehead, then pointed urgently behind her.

I didn't understand, and shook my head to convey this.

She repeated the gestures more emphatically, and this time I realized she was actually pointing down and behind her. The stables! Something about the stables. But what about the stables?

I considered her first gesture again. She appeared to be stabbing herself in the forehead. Something had hit her in the stables? She had killed something in the stables?

I shook my head again. She bared her teeth at me in frustration.

"Innkeep!"

I jumped a foot at the bellow.

Aahz and Quigley had just walked through the door. Whatever Tanda was trying to tell me would just have to wait. Our attack had begun.

"Two flagons of your best wine . . . and send someone to see to my unicorn."

Aahz was doing all the talking, of course. It had been agreed that he would take the lead in the conversation. Quigley hadn't been too happy about that, but in the end had consented to speaking only when absolutely necessary.

Their entrance had had surprisingly little impact on the assemblage below. In fact, Isstvan was the only one to even look in their direction.

"Come in. Come in, gentlemen," he smiled, spreading his arms wide in welcome. "We've been expecting you!"

"You have?" blurted Quigley, echoing my thoughts.

"Of course, of course. You shouldn't try to fool old Isstvan." He shook a finger at them in mock sternness. "Word was just brought to us by . . . oh, I'm sorry. I haven't introduced you to my new purchasing agent yet."

"We've met," came the voice of the hunched figure as he turned to face them.

Frumple!

That's what Tanda had been trying to tell me! The war unicorn, Quigley's unicorn, was down in the stable. For all our speed, Frumple had gotten here ahead of us.

"Who are you?" asked Quigley, peering at the Deveel.

For some reason this seemed to set Isstvan off into peals of laughter from his eyes. "We are going to have such fun this afternoon!"

He gestured absently and the inn door slammed shut. There was a sudden ripple of dull clunks behind me, and I realized the room doors were locking themselves. We were sealed in! All of us.

"I don't believe I've had such a good time since I made love to my week-dead sister."

Isstvan's voice was still jovial, but it struck an icy note of fear within me. I realized that not only was he a powerful magician, he was quite insane.

Chapter Twenty-Four:

"Ya gotta be subtle!"

—M. HAMMER

THERE was a tense, expectant silence as the foursome leaned forward to study their captives. It was as if two songbirds had tried to edge through a crowd of vultures to steal a snack only to find they were the intended meal.

I knelt, watching in frozen horror, fully expecting to witness the immediate demise of my two allies.

"Since Frumple's already announced us," Aahz said smoothly, "I guess there's no need to maintain this disguise."

The confident tone of his voice steadied my shattered nerve. We were in it now, and win or lose we'd just have to keep going.

Quickly, I shut my eyes and removed Aahz's Garkin disguise.

"Aahz!" cried Isstvan in delight. "I should have known it was you."

"He's the one who. . . ." Brockhurst began.

"Do you two know each other?" Frumple asked, ignoring the Imp.

"Know each other?" Isstvan chortled. "We're *old*

181

enemies. He and a couple other scalawags nearly destroyed me the last time we met.''

"Well it's our turn now, right Isstvan?" smiled Higgens, leisurely reaching for his crossbow.

"Now, now!" said Isstvan, picking the Imp up by his head and shaking him gently. "Mustn't rush things."

"Seems to me," Aahz sneered, "that you're having trouble finding decent allies, Isstvan."

"Oh, Aahz," Isstvan laughed. "Still the sharp tongue, eh?"

"Imps?" Aahz's voice was scornful. "C'mon, Isstvan. Even you can do better than that."

Isstvan sighed and dropped Higgens back in his chair.

"Well, one does what one can. Inflation, you know."

He shook his head sadly, then brightened again.

"Oh you don't know how glad I am to see you, Aahz. I thought I was going to have to wait until we conquered Perv before I got my revenge, and here you just walk in. Now don't you dare pop off before we've settled our score."

"I told you before," Frumple interrupted. "He's lost his powers."

"Powers. Hmph! He never had any powers," Quigley chimed in, baited from his frightened silence at the insult of having been ignored.

"Well, who do we have here?" Isstvan smiled, looking at Quigley for the first time. "Have we met?"

"Say Isstvan," interrupted Aahz. "Mind if I have some of that wine? No reason to be barbaric about this."

"Certainly, Aahz." Isstvan waved him forward. "Help yourself."

It was eerie listening to the conversation: apparently civilized and friendly, it had a cat-and-mouse undercurrent which belied the casual tones.

"Watch him!" Frumple hissed, glaring at Aahz.

"Oh Frumple! You are such a wart," Isstvan scolded. "Why you were the one who assured me that he had lost his powers."

"Well, I think he makes sense," Brockhurst grumbled, rising and backing away as Aahz approached the table. "If you don't mind, Isstvan, I'll watch from over here."

He sat on the bottom steps of the flight of stairs heading up to the mezzanine where Tanda and I were hidden. His tone was conversational, but it was clear he was only waiting for Isstvan's signal to loose him on the helpless pair.

"Oh, you Imps are worse than the Deveels!" Isstvan scowled.

"That's a given," Frumple commented dryly.

"Now look, Frumple. . . ." Higgens began angrily.

"As to who this figure is," Frumple pointed to Quigley, ignoring the Imps. "That is Garkin's apprentice. He's the one who's been handling the magik for our Pervert since he lost his powers."

"Really?" asked Isstvan eagerly. "Can you do the cups and balls trick? I love the cups and balls trick."

"I don't understand," mumbled Quigley vacantly, backing away from the assemblage.

Well, if we were ever going to have a diversion, it would have to be now. Closing my eyes, I changed Quigley's features. The obvious choice for his disguise was . . . me!

"See," said Frumple pointing proudly. "I told you so."

"Throckwoddle!" exclaimed the two Imps simultaneously.

"What?" said Frumple narrowing his eyes suspiciously.

I was ready for them. As the exclamations rose, I changed Quigley again. This time, I gave him Throckwoddle features.

"Why, it *is* Throckwoddle," cried Isstvan. "Oh that's funny."

"Wait a minute!" Brockhurst hissed. "How could you be Throckwoddle when we turned you into a statue before we caught up with Throckwoddle?"

This set Isstvan off into even greater peals of laughter.

"Stop," he called breathless. "Oh stop. Oh! My ribs hurt. Aahz, you've outdone yourself this time."

"It's nothing really," Aahz acknowledged modestly.

"There's something wrong here!" Frumple declared.

He plunged a hand deep into his robe, never taking his eyes from Quigley. Almost too late I realized what he was doing. He was going for his crystal, the one that let him detect disguises. As the glittering bauble emerged, I swung into action.

A simple levitation, a small flick with my mind, and the crystal popped out of Frumple's grasp and plopped into the wine jug.

"Framitz!" Frumple swore, starting to fish for his possession.

"Get your hands out of the wine, Frumple!" Aahz chided slapping his wrist. "You'll get your toy when we finish the jug!"

As if to illustrate his point, he hefted the jug and began refilling the flagons around the table.

"Enough of this insanity!" Quigley exploded.

I winced at the use of the word "insanity," but Isstvan didn't seem to mind. He merely leaned forward to watch Quigley.

"I am neither Skeeve nor Throckwoddle," Quigley continued, "I am Quigley, demon hunter extraordinaire! Let any dispute who dare, and man or demon I'll show him who I am!"

This proved too much for Isstvan, who actually collapsed in laughter.

"Oh he's funny, Aahz," he gasped. "Where did you find this funny man?"

"You sent him to me, remember?" Aahz prompted.

"Why so I did, so I did," Isstvan mused, and even this fact he seemed to find hysterically funny.

The others were not so amused.

"So you're a demon hunter, eh?" Frumple snarled. "What's your gripe anyway?"

"The offenses of demons are too numerous to list," Quigley retorted haughtily.

"We aren't going anywhere for a while," Brockhurst

chimed in from the stairs. "And neither are you. List us a few of these offenses."

"Well . . ." began Quigley, "you stole my magik pendant and my magik sword. . . ."

"We don't know anything about a magik pendant." Higgens bristled. "And we gave your so-called magik sword to. . . ."

"What else do demons do?" Frumple interrupted, apparently none too eager to have the discussion turn to swords.

"Well . . . you bewitched my war unicorn into thinking he's a dragon!" Quigley challenged.

"Your war unicorn is currently tethered in the stable," Higgens stated flatly. "Frumple brought him in."

"My unicorn is tethered outside the door!" Quigley insisted. "And he thinks he's a dragon!"

"Your unicorn is tethered in the stable," Higgens barked back. "And we think you're a fruitcake!"

"Gentlemen, gentlemen," Isstvan managed to hold up his hands despite his laughter. "All this is quite amusing, but . . . well, will you look at that!"

This last was said in such a tone of wonder that the attention of everyone in the room was immediately drawn to the spot he was looking at.

Suspended in midair, not two hand-spans from Isstvan's head, was a small red dart with gold and black fletchings.

"An assassin's dart!" Isstvan marveled, gently plucking the missile from where it was hovering. "Now who would be naughty enough to try to poison me from behind?"

His eyes slowly moved to Brockhurst sitting casually on the stairs.

Brockhurst suddenly realized he was the object of everyone's attention. His eyes widened in fright.

"No! I . . . Wait! Isstvan!" he half-rose holding out a hand as if to ward off a blow. "I didn't . . . No! Don't. Glaag!"

This last was said as his hands suddenly flew to his

throat and began choking him violently.

"Glaak . . . eak . . . urk. . . ."

He fell back on the stairs and began rolling frantically back and forth.

"Isstvan," Higgens began hesitantly, "normally I wouldn't interfere, but don't you think you should hear what he has to say, first?"

"But I'm not doing anything," Isstvan blinked with hurt innocence.

My eyes flashed to the other end of the mezzanine. Tanda was crouched there, her eyes closed. She seemed to be choking an invisible person on the floor in front of her. With dawning realization, I began to appreciate more and more the subtleties of a trained assassin.

"You aren't doing anything?" Higgens shrilled, "Well, then do something! He's dying!"

I thought for a moment that the ludicrous statement would set Isstvan to laughing again, but not this time.

"Oh," he sighed. "This is all so confusing. Yes, I guess you're right."

He clicked his fingers and Brockhurst stopped thrashing about and began breathing again in long, ragged breaths.

"Here, old boy," said Aahz. "Have some wine."

He offered Brockhurst a brimming flagon which the Imp began to gulp gratefully.

"Aahz," Isstvan said sternly. "I don't think you've been honest with us."

"Me?" Aahz asked innocently.

"Even you couldn't have caused this much havoc without assistance. Now where is it coming from?"

He closed his eyes and turned his face toward the ceiling for a moment.

"Aah!" he suddenly proclaimed. "Here it is."

There was a squawk from the other end of the mezzanine and Tanda was suddenly lifted into view by unseen hands.

"Higgens!" exclaimed Isstvan, "Another one! Well, well, the day is full of surprises."

Tanda held her silence as she was floated down to a chair on a level with the others.

"Now let's see." Isstvan mumbled to himself. "Have we missed anybody?"

I felt the sudden pressure of invisible forces and realized I was next. I tried desperately to think of a disguise, but the only thing that came to mind was Gleep . . . so I tried it.

"A dragon!" cried Brockhurst as I floated into view.

"Gleep!" I said, rolling my eyes desperately.

"Oh now that's too much," Isstvan pouted. "I want to see who I'm dealing with."

He gave a vacant wave of his hand, and the disguises disappeared . . . all of them. I was me, Quigley was Quigley, Tanda was Tanda, the Imps were Imps, and the Deveel was a Deveel. Aahz, of course, was Aahz. Apparently a moratorium had been declared on disguises . . . by a majority of one . . . Isstvan.

I came drifting down to join the others, but my entrance was generally ignored in the other proceedings.

"Tanda!" Isstvan cried enthusiastically. "Well, well. This *is* a reunion, isn't it?"

"Bark at the moon, Isstvan," Tanda snarled defiantly.

Quigley was looking at everyone else with such speed I thought his head would fall off.

"I don't understand!" he whimpered plaintively.

"Shut up, Quigley," Aahz growled. "We'll explain later."

"That's assuming there is a later," Frumple sneered.

I tended to agree with Frumple. The atmosphere in the room no longer had even the semblance of joviality. It was over. We had lost. We were all exposed and captured, and Isstvan was as strong as ever. Whatever Aahz's secret weapon was, it apparently hadn't worked.

"Well, I'm afraid all good things must come to an end," Isstvan sighed, draining his flagon. "Now I'm afraid I'll have to dispose of you."

He sounded genuinely sad, but somehow I couldn't

muster any sympathy for his plight.

"Just one question before we begin, Aahz," he asked in surprisingly sane tones.

"What's that?" Aahz responded.

"Why did you do it? I mean, with as feeble a team as this, how did you possibly hope to beat me?"

Isstvan sounded genuinely sincere.

"Well, Isstvan," Aahz drawled, "that's a matter of opinion."

"What's that supposed to mean?" Isstvan asked suspiciously.

"I don't 'hope' we can beat you," Aahz smiled. "I know we can."

"Really?" Isstvan chuckled. "And upon what are you basing your logic?"

"Why, I'm basing it on the fact that we've already won," Aahz blinked innocently. "It's all over, Isstvan, whether you realize it or not."

Chapter Twenty-Five:

"Just because you've beaten a sorcerer, doesn't mean you've beaten a sorcerer."

—TOTH-AAMON

"AAHZ," Isstvan said sternly, "there comes a time when even your humor wears a little thin."

"I'm not kidding, Isstvan," Aahz assured him. "You've lost your powers. Go ahead, try something. Anything!"

Isstvan hesitated. He closed his eyes.

Nothing happened.

"You see?" Aahz shrugged. "You've lost your powers. All of them. And don't look to your associates for help. They're all in the same boat."

"You mean we've really won?" I blurted out, the full impact of what was transpiring finally starting to sink in.

"That's right, kid."

Aahz suddenly leaned forward and clapped Frumple on the shoulder.

"Congratulations, Frumple," he exclaimed. "I've got to admit I didn't think you could do it."

"What?" blinked the Deveel.

"I'm just glad this squares our debt with you," Aahz continued without pause. "You won't try to back out on it now, will you?"

"Frumple!" Isstvan's voice was dark with menace. "Did you do this to us?"

"I . . . I. . . ." Frumple stammered.

"Go ahead, Frumple. Gloat!" Aahz encouraged. "He can't do anything to you now. Besides, you can teleport out of here anytime you want."

"No, he can't!" snarled Higgens, and his arm flashed forward.

I caught a glimpse of a small ball flying through the air before it exploded against Frumple's forehead in a cloud of purple dust.

"But. . . ." began Frumple, but it was too late.

In mid-gesture his limbs became rigid and his face froze. We had another statue on our hands.

"Good move, Higgens," applauded Aahz.

"If it wouldn't be too much trouble, Aahz," interrupted Isstvan. "Could you explain what's going on here?"

"Aah!" said Aahz, "therein lies the story."

"This sounds familiar," Quigley mumbled.

I poked him in the ribs with my elbow. We weren't out of this yet.

"It seems that Frumple learned about your plans from Throckwoddle. Apparently he was afraid that if you succeeded in taking over the dimensions, you would implement price controls, thereby putting him out of business as a merchant. You know how those Deveels are."

The Imps snorted. Isstvan nodded thoughtfully.

"Anyway, he decided to try to stop you. To accomplish this, he blackmailed the four of us into assisting him. We were to create a diversion while he effected the actual attack."

"Well, what did he do?" prompted Higgens.

"He drugged the wine!" explained Aahz. "Don't you remember?"

"When?" asked Brockhurst.

"When he dropped that phony crystal into the jug, remember?"

"But he drank from the jug, too!" exclaimed Higgens.

"That's right, but he had taken an antidote in advance," Aahz finished with a flourish.

"So we're stuck here!" Brockhurst spat in disgust.

"You know, Aahz," Isstvan said slowly. "It occurs to me that even if everything happened exactly as you described it, you and your friends here played a fairly large part in the plot."

"You're right, Isstvan," Aahz admitted, "but I'm prepared to offer you a bargain."

"What kind of a bargain?" Isstvan asked suspiciously.

"It's in two parts. First, to clear Tanda and myself from having opposed you in your last bid for power, I can offer transportation for you and your allies out of this dimension."

"Hmm. . . ." said Isstvan. "And the second part?"

"For the second part, I can give you the ultimate vengeance to visit on Frumple here. In exchange, I want your promise you'll bear no grudge against the four of us for our part in today's misfortune."

"Pardon for four in exchange for vengeance on one?" Isstvan grunted. "That doesn't sound like much of a deal."

"I think you're overlooking something, Isstvan," Aahz cautioned.

"What's that?"

"You've lost your powers. That makes it four of us against three of you."

"Look at your four," Brockhurst sneered. "A woman, a half-trained apprentice, a broken-down demon hunter and a Pervert."

"Broken-down?" Quigley scowled.

"Easy, Quigley . . . and you too, Tanda," Aahz ordered. "Your three are nothing to brag about either, Brockhurst. Two Imps who've lost their powers and a fat madman."

Surprisingly, this seemed to revive Isstvan's humor. The Imps were not amused.

"Now look, Aahz," Higgens began, "if you want a fight. . . ."

"You miss the point entirely, gentlemen," Aahz said soothingly. "I'm trying to avoid a fight. I'm merely trying to point out that if this comes to a fight, you'll lose."

"Not necessarily," Brockhurst bristled.

"Inescapably," Aahz insisted. "Look, if we fight and we win, you lose. On the other hand, if we fight and we lose, you lose."

"How do you figure that?" Higgens asked suspiciously.

"Simple!" said Aahz smugly, "If you kill us, you'll have lost your only way to get out of this dimension. You'll be stuck forever on Klah. By my figuring, that's losing."

"We're in agreement there," Brockhurst mumbled.

"Oh, stop this bickering!" Isstvan interrupted with a chuckle. "Aahz is right, as usual. He may have lost a couple of fights, both magical and physical, but I've never heard of anyone out-arguing him."

"Then it's a deal?" Aahz asked.

"It's a deal!" Isstvan said firmly. "As if we had any choice in the matter."

They shook hands ceremoniously.

I noticed the Imps were whispering together and shooting dark glances in our direction. I wondered if a deal with Isstvan was binding on the Imps. I wondered if a handshake was legally binding in a situation such as this. But most of all, I wondered what Aahz had up his sleeve this time.

"Well, Aahz?" Isstvan asked, "Where is this escape clause you promised?"

"Right here!" Aahz said, fishing a familiar object from inside his shirt and tossing it to Isstvan.

"A D-Hopper!" Isstvan cried with delight. "I haven't seen one of these since. . . ."

"What is it?" Higgens interrupted.

Isstvan scowled at him.

"It's our ticket off this dimension," he exclaimed grudgingly.

"How does it work?" Brockhurst asked suspiciously.

"Trust me, gentlemen." Isstvan's distasteful expression gave lie to the joviality of his words. "It works."

He turned to Aahz again.

"Imps!" he mumbled to himself.

"You hired 'em," Aahz commented, unsympathetically.

"So I did. Well, what is this diabolical vengeance you have in mind for Frumple?"

"That's easy," smiled Aahz. "Use the D-Hopper and take him back to Deva."

"Why Deva?" Isstvan asked.

"Because he's been banned from Deva," Higgens answered, the light dawning.

". . . and the Deveels are unequaled at meting out punishment to those who break their laws," Brockhurst finished with an evil smile.

"Why was Frumple banned from Deva?" Tanda whispered to me.

"I don't know," I confided. "Maybe he gave a refund or something."

"I don't believe it," she snorted, "I mean he *is* a Deveel."

"Aahz," Isstvan smiled, regarding the D-Hopper, "I've always admired your sense of humor. It's even nastier than mine."

"What do you expect from a Pervert?" snorted Brockhurst.

"Watch your mouth, Imp," I snarled.

He was starting to get on my nerves.

"Then it's settled!" Isstvan chortled, clapping his hands together gleefully. "Brockhurst! Higgens! Come gather around Frumple here. We're off to Deva."

"Right now?" asked Brockhurst.

"With . . . things here so unsettled?" Higgens added, glancing at us again.

"Oh, we won't be long," Isstvan assured them.

"There's nothing here we can't come back and pick up later."

"That's true," admitted Brockhurst, staring at me thoughtfully.

"Umm . . . Isstvan?"

It was Quigley.

"Are you addressing me?" Isstvan asked with mock formality.

"Yes." Quigley looked uncomfortable. "Am I to understand you are all about to depart for some place completely populated with demons?"

"That is correct," Isstvan nodded.

"Could . . . that is . . . would you mind if I accompanied you?"

"What?" I exclaimed, genuinely startled. "Why?"

"Well . . ." Quigley said hesitantly, "if there is one thing I have learned this day, it's that I really know very little about demons."

"Hear, hear!" mumbled Aahz.

"I am undecided as to whether or not to continue in my chosen profession," Quigley continued, "but in any case it behooves me to learn more about demons. What better place could there be for such study than in a land completely populated with demons?"

"Why should we burden ourselves with a demon hunter of all things?" Brockhurst appealed to Isstvan.

"Maybe we could teach him a few things about demons," Higgens suggested in an overly innocent voice, giving his partner a covert poke in the side.

"What? Hmm . . . You know, you're right, Higgens." Brockhurst was suddenly smiling again.

"Good!" exclaimed Isstvan. "We'll make a party of it."

"In that case," purred Tanda, "you won't mind if I tag along, too."

"What?" exclaimed Brockhurst.

"Why?" challenged Higgens.

"To help, of course," she smiled. "I want to be there when you teach Quigley about demons. Maybe I can help him learn."

"Wonderful, wonderful," Isstvan beamed, overriding the Imps' objections. "The more the merrier. Aahz? Skeeve? Will you be joining us?"

"Not this time, thanks," Aahz replied before I could open my mouth. "The kid here and I have a few things to go over that won't wait."

"Like what?" I asked.

"Shut up, kid," Aahz hissed, then smiled again at the group. "You all run along. We'll be here when you come back."

"We'll be looking forward to it." Brockhurst smiled grimly.

"G'bye, Aahz, Skeeve!" Tanda waved. "I'll look for you next time around."

"But Tanda. . . ." I began.

"Don't worry, lad," Quigley assured me. "I'll make sure nothing happens to her."

Behind him, Tanda shot me a bawdy wink.

"Aahz!" Isstvan chuckled. "I do enjoy your company. We must work together more often."

He adjusted the settings on the D-Hopper and prepared to trigger it.

"Good-bye, Isstvan." Aahz smiled and waved. "Remember me!"

There was a rippling in the air and they were gone. All of them.

"Aahz!" I said urgently. "Did you see how those Imps looked at us?"

"Hmm? Oh. Yeah, kid. I told you they were vicious little creatures."

"But what are we going to do when they get back?"

"Don't worry about it, kid."

"Don't worry about it!" I shrieked. "We've got to. . . ."

". . . because they aren't coming back," Aahz finished.

That stopped me.

"But . . . when they get done on Deva. . . ."

"That's the joke, kid," Aahz grinned at me. "They aren't going to Deva."

Chapter Twenty-Six:

*"A woman, like a good piece of music,
should have a solid end."*

—F. SCHUBERT

"THEY aren't going to Deva?"

I was having a rough time dealing with the concept.

"That's right, kid," Aahz said, pouring himself some more wine.

"But Isstvan set the D-Hopper himself."

"Yeah!" Aahz grinned smugly. "But last night I made one extra preparation for this sortie. I changed the markings on the dials."

"Then where are they going?"

"Beats me!" Aahz shrugged, taking a deep draught of the wine. "But I'm betting it'll take 'em a long time to find their way back. There are a lot of settings on a D-Hopper."

"But what about Tanda and Quigley?"

"Tanda can take care of Quigley," Aahz assured me. "Besides, she has the powers to pull them out anytime she wants."

"She does?"

"Sure. But she'll probably have a few laughs just tagging along for a while. Can't say as I blame her. I'd love to see Quigley deal with a few dimensions myself."

He took another generous gulp of the wine.

"Aahz!" I cried in sudden realization. "The wine!"

"What about it? Oh. Don't worry kid," he smiled. "I've already lost my powers, remember? Besides, you don't think I'd drug my own wine, do you?"

"You drugged the wine?"

"Yeah. That was my secret weapon. You didn't really believe all that bunk about Frumple, did you?"

"Ahh . . . of course not," I said, offended.

Actually, even though I knew Frumple hadn't done it, I had completely lost track of actually who had done what and to whom.

"Here, kid." Aahz handed me his flagon and picked up the jug. "Have some yourself. You did pretty good this afternoon."

I took the flagon, but somehow couldn't bring myself to drink any.

"What did you put in the wine, anyway?" I asked.

"Joke powder," Aahz replied. "As near as I can tell, it's the same stuff Garkin used on me. You can put it in a drink, sprinkle it over food, or burn it and have your victim inhale the smoke."

I had a sudden flash recollection of the brazier billowing smoke as Aahz materialized.

"What does it do?"

"Weren't you paying attention, kid?" Aahz cocked his head at me. "It takes away your powers."

"Permanently?"

"Of course not!" Aahz scoffed. "Only for a century."

"What's the antidote?"

"There isn't one . . . at least I couldn't get the stall-proprietor to admit to having one. Maybe when you get a little better with the magik, we'll go back to Deva and beat an answer out of him."

I thought for a few minutes. That seemed to answer all my questions . . . except one.

"Say . . . um, Aahz?"

"Yeah, kid?"

"What do we do now?"

"About what?" Aahz asked.

"I mean, what do we do? We've been spending all the time since we met getting ready to fight Isstvan. Well, it's over. Now what do we do?"

"What *you* do, apprentice," Aahz said sternly, "is devote your time to your magik. You've still got a long way to go before you're even close to Master status. As for me . . . well, I guess most of my time will be spent teaching you."

He poured a little more wine down his throat.

"Actually, we're in pretty good shape," he stated. "We've got a magik crystal courtesy of Frumple . . . and that crummy sword if we search his gear."

"And a malfunctioning fire-ring," I prompted.

"Um. . . ." said Aahz. "Actually, I . . . ahh . . . well, I gave the ring to Tanda."

"Gave?" I asked. "You *gave* something away?"

Aahz shrugged.

"I'm a soft touch. Ask anybody."

"Hmm. . . ." I said.

"We've, um, also got a war unicorn if we want to go anywhere," Aahz hastened on, "and that stupid dragon of yours."

"Gleep isn't stupid!" I insisted hotly.

"Okay, okay," Aahz amended, ". . . your intelligent, personable dragon."

"That's better," I mumbled.

". . . Even though it beats me why we'd want to go anyplace," Aahz commented, looking around him. "This place seems sound enough. You'd have some good force lines to play with, and the wine cellar will be well stocked if I know Isstvan. We could do lots worse for a base of operations."

Another question occurred to me.

"Say, Aahz?"

"Yeah, kid?"

"A few minutes ago you said you wanted to see Quigley when he visited other dimensions . . . and you seem to have a weak spot for Tanda. . . ."

"Yeah?" Aahz growled. "So?"

"So why didn't you go along with them? You didn't have to get stranded in this dimension."

"Isstvan's a fruitcake," Aahz declared pointedly, "and I don't like Imps. You think I'd like having them for traveling companions?"

"But you said Tanda could travel the dimensions by herself. Couldn't you and she have. . . ."

"All right, all right," interrupted Aahz. "You want me to say it? I stayed here because of you."

"Why?"

"Because you're not up to traveling the dimensions yet. Not until you. . . ."

"I mean, why stay with me at all?"

"Why? Because you're my apprentice! That's why." Aahz seemed genuinely angry. "We made a deal, remember? You help me against Isstvan and I teach you magik. Well, you did your part and now I'm going to do mine. I'm going to teach you magik if it kills you . . . or me, which is more probable!"

"Yes, Aahz!" I agreed hastily.

"Besides," he mumbled, taking another drink. "I like you."

"Excuse me?" I said. "I didn't quite hear that."

"Then pay attention!" Aahz barked. "I said drink your wine, and give some to that stupid dragon of yours. I will allow you one . . . count it, one . . . night of celebration. Then bright and early tomorrow, we start working in earnest."

"Yes, Aahz," I said obediently.

"And kid," Aahz grinned, "don't worry about it being boring. We don't have to go looking for adventure. In our profession, it usually comes looking for us."

I had an ugly feeling he was right.

MYTH CONCEPTIONS

Robert Asprin

This book is dedicated to

Laurie Oshrin and Judith Sampson

*a modern day student-teacher team who
unwittingly guaranteed the myth-adventures
of Aahz and Skeeve would continue to be written!*

Chapter One:

"Life is a series of rude awakenings."
—R. V. WINKLE

OF all the various unpleasant ways to be aroused from a sound sleep, one of the worst is the noise of a dragon and a unicorn playing tag.

I pried one eye open and blearily tried to focus on the room. A chair toppled noisily to the floor, convincing me the blurred images my mind was receiving were due at least in part to the irregular vibrations coming from the floor and walls. One without my vast storehouse of knowledge (hard won and painfully endured) might be inclined to blame the pandemonium on an earthquake. I didn't. The logic behind this conclusion was simple. Earthquakes were extremely uncommon in this area. A dragon and a unicorn playing tag wasn't.

It was starting out as an ordinary day . . . that is, ordinary if you're a junior magician apprenticed to a demon.

If I had been able to predict the future with any

1

degree of accuracy and thus forsee the events to
come, I probably would have stayed in bed. I mean,
fighting has never been my forte, and the idea of taking on a whole army . . . but I'm getting ahead of
myself.

The thud that aroused me shook the building, accompanied by the crash of various dirty dishes shat-
tering on the floor. The second thud was even more
spectacular.

I considered doing something. I considered going
back to sleep. Then I remembered my mentor's condition when he had gone to bed the night before.

That woke me up fast. The only thing nastier than
a demon from Perv is a demon from Perv with a
hangover.

I was on my feet and headed for the door in a
flash. (My agility was a tribute more to my fear
rather than to any inborn talent.) Wrenching the
door open, I thrust my head outside and surveyed the
terrain. The grounds outside the inn seemed normal.
The weeds were totally out of hand, more than chest
high in places. Something would have to be done
about them someday, but my mentor didn't seem to
mind their riotous growth, and since I was the logical
candidate to cut them if I raised the point, I decided
once again to keep silent on the subject.

Instead, I studied the various flattened patches and
newly torn paths in the overgrowth, trying to determine the location or at least the direction of my quar-
ries' movement. I had almost convinced myself that
the silence was at least semipermanent and it would
be all right to go back to sleep, when the ground
began to tremble again. I sighed and shakily drew
myself up to my full height, what there was of it, and
prepared to meet the onslaught.

The unicorn was the first to come into view, great clumps of dirt flying from beneath his hooves as he ducked around the corner of the inn on my right.

"Buttercup!" I shouted in my most authoritative tone.

A split second later I had to jump back into the shelter of the doorway to avoid being trampled by the speeding beast. Though a bit miffed at his disobedience, I didn't really blame him. He had a dragon chasing him, and dragons are not notoriously agile when it comes to quick stops.

As if acting on a cue from my thoughts, the dragon burst into view. To be accurate, he didn't really burst, he thudded, shaking the inn as he rebounded off the corner. As I said, dragons are not notoriously agile.

"Gleep!" I shouted. "Stop it this instant!"

He responded by taking an affectionate swipe at me with his tail as he bounded past. Fortunately for me, the gesture went wide of its mark, hitting the inn with another jarring thud instead.

So much for my most authoritative tone. If our two faithful charges were any more obedient, I'd be lucky to escape with my life. Still I had to stop them. Whoever came up with the immortal quote about waking sleeping dragons had obviously never had to contend with a sleeping demon.

I studied the two of them chasing each other through the weeds for a few moments, then decided to handle this the easy way. Closing my eyes, I envisioned both of them, the dragon and the unicorn. Then I superimposed the image of the dragon over that of the unicorn, fleshed it out with a few strokes of my mental paintbrush, then opened my eyes.

To my eyes, the scene was the same, a dragon and

a unicorn confronting each other in a field of weeds. But, of course, I had cast the spell, so naturally I wouldn't be taken in. Its true effect could be read in Gleep's reaction.

He cocked his head and peered at Buttercup, first from this angle, then that, stretching his long serpentine neck to its limits. Then he swiveled his head until he was looking backward and repeated the process, scanning the surrounding weeds. Then he looked at Buttercup again.

To his eyes, his playmate had suddenly disappeared, to be replaced by another dragon. It was all very confusing, and he wanted his playmate back.

In my pet's defense, when I speak of his lack of agility, both physically and mentally, I don't mean to imply he is either clumsy or stupid. He's young, which also accounts for his mere ten-foot length and half-formed wings. I fully expect that when he matures—in another four or five hundred years—he will be very deft and wise, which is more than I can say for myself. In the unlikely event I should live that long, all I'll be is old.

"Gleep?"

The dragon was looking at me now. Having stretched his limited mental abilities to their utmost, he turned to me to correct the situation or at least provide an explanation. As the perpetrator of the situation causing his distress, I felt horribly guilty. For a moment, I wavered on the brink of restoring Buttercup's normal appearance.

"If you're *quite* sure you're making enough noise. . . ."

I winced at the deep, sarcastic tones booming close behind me. All my efforts were for naught. Aahz was awake.

I assumed my best hangdog attitude and turned to face him.

Needless to say, he looked terrible.

If, perchance, you think a demon covered with green scales already looks terrible, you've never encountered one with a hangover. The normal gold flecks in his yellow eyes were now copper, accented by a throbbing network of orange veins. His lips were drawn back in a painful grimace which exposed even more of his pointed teeth than his frightening, *reassuring* smile. Looming there, his fists clenched on his hips, he presented a picture terrifying enough to make a spider-bear faint.

I wasn't frightened, however. I had been with Aahz for over a year now, and knew his bark was worse than his bite. Then again, he had never bitten me.

"Gee, Aahz," I said, digging a small hole with my toe. "You're always telling me if I can't sleep through anything, I'm not really tired."

He ignored the barb, as he so frequently does when I catch him on his own quotes. Instead he squinted over my shoulder at the scene outside.

"Kid," he said. "Tell me you're practicing. Tell me you haven't really scrounged up another stupid dragon to make our lives miserable."

"I'm practicing!" I hastened to reassure him.

To prove the point, I quickly restored Buttercup's normal appearance.

"Gleep!" said Gleep happily, and the two of them were off again.

"Really, Aahz," I said innocently to head off his next caustic remark. "Where would I find another dragon in this dimension?"

"If there was one to be found here on Klah, you'd

find it,'' he snarled. ''As I recall, you didn't have that much trouble finding this one the first time I turned my back on you. Apprentices!''

He turned and retreated out of the sunlight into the dim interior of the inn.

''If I recall,'' I commented, following him, ''that was at the Bazaar on Deva. I couldn't get another dragon there because you won't teach me how to travel through the dimensions.''

''Get off my case, kid!'' he moaned. ''We've been over it a thousand times. Dimension traveling is dangerous. Look at me! Stranded without my powers in a back-assward dimension like Klah, where the lifestyle is barbaric and the food is disgusting.''

''You lost your powers because Garkin laced his special effects cauldron with that joke powder and then got killed before he could give you the antidote,'' I pointed out.

''Watch out how you talk about your old teacher,'' Aahz warned. ''The old slime-monger was inclined to get carried away with practical jokes once in a while, true. But he was a master magician . . . and a friend of mine. If he wasn't, I wouldn't have saddled myself with his mouthy apprentice,'' he finished, giving me a meaningful look.

''I'm sorry, Aahz,'' I apologized. ''It's just that I—''

''Look, kid,'' he interrupted wearily, ''if I had my powers—which I don't—and if you were ready to learn dimension hopping—which you aren't—we could give it a try. Then, if you miscalculated and dumped us into the wrong dimension, I could get our tails out before anything bad happened. As things stand, trying to teach you dimension hopping would be more dangerous than playing Russian roulette.''

"What's russian?" I asked.

The inn shook as Gleep missed the corner turn again.

"When are you going to teach your stupid dragon to play on the other side of the road?" Aahz snarled, craning his neck to glare out a window.

"I'm working on it, Aahz," I insisted soothingly. "Remember, it took me almost a whole year to housebreak him."

"Don't remind me," Aahz grumbled. "If I had my way, we'd . . ."

He broke off suddenly and cocked his head to one side.

"You'd better disguise that dragon, kid," he announced suddenly. "And get ready to do your 'dubious character' bit. We're about to have a visitor."

I didn't contest the information. We had established long ago that Aahz's hearing was much more acute than mine.

"Right, Aahz," I acknowledged and hurried about my task.

The trouble with using an inn for a base of operations, however abandoned or weather-beaten it might be, was that occasionally people would stop here seeking food and lodging. Magik was still outlawed in these lands, and the last thing we wanted was witnesses.

Chapter Two:

"First impressions, being the longest lasting, are of utmost importance."

—J. CARTER

AAHZ and I had acquired the inn under rather dubious circumstances. Specifically, we claimed it as our rightful spoils of war after the two of us (with the assistance of a couple of allies, now absent) had routed Isstvan, a maniac magician, and sent him packing into far dimensions along with all his surviving accomplices. The inn had been Isstvan's base of operations. But now it was ours. Who Isstvan had gotten it from and how, I didn't want to know. Despite Aahz's constant assurances, I lived in dread of encountering the inn's rightful owner.

I couldn't help remembering all this as I waited outside the inn for our visitor. As I said, Aahz has very good hearing. When he tells me he hears something "close by," he frequently forgets to mention that "close by" may be over a mile away.

I have also noted, over the course of our friendship, that his hearing is curiously erratic. He can hear

8

a lizard-bird scratching itself half a mile away, but occasionally seems unable to hear the politest of requests no matter how loudly I shout them at him.

There was still no sign of our rumored visitor. I considered moving back inside the inn out of the late morning sun, but decided against it. I had carefully arranged the scene for our guest's arrival, and I hated to disrupt it for such a minor thing as personal comfort.

I had used the disguise spell liberally on Buttercup, Gleep, and myself. Gleep now looked like a unicorn, a change that did not seem to bother Buttercup in the slightest. Apparently unicorns are less discriminating about their playmates than are dragons. I had made them both considerably more disheveled and unkempt-looking than they actually were. This was necessary to maintain the image set forth by my own appearance.

Aahz and I had decided early in our stay that the best way to handle unwanted guests was not to threaten them or frighten them away, but rather to be so repulsive that they left of their own accord. To this end, I had slowly devised a disguise designed to convince strangers they did not want to be in the same inn with me, no matter how large the inn was or how many other people were there. In this disguise, I would greet wayward travelers as the proprietor of the inn.

Modestly, I will admit the disguise was a screaming success. In fact, that was the specific reaction many visitors had to it. Some screamed, some looked ill, others sketched various religious symbols in the air between themselves and me. None of them elected to spend the night.

When I experimented with various physical defects, Aahz correctly pointed out that many people did not find any single defect revolting. In fact, in a dimension such as Klah, most would consider it normal. To guarantee the desired effect, I adopted many of them.

When disguised, I walked with a painful limp, had a hump-back, and a deformed hand which was noticeably diseased. What teeth remained were twisted and stained, and the focus of one of my eyes had a tendency to wander about independently of the other. My nose—in fact, my entire face—was not symmetrical, and as a masterstroke of my disguise abilities, there appeared to be vicious-looking bugs crawling about my mangy hair and tattered clothes.

The overall effect was horrifying. Even Aahz admitted he found it disquieting, which, considering the things he's seen in his travels through the dimensions, was high praise indeed.

My thoughts were interrupted as our visitor came into view. He sat ramrod-straight astride a huge, flightless riding bird. He carried no visible weapons and wore no uniform, but his bearing marked him as a soldier much more than any outer trappings could have. His eyes were wary, constantly darting suspiciously about as he walked his bird up to the inn in slow, deliberate steps. Surprisingly enough, his gaze passed over me several times without registering my presence. Perhaps he didn't realize I was alive.

I didn't like this. The man seemed more the hunter than the casual traveler. Still, he was here and had to be dealt with. I went into my act.

"Does the noble sahr require a room?"

As I spoke I moved forward in my practical, rolling gait. In case the subtlety of my disguise escaped him, I allowed a large gob of spittle to ooze from the corner of my mouth where it rolled unhindered down to my chin.

For a moment the man's attention was occupied controlling his mount. Flightless or not, the bird was trying to take to the air.

Apparently my disguise had touched a primal chord in the bird's mind that went back prior to its flightless ancestry.

I waited, head cocked curiously, while the man fought the bird to a fidgety standstill. Finally, he turned his attention to me for a moment. Then he averted his eyes and stared carefully at the sky.

"I come seeking the one known as Skeeve the magician," he told me.

Now it was my turn to jump. To the best of my knowledge, no one knew who I was and what I was, much less where I was, except for Aahz and me.

"That's me!" I blurted out, forgetting myself and using my real voice.

The man turned horrified eyes on me, and I remembered my appearance.

"That's me master!" I amended hastily. "You wait . . . I fetch."

I turned and scuttled hastily into the inn. Aahz was waiting inside.

"What is it?" he demanded.

"He's . . . he wants to talk to Skeeve . . . to me!" I babbled nervously.

"So?" he asked pointedly. "What are you doing in here? Go outside and talk to the man."

"Looking like this?"

Aahz rolled his eyes at the ceiling in exasperation.

"Who cares what you look like?" he barked. "C'mon, kid. The man's a total stranger!"

"I care!" I declared, drawing myself up haughtily.

"The man asked for Skeeve the magician, and I think—"

"He what?" Aahz interrupted.

"He asked for Skeeve the magician," I repeated, covertly studying the figure waiting outside.

"He looks like a soldier to me," I supplied.

"He looks scared to me," Aahz retorted. "Maybe you should tone down your disguise a bit next time."

"Do you think he's a demon-hunter?" I asked nervously.

Instead of answering my question, Aahz turned abruptly from the window.

"If he wants a magician, we'll give him a magician," he murmured. "Quick, kid, slap the Garkin disguise on me."

As I noted earlier, Garkin was my first magik instructor. An imposing figure with a salt-and-pepper beard, he was one of our favorite and most oft-used disguises. I could do Garkin in my sleep.

"Good enough, kid," Aahz commented, surveying the results of my work. "Now follow close and let me do the talking."

"Like this?" I exclaimed.

"Relax, kid," he reassured me. "For this conversation I'm you. Understand?"

Aahz was already heading out through the door without waiting for my reply, leaving me little choice other than to follow along behind him.

"Who seeks an audience with the great Skeeve?" Aahz bellowed in a resonant bass voice.

The man shot another nervous glance at me, then drew himself up in stiff formality.

"I come as an emissary from his most noble Majesty, Rodrick the Fifth, King of Possiltum, who—"

"Where's Possiltum?" Aahz interrupted.

"I beg your pardon?" the man blinked.

"Possiltum," Aahz repeated. "Where is it?"

"Oh!" the man said with sudden understanding. "It's the kingdom just east of here . . . other side of the Ember River . . . you can't miss it."

"Okay," Aahz nodded. "Go on."

The man took a deep breath, then hesitated, frowning.

"King of Possiltum," I prompted.

"Oh yes! Thanks." The man shot a quick smile, then another quick stare, then continued, "King of Possiltum, who sends his respects and greetings to the one known as Skeeve the magician . . ."

He paused and looked at Aahz expectantly. He was rewarded with a polite nod of the head. Satisfied, the man continued.

"His Majesty extends an invitation to Skeeve the magician to appear before the court of Possiltum that he might be reviewed for his suitability for the position of court magician."

"I don't really feel qualified to pass judgment on the king's suitability as a court magician," Aahz said modestly, eyeing the man carefully. "Isn't he content just to be king?"

"No, no!" the man corrected hastily. "The king wants to review *your* suitability."

"Oh!" Aahz said with the appearance of sudden understanding. "That's a different matter entirely. Well, well. An invitation from . . . who was it again?"

"Rodrick the Fifth," the man announced, lifting his head haughtily.

"Well," Aahz said, grinning broadly. "I've never been one to refuse a *fifth!*"

The man blinked and frowned, then glanced at me quizzically. I shrugged, not understanding the joke myself.

"You may tell His Majesty," Aahz continued, unaware of our confusion. "I shall be happy to accept his kind invitation. I shall arrive at his court at my earliest convenience."

The man frowned.

"I believe His Majesty requires your immediate presence," he commented darkly.

"Of course," Aahz answered smoothly. "How silly of me. If you will accept our hospitality for the night, I and my assistant here will be most pleased to accompany you in the morning."

I knew a cue when I heard one. I drooled and bared my teeth at the messenger.

The man shot a horrified look in my direction.

"Actually," he said hastily, "I really must be going. I'll tell His Majesty you'll be following close behind."

"You're sure you wouldn't like to stay?" Aahz asked hopefully.

"Positive!" The man nearly shouted his reply as he began backing the bird away from us.

"Oh, well," Aahz said. "Perhaps we'll catch up with you on the road."

"In that case," the man said, turning his bird, "I'll want a head . . . that is, I'd best be on my way to announce your coming."

I raised my hand to wave good-bye, but he was already moving at a rapid pace, urging his mount to still greater speeds and ignoring me completely.

"Excellent!" Aahz exclaimed, rubbing his hands together gleefully. "A court magician! What a soft job! And the day started out so miserably."

"If I can interrupt," I interrupted. "There's one minor flaw in your plan."

"Hmm? What's that?"

"I don't want to be a court magician!"

As usual, my protest didn't dampen his enthusiasm at all.

"You didn't want to be a magician, either," he reminded me bluntly. "You wanted to be a thief. Well, here's a good compromise for you. As a court magician, you'll be a civil servant . . . and civil servants are thieves on a grander scale than you ever dreamed possible!"

Chapter Three:

"Ninety percent of any business transaction is selling yourself to the client."
—X. HOLLANDER

"Now let me see if I've got this right," I said carefully. "You're saying they probably *won't* hire me on the basis of my abilities?"

I couldn't believe I'd interpreted Aahz's lecture correctly, but he beamed enthusiastically.

"That's right, kid," he approved. "Now you've got it."

"No, I don't," I insisted. "That's the craziest thing I've ever heard!"

Aahz groaned and hid his face in his hand.

It had been like this ever since we left the inn, and three days of a demon's groaning is a bit much for anyone to take.

"I'm sorry, Aahz," I said testily, "but I don't believe it. I've taken a lot of things you've told me on faith, but this . . . this goes against common sense."

"What does common sense have to do with it?" he exploded. "We're talking about a job interview!"

16

At this outburst, Buttercup snorted and tossed his head, making it necessary for us to duck out of range of his horn.

"Steady, Buttercup!" I admonished soothingly.

Though he still rolled his eyes, the unicorn resumed his stoic plodding, the travois loaded with our equipment dragging along behind him still intact. Despite incidents such as had occurred back at the inn, Buttercup and I got along fairly well, and he usually obeyed me. In contrast, he and Aahz never really hit it off, especially when the latter chose to raise his voice angrily.

"All it takes is a little gentleness," I informed Aahz smugly. "You should try it sometime."

"While you're showing off your dubious rapport with animals," Aahz retorted, "you might call your dragon back. All we need is to have him stirring up the countryside."

I cast a quick glance about. He was right. Gleep had disappeared . . . again.

"Gleep!" I called. "Come here, fella!"

"Gleep!" came an answering cry.

The bushes off to our left parted, and the dragon's head emerged.

"Gleep?" he said, cocking his head.

"Come here!" I repeated.

My pet needed no more encouragement. He bounded into the open and trotted to my side.

"I still say we should have left that stupid dragon back at the inn," Aahz grumbled.

I ignored him, checking to be sure that the gear hung saddlebag fashion over the dragon's back was still secure. Personally, I felt we were carrying far too much in the way of personal belongings, but Aahz had insisted. Gleep tried to nuzzle me affectionately with his head, and I caught a whiff of his breath. For a moment, I wondered if Aahz had been right about leaving the dragon behind.

"What were you saying about job interviews?" I asked, both to change the subject and to hide the fact I was gagging.

"I know it sounds ridiculous, kid," Aahz began with sudden sincerity, "and it is, but a lot of things are ridiculous, particularly in this dimension. That doesn't mean we don't have to deal with them."

That gave me pause to think. To a lot of people, having a demon and a dragon for traveling companions would seem ridiculous. As a matter of fact, if I took time to think it through, it seemed pretty ridiculous to me!

"Okay, Aahz," I said finally, "I can accept the existence of ridiculousness as reality. Now try explaining the court magician thing to me again."

We resumed walking as Aahz organized his thoughts. For a change, Gleep trailed placidly along beside Buttercup instead of taking off on another of his exploratory side trips.

"See if this makes any sense," Aahz said finally. "Court magicians don't do much . . . magically at least. They're primarily kept around for show, as a status symbol to demonstrate a court is advanced enough to rate a magician. It's a rare occasion when they're called upon to do anything. If you were a jester, they'd work your tail off, but not as a magician. Remember, most people are skittish about magik, and use it as seldom as possible."

"If that's the case," I said confidently, "I'm qualified. I'll match my ability to do nothing against any magician on Klah."

"No argument there," Aahz observed dryly. "But

it's not quite that easy. To hold the job takes next to no effort at all. Getting the job can be an uphill struggle.''

"Oh!" I said, mollified.

"Now to get the job, you'll have to impress the king and probably his advisors," Aahz continued. "You'll have to impress them with *you*, not with your abilities."

"How's that again?" I frowned.

"Look, kid. Like I said, a court magician is window dressing, a showpiece. They'll be looking for someone they want to have hanging around their court, someone who is impressive whether or not he ever does anything. You'll have to exude confidence. Most important, you'll have to look like a magician . . . or at least, what they think a magician looks like. If you can dress like a magician, talk like a magician, and act like a magician, maybe no one will notice you don't have the abilities of a magician."

"Thanks, Aahz," I grimaced. "You're really doing wonders towards building my confidence."

"Now don't sulk," Aahz admonished. "You know how to levitate reasonably large objects, you can fly after a fashion, and you've got the disguise spell down pat. You're doing pretty well for a rank novice, but don't kid yourself into believing you're anywhere near full magician's status."

He was right, of course, but I was loath to admit it.

"If I'm such a bumbling incompetent," I said stiffly, "why are we on our way to establish me as a court magician?"

Aahz bared his teeth at me in irritation.

"You aren't listening, kid," he snarled. "Holding the job once you've got it will be a breeze. You can handle that now. The tricky part will be getting you hired. Fortunately, with a few minor modifications and a little coaching, I think we can get you ready for polite society.''

"Modifications such as what?" I asked, curious despite myself.

Aahz made a big show of surveying me from head to foot.

"For a start," he said, "there's the way you dress.''

"What's wrong with the way I dress?" I countered defensively.

"Nothing at all," he replied innocently. "That is, if you want people to see you as a bumpkin peasant with dung on his boots. Of course, if you want to be a court magician, well, that's another story. No respectable magician would be caught dead in an outfit like that.''

"But I am a respectable magician!" I argued.

"Really? Respected by who?"

He had me there, so I lapsed into silence.

"That's specifically the reason I had the foresight to bring along a few items from the inn," Aahz continued, indicating Buttercup's burdens with a grand sweep of his hand.

"And here I thought you were just looting the place," I said dryly.

"Watch your mouth, kid," he warned. "This is all for your benefit.''

"Really? You aren't expecting anything at all out of this deal?"

My sarcasm, as usual, was lost on him.

"Oh, I'll be around," he acknowledged. "Don't worry about that. Publicly, I'll be your apprentice.''

"My apprentice?"

This job was suddenly sounding much better.

"Publicly!" Aahz repeated hastily. "Privately, you'll continue your lessons as normal. Remember that before you start getting frisky with your 'apprentice.'"

"Of course, Aahz," I assured him. "Now, what was it you were saying about changing the way I dress?"

He shot me a sidelong glance, apparently suspicious of my sudden enthusiasm.

"Not that there's anything wrong with me the way I am," I added with a theatrical scowl.

That seemed to ease his doubts.

"Everything's wrong with the way you dress," he growled. "We're lucky those two Imps left most of their wardrobe behind when we sent 'em packing along with Isstvan."

"Higgens and Brockhurst?"

"Yeah, those two," Aahz grinned evilly at the memory. "I'll say one thing for Imps. They may be inferior to Deveels as merchants, but they *are* snappy dressers."

"I find it hard to believe that all that stuff you bundled along is wardrobe," I observed skeptically.

"Of course it isn't," my mentor moaned. "It's special effects gear."

"Special effects?"

"Don't you remember anything, kid?" Aahz scowled. "I told you all this when we first met. However easy magik is, you can't let it *look* easy. You need a few hand props, a line of patter . . . you know, like Garkin had."

Garkin's hut, where I had first been introduced to magik, had been full of candles, vials of strange powders, dusty books . . . now there was a magician's lair! Of course, I had since discovered most of what he had was unnecessary for the actual working of magik itself.

I was beginning to see what Aahz meant when he said I'd have to learn to put on a show.

"We've got a lot of stuff we can work into your presentation," Aahz continued. "Isstvan left a lot of his junk behind when he left. Oh, and you might find some familiar items when we unload. I think the Imps helped themselves to some of Garkin's equipment and brought it back to the inn with them."

"Really?" I said, genuinely interested. "Did they get Garkin's brazier?"

"Brazier?" My mentor frowned.

"You remember," I prompted. "You used it to drink wine out of when you first arrived."

"That's right! Yeah, I think I saw it in there. Why?"

"No special reason," I replied innocently. "It was always a favorite of mine, that's all."

From watching Garkin back in my early apprentice days, I knew there were secrets to that brazier I was dying to learn. I also knew that, if possible, I wanted to save it as a surprise for Aahz.

"We're going to have to do something about your physical appearance, too," Aahz continued thoughtfully.

"What's—"

"You're too young!" he answered, anticipating my question. "Nobody hires a young magician. They want one who's been around for a while. If we—"

He broke off suddenly and craned his neck to look around.

"Kid," he said carefully, studying the sky. "Your dragon's gone again."

I did a fast scan. He was right.

"Gleep!" I called. "Here, fella!"

The dragon's head appeared from the depths of a bush behind us. There was something slimy with legs dangling from his mouth, but before I could manage an exact identification, my pet swallowed and the whatzit disappeared.

"Gleep!" he said proudly, licking his lips with his long forked tongue.

"Stupid dragon," Aahz muttered darkly.

"He's cheap to feed," I countered, playing on what I knew to be Aahz's tight-fisted nature.

As we waited for the dragon to catch up, I had time to reflect that for once I felt no moral or ethical qualms about taking part in one of Aahz's schemes. If the unsuspecting Rodrick the Fifth was taken in by our charade and hired us, I was confident the king would be getting more than he bargained for.

Chapter Four:

"If the proper preparations have been made and the necessary precautions taken, any staged event is guaranteed success."

—ETHELRED THE UNREADY

THE candle lit at the barest flick from my mind.

Delighted, I snuffed it and tried again.

A sidelong glance, a fleeting concentration of my will, and the smoldering wick burst into flame again.

I snuffed the flame and sat smiling at the familiar candle.

This was the first real proof I'd had as to how far my magical powers had developed in the past year. I knew this candle from my years as Garkin's apprentice. In those days, it was my arch nemesis. Even focusing all my energies failed to light it then. But now . . .

I glanced at the wick again, and again it rewarded me with a burst of flame.

I snuffed it and repeated the exercise, my confidence growing as I realized how easily I could now do something I once thought impossible.

"Will you knock it off with the candle!"

I jumped at the sound of Aahz's outburst, nearly upsetting the candle and setting the blanket afire.

"I'm sorry, Aahz," I said, hastily snuffing the candle for the last time. "I just—"

"You're here to audition for court magician," he interrupted. "Not for town Christmas tree!"

I considered asking what a Christmas tree was, but decided against it. Aahz seemed uncommonly irritable and nervous, and I was pretty sure, however I chose to phrase my question, that the answer would be both sarcastic and unproductive.

"Stupid candle blinking on and off," Aahz grumbled half to himself. "Attract the attention of every guard in the castle."

"I thought we were trying to attract their attention," I pointed out, but Aahz ignored me, peering at the castle through the early-morning light.

He didn't have to peer far, as we were camped in the middle of the road just short of the castle's main gates.

As I said, I was under the impression our position was specifically chosen to attract attention to ourselves.

We had crept into position in the dead of night, clumsily picking our way through the sleeping buildings clustered about the main gate. Not wishing to show a light, unpacking had been minimal, but even in the dark, I had recognized Garkin's candle.

All of this had to do with something Aahz called a "dramatic entrance." As near as I could tell, all this meant was we couldn't do anything the easy way.

Our appearance was also carefully designed for effect, with the aid of the Imps' abandoned wardrobe and my disguise spells.

Aahz was outfitted in my now traditional "dubious character'' disguise. Gleep was standing placidly beside Buttercup disguised as a unicorn, giving us a matched pair. It was my own appearance, however, which had been the main focus of our attentions.

Both Aahz and I had agreed that the Garkin disguise would be unsuitable for this effort. While my own natural appearance was too young, Garkin's would be too old. Since we could pretty much choose the image we wanted, we decided to field a magician in his mid to late thirties; young without being youthful, experienced without being old, and powerful but still learning.

To achieve this disguise involved a bit more work than normal, as I did not have an image in mind to superimpose over my own. Instead, I closed my eyes and envisioned myself as I appeared normally, then slowly erased the features until I had a blank face to begin on. Then I set to work with Aahz watching carefully and offering suggestions and modifications.

The first thing I changed was my height, adjusting the image until the new figure stood a head and a half taller than my actual diminutive stature. My hair was next and I changed my strawberry-blond thatch to a more sinister black, at the same time darkening my complexion several shades.

The face gave us the most trouble.

''Elongate the chin a little more,'' Aahz instructed. ''Put on a beard . . . not that much, stupid! Just a little goatee! . . . That's better! . . . Now lower the sideburns . . . okay, build up the nose . . . narrow it . . . make the eyebrows bushier . . . no, change 'em back and sink the eyes a little instead . . . for crying out loud change the eye color! Make 'em brown . . . okay, now a couple of frown wrinkles in the middle of the forehead. . . . Good. That should do it.''

I stared at the figure in my mind, burning the image into my memory. It was effective, maybe a bit more sinister than I would have designed if left to my own devices, but Aahz was the expert and I had to trust his judgment. I opened my eyes.

"Terrific, kid!" Aahz beamed. "Now put on that black robe with the gold and red trim the Imps left, and you'll cut a figure fit to grace any court."

"Move along there! You're blocking the road!"

The rude order wrenched my thoughts back to the present.

A soldier, resplendent in leather armor and brandishing an evil-looking pike, was angrily approaching our crude encampment. Behind him the gates stood slightly ajar, and I could see the heads of several other soldiers watching us curiously.

Now that the light was improving, I could see the wall better. It wasn't much of a wall, barely ten feet high. That figured. From what we had seen since we crossed the border, it wasn't much of a kingdom, either.

"You deaf or something?" the soldier barked drawing close. "I said move along!"

Aahz scuttled forward and planted himself in the soldier's path.

"Skeeve the Magnificent has arrived," he announced. "And he—"

"I don't care who you are!" the soldier snarled, wasting no time placing his pike between himself and the figure addressing him. "You can't—"

He broke off abruptly as his pike leaped from his grasp and floated horizontally in mid-air until it was forming a barricade between him and Aahz.

The occurrence was my doing, a simple feat of levitation. Regardless of our planned gambit, I felt I

should take a direct hand in the proceedings before
things got completely out of hand.

"I am Skeeve!" I boomed, forcing my voice into a
resonant bass. "And that is my assistant you are attempting to threaten with your feeble weapon. We
have come in response to an invitation from Rodrick
the Fifth, King of Possiltum!"

"That's right, Bosco!" Aahz leered at the soldier.
"Now just run along like a good fellow and pass the
word we're here . . . eh?"

As I noted earlier, all this was designed to impress
the hell out of the general populace. Apparently the
guard hadn't read the script. He did not cower in
terror or cringe with fear. If anything, our little act
seemed to have the exact opposite effect on him.

"A magician, eh?" he said with a mocking sneer.
"For that I've got standing orders. Go around to the
back where the others are."

This took us aback. Well, at least it took *me*
aback. According to our plan, we would end up arguing whether we entered the palace to perform in the
king's court, or if the king had to bring his court outside to where we were. Being sent to the back door
was not an option we had considered.

"To the back?" Aahz glowered. "You dare to suggest a magician of my master's stature go to the back
door like a common servant?"

The soldier didn't budge an inch.

"If it were up to me, I'd 'dare to suggest' a far less
pleasant activity for you. As it is, I have my orders.
You're to go around to the back like all the others."

"Others?" I asked carefully.

"That's right," the guard sneered. "The king is
holding an open air court to deal with all you
'miracle workers.' Every hack charm-peddler for

eight kingdoms is in town. Some of 'em have been in line since noon yesterday. Now get around to the back and quit blocking the road!''

With that he turned on his heel and marched back to the gate, leaving his pike hanging in mid-air.

For once, Aahz was as speechless as I was. Apparently I wasn't the only one the king had invited to drop by. Apparently we were in big trouble.

Chapter Five:

". . . Eye of newt, toe of frog . . ."
—Believed to be the first recipe
for an explosive mixture . . .
The forerunner of gunpowder.

"WHAT are we going to do, Aahz?"

With the guard out of earshot, I could revert to my normal voice and speech patterns, though it was still necessary to keep my physical disguise intact.

"That's easy," he responded. "We pack up our things and go around the back. Weren't you listening, kid?"

"But what are we going to do about . . ."

But Aahz was already at work, rebinding the few items we had unpacked.

"Don't do anything, kid," he warned over his shoulder. "We can't let anyone see you doing menial work. It's bad for the image."

"He said there were other magicians here!" I blurted at last.

"Yeah. So?"

"Well, what are we going to do?"

Aahz scowled. "I told you once. We're going to pack our things and—"

"What are we going to do about the other magicians?"

"Do? We aren't going to *do* anything. You aren't up to dueling, you know."

He had finished packing and stepped back to survey his handiwork. Nodding in satisfaction, he turned and shot a glance over my shoulder.

"Do something about the pike, will ya, kid?"

I followed his gaze. The guard's pike was still hanging suspended in mid-air. Even though I hadn't been thinking about it, part of my mind had been keeping it afloat until I decided what to do with it. The question was, what should I do with it?

"Say, Aahz . . ." I began, but Aahz had already started walking along the wall.

For a moment I was immobilized with indecision. The guard had gone so I couldn't return his weapon to him. Still, simply letting it drop to the ground seemed somehow anticlimatic.

Unable to think of anything to do that would have the proper dramatic flair, I decided to postpone the decision. For the time being, I let the pike float along behind me as I hurried after Aahz, first giving it additional elevation so it would not be a danger to Gleep and Buttercup.

"Were you expecting other magicians to be here?" I asked, drawing abreast of my mentor.

"Not really," Aahz admitted. "It was a possibility, of course, but I didn't give it a very high probability rating. Still, it's not all that surprising. A job like this is bound to draw competition out of the woodwork."

He didn't seem particularly upset, so I tried to take

this new development in stride.

"Okay," I said calmly. "How does this change our plans?"

"It doesn't. Just do your thing like I showed you and everything should come out fine."

"But if the other magicians—"

Aahz stopped short and turned to face me.

"Look, kid," he said seriously, "just because I keep telling you you've got a long way to go before you're a master magician doesn't mean you're a hack! I wouldn't have encouraged you to show up for this interview if I didn't think you were good enough to land the job."

"Really, Aahz?"

He turned and started walking again.

"Just remember, as dimensions go, Klah isn't noted for its magicians. You're no master, but masters are few and far between. I'm betting that compared to the competition, you'll look like a real expert."

That made sense. Aahz was quite outspoken in his low opinion of Klah and the Klahds that inhabited it, including me. That last thought made me fish for a bit more reassurance.

"Aahz?"

"Yeah, kid?"

"What's your honest appraisal of my chances?"

There was a moment of silence before he answered.

"Kid, you know how you're always complaining that I keep tearing down your confidence?"

"Yeah?"

"Well, for both our sakes, don't push too hard for my honest appraisal."

I didn't.

Getting through the back gate proved to be no problem . . . mostly because there wasn't a back gate. To my surprise and Aahz's disgust, the wall did not extend completely around the palace. As near as I could see, only the front wall was complete. The two side walls were under construction, and the back wall was nonexistent. I should clarify that. My statement that the side walls were under construction was an assumption based on the presence of scaffolding at the end of the wall rather than by the observation of any activity going on. If there was any work being performed, it was being done carefully enough not to disturb the weeds which abounded throughout the scaffolding.

I was beginning to have grave doubts about the kingdom I was about to ally myself with.

It was difficult to tell if the court was being convened in a garden, or if this was a courtyard losing its fight with the weeds and underbrush which crowded in through the opening where the back wall should have been. (Having grown up on a farm, my basic education in plants was that if it wasn't edible and growing in neat rows, it was a weed.)

As if in answer to my thoughts, Buttercup took a large mouthful of the nearest clump of growth and began chewing enthusiastically. Gleep sniffed the same bush and turned up his nose at it.

All this I noted only as an aside. My main attention was focused on the court itself.

There was a small open-sided pavilion set against the wall of the palace sheltering a seated figure, presumably the king. Standing close beside him on either side were two other men. The crowd, such as it was, was split into two groups. The first was standing in a somewhat orderly line along one side of the garden. I assumed this was the waiting line . . . or rather I hoped it was as that was the group we joined. The second group was standing in a disorganized mob on the far side of the garden watching the proceedings. Whether these were rejected applicants or merely interested hangers-on, I didn't know.

Suddenly, a young couple in the watching group caught my eye. I hadn't expected to encounter any familiar faces here, but these two I had seen before. Not only had I seen them, Aahz and I had impersonated them at one point, a charade which had resulted in our being hanged.

"Aahz!" I whispered urgently. "Do you see those two over there?"

"No," Aahz said bluntly, not even turning his head to look.

"But they're the—"

"Forget 'em," he insisted. "Watch the judges. They're the ones we have to impress."

I had to admit that made a certain amount of sense. Grudgingly, I turned my attention to the figures in the pavilion.

The king was surprisingly young, perhaps in his mid-twenties. His hair was a tumble of shoulder-length curls, which combined with his slight build almost made him look effeminate. Judging from his posture, either the interviews had been going on for some time, or he had mastered the art of looking totally bored.

The man on his left bent and urgently whispered something in the king's ear and was answered by a vague nod.

This man, only slightly older than the king but balding noticeably, was dressed in a tunic and cloak

of drab color and conservative cut. Though relaxed
in posture and quiet in bearing, there was a watchful
brightness to his eyes that reminded me of a feverish
weasel.

There was a stirring of the figure on the king's
right, which drew my attention in that direction. I
had a flash impression of a massive furry lump, then
I realized with a start that it was a man. He was tall
and broad, his head crowned with thick, black,
unkempt curls, his face nearly obscured by a full
beard and mustache. This, combined with his heavy
fur cloak, gave him an animal-like appearance which
had dominated my first impression. He spoke briefly
to the king, then recrossed his arms in a gesture of
finality and glared at the other advisor. His cloak
opened briefly during his oration, giving me a
glimpse of a glittering shirt of mail and a massive
double-headed hand-axe hung on a belt at his waist.
Clearly this was not a man to cross. The balding
figure seemed unimpressed, matching his rival's glare
with one of his own.

There was a sharp nudge in my ribs.

"Did you see that?" Aahz whispered urgently.

"See what?" I asked.

"The king's advisors. A general and a chancellor
unless I miss my guess. Did you see the gold medal-
lion on the general?"

"I saw his axe!" I whispered back.

The light in the courtyard suddenly dimmed.

Looking up, I saw a mass of clouds forming overhead, blotting out the sun.

"Weather control," Aahz murmured half to himself. "Not bad."

Sure enough, the old man in the red cloak cur-

rently before the throne gestured wildly and tossed a
cloud of purple powder into the air, and a light drizzle began to fall.

My spirits fell along with the rain. Even with
Aahz's coaching on presentation, my magik was not
this powerful or impressive.

"Aahz . . ." I whispered urgently.

Instead of responding, he waved me to silence, his
eyes riveted on the pavilion.

Following his gaze, I saw the general speaking
urgently with the king. The king listened for a moment, then shrugged and said something to the magician.

Whatever he said, the magician didn't like it.
Drawing himself up haughtily, he turned to leave,
only to be called back by the king. Pointing to the
clouds, the king said a few more words and leaned
back. The magician hesitated, then shrugged, and
began gesturing and chanting once more.

"Turned him down," Aahz said smugly.

"Then what's he doing now?"

"Clearing up the rain before the next act goes on,"
Aahz informed me.

Sure enough, the drizzle was slowing and the
clouds began to scatter, much to the relief of the audience who, unlike the king, had no pavilion to protect them from the storm. This further display of the
magician's power, however, did little to bolster my
sagging confidence.

"Aahz!" I whispered. "He's a better magician
than I am."

"Yeah," Aahz responded. "So?"

"So if they turned him down, I haven't got a
chance!"

"Maybe yes, maybe no," came the thoughtful

reply. "As near as I can tell, they're looking for something specific. Who knows? Maybe you're it. Remember what I told you, cushy jobs don't always go to the most skillful. In fact, it usually goes the other way."

"Yeah," I said, trying to sound optimistic. "Maybe I'll get lucky."

"It's going to take more than luck," Aahz corrected me sternly. "Now, what have you learned watching the king's advisors?"

"They don't like each other," I observed immediately.

"Right!" Aahz sounded surprised and pleased. "Now that means you probably won't be able to please them both. You'll have to play up to one of them . . . or better still insult one. That'll get the other one on your side faster than anything. Now, which one do you want on your side?"

That was easier than his first question.

"The general," I said firmly.

"Wrong! You want the chancellor."

"The chancellor!" I exclaimed, blurting the words out louder than I had intended. "Did you see the size of that axe the general's carrying?"

"Uh-huh," Aahz replied. "Did you hear what happened to the guy who interviewed before old Red Cloak here got his turn?"

I closed my eyes and controlled my first sharp remark.

"Aahz," I said carefully, "remember me? I'm Skeeve. I'm the one who can't hear whispers a mile away."

As usual Aahz ignored my sarcasm.

"The last guy didn't even get a chance to show his stuff," he informed me. "The chancellor took one look at the crowd he brought with him and asked how many were in his retinue. 'Eight,' the man said. 'Too many!' says the chancellor and the poor fool was dismissed immediately."

"So?" I asked bluntly.

"So the chancellor is the one watching the purse strings," concluded Aahz. "What's more, he has more influence than the general. Look at these silly walls. Do you think a military man would leave walls half-finished if he had the final say? Somebody decided too much money was being spent constructing them and the project was canceled or delayed. I'm betting that somebody was the chancellor."

"Maybe they ran out of stones," I suggested.

"C'mon, kid. From what we've seen since we crossed the border this kingdom's principal crop is stones."

"But the general . . ."

As I spoke, I glanced in the general's direction again. To my surprise and discomfort, he was staring directly at me. It wasn't a friendly stare.

I hesitated for a moment, hoping I was wrong. I wasn't. The general's gaze didn't waver, nor did his expression soften. If anything, it got uglier.

"Aahz," I hissed desperately, unable to tear my eyes from the general.

Now the king and the chancellor were staring in my direction too, their attention drawn by the general's gaze.

"Kid!" Aahz moaned beside me. "I thought I told you to do something about that pike!"

The pike! I had completely forgotten about it!

I pulled my eyes from the general's glare and glanced behind me as casually as I could.

Buttercup and Gleep were still standing patiently

to our rear, and floating serenely above them was the guard's pike. I guess it was kind of noticeable.

"You!"

I turned toward the pavilion and the sound of the bellow. The general had stepped forward and was pointing a massive finger at me.

"Yes, you!" he roared as our eyes met once more. "Where did you get that pike? It belongs to the palace guards."

"I think you're about to have your interview, kid," Aahz murmured. "Give it your best and knock 'em stiff."

"But—" I protested.

"It beats standing in line!"

With that, Aahz took a long leisurely step backward. The effect was the same as if I had stepped forward, which I definitely hadn't. With the attention of the entire courtyard now centered on me, however, I had no choice but to take the plunge.

Chapter Six:

"That's entertainment!"
—VLAD THE IMPALER

CROSSING my arms, I moved toward the pavilion, keeping my pace slow and measured.

Aahz had insisted I practice this walk. He said it would make me look confident and self-possessed. Now that I was actually appearing before a king, I found I was using the walk, not as a show of arrogance, but to hide the weakness in my legs.

"Well?" the general rumbled, looming before me. "I asked you a question! Where did you get that pike? You'd best answer before I grow angry!"

Something in me snapped. Any fear I felt of the general and his axe evaporated, replaced by a heady glow of strength.

I had discovered on my first visit to the Bazaar at Deva that I didn't like to be pushed by big, loud Deveels. I discovered now that I also didn't like it any better when the arrogance came from a big, loud fellow Klahd.

So the big man wanted to throw his weight around, did he?

With a twitch of my mind, I summoned the pike. Without turning to look, I brought it arrowing over my shoulder in a course destined to embed it in the general's chest.

The general saw it coming and paled. He took an awkward step backward, realized it was too late for flight, and groped madly for his axe.

I stopped the pike three feet from his chest, floating it in front of him with its point leveled at his heart.

"This pike?" I asked casually.

"Ahh . . ." the general responded, his eyes never leaving the weapon.

"I took this pike from an overly rude soldier. He said he was following orders. Would those orders come from you, by any chance?"

"I . . . um. . . ." The general licked his lips. "I issued orders that my men deal with strangers in an expedient fashion. I said nothing about their being less then polite."

"In that case . . ."

I moved the pike ninety degrees so that it no longer threatened the general.

". . . I return the pike to you so that you might give it back to the guard along with a clarification of your orders. . . ."

The general hesitated, scowling, then extended his hand to grasp the floating pike. Just before he reached it, I let it fall to the ground where it clattered noisily.

". . . and hopefully additional instructions as to how to handle their weapons," I concluded.

The general flushed and started to pick up the

pike. Then the chancellor snickered, and the general spun around to glare at him. The chancellor smirked openly and whispered something to the king, who tried to suppress a smile at his words.

The general turned to me again, ignoring the pike, and glared down from his full height.

"Who are you?" he asked in a tone which implied my name would be immediately moved to the head of the list for public execution.

"Who's asking?" I glared back, still not completely over my anger.

"The man you are addressing," the king interceded, "is Hugh Badaxe, Commander of the Royal Armies of Possiltum."

"And I am J. R. Grimble," the chancellor added hastily, afraid of being left out. "First Advisor to His Majesty."

The general shot another black look at Grimble. I decided it was time to get down to business.

"I am the magician known as Skeeve," I began grandly. "I have come in response to a gracious invitation from His Most Noble Majesty, Rodrick the Fifth."

I paused and inclined my head slightly to the king who smiled and nodded in return.

"I have come to determine for myself if I should consider accepting a position at the court of Possiltum."

The phrasing of that last part had been chosen very carefully by Aahz. It was designed to display my confidence by implying the choice was mine rather than theirs.

The subtlety was not lost on the chancellor, who raised a critical eyebrow at my choice of words.

"Now, such a position requires confidence on both

sides," I continued. "I must feel that I will be amply rewarded for my services, and His Majesty must be satisfied that my skills are worthy of his sponsorship."

I turned slightly and raised my voice to address the entire court.

"The generosity of the crown of Possiltum is known to all," I declared. "And I have every confidence His Majesty will reward his retainers in proportion to their service to him."

There was a strangled sound behind me, from the general, I think. I ignored it.

"Therefore, all that is required is that I satisfy His Majesty . . . and his advisors . . . that my humble skills will indeed suffice his needs."

I turned to the throne once more, letting the king see my secret smile which belied the humility of my words.

"Your Majesty, my powers are many and varied. However, the essence of power is control. Therefore realizing you are a busy man, rather than waste time with mere commercial trickeries and minor demonstrations such as we have already seen, I shall weave but three spells and trust in your wisdom to perceive the depths behind them."

I turned and stretched forth a finger to point at Buttercup and Gleep.

"Yonder are my prize pair of matched unicorns," I said dramatically. "Would Your Majesty be so kind as to choose one of them?"

The king blinked in surprise at being invited to participate in my demonstration. For a moment he hesitated.

"Umm . . . I choose the one on the left," he said, finally indicating Buttercup.

I bowed slightly.

"Very well, Your Majesty. By your word shall that creature be spared. Observe the other closely."

Actually, that was another little stunt Aahz had taught me. It's called a "magician's force," and allows a performer to offer his audience a choice without really giving them a choice. Had the king chosen Gleep, I would have simply proceeded to work on "the creature he had doomed with a word."

Slowly, I pointed a finger at Gleep and lowered my head slightly.

"Walla walla Washington!" I said somberly.

I don't know what the words meant, but Aahz assured me they had historic precedence and would convince people I was actually doing something complex.

"Alla kazam shazam," I continued, raising my other arm. *"Bibbity bobbity . . ."*

I mentally removed Gleep's disguise.

The crowd reacted with a gasp, drowning out my final *"goo-gleep."*

My dragon heard his name, though, and reacted immediately. His head came up and he lumbered forward to stand docilely at my side. As planned, Aahz immediately shambled forward to a position near Gleep's head and stood watchful and ready.

This was meant to imply that we were prepared to handle any difficulty which might arise with the dragon. The crowd's reaction to him, however, overshadowed their horror at seeing a unicorn transformed to a dragon. I had forgotten how effective the "disreputable character" disguise was. Afraid of losing the momentum of my performance, I hurried on.

"This misshapen wretch is my apprentice Aahz," I

announced. "You may wonder if it is within his power to stop the dragon should the beast grow angry. I tell you now . . . it is not!"

The crowd edged back nervously. From the corner of my eye, I saw the general's hand slide to the handle of his axe.

"But it *is* within my power! Now you know that the forces of darkness are no strangers to Skeeve!"

I spun and stabbed a finger at Aahz.

"*Bobbelty gook, crumbs and martyrs!*"

I removed Aahz's disguise.

There was a moment of stunned silence, then Aahz smiled. Aahz's smile has been known to make strong men weak, and there were not many strong men in the crowd.

The audience half trampled each other in their haste to backpedal from the demon, and the sound of screeches was intermixed with hastily chanted protection spells.

I turned to the throne once more. The king and the chancellor seemed to be taking it well. They were composed, though a bit pale. The general was scowling thoughtfully at Aahz.

"As a demon, my apprentice can suppress the dragon if need be . . . nay, ten dragons. Such is my power. Yet power must be tempered with gentleness . . . gentility if you will."

I allowed my expression to grow thoughtful.

"To confuse one's enemies and receive one's allies, you need no open show of power or menace. For occasions such as those, one's powers can be masked until one is no more conspicuous than . . . than a stripling."

As I spoke the final words, I stripped away my own disguise and stood in my youthful unsplendor. I probably should have used some fake magik words, but I had already used up all the ones Aahz had taught me and was afraid of experimenting with new ones.

The king and the chancellor were staring at me intently as if trying to penetrate my magical disguise with willpower alone. The general was performing a similar exercise staring at Aahz, who folded his arms and bared his teeth in a confident smile.

For a change, I shared his confidence. Let them stare. It was too late to penetrate my magik because I wasn't working any more. Though the royal troupe and the entire audience was convinced they were witnessing a powerful spell, in actuality all I had done was remove the spells which had been distorting their vision. At the moment, all of us, Aahz, Buttercup, Gleep, and myself, were our normal selves, however abnormal we appeared. Even the most adept magical vision could not penetrate a nonexistent spell.

"As you see, Your Majesty," I concluded. "My powers are far from ordinary. They can make the gentle fearsome, or the mighty harmless. They can destroy your enemies or amuse your court, depending upon your whim. Say the word, speak your approval, and the powers of Skeeve are yours to command."

I drew myself up and bowed my head respectfully, and remained in that position awaiting judgment from the throne.

Several moments passed without a word. Finally, I risked a peek at the pavilion.

The chancellor and the general were exchanging heated whispers over the head of the king, who inclined his head this way and that as he listened. Realizing this could take a while, I quietly eased my head to an upright position as I waited.

"Skeeve!" the king called suddenly, interrupting his advisor's arguments. "That thing you did with the pike. Can you always control weapons so easily?"

"Child's play, Your Majesty," I said modestly. "I hesitate to even acknowledge it as a power."

The king nodded and spoke briefly to his advisors in undertones. When he had finished, the general flushed and, turning on his heel, strode off into the palace. The chancellor looked smug.

I risked a glance at Aahz, who winked at me. Even though he was further away, apparently his acute hearing had given him advance notice of the king's decision.

"Let all here assembled bear witness!" the chancellor's ringing voice announced. "Rodrick the Fifth, King of Possiltum, does hereby commend the magical skill and knowledge of one Skeeve and does formally name him Magician to the Court of Possiltum. Let all applaud the appointment of this master magician . . . and then disperse!"

There was a smattering of halfhearted applause from my vanquished rivals, and more than a few glares. I acknowledged neither as I tried to comprehend the chancellor's words.

I did it! Court Magician! Of the entire selection of magicians from five kingdoms, I had been chosen! Me! Skeeve!

I was suddenly aware of the chancellor beckoning me forward. Trying to be nonchalant, I approached the throne.

"Lord Magician," the chancellor said with a smile. "If you will, might we discuss the matter of your wages?"

"My apprentice handles such matters," I informed him loftily. "I prefer not to distract myself with such mundane matters."

Again, we had agreed that Aahz would handle the wage negotiations, his knowledge of magik being surpassed only by his skill at haggling. I turned and beckoned to him. He responded by hurrying forward, his eavesdropping having forewarned him of the situation.

"That can wait, Grimble," the king interrupted. "There are more pressing matters which command our magician's attention."

"You need only command, Your Majesty," I said, bowing grandly.

"Fine," the king beamed. "Then report to General Badaxe immediately for your briefing."

"Briefing about what?" I asked, genuinely puzzled.

"Why, your briefing about the invading army, of course," the king replied.

An alarm gong went off in the back of my mind.

"Invading army?" I blurted, forgetting my rehearsed pompous tones. "What invading army?"

"The one which even now approaches our borders," the chancellor supplied. "Why else would we suddenly need a magician?"

Chapter Seven:

"Numerical superiority is of no consequence. In battle, victory will go to the best tactician."

—G. A. CUSTER

"CUSHY job, he said! Chance to practice, he said! Piece of cake, he said!"

"Simmer down, kid!" Aahz growled.

"Simmer down? Aahz, weren't you listening? I'm supposed to stop an army! Me!"

"It could be worse," Aahz insisted.

"How?" I asked bluntly.

"You could be doing it without me," he replied. "Think about it."

I did, and cooled down immediately. Even though my association with Aahz seemed to land me in an inordinate amount of trouble, he had also been unfailing in his ability to get me out . . . so far. The last thing I wanted to do was drive him away just when I needed him the most.

"What am I going to do, Aahz?" I moaned.

"Since you ask"—Aahz smiled—"my advice would be to not panic until we get the whole story.

Remember, there are armies and there are armies. For all we know, this one might be weak enough for us to beat fair and square."

"And if it isn't?" I asked skeptically.

"We'll burn that bridge when we come to it," Aahz sighed. "First, let's hear what old Badaxe has to say."

Not being able to think of anything to say in reply to that, I didn't. Instead, I kept pace with my mentor in gloomy silence as we followed the chancellor's directions through the corridors of the palace.

It would have been easier to accept the offered guide to lead us to our destination, but I had been more than a little eager to speak with Aahz privately. Consequently, we had left Buttercup and Gleep in the courtyard with our equipment and were seeking out the general's chambers on our own.

The palace was honeycombed with corridors to the point where I wondered if there weren't more corridors than rooms. Our trek was made even more difficult by the light, or lack thereof. Though there were numerous mountings for torches set in the walls, it seemed only about one out of every four was being used, and the light shed by those torches was less than adequate for accurate navigation of the labyrinth.

I commented on this to Aahz as further proof of the tightfisted nature of the kingdom. His curt response was that the more money they saved on overhead and maintenance, the more they would have to splurge on luxuries . . . like us.

He was doggedly trying to explain the concept of an "energy crisis" to me, when we rounded a corner and sighted the general's quarters.

They were fairly easy to distinguish, since this was

the only door we had encountered which was bracketed by a pair of matching honor guards. Their polished armor gleamed from broad shoulders as they observed our approach through narrowed eyes.

"Are these the quarters of General Badaxe?" I inquired politely.

"Are you the magician called Skeeve?" the guard challenged back.

"The kid asked you a question, soldier!" Aahz interceded. "Now are you going to answer or are you so dumb you don't know what's on the other side of the door you're guarding?"

The guard flushed bright red, and I noticed his partner's knuckles whitening on the pike he was gripping. It occurred to me that now that I had landed the magician's job, it might not be the wisest course to continue antagonizing the military.

"Um, Aahz . . ." I murmured.

"Yes! These are the quarters of General Badaxe . . . sir!" the guard barked suddenly.

Apparently the mention of my colleague's name had confirmed my identity, though I wondered how many strangers could be wandering the halls accompanied by large scaly demons. The final, painful, "sir" was a tribute to my performance in the courtyard. Apparently the guards had been instructed to be polite, at least to me, no matter how much it hurt . . . which it obviously did.

"Thank you, guard," I said loftily, and hammered on the door with my fist.

"Further," the guard observed, "the general left word that you were to go right in."

The fact that he had withheld that bit of information until after I had knocked indicated that the guards hadn't completely abandoned their low regard for magicians. They were simply finding more subtle ways of being annoying.

I realized Aahz was getting ready to start a new round with the guard, so I hastily opened the door and entered, forcing him to follow.

The general was standing at the window, silhouetted by the light streaming in from outside. As we entered, he turned to face us.

"Ah! Come in, gentlemen," he boomed in a mellow tone. "I've been expecting you. Do make yourselves comfortable. Help yourselves to the wine if you wish."

I found his sudden display of friendliness even more disquieting than his earlier show of hostility. Aahz, however, took it all in stride, immediately taking up the indicated jug of wine. For a moment I thought he was going to pour a bit of it into one of the goblets which shared the tray with the jug and pass it to me. Instead, he took a deep drink directly from the jug and kept it, licking his lips in appreciation. In the midst of the chaos my life had suddenly become, it was nice to know some things remained constant.

The general frowned at the display for a moment, then forced his features back into the jovial expression he had first greeted us with.

"Before we begin the briefing," he smiled, "I must apologize for my rude behavior during the interview. Grimble and I have . . . differed in our opinions on the existing situation, and I'm afraid I took it out on you. For that I extend my regrets. Ordinarily, I would have nothing against magicians as a group, or you specifically."

"Whoa! Back up a minute, General," Aahz interrupted. "How does your feud with the chancellor involve us?"

The general's eyes glittered with a fierceness that belied the gentility of his oration.

"It's an extension of our old argument concerning allocation of funds," he said. "When news reached us of the approaching force, my advice to the king was to immediately strengthen our own army that we might adequately perform our sworn duty of defending the realm."

"Sounds like good advice to me," I interjected, hoping to improve my status with the general by agreeing with him.

Badaxe responded by fixing me with a hard glare.

"Strange that you should say that, magician," he observed stonily. "Grimble's advice was to invest the money elsewhere than in the army, specifically in a magician."

It suddenly became clear why we had been received by the guards and the general with something less than open-armed camaraderie. Not only were they getting us instead of reinforcements, our presence was a slap at their abilities.

"Okay, General," Aahz acknowledged. "All that's water under the drawbridge. What are we up against?"

The general glanced back and forth between me and Aahz, apparently surprised that I was allowing my apprentice to take the lead in the briefing. When I failed to rebuke Aahz for his forwardness, the general shrugged and moved to a piece of parchment hanging on the wall.

"I believe the situation is shown clearly by this—" he began.

"What's that?" Aahz interrupted.

The general started to respond sharply, then caught himself. "This," he said evenly, "is a map of the kingdom you are supposed to defend. It's called Possiltum."

"Yes, of course," I nodded. "Continue."

"This line here to the north of our border represents the advancing army you are to deal with."

"Too bad you couldn't get it to scale," Aahz commented. "The way you have it there, the enemy's front is longer than your border."

The general bared his teeth.

"The drawing *is* to scale," he said pointedly. "Perhaps now you will realize the magnitude of the task before you."

My mind balked at accepting his statement.

"Really, General," I chided. "Surely you're overstating the case. There aren't enough fighting men in any kingdom to form a front that long."

"Magician," the general's voice was menacing, "I did not reach my current rank by overstating military situations. The army you are facing is one of the mightiest forces the world has ever seen. It is the striking arm of a rapidly growing empire situated far to the north. They have been advancing for three years now, absorbing smaller kingdoms and crushing any resistance offered. All able-bodied men of conquered lands are conscripted for military service, swelling their ranks to the size you see indicated on the map. The only reason they are not advancing faster is that in addition to limitless numbers of men, they possess massive war machines which, though effective, are slow to transport."

"Now tell us the bad news," Aahz commented dryly.

The general took him seriously.

"The bad news," he growled, "is that their leader is a strategist without peer. He rose to power trouncing forces triple the size of his own numbers, and now that he has a massive army at his command, he is virtually unbeatable."

"I'm beginning to see why the king put his money into a magician," my mentor observed. "It doesn't look like you could have assembled a force large enough to stop them."

"That wasn't my plan!" the general bristled. "While we may not have been able to crush the enemy, we could have made them pay dearly enough for crossing our border that they might have turned aside for weaker lands easier to conquer."

"You know, Badaxe," Aahz said thoughtfully, "that's not a bad plan. Working together we might still pull it off. How many men can you give us for support?"

"None," the general said firmly.

I blinked.

"Excuse me, General," I pressed. "For a moment there, I thought you said—"

"None," he repeated. "I will not assign a single soldier of mine to support your campaign."

"That's insane!" Aahz exploded. "How do you expect us to stop an army like that with just magik?"

"I don't," the general smiled.

"But if we fail," I pointed out, "Possiltum falls."

"That is correct," Badaxe replied calmly.

"But—"

"Allow me to clarify my position," he interrupted. "In my estimation, there is more at stake here than one kingdom. If you succeed in your mission, it will establish that magik is more effective than military force in defending a kingdom. Eventually, that could lead to all armies being disbanded in preference to hiring magicians. I will have no part in establishing a precedent such as that. If you want to show that magicians are superior to armies, you will have to do it with magik alone. The military will not lift a finger to assist you.''

As he spoke, he took the jug of wine from Aahz's unresisting fingers, a sign in itself that Aahz was as stunned by the general's words as I was.

''My feelings on this subject are very strong, gentlemen,'' Badaxe continued, pouring himself some wine. ''So strong, in fact, I am willing to sacrifice myself and my kingdom to prove the point. What is more, I would strongly suggest that you do the same.''

He paused, regarding us with those glittering eyes.

''Because I tell you here and now, should you emerge victorious from the impending battle, you will not live to collect your reward. The king may rule the court, but word of what happens in the kingdom comes to him through my soldiers, and those soldiers will be posted along your return path to the palace, with orders to bring back word of your accidental demise, even if they have to arrange it. Do I make myself clear?''

Chapter Eight:

"Anything worth doing, is worth doing for a profit."

—TERESIAS

WITH a massive effort of self-control, I contained myself not only after we had left the general's quarters, but until we were out of earshot of the honor guard. When I finally spoke, I managed to keep the telltale note of hysteria out of my voice which would have betrayed my true feelings.

"Like you said, Aahz," I commented casually, "there are armies and there are armies. Right?"

Aahz wasn't fooled for a minute.

"Hysterics won't get us anywhere, kid," he observed. "What we need is sound thinking."

"Excuse me," I said pointedly, "but isn't 'sound thinking' what got us into the mess in the first place?"

"Okay, okay!" Aahz grimaced. "I'll admit I made a few oversights when I originally appraised the situation."

"A few oversights?" I echoed incredulously. "Aahz, this 'cushy job' you set me up for doesn't bear even the vaguest resemblance to what you described when you sold me on the idea."

"I know, kid," Aahz sighed. "I definitely owe you an apology. This sounds like it's actually going to be work."

"Work!" I shrieked, losing control slightly. "It's going to be suicide."

Aahz shook his head sadly.

"There you go overreacting again. It doesn't have to be suicide. We've got a choice, you know."

"Sure," I retorted sarcastically. "We can get killed by the invaders or we can get killed by Badaxe's boys. How silly of me not to have realized it. For a moment there I was getting worried."

"Our choice," Aahz corrected sternly, "is to go through with this lame-brained mission, or to take the money and run."

A ray of hope broke through the dismal gloom that had burdened my mind.

"Aahz," I said in genuine awe, "you're a genius. C'mon, let's get going."

"Get going where?" Aahz asked.

"Back to the inn, of course," I replied. "The sooner the better."

"That wasn't one of our options," my mentor sneered.

"But you said—"

"I said 'take the money *and* run' not just 'run,' " he corrected. "We aren't going anywhere until we've seen Grimble."

"But Aahz—"

" 'But Aahz' nothing," he interrupted fiercely. "This little jaunt has cost us a bundle. We're going to

at least make it break even, if not show a small profit."

"It hasn't cost us anything," I said bluntly.

"It cost us travel time and time away from your
studies," Aahz countered. "That's worth something."

"But—"

"Besides," he continued loftily, "there are more
important issues at stake here."

"Like what?" I pressed.

"Well . . . like, um . . ."

"There you are, gentlemen!"

We turned to find Grimble approaching us rapidly
from behind.

"I was hoping to catch you after the briefing," the
chancellor continued, joining us. "Do you mind if I
watch with you? I know you'll be eager to start off
on your campaign, but there are certain matters we
must discuss before you leave."

"Like our wages," Aahz supplied firmly.

Grimble's smile froze.

"Oh! Yes, of course. First, however, there are
other things to deal with. I trust the general supplied
you with the necessary information for your mission."

"Down to the last gruesome detail," I confirmed.

"Good, good," the chancellor chortled, his enthusiasm undimmed by my sarcasm. "I have every confidence you'll be able to deal with the riffraff from
the North. I'll have you know you were my personal
choice even before the interviews. In fact, I was the
one responsible for sending you the invitation in the
first place."

"We'll remember that," Aahz smiled, his eyes narrowing dangerously.

A thought occurred to me.

"Say . . . um, Lord Chancellor," I said casually, "how did you happen to hear of us in the first place?"

"Why do you ask?" Grimble countered.

"No special reason," I assured him. "But as the interview proved so fruitful, I would like to send a token of my gratitude to that person who spoke so highly of me to you."

It was a pretty flimsy story, but the chancellor seemed to accept it.

"Well . . . um, actually it was a wench," he admitted. "Rather comely, but I don't recall her name just offhand. She may have dyed her hair since you met her. It was green at the time we . . . er . . . met. Do you know her?"

Indeed I did. There was only one woman who knew of Aahz and me, much less our whereabouts. Then again, there was only one woman I knew who fit the description of being voluptuous with green hair. Tanda!

I opened my mouth to acknowledge my recognition, when Aahz dug a warning elbow into my rib.

"Glah!" I said intelligently.

"How's that again?" Grimble inquired.

"I . . . um, I can't place the person, just offhand," I lied. "But you know how absentminded we magicians are."

"Of course," the chancellor smiled, for some reason relieved.

"Now that that's settled," Aahz interrupted, "I believe you mentioned something about our wages."

Grimble scowled for a moment, then broke into a good-natured grin.

"I can see why Master Skeeve leaves his business dealings to you, Aahz," he conceded.

"Flattery's nice," Aahz observed, "but you can't spend it. The subject was our wages."

"You must realize we are a humble kingdom," Grimble sighed, "though we try to reward our retainers as best we can. There have been quarters set aside for the court magician which should be spacious enough to accommodate both of you. Your meals will be provided . . . that is, of course, assuming you are on time when they are served. Also, there is a possibility . . . no, I'd go so far as to say it is a certainty that His Majesty's generosity will be extended to include free stable space and food for your unicorns. How does that sound?"

"So far, pretty cheap," Aahz observed bluntly.

"What do you mean, 'cheap?' " the chancellor snarled, losing his composure for a moment.

"What you've offered so far," Aahz sneered, "is a room we won't be sleeping in, meals we won't be eating, and stable space we won't be using because we'll be in the field fighting your war for you. In exchange, you want Skeeve here to use his skills to save your kingdom. By my calculations, that's cheap!"

"Yes, I see your point," Grimble conceded. "Well, there will, of course, be a small wage paid."

"How small?" Aahz pressed.

"Sufficient to cover your expenses," the chancellor smiled. "Shall we say fifty gold pieces a month?"

"Let's say two hundred," Aahz smiled back.

"Perhaps we could go as high as seventy-five," Grimble countered.

"And we'll come down to two-twenty-five," Aahz offered.

"Considering his skills, we could pay . . . excuse me," the chancellor blinked. "Did you say two-twenty-five?"

"Actually," Aahz conceded, "I misspoke."

"I thought so." Grimble smiled.

"I meant two-fifty."

"Now see here—" the chancellor began.

"Look, Grimble," Aahz met him halfway, "you had three choices. You could double the size of your army, hire a magician, or lose the kingdom. Even at three hundred a month, Skeeve here is your best deal. Don't look at what you're spending, look at what you're saving."

Grimble thought about it for a few moments.

"Very well," he said, grimacing. "Two-fifty it is."

"I believe the figure under discussion was three hundred," I observed pointedly.

That earned me a black look, but I stood my ground and returned his stare levelly.

"Three hundred," he said, forcing the words out through gritted teeth.

"Payable in advance," Aahz added.

"Payable at the end of the pay period," Grimble corrected.

"C'mon, Grimble," Aahz began, but the chancellor interrupted him, holding up his hand.

"No! On that point I must remain inflexible," he insisted. "Everyone in the Royal Retinue is paid at the same time, when the vaults are opened at the end of the pay period. If we break that rule and start allowing exceptions, there will be no end to it."

"Can you at least give us a partial advance?" Aahz pressed. "Something to cover expenses on the up-coming campaign?"

"Definitely not!" Grimble retorted. "If I paid out

monies for services not yet rendered, certain people, specifically Hugh Badaxe, would suspect you intended to take the money and flee without entering battle at all!"

That hit uncomfortably close to home, and I found myself averting my eyes for fear of betraying my guilt. Aahz, however, never even blinked.

"What about bribes?" he asked.

Grimble scowled.

"It is unthinkable that one of the king's retainers would accept a bribe, much less count on it as part of his income. Any attempt to bribe you should be reported immediately to His Majesty!"

"Not *taking* bribes, Grimble," Aahz snarled. "*Giving* them. When we give money out to the enemy, does that come out of our wages, or does the kingdom pay for it?"

"I seriously doubt you could buy off the army facing you," the chancellor observed skeptically. "Besides, you're supposed to carry the day with magik. That's what we're paying you for."

"Even magik is aided by accurate information," Aahz replied pointedly. "C'mon Grimble, you know court intrigue. A little advance warning can go a long way in any battle."

"True enough," the chancellor admitted. "Very well, I guess we can give you an allowance for bribes, assuming it will be kept within reason."

"How much in reason?" Aahz inquired.

"Say . . . five gold pieces."

"Twenty-five would—"

"Five!" Grimble said firmly.

Aahz studied his adversary for a moment, then sighed.

"Five," he said, extending his palm.

The chancellor grudgingly dug into his purse and counted out five gold pieces. In fact, he counted them twice before passing them to Aahz.

"You realize, of course," he warned, "I will require an accounting of those funds after your victory."

"Of course," Aahz smiled, fondling the coins.

"You seem very confident of our victory, Lord Chancellor," I observed.

Grimble regarded me with cocked eyebrow for a moment.

"Of course I am confident, Lord Magician," he said at last. "So confident, I have staked my kingdom, and more importantly, my reputation, on your success. You will note I rate my reputation above the kingdom. That is no accident. Kingdoms rise and fall, but a chancellor can always find employment. That is, of course, providing it was not his advice which brought the kingdom to ruin. Should you fail in your campaign to save Possiltum, my career is finished. If that should happen, gentlemen, your careers fall with mine."

"That has the sound of a threat to it, Grimble," Aahz observed dryly.

"Does it?" the chancellor responded with mock innocence. "That was not my intent. I am not threatening, I am stating a fact. I maintain very close contact with the chancellors of all of the surrounding kingdoms; in fact I am related to several. They are all aware of my position in this magik versus the military issue. Should I prove wrong in my judgment, should you fail in your defense of Possiltum, they will note it. Thereafter, any magician—and you specifically, Skeeve—will be denounced as a fraud and a charlatan should you seek further employment. In fact, as the chancellors frequently control the courts, I would not be surprised if they found an excuse or a trumped-up charge which would allow them to have you put to death as a favor to me. The method of death varies from kingdom to kingdom, but the end result is the same. I trust you will keep that in mind as you plan your campaign.''

With that, he turned on his heel and strode away, leaving us standing in silence.

''Well, Aahz,'' I said finally, ''do you have any sound advice on our situation now?''

''Of course,'' he retorted.

''What?'' I asked.

''Now that we've got the whole story,'' he said solemnly, ''now you can panic.''

Chapter Nine:

"There is more at stake here than our lives."

—COL. TRAVIS
Alamo Pep Talk

ON the third night after leaving Possiltum's capital, we camped on a small knoll overlooking the kingdom's main north-south trail.

Actually, I use the phase "north-south" rather loosely in this instance. In three days' travel, our progress was the only northward movement we had observed on this particular strip of beaten dirt. The dearth of northbound traffic was emphasized by the high volume of people bound in the opposite direction.

As we traveled we were constantly encountering small groups and families picking their way steadily toward the capital in that unhurried yet ground-eating pace that typifies people accustomed to traveling without means of transport other than their feet. They did not seem particularly frightened or panicky, but two common characteristics marked them all as being more than casual travelers.

First, the great amount of personal effects they carried was far in excess of that required for a simple pilgrimage. Whether bound in cumbersome backpacks or heaped in small, hand-pushed carts, it was obvious the southbound travelers were bringing with them as much of their worldly possessions as they could carry or drag.

Second, no one paid us any heed other than a passing glance. This was even more noteworthy than the prior observation.

Currently, our party consisted of three: myself, Aahz, and Gleep. We had left Buttercup at the palace, much to Aahz's disgust. He would have preferred to leave Gleep and bring Buttercup, but the royal orders had been firm on this point. The dragon was not to remain at the palace unless one or both of us also stayed behind to handle him. As a result, we traveled as a trio—a youth, a dragon, and a grumbling demon—not exactly a common sight in these or any other parts. The peasants flowing south, however, barely noticed us other than to give us clear road space when we passed.

Aahz maintained that this was because whatever they were running from inspired such fear that they barely noted anything or anybody in their path. He further surmised that the motivating force for this exodus could only be the very army we were on our way to oppose.

To prove his point, we attempted to question several of the groups when we encountered them. We stopped doing this after the first day due to the similarities of the replies we received. Sample:

Aahz: Hold, stranger! Where are you going?
Answer: To the capital!

Aahz: Why?

Answer: To be as near as possible to the king when he makes his defense against the invaders from the North. He'll have to try to save himself even if he won't defend the outlands.

Aahz: Citizen you need flee no more. You have underestimated your king's concern for your safety. You see before you the new court magician, retained by His Majesty specifically for the purpose of defending Possiltum from the invading army. What say you to that?

Answer: One magician?

Aahz: With my own able assistance, of course.

Answer: I'd say you were crazy.

Aahz: Now look—

Answer: No, *you* look, whoever or whatever you are. Meaning no disrespect to this or any other magician, you're fools to oppose that army. Magik may be well and good against an ordinary force, but you aren't going to stop *that* army with one magician . . . or twenty magicians for that matter.

Aahz: We have every confidence—

Answer: Fine, then *you* go north. Me, I'm heading for the capital!

Though this exchange had eventually quelled our efforts to reassure the populace, it had given rise to an argument which was still unresolved as we prepared to sleep on the third night.

"What happened to your plan to take the money and run?" I grumbled.

"Big deal," Aahz shot back. "Five whole gold pieces."

"You said you wanted a profit," I pressed. "Okay! We've got one. So it's small . . . but so was the effort we put into it. Considering we didn't spend anything—"

"What about the unicorn?" Aahz countered. "While they're still holding the unicorn, we've lost money on the deal."

"Aahz," I reminded him. "Buttercup didn't cost us anything, remember? He was a gift from Quigley."

"It would cost money to replace him," Aahz insisted. "That means that we lost money on the deal unless we get him back. I've told you, I want a profit . . . and definitely refuse to accept a loss."

"Gleep?"

Aahz's heated words had awakened my dragon, who raised his head in sleepy inquiry.

"Go back to sleep, Gleep!" I said soothingly. "Everything's all right."

Reassured, he rolled onto his back and laid back his head.

Ridiculous as he looked, lying there with his four legs sticking up in the air, he had reminded me of something.

I pondered the memory for a moment, then decided to change my tactics.

"Aahz," I said thoughtfully, "what's the real reason for your wanting to go through with this?"

"Weren't you listening, kid? I said—"

"I know, I know," I interrupted. "You said it was for the profit. The only thing wrong with that is you tried to leave Gleep behind, who cost us money, instead of Buttercup, who didn't cost us anything! That doesn't ring true if you're trying to show a profit with the least possible effort."

"Um, you know how I feel about that stupid dragon—" Aahz began.

"And you know how I feel about him," I interrupted, "As such, you also know I'd never abandon him to save my own skin, much less for money. For some reason, you wanted to be sure I'd see this thing through . . . and that reason has nothing at all to do with money. Now, what is it?"

It was Aahz's turn to lapse into thoughtful silence.

"You're getting better at figuring things out, kid," he said finally.

Normally, I would have been happy to accept the compliment. This time, however, I saw it as what it was: an attempt to distract me.

"The reason, Aahz," I said firmly.

"There are several reasons, kid," he said with uncharacteristic solemnity. "The main one is that you're not a master magician yet."

"If you don't mind my saying so," I commented dryly, "that doesn't make a whole lot of sense. If I'm short on ability, why are you so eager to shove me into this mission?"

"Hear me out, kid," Aahz said, raising a restraining hand. "I made a mistake, and that mistake has dumped us into a situation that needs a master magician. More than a master magician's abilities, we need a master magician's conscience. Do you follow me?"

"No," I admitted.

"Not surprising," Aahz sighed. "That's why I tried to trick you into completing this mission instead of explaining it. So far, all your training has been on physical abilities without developing your professional conscience."

"You've taught me to keep one eye on the

profits," I pointed out defensively.

"That's not what I mean, kid. Look, for a minute forget about profits."

"Are you feeling okay, Aahz?" I asked with genuine concern. "You don't sound like yourself at all."

"Will you get off my back, kid," he snarled. "I'm trying to explain something important!"

I sank into a cowed silence. Still I was reassured. Aahz was definitely Aahz.

"When you were apprenticed to Garkin," Aahz began, "and even when you first met me, you didn't want to be a magician. You wanted to be a thief. To focus your energies behind your lessons, I had to stress how much benefit you could reap from learning magik."

He paused. I didn't say anything. There was nothing to say. He was right, both in his recollections and his interpretation of them.

"Well," he sighed, "there's another side to magik. There's a responsibility . . . a responsibility to your fellow practitioners, and, more importantly, to magik itself. Even though we have rivals and will probably acquire more if we live that long, and even though we may fight with them or beat them out for a job, we are all bound by a common cause. Every magician has a duty to promote magik, to see that its use is respected and reputable. The greater the magician, the greater his sense of duty."

"What's that got to do with our current situation?" I prompted.

"There's an issue at stake here, kid," he answered carefully. "You heard it from Badaxe and Grimble both. More importantly, you heard it from the populace when we talked to the peasants. Rodrick is gambling his entire kingdom on the ability of magik to do a job. Now, no one but a magician can tell how reasonable or unreasonable a task that might be. If we fail, all the laymen will see is that magik failed, and they'll never trust it again. That's why we can't walk away from this mission. We're here representing magik . . . and we've got to give it our best shot.''

I thought about that for a few moments.

"But what can we do against a whole army?" I asked finally.

"To be honest with you," Aahz sighed, "I really don't know. I'm hoping we can come up with an idea after we've seen exactly what it is we're up against."

We sat silently together for a long time after that, each lost in his own thoughts of the mission and what was at stake.

Chapter Ten:

"One need not fear superior numbers if the opposing force has been properly scouted and appraised."

—S. BULL

MY last vestige of hope was squashed when we finally sighted the army. Reports of its massive size had not been overstated; if anything, they had failed to express the full impact of the force's might.

Our scouting mission had taken us across Possiltum's northern border and several days' journey into its neighbor's interior. The name of this kingdom was inconsequential. If it was not already considered part of the new empire, it would be as soon as the news spread.

We weren't sure if we had just missed the last battle, or if the kingdom had simply surrendered. Whichever the case, there were no defending troops in evidence, just large encampments of the Empire's forces spread out in a rough line which disappeared over the horizon in either direction.

Fortunately, the army was not currently on the move, which made our scouting considerably easier.

There were sentries posted at regular intervals all
along the front line, but as they were not more than a
given distance from the encampments, we simply
traversed the line without approaching them too
closely, and thus escaped detection.

Periodically, we would creep closer to an encampment or climb a tree to improve our view. Aahz
seemed very absorbed in his own thoughts, both
when we were actually viewing the troops and as we
were traveling to new locations. Since I couldn't get
more than an occasional grunt or monosyllable out
of him, I occupied myself making my own observa-
tions.

The soldiers were clothed roughly the same. Standard equipment seemed to include a leather helmet
and breastplate, a rough knee-length cloth tunic, san-
dals, sword, two javelins, and a large rectangular
shield. Apparently they were not planning to move
immediately, for they had pitched their tents and
spent most of their time sharpening weapons, repair-
ing armor, eating, or simply lolling about. Occasionally, a metal-encrusted soldier, presumably an
officer, would appear and shout at the others, whereupon they would listlessly form ranks and drill. Their
practice would usually grind to a halt as soon as the
officer passed from view.

There were occasional pieces of siege equipment
designed to throw large rocks or spears long
distances, though we never saw them in operation.
The only pieces of equipment that seemed to be used
with any regularity were the signal towers. Each encampment had one of these, a rickety affair of lashed
together poles stretching roughly twenty feet in the
air and surmounted by a small, square platform.
Several times a day, one soldier in each encampment

would mount one of these structures, and they would signal to each other with pennants or standards. The towers also did duty as clotheslines, and were periodically draped with drying tunics.

All in all, it looked like an incredibly boring existence. In fact, from my appraisal, the only thing duller than being a soldier of the Empire was spending days on end watching soldiers of the Empire!

I commented on this to Aahz as we lay belly-down on a grassy knoll, surveying yet another encampment.

"You're right, kid," he admitted absently. "Being a soldier is pretty dull work."

"How about us?" I probed, eager to keep him talking. "What we're doing isn't exactly exciting, you know!"

"You want excitement?" he asked, focusing on me for the first time in days. "Tell you what. Why don't you just stroll down there and ask the Officer of the Day for a quick rundown on how their army operates? I bet that'll liven things up for you."

"I'm not *that* bored!" I amended hastily.

"Then what say you just keep quiet and let me do this my way." Aahz smiled and resumed his studies.

"Do what your way?" I persisted. "Exactly what is it we're trying to accomplish anyway?"

Aahz sighed.

"We're scouting the enemy," he explained patiently. "We've got enough going against us on this campaign without rushing in uninformed."

"How much information do we need?" I grumbled. "This encampment doesn't look any different from the last five we looked at."

"That's because you don't know what you're looking for," Aahz scoffed. "What have you learned so far about the opposition?''

I wasn't ready for the question but I gamely rose to the challenge.

"Um . . . there are a lot of them . . . they're well armed . . . um . . . and they have catapults . . ."

"That's all?" Aahz sneered. "Brilliant! You and Badaxe make a great team of tacticians."

"Okay, so teach me!" I shot back. "What have you learned?"

"You can spend years trying to learn military theory without scratching the surface," my mentor replied sternly. "But I'll try to give you the important parts in a nutshell. To appraise a force, such as we're doing now, remember two words: 'Sam' and 'Doc.' ''

" 'Sam' and 'Doc,' '' I repeated dutifully.

"Some folks prefer to remember 'Salute' but I like 'Sam' and 'Doc,' '' Aahz added as an aside.

"Terrific," I said, grimacing. "Now tell me what it means."

"They're to help you remember an information checklist," Aahz confided. " 'Salute's stands for Size, Activity, Location, Unit, Time, and Equipment. That's fine as far as it goes, but it assumes no judgmental ability on the part of the scout. I prefer 'Sam' and 'Doc.' That stands for Strength, Armament, Movement, and Deployment, Organization, and Communications."

"Oh," I said, hoping he wasn't expecting me to remember all this.

"Now, using that framework," Aahz continued, "let's summarize what we've seen so far. Size: there are lots of them, enough so it's kind of pointless to try for an exact count. Movement: currently, they're just sitting there."

"I got that far all by myself," I pointed out sarcastically.

"The big key, however," Aahz continued, ignoring me, "is in their Armament and Equipment. When you look at this, consider both what is there and what isn't."

"How's that again?" I asked.

"What there is is a lot of foot-schloggers, infantry, a little artillery in the form of catapults and archers, but nothing even vaguely resembling cavalry. That means they're going to go slow when they move, particularly in battle. We don't have to worry about any fast, flanking moves; it'll be a toe-to-toe slugfest."

"But, Aahz—" I began.

"As to the Deployment and Organization," he pushed on undaunted, "they're strung out all over the place, probably because it's easier to forage for food that way. Then again, it displays a certain confidence on their part that they don't feel it's necessary to mass their forces. I think we're looking at their Organization, a collection of companies or battalions each under the leadership of two or three officers, all under the guidance of a super-leader or general."

"Aahz—" I tried again.

"Communications seems to be their most vulnerable point," Aahz pushed on doggedly. "If an army this size doesn't coordinate its movements, it's in big trouble. If they're really using signal towers and runners to pass messages, we might be able to jinx the works for them."

"All of which means what?" I interrupted finally.

"Hmm? Oh, that's a capsule summary of what we're up against," Aahz replied innocently.

"I know. I know," I sighed. "But for days you've been saying you'll formulate a plan after you've seen what we're up against. Well, you've seen it. What's the plan? How can we beat 'em?''

"There's no way, kid," Aahz admitted heavily. "If I had seen one, I would have told you, but I haven't, and that's why I keep looking."

"Maybe there isn't one," I suggested cautiously.

Aahz sighed.

"I'm starting to think you're right. If so, that means we'll have to do something I really don't want to do."

"You mean give up?" I said, genuinely startled. "After that big speech you gave me about responsibility and—"

"Whoa," Aahz interrupted. "I didn't say anything about giving up. What we're going to do is—"

"Gleep!"

The unmistakable sound came to us from behind, rolling up the hill from the brush-filled gully where we'd left my pet.

"Kid," Aahz moaned, "will you keep that stupid dragon quiet? All we need now is to have him pull the army down our necks."

"Right, Aahz!" I agreed, worming away backward as fast as I could.

As soon as I was clear of the crest of the hill, I rose to a low crouch and scuttled down the slope in that position. Crawling is neither a fast nor comfortable means of travel for me.

As per our now normal procedure, we had tethered Gleep to a tree . . . a large tree after he had successfully uprooted several small ones. Needless to say, he wasn't wild about the idea, but it was necessary considering the delicate nature of our current work.

"Gleep!"

I could see him now, eagerly straining at the end of

his rope. Surprisingly, however, for a change he wasn't trying to get to me. In fact, he was trying his best to get at a large bush which stood some distance from his tree . . . or at something hidden in the bush!

Cold sweat suddenly popped out on my brow. It occurred to me that Gleep might have been discovered by one of the enemy army scouts. That would be bad enough, but even worse was the possibility said scout might still be around.

I hurriedly stepped sideways into the shadow of a tree and reviewed the situation. I hadn't actually *seen* a scout. In fact, there was no movement at all in the indicated bush. I could sneak back and get Aahz, but if I were wrong he wouldn't be very happy over being called to handle a false alarm. I could set Gleep loose and let him find the intruder, but that would mean exposing myself.

As I stood debating my next course of action, someone slipped up behind me and put hands over my eyes.

"Surprise!" came a soft voice in my ear.

Chapter Eleven:

"Should old acquaintance be forgot. . . . "

—COUNT OF MONTE CRISTO

I JUMPED!

Perhaps I should clarify. When I say "I jumped," I mean I really jumped. Over a year ago, Aahz had taught me to fly, which is actually controlled hovering caused by reverse levitation.

Whatever it was, I did it. I went straight up in the air about ten feet and stayed there. I didn't know what had snuck up behind me, and didn't want to know. I wanted help! I wanted Aahz!

I drew a mighty breath to express this desire.

"Kinda jumpy, aren't you, handsome?"

That penetrated my panic.

Stifling my shout before it truly began, I looked down on my attacker. From my vantage point, I was treated to a view of a gorgeous golden-olive complexioned face, accented by almond-shaped cat's eyes, framed by a magnificent tumble of light green hair. I could also see a generous expanse of cleavage.

"Tanda!" I crowed with delight, forcing my eyes back to her face.

"Do you mind coming down?" she called. "I can't come up."

I considered swooping down on her dramatically, but decided against it. I'm still not all that good at flying, and the effect would be lost completely if I crashed into her.

Instead, I settled for lowering myself gently to the ground a few paces from her.

"Gee, Tanda, I . . . *glack!*"

The last was squeezed forcefully from me as she swept me into a bone-crushing embrace.

"Gee, it's good to see you, handsome," she murmured happily. "How have you been?"

"I *was* fine," I noted, untangling myself briefly. "What are you doing here?"

The last time I had seen her, Tanda was part of the ill-fated group Aahz and I had seen off to dimensions unknown. Of the whole crowd, she had been the only one I was sorry to see go.

"I'm waiting for you, silly," she teased, slipping an affectionate arm around my waist. "Where's Aahz?"

"He's—" I started to point up the hill when a thought occurred to me. "Say . . . how did you know I had Aahz with me?"

"Oh! Don't get mad," she scolded, giving me a playful shake. "It stands to reason. Even Aahz wouldn't let you face that army alone."

"But how did you—"

"Gleep!"

My dragon had discovered his quarry was no longer hiding behind the bush. As a result, he was now straining at the end of his rope trying to reach

us. The tree he was tethered to was swaying dangerously.

"Gleep!" Tanda called in a delighted voice. "How
are ya, fella?"

The tree dipped to new lows as my dragon quivered
with glee at having been recognized. I was quivering a
little myself. Tanda had that affect on males.

Heedless of her own safety, Tanda bounded forward to kneel before the dragon, pulling his whiskers
and scratching his nose affectionately.

Gleep loved it. I loved it, too. In addition to her
usual soft, calf-high boots, Tanda was wearing a
short green tunic which hugged her generous curves
and showed off her legs just swell. What's more,
when she knelt down like that, the hem rode up
until. . . .

"What's wrong with that dragon?" Aahz boomed,
bursting out of the brush behind me.

This time I didn't jump . . . much.

"Gee, Aahz," I began. "It's . . ."

I needn't have bothered trying to explain.

Tanda uncoiled and came past me in a bound.

"Aahz!" she exclaimed, flinging herself into his
arms.

For a change, my mentor was caught as flat-footed
as I had been. For a moment, the tangle of arms
teetered on the brink of collapse, then down it went.

They landed with a resounding thump, Aahz on
the bottom and therefore soaking up most of the impact.

"Still impulsive, aren't you?" Tanda leered.

"Whoosh . . . hah . . . ah . . ." Aahz responded ur-
banely.

Tanda rolled to her feet and began rearranging her
tunic.

"At least I don't have to ask if you're glad to see me," she observed.

"Tanda!" Aahz gasped at last.

"You remembered?" Tanda beamed.

"She's been waiting for us, Aahz," I supplied brightly.

"That's right!" Aahz scowled. "Grimble said you set us up for this job."

Tanda winced.

"I can explain that," she said apologetically.

"I can hardly wait," Aahz intoned.

"I'm kind of curious about that myself," I added.

"Um . . . this could take a while, guys," she said thoughtfully. "Got anything around to drink?"

That was easily the most reasonable question asked so far today. We broke out the wine, and in no time were sitting around in a small circle quenching our thirst. Much to Aahz's disgust, I insisted we sit close enough to Gleep that he not be left out. This meant, of course, his rather aromatic breath flavored our discussion, but as I pointed out it was the only way to keep him quiet while we talked.

"What happened after you left?" I prodded. "Where are Isstvan and Brockhurst and Higgins? What happened to Quigley? Did they ever bring Frumple back to life, or is he still a statue?"

"Later, kid," Aahz interrupted. "First things first. You were about to explain about Grimble."

"Grimble," Tanda responded, wrinkling her nose. "Did you ever notice the 'crookeder' a person is, the more possessive he is? He's the main reason I didn't wait for you at Possiltum."

"From the beginning," Aahz instructed.

"From the beginning." Tanda pursed her lips thoughtfully. "Well, I picked him up in a singles bar

. . . he's married, but I didn't know that till later.''

"What's a singles bar?" I interrupted.

"Shut up, kid," Aahz snarled.

"Well, it wasn't actually a singles bar," Tanda corrected. "It was more of a tavern. I should have known he was married. I mean, nobody that young is *that* bald unless he's got a wife at home."

"Skip the philosophy," Aahz moaned. "Just tell us the story, huh?"

Tanda cocked an eyebrow at him.

"You know, Aahz," she accused, "for someone as long-winded as you are when it comes to telling stories, you're awfully impatient when it comes to listening to someone else."

"She's right, you know," I commented.

"Enough!" Aahz bellowed. "The story!"

"Well, one of the things Grimble mentioned while he was trying to impress me with how important his job was, was that he was trying to find a court magician. He said he had convinced the king to hire one, but now he couldn't find one and was going to end up looking like an idiot."

"And when he mentioned idiots," I supplied, "naturally you thought of us."

"Now, don't be that way," Tanda scolded. "I thought it was a good way to help out a couple of friends. I knew you two were hanging out in this neck of the woods . . . and everybody knows what a cushy job being a court magician is."

"What did I tell you, kid," Aahz commented.

"We must be talking about different jobs," I retorted.

"Hey," Tanda interrupted, laying a soft hand on my arm. "When I gave him your names, I didn't know about the invading army. Honest!"

My anger melted away at her touch. Right then, she could have told me she had sold my head as a centerpiece and I would have forgiven her.

"Well . . ." I began, but she persisted, which was fine by me.

"As soon as I found out what the real story was, I knew I had gotten you into a tight spot," she said with soft sincerity. "Like I said, I would have waited at Possiltum, but I was afraid what with your disguises and all, that you'd recognize me before I spotted you. If you gave me the kind of greeting I've grown to expect, it could have really queered the deal. Grimble's a jealous twit, and if he thought we were more than nodding acquaintances, he would have held back whatever support he might normally give."

"Big deal," Aahz grumbled. "Five whole gold pieces."

"That much?" Tanda sounded honestly surprised. "Which arm did you break?"

"Aahz always gets us the best possible deal," I said proudly. "At least, monetarily."

"Well," Tanda concluded, "at least I won't dig into your war funds. When I found out the mess I had gotten you into, I decided I'd work this one for free. Since I got you into it, the least I can do is help get you out."

"That's terrific," I exclaimed.

"It sure is!" Aahz agreed.

Something in his voice annoyed me.

"I meant that she was helping us," I snarled. "Not that she was doing it for free."

"That's what I meant, too, apprentice," Aahz glowered back. "But unlike some, I know what I'm talking about!"

"Boys, boys," Tanda said, separating us with her hands. "We're on the same side. Remember?"

"Gleep!" said the dragon, siding with Tanda.

As I have said, Gleep's breath is powerful enough to stop any conversation, and it was several minutes before the air cleared enough for us to continue.

"Before we were so rudely interrupted," Tanda gasped at last, "you were starting to say something, Aahz. Have you got a plan?"

"Now I do," Aahz smiled, chucking her under the chin. "And believe me, doing it without you would have been rough."

That had an anxious sound to it. Tanda's main calling, at least the only one mentionable in polite company, was Assassin.

"C'mon, Aahz," I chided. "Tanda's good, but she's not good enough to take on a whole army."

"Don't bet on it, handsome," she corrected, winking at me.

I blushed but continued with my argument.

"I still say the job's too big for one person, or three people for that matter," I insisted.

"You're right, kid," Aahz said solemnly.

"We just can't . . . what did you say, Aahz?"

"I said you were right," Aahz repeated.

"I thought so," I marveled. "I just wanted to hear it again."

"You'd *hear* it more often if you were *right* more often," Aahz pointed out.

"C'mon, Aahz," Tanda interrupted. "What's the plan?"

"Like the kid says," Aahz said loftily, "we need more help. We need an army of our own."

"But Aahz," I reminded him, "Badaxe said—"

"Who said anything about Badaxe?" Aahz replied

innocently. "We're supposed to win this war with magik, aren't we? Well, fine. With Tanda on our team, we've got a couple of extra skills to draw on. Remember?"

I remembered. I remembered Aahz saying he wasn't worried about Tanda leaving with Isstvan because she could travel the dimensions by herself if things got rough. The light began to dawn.

"You mean . . ."

"That's right, kid," Aahz smiled. "We're going back to Deva. We're going to recruit a little invasionary force of our own!"

Chapter Twelve:

"This is no game for old men! Send in the boys!"

—W. HAYS

I DON'T know how Tanda transported us from Klah to Deva. If I did, we wouldn't have needed her. All I know is that at the appropriate time she commenced to chant and shift her shoulders (a fascinating process in itself), and we were there.

"There," in this case, was at the Bazaar at Deva. That phrase alone, however, does not begin to describe our new surroundings as they came into focus.

A long time ago, the dimension of Deva had undergone an economic collapse. To survive, the Deveels (who I once knew as devils) used their ability to travel the dimensions and become merchants. Through the process of natural selection, the most successful Deveels were not the best fighters, but the best traders. Now, after countless generations of this process, the Deveels were acknowledged as the best merchants in all the dimensions. They were also acknowledged as being the shrewdest, coldest, most profit-hungry cheats ever to come down the pike.

The Bazaar at Deva was their showcase. It was an all-day, all-night, year-round fair where the Deveels met to haggle with each other over the wares fetched back from the various dimensions. Though it was originally established and maintained by Deveels, it was not unusual to find travelers from many dimensions shopping the endless rows of displays and booths. The rule of thumb was, "If it's to be found anywhere, you'll find it at the Bazaar at Deva."

I had been here once before with Aahz. At the time, we were searching for a surprise weapon to use against Isstvan. What we ended up with was Gleep and Tanda! . . . Distractions abound at the Bazaar.

I mention this in part to explain why, as unusual as our foursome must have appeared, no one paid us the slightest attention as we stood watching the kaleidoscope of activity whirling about us.

Gleep pressed against me for reassurance, momentarily taken aback at the sudden change of surroundings. I ignored him. My first visit to this place had been far too brief for my satisfaction. As such, I was rubbernecking madly, trying to see as much as possible as fast as possible.

Tanda was more businesslike.

"Now that we're here, Aahz," she drawled, "do you know where we're going?"

"No," Aahz admitted. "But I'll find out right now."

Without further warning, he casually reached out and grabbed the arm of the nearest passerby, a short, ugly fellow with tusks. Spinning his chosen victim around, Aahz bent to scowl in his face.

"You!" he snarled. "Do you like to fight?"

For a moment my heart stopped. All we needed now was to get into a brawl.

Fortunately, instead of producing a weapon, the tusker gave ground a step and eyed our party suspiciously.

"Not with a Pervert backed by a dragon, I don't," he retorted cautiously.

"Good!" Aahz smiled. "Then if you wanted to hire someone to do your fighting for you, where would you go?"

"To the Bazaar at Deva," the tusker shrugged.

"I know that!" Aahz snarled. "But *where* at the Bazaar?"

"Oh," the tusker exclaimed with sudden understanding. "About twenty rows in that direction, then turn right for another thirty or so. That's where the mercenaries hang out."

"Twenty, then up thirty," Aahz repeated carefully. "Thanks."

"A finder's fee would be appreciated more than any thanks," the tusker smiled, extending a palm.

"You're right!" Aahz agreed, and turned his back on our benefactor.

The tusker hesitated for a moment, then shrugged and continued on his way. I could have told him that Perverts in general and Aahz specifically are not noted for their generosity. "We go twenty rows that way, then up thirty," Aahz informed us.

"Yeah, we heard," Tanda grimaced. "Why didn't you just ask him flat out?"

"My way is quicker," Aahz replied smugly.

"Is it?" I asked skeptically.

"Look kid," Aahz scowled. "Do you want to lead us through this zoo?"

"Well . . ." I hesitated.

"Then shut up and let me do it, okay?"

Actually, I was more than willing to let Aahz lead the way to wherever it was we were going. For one thing, it kept him busy navigating a path through the crowd. For another, it left me with next to nothing to do except marvel at the sights of the Bazaar as I followed along in his wake.

Try as I might, though, there was just too much for one set of eyes to see.

In one booth, two Deveels argued with an elephant-headed being over a skull; at least, I think it was a skull. In another, a Deveel was putting on a demonstration for a mixed group of shoppers, summoning clouds of floating green bubbles from a tiny wooden box.

At one point, our path was all but blocked by a booth selling rings which shot bolts of lightning. Between the salesman's demonstrations and the customers trying out their purchases, the way was virtually impassable.

Aahz and Tanda never broke stride, however, confidently maintaining their pace as they walked through the thick of the bolts. Miraculously, they passed through unscathed.

Gritting my teeth, I seized one of Gleep's ears and followed in their footsteps. Again, the bolts of energy failed to find us. Apparently no Deveel would bring injury or allow anyone in his shop to bring injury to a potential customer. It was a handy fact to know.

The lightning rings brought something else to mind, however. The last time we parted company with Tanda, Aahz had given her a ring that shot a heat ray capable of frying a man-sized target on the spot. That's right . . . I said he *gave* it to her. You might think this was proof of the depth of his feelings for her. It's my theory he was sick. Anyway, I was reminded of the ring and curious as to what had become of it.

Increasing my pace slightly, I closed the distance between myself and the pair in the lead, only to find they were already deeply engrossed in conversation. The din that prevails at the Bazaar stymies any attempt at serious eavesdropping, but I managed to catch occasional bits and pieces of the conversation as we walked.

". . . heard . . . awfully expensive, aren't they?" Tanda was saying.

". . . lick their weight in . . ." Aahz replied smugly.

I moved in a little closer, trying to hear better.

". . . makes you think they've got anyone here?" Tanda asked.

"With the number of bars here?" Aahz retorted. "The way I hear it, this is one of their main . . ."

I lost the rest of that argument. A knee-high, tentacled mass suddenly scuttled across my boots and ducked through a tent flap, closely pursued by two very frustrated-looking Deveels.

I ignored the chase and the following screams, hurrying to catch up with Aahz and Tanda again. Apparently they were discussing mercenaries, and I wanted to hear as much as possible, both to further my education, and because I might have to lead them into battle eventually.

". . . find them?" Tanda was asking. "All we have is a general area."

". . . easy," Aahz replied confidently. "Just listen for the singing."

"Singing?" Tanda was skeptical.

"It's their trademark," Aahz pronounced. "It also lands them in most of their . . ."

A Deveel stepped in front of me, proudly displaying a handful of seeds. He threw them on the ground with a flourish, and a dense black thornbush sprang up to block my path. Terrific. Normally, I would have been fascinated, but at the moment I was in a hurry.

Without even pausing to upbraid the Deveel, I took to the air, desperation giving wings to my feet . . . desperation assisted by a little levitation. I cleared the thornbush easily, touched down lightly on the far side, and was practically trampled by Gleep as he burst through the barrier.

"Gleep?" he said, cocking his head at me curiously.

I picked myself up from the dust where I had been knocked by his enthusiasm and cuffed him.

"Watch where you're going next time," I ordered angrily.

He responded by snaking out his long tongue and licking my face. His breath was devastating and his tongue left a trail of slime. Obviously my admonishment had terrified him.

Heaving a deep sigh, I sprinted off after Aahz with Gleep lumbering along in hot pursuit.

I was just overtaking them when Aahz stopped suddenly in his tracks and started to turn. Unable to halt my headlong sprint, I plowed into him, knocking him sprawling.

"In a hurry, handsome?" Tanda asked, eyeing me slyly.

"Gee, Aahz," I stammered, bending over him, "I didn't mean to—"

From a half sitting position, his hand lashed out in

a cuff that spun me halfway around.

"Watch where you're going next time," he growled.

"Gleep!" said the dragon and licked my face.

Either my head was spinning more than I thought, or I had been through this scene before.

"Now quit clowning around and listen, kid."

Aahz was on his feet again, and all business.

"Here's where we part company for a while. You wait here while I go haggle with the mercenaries."

"Gee, Aahz," I whined. "Can't I—"

"No, you can't!" he said firmly. "The crew I'm going after is sharp. All we need is one of your dumb questions in the middle of negotiations and they'll triple their prices."

"But—" I began.

"You will wait here," Aahz ordered. "I repeat, *wait*. No fights, no window shopping for dragons, just wait!"

"I'll stay here with him, Aahz," Tanda volunteered.

"Good," Aahz nodded. "And try to keep him out of trouble, okay?"

With that, he turned and disappeared into the crowd. Actually, I wasn't too disappointed. I mean, I would have liked to have gone with him, but I liked having some time alone with Tanda even more . . . that is, if you can consider standing in the middle of the Bazaar at Deva being alone with someone.

"Well, Tanda," I said, flashing my brightest smile.

"Later, handsome," she replied briskly. "Right now I've got some errands to run."

"Errands?" I blinked.

"Yeah. Aahz is big on manpower, but I'd just as

soon have a few extra tricks up my sleeve in case the going gets rough," she explained. "I'm going to duck over to the special effects section and see what they have in stock."

"Okay," I agreed. "Let's go."

"No, you don't," she said, shaking her head. "I think I'd better go this one alone. The kind of places I have in mind aren't fit for civilized customers. You and the dragon wait here."

"But you're supposed to be keeping me out of trouble!" I argued.

"And that's why I'm not taking you along," she said, smiling. "Now, what do you have along in the way of weaponry?"

"Well . . ." I said hesitantly, "there's a sort of a sword in one of Gleep's packs."

"Fine!" she said. "Get it out and wear it. It'll keep the riffraff at a distance. Then . . . um . . . wait for me in there!"

She pointed at a strange-looking stone structure with a peeling sign on its front.

"What is it?" I asked, peering at it suspiciously.

"It's a 'Yellow Crescent Inn,' " she explained. "It's sort of a restaurant. Get yourself something to eat. The food's unappetizing, but vaguely digestible."

I studied the place for a moment.

"Actually," I decided finally, "I think I'd rather . . ."

Right about there I discovered I was talking to myself. Tanda had disappeared without a trace.

For the second time in my life I was alone in the Bazaar at Deva.

Chapter Thirteen:

"Hold the pickles, hold the lettuce."
—HENRY VIII

FASCINATING as the Bazaar is, facing it alone can be rather frightening.

Being particularly susceptible to fear, I decided to follow Tanda's advice and entered the inn.

First, however, I took the precaution of tethering Gleep to the inn's hitching post and unpacking the sword. We had one decent sword. Unfortunately, Aahz was currently wearing it. That left me with Garkin's old sword, a weapon which has been sneered at by demon and demon-hunter alike. Still, its weight was reassuring on my hip, though it might have been more reassuring if I had known anything about how to handle it. Unfortunately, my lessons with Aahz to date had not included swordsmanship. I could only hope it would not be apparent to the casual observer that this was my first time to wear a sword.

Pausing in the door, I surveyed the inn's interior. Unaccustomed as I was to gracious dining, I realized in a flash that this wasn't it.

One of the few pieces of advice my farmer father had given me before I ran away from home was not to trust any inn or restaurant that appeared overly clean. He maintained the cleaner a place was, the more dubious the quality and origin of their food would be. If he were even vaguely right, this inn must be the bottom of the barrel. It was not only clean, it gleamed.

I do not mean that figuratively. Harsh overhead lights glinted off a haphazard arrangement of tiny tables and uncomfortable-looking chairs constructed of shiny metal and a hard white substance I didn't recognize. At the far end of the inn was a counter behind which stood a large stone gargoyle, the only decorative feature in the place. Behind the gargoyle was a door, presumably leading into the kitchen. There was a small window in the door through which I caught glimpses of the food being prepared. Preparation consisted of passing patties of meat over a stove, cramming them into a split roll, slopping a variety of colored pastes on top of the meat, and wrapping the whole mess in a piece of paper.

Watching this process confirmed my earlier fears. I do all the cooking for Aahz and myself, as I did before that for Garkin and myself, and before that just for myself. While I have no delusions as to the high quality of my cooking, I do know that what they were doing to that meat could only yield a meal the consistency and flavor of charred glove leather.

Despite the obvious low quality of the food, the inn seemed nearly full of customers. I noticed this out of the corner of my eye. I also noticed that a high percentage of them were staring at me. It occurred to me that this was probably because I had been stand-

ing in the door for some time without entering while
working up my courage to go in.

Feeling slightly embarrassed, I stepped inside and
let the door swing shut behind me. With fiendish accuracy, the door closed on my sword, pinning it
momentarily and forcing me to break stride clumsily
as I started forward. So much for my image as a
swordsman.

Humiliated, I avoided looking at the other customers and made my way hurriedly to the inn's
counter. I wasn't sure what I was going to do once I
got there, since I didn't trust the food, but hopefully
people would stop staring at me if I went through the
motions of ordering.

Still trying to avoid eye contact with anyone, I
made a big show of studying the gargoyle. There was
a grinding noise, and the statue turned its head to
return my stare. If wasn't a statue! They really had a
gargoyle tending the counter!

The gargoyle seemed to be made of coarse gray
stone, and when he flexed his wings, small pieces of
crushed rock and dust showered silently to the floor.
His hands were taloned, and there were curved spikes
growing out of his elbows. The only redeeming feature I could see was his smile, which in itself was a bit
unnerving. Dominating his wrinkled face, the smile
seemed permanently etched in place, stretching well
past his ears and displaying a set of pointed teeth
even longer than Aahz's.

"Take your order?" the gargoyle asked politely,
the smile never twitching.

"Um . . ." I said taking a step back. "I'll have to
think about it. There's so much to choose from."

In actuality I couldn't read the menu . . . if that's
what it was. There was something etched in the wall

behind the gargoyle in a language I couldn't decipher. I assume it was a menu because the prices weren't etched in the wall, but written in chalk over many erasures.

The gargoyle shrugged.

"Suit yourself," he said indifferently. "When you make up your mind, just holler. The name's Gus."

"I'll do that . . . Gus," I smiled, backing slowly toward the door.

Though it was my intent to exit quietly and wait outside with Gleep, things didn't work out that way. Before I had taken four steps, a hand fell on my shoulder.

"Skeeve, isn't it?" a voice proclaimed.

I spun around, or started to. I was brought up short when my sword banged into a table leg. My head kept moving, however, and I found myself face to face with an Imp.

"Brockhurst!" I exclaimed, recognizing him immediately.

"I thought I recognized you when you . . . *hey!*" The Imp took a step backward and raised his hands defensively. "Take it easy! I'm not looking for any trouble."

My hand had gone to my sword hilt in an involuntary effort to free it from the table leg. Apparently Brockhurst had interpreted the gesture as an effort to draw my weapon.

That was fine by me. Brockhurst had been one of Isstvan's lieutenants, and we hadn't parted on the best of terms. Having him a little afraid of my "ready sword" was probably a good thing.

"I don't hold any grudges," Brockhurst continued insistently. "That was just a job! Right now I'm between jobs . . . permanently!"

That last was added with a note of bitterness which piqued my curiosity.

"Things haven't been going well?" I asked cautiously.

The Imp grimaced.

"That's an understatement. Come on, sit down. I'll buy you a milkshake and tell you all about it."

I wasn't certain what a milkshake was, but I was sure I didn't want one if they were sold here.

"Um . . . thanks anyway, Brockhurst," I said, forcing a smile, "but I think I'll pass."

The Imp arched an eyebrow at me.

"Still a little suspicious, eh?" he murmured. "Well, can't say as I blame you. Tell you what we'll do."

Before I could stop him, he strolled to the counter.

"Hey, Gus!" he called. "Mind if I take an extra cup?"

"Actually . . ." the gargoyle began.

"Thanks!"

Brockhurst was already on his way back, bearing his prize with him, some kind of a thin-sided, flimsy cannister. Plopping down at a nearby table, he beckoned to me, indicating the seat opposite him with a wave of his hand.

There was no gracious course for me to follow other than to join him, though it would later occur to me I had no real obligation to be gracious. Moving carefully to avoid knocking anything over with my sword, I maneuvered my way to the indicated seat.

Apparently, Brockhurst had been sitting here before, as there was already a cannister on the table identical to the one he had fetched from the counter. The only difference was that the one on the table was three-quarters full of a curious pink liquid.

With great ceremony, the Imp picked up the can-nister from the table and poured half its contents into the new vessel. The liquid poured with the consistency of swamp muck.

"Here!" he said, pushing one of the cannisters across the table to me. "Now you don't have to worry about any funny business with the drinks. We're both drinking the same thing."

With that, he raised his vessel in a mock toast and took a healthy swallow from it. Apparently he expected me to do the same. I would have rather sucked blood.

"Um . . . it's hard to believe things aren't going well for you," I stalled. "You look well enough."

For a change, I was actually sincere. Brockhurst looked good . . . even for an Imp. As Aahz had said, Imps are snappy dressers, and Brockhurst was no exception. He was outfitted in a rust-colored velvet jerkin trimmed in gold, which set off his pink complexion and sleek black hair superbly. If he were starving, you couldn't tell it from looking at him. Though still fairly slender, he was as well muscled and adroit as when I had first met him.

"Don't let appearances fool you," Brockhurst insisted, shaking his head. "You see before you an Imp pushed to the wall. I've had to sell everything—my crossbow, my pouch of magic tricks—I couldn't even raise enough money to pay my dues to the Assassins Guild."

"It's that hard to find work?" I sympathized.

"I'll tell you, Skeeve," he whispered confidentially, "I haven't worked since that fiasco with Isstvan."

The sound of that name still sent chills down my back.

"Where is Isstvan, anyway?" I asked casually.

"Don't worry about him," Brochkurst said grimly. "We left him working concession stands on the Isle of Coney, a couple of dimensions from here."

"What happened to the others?"

I was genuinely curious. I hadn't had much of a chance to talk with Tanda since our reunion.

"We left Frumple under a cloud of birds in some park or other . . . figured he looked better as a statue than he did alive. The demon hunter and the girl took off for parts unknown one night while we were asleep. My partner, Higgens, headed back to Imper. He figured his career was over and that he might as well settle down. Me, I've been looking for work ever since, and I'm starting to think Higgens was right."

"Come on, Brochkurst," I chided. "There must be something you can do. I mean, this is the Bazaar."

The Imp heaved a sigh and took another sip of his drink.

"It's nice of you to say that, Skeeve," he smiled. "But I've got to face the facts. There's not a big demand for Imps anyway, and none at all for an Imp with no powers."

I knew what he meant. All the dimension travelers I had met so far—Aahz, Isstvan, Tanda, and even the Deveel Frumple—seemed to regard Imps as inferior beings. The nicest thing I had heard said about them was that they were styleless imitators of the Deveels.

I felt sorry for him. Despite the fact we had first met as enemies, it wasn't that long ago I had been a loser nobody wanted.

"You've got to keep trying," I encouraged.

"Somewhere, there's someone who wants to hire you."

"Not very likely," the Imp grimaced. "The way I am now, *I* wouldn't hire me. Would you?"

"Sure I would," I insisted. "In a minute."

"Oh, well," he sighed. "I shouldn't dwell on myself. How have things been with you? What brings you to the Bazaar?"

Now it was my turn to grimace.

"Aahz and I are in a bad spot," I explained. "We're here trying to recruit a force to help us out."

"You're hiring people?" Brockhurst was suddenly intense.

"Yeah. Why?" I replied.

Too late, I realized what I was saying.

"Then you weren't kidding about hiring me!" Brockhurst was beside himself with glee.

"Um . . ." I said.

"This is great," the Imp chortled, rubbing his hands together. "Believe me, Skeeve, you won't regret this."

I was regretting it already.

"Wait a minute, Brockhurst," I interrupted desperately. "There are a few things you should know about the job."

"Like what?"

"Well . . . for one thing, the odds are bad," I said judiciously. "We're up against an army. That's pretty rough fare considering how low the pay is."

I thought I would touch a nerve with that remark about the pay. I was right.

"How low *is* the pay?" the Imp asked bluntly.

Now I was stuck. I didn't have the vaguest idea how much mercenaries were normally paid.

"We . . . um . . . we couldn't offer you more than

one gold piece for the whole job,'' I shrugged.

"Done!" Brockhurst proclaimed. "With the current state of my finances, I can't turn down an offer like that no matter how dangerous it is."

It occurred to me that sometime I should have Aahz give me a quick course in rates of exchange.

"Um . . . there's one other problem," I murmured thoughtfully.

"What's that?"

"Well, my partner, you remember Aahz?"

The Imp nodded.

"Well, he's out right now trying to hire a force, and he's got the money," I continued. "There's a good chance that if he's successful, and he usually is, there won't be enough money left to hire you."

Brockhurst pursed his lips for a moment, then shrugged.

"Well," he said, "I'll take the chance. I wasn't going anywhere anyway. As I said, they haven't exactly been beating my door down with job offers."

I had run out of excuses.

"Well"—I smiled lamely—"as long as you're aware—"

"Heads up, boss," the Imp's murmur interrupted me. "We've got company."

I'm not sure which worried me more, Brockhurst calling me "boss" or the specterlike character who had just stepped up to our table.

Chapter Fourteen:

"We're looking for a few good men."
—B. CASSIDY

FOR a moment I thought we were being confronted by a skeleton. Then I looked closer and realized there really *was* skin stretched over the bones, though its dusty-white color made it seem very dead indeed.

The figure's paleness was made even more corpse-like by the blue-black hooded robe that enshrouded it. It wasn't until I noted the wrinkled face with a short, bristly white beard that I realized our visitor was actually a very old man . . . very old.

He looked weak to the point of near collapse, desperately clutching a twisted black walking staff which seemed to be the only thing keeping him erect. Still, his eyes were bright and his smile confident as he stood regarding us.

"Did I hear you boys right?" he asked in a crackling voice.

"I beg your pardon?" Brockhurst scowled at him.

The ancient figure sneered and raised his voice.

"I said, 'Did I hear you boys right?'!" he barked.

"What's the matter? Are you deaf?"

"Um . . . excuse me," I interrupted hastily. "Before we can answer you, we have to know what you thought we said."

The old man thought for a minute, then bobbed his head in a sudden nod.

"You know, yer right!" he cackled. "Pretty smart, young fella."

He began to list, but caught himself before he fell.

"Thought I heard you tell Pinko here you were looking for a force to take on an army," he pronounced, jerking a thumb at Brockhurst.

"The name's Brockhurst, not Pinko!" the Imp snarled.

"All right, Bratwurst," the old man nodded. "No need to get your dander up."

"That's Brockhurst!"

"You heard right," I interrupted again, hoping the old man would go away as soon as his curiosity was satisfied.

"Good!" the man declared. "Count me in! Me and Blackie haven't been in a good fight for a long time."

"How long is that in centuries?" Brockhurst sneered.

"Watch your mouth, Bratwurst!" the old man warned. "We may be old, but we can still teach you a thing or two about winnin' wars."

"Who's Blackie?" I asked, cutting off Brockhurst's reply.

In reply, the old man drew himself erect . . . well, nearly erect, and patted his walking staff.

"This is Blackie!" he announced proudly. "The finest bow ever to come from Archiah, and that takes in a lot of fine bows!"

I realized with a start that the walking staff was a bow, unstrung, with its bowstring wrapped around it. It was unlike any bow I had ever seen, lumpy and uneven, but polished to a sheen that seemed to glimmer with a life all its own.

"Wait a minute!" Brockhurst was suddenly attentive. "Did you say you come from Archiah?"

"That I did," the old man grinned. "Ajax's the name, fighting's my game. Ain't seen a war yet that could lay old Ajax low, and I've seen a lot of 'em."

"Um . . . could you excuse us for just a minute, sir?" Brockhurst smiled apologetically.

"Sure, son," Ajax nodded. "Take your time."

I couldn't understand the Imp's sudden change in attitude, but he seemed quite intense as he jerked his head at me, so I leaned close to hear what he had to say.

"Hire him, boss!" he hissed in my ear.

"What?" I gasped, not believing I had heard him right.

"I said hire him!" the Imp repeated. "I may not have much to offer you, but I can give you advice. Right now, my advice is to hire him."

"But he's—"

"He's from Archiah!" Brockhurst interrupted. "Boss, that dimension *invented* archery. You don't find many genuine Archers of any age for hire. If you've really got a war on your hands, hire him. He could tip the balance for us."

"If he's that good," I whispered back, "can we afford him?"

"One gold piece will be adequate," Ajax smiled toothily, adding his head to our conference. "I accept your offer."

"Excellent!" Brockhurst beamed.

"Wait a minute," I shrieked desperately, "I have a partner that—"

"I know, I know," Ajax sighed, holding up a restraining hand. "I heard when you told Bratwurst here."

"That's Brockhurst," the Imp growled, but he did it smiling.

"If your partner can't find help, then we're hired!" the old man laughed, shaking his head. "It's a mite strange, but these are strange times."

"You can say that again," I muttered.

I was beginning to think I had spoken too loud in my conversation with Brockhurst.

"One thing you should know, though, youngster," Ajax murmured confidentially. "I'm bein' followed."

"By who?" I asked.

"Don't rightly know," he admitted. "Haven't figured it out yet. It's the little blue fella in the corner behind me."

I craned my neck to look at the indicated corner. It was empty.

"What fella? I mean, fellow," I corrected myself.

Ajax whipped his head around with a speed that belied his frail appearance.

"Dang it," he cursed. "He did it again. I'm telling you, youngster, that's why I can't figure what he's after!"

"Ah . . . sure, Ajax," I said soothingly. "You'll catch him next time."

Terrific. An Imp with no powers, and now an old Archer who sees things.

My thoughts were interrupted by a gentle tap on my shoulder. I turned to find the gargoyle looming over me.

"Your order's ready, sir," he said through his perma-smile.

"My order?"

"Yes, if you'll step this way."

"There must be some mistake," I began, "I didn't . . ."

The gargoyle was already gone, lumbering back to his counter. I considered ignoring him. Then I considered his size and countenance, and decided I should straighten out this misunderstanding in a polite fashion.

"Excuse me," I told my charges. "I'll be right back."

"Don't worry about us, boss," Brockhurst waved.

I wasn't reassured.

I managed to make my way to the counter without banging my sword against anything or anyone, a feat that raised my spirits for the first time that afternoon. Thus bolstered, I approached the gargoyle.

"I . . . um . . . I don't recall ordering anything," I stated politely.

"Don't blame you, either," the gargoyle growled through his smile. "Beats me how anyone or anything can eat the slop they serve here."

"But—"

"That was just to get you away from those two," the gargoyle shrugged. "You see, I'm shy."

"Shy about what?"

"About asking you for a job, of course!"

I decided I would definitely have to keep my voice down in the future. My quiet conversation with Brockhurst seemed to have attracted the attention of half the Bazaar.

"Look . . . um . . ."

"Gus!" the gargoyle supplied.

"Yes, well, ah, Gus, I'm really not hiring—"

"I know. Your partner is," Gus interrupted. "But you're here and he isn't, so I figured I'd make our pitch to you before the second team roster is completely filled."

"Oh!" I said, not knowing what else to say.

"The way I see it," the gargoyle continued, "we could do you a lot of good. You're a Klahd, aren't you?"

"I'm from Klah," I acknowledged stiffly.

"Well, if my memory serves me correctly, warfare in that dimension isn't too far advanced technologically."

"We have crossbows and catapults," I informed him. "At least the other side does."

"That's what I said," Gus agreed. "Primitive. To stop that force, all you need is air support and a little firepower. We can supply both, and we'll work cheap, both of us for one gold piece."

Now I was sure I had underestimated the market value of gold pieces. Still, the price was tempting.

"I dunno, Gus," I said cagily. "Ajax there is supposed to be a pretty good Archer."

"Archers," the gargoyle snorted. "I'm talking about *real* firepower. The kind my partner can give you."

"Who *is* your partner?" I asked. "He isn't short and blue by any chance, is he?"

"Naw," Gus replied, pointing to the far corner. "That's the Gremlin. He came in with the Archer."

"A Gremlin?" I said, following his finger.

Sure enough, perched on a chair in the corner was a small, elfish character. Mischievous eyes danced in his soft blue face as he nodded to me in silent recognition. Reflexively, I smiled and nodded back. Apparently I owed Ajax an apology.

"I thought Gremlins didn't exist," I commented casually to Gus.

"A lot of folks think that," the gargoyle agreed. "But you can see for yourself, they're real."

I wasn't sure. In the split second I had taken my eyes off the Gremlin to speak with Gus, he had vanished without a trace. I was tempted to go looking for him, but Gus was talking again.

"Just a second and I'll introduce you to my partner," he was saying. "He's here somewhere."

As he spoke, the gargoyle began rummaging about his own body, feeling his armpits and peering into the wrinkles on his skin.

I watched curiously, until my attention was arrested by a small lizard that had crawled out of one of the gargoyle's wing folds and was now regarding me fixedly from Gus's right shoulder. It was only about three inches long, but glowed with a brilliant orange hue. There were blotchy red patterns which seemed to crawl about the lizard's skin with a life of their own. The overall effect was startlingly beautiful.

"Is that your lizard?" I asked.

"There he is!" Gus crowed triumphantly, snatching the reptile from his shoulder and cupping it in his hands. "Meet Berfert. He's the partner I was telling you about."

"Hello, Berfert," I smiled, extending a finger to stroke him.

The gargoyle reacted violently, jerking the lizard back out of my reach.

"Careful, there," he warned. "That's a good way to lose a finger."

"I wasn't going to hurt him," I explained.

"No, he was about to hurt you!" Gus countered. "Berfert's a salamander, a walking firebomb. We get along because I'm one of the few beings around that won't burn to a crisp when I touch him."

"Oh," I said with sudden understanding. "So when you said 'firepower'—"

"I meant *firepower*," Gus finished. "Berfert cleans 'em out on the ground, and I work 'em over from the air. Well, what do you say? Have we got a deal?"

"I'll . . . um . . . have to talk it over with my partner," I countered.

"Fine," Gus beamed. "I'll start packing."

He was gone before I could stop him.

I sagged against the counter, wishing fervently for Aahz's return. As if in answer to my thoughts, my mentor burst through the door, following closely by Tanda.

My greeting died in my throat when I saw his scowl. Aahz was not in a good mood.

"I thought I told you to wait outside," he bellowed at me.

"Calm down, Aahz," Tanda soothed. "I thought he'd be more comfortable waiting in here. Besides, there's no reason to get upset. We're here and he's here. Nothing has gone wrong."

"You haven't been dealing with any Deveels?" Aahz asked suspiciously.

"I haven't even talked with any," I protested.

"Good!" he retorted, slightly mollified. "There's hope for you yet, kid."

"I told you he could stay out of trouble," Tanda smiled triumphantly. "Isn't that right, handsome?"

Try as I might, I couldn't bring myself to answer her.

Chapter Fifteen:

"I'll worry about it tomorrow."
—S. O'HARA

"UM . . . are the mercenaries waiting outside?" I asked finally.

"You didn't answer her question, kid," Aahz observed, peering at me with renewed suspicion.

"Don't strain your neck looking for your troops, handsome," Tanda advised me. "There weren't any. It seems our mighty negotiator has met his match."

"Those bandits!" Aahz exploded. "Do you have any idea what it would cost us if I had agreed to pay their bar bill as part of the contract? If that's a non-profit group, I want to audit their books."

My hopes for salvation sank like a rock.

"You didn't hire them?" I asked.

"No, I didn't," Aahz scowled. "And that moves us back to square one. Now we've got to recruit a force one at a time."

"Did you try—" I began.

"Look, kid," Aahz interrupted with a snarl, "I

did the best I could, and I got nowhere. I'd like to see you do better.''

"He already has!" Brockhurst announced, rising from his seat. "While you were wasting time, Skeeve here has hired himself a fighting team."

"He what?" Aahz bellowed, turning on his critic. "Brockhurst! What are you doing here?"

"Waiting for orders in our upcoming campaign," the Imp replied innocently.

"What campaign?" Aahz glowered.

"The one on Klah, of course," Brockhurst blinked. "Haven't you told him yet, boss?"

"Boss?" Aahz roared. "Boss?"

"No need ta shout," Ajax grumbled, turning to face the assemblage. "We hear ya plain enough."

"Ajax!" Tanda exclaimed gleefully.

"Tanda!" the old man yelped back.

She was at him in a bound, but he smoothly interposed his bow between them.

"Easy, girl," he laughed. "None of your athletic greetings. I'm not as young as I used to be, ya know."

"You old fraud!" Tanda teased. "You'll outlive us all."

Ajax shrugged dramatically. "That kinda depends on how good a general the youngster there is," he commented.

"Kid," Aahz growled through gritted teeth, "I want to talk to you! *Now!*"

"I know that temper!" Gus announced, emerging from the back room.

"Gus!" Aahz exclaimed.

"In the stone!" the gargoyle confirmed. "Are you in on this expedition? The boss didn't say anything about working with Perverts."

Instead of replying, Aahz sank heavily into a chair and hid his face in his hands.

"Tanda!" he moaned. "Tell me again about how this kid can stay out of trouble."

"Um . . . Aahz," I said cautiously, "could I talk to you for a minute . . . privately?"

"Why, I think that's an excellent idea . . . boss," he said.

The smile he gave me wasn't pleasant.

"Kid!" Aahz moaned after I had finished my tale. "How many times do I have to tell you? This is the Bazaar at Deva! You've *got* to be careful what you say and to whom, especially when there's money involved."

"But I told them nothing was definite until we found out if you had hired someone else," I protested.

"But I didn't hire anyone else, so now the deal is final," Aahz sighed.

"Can't we get out of it?" I asked hopefully.

"Back out of a deal on Deva?" Aahz shook his head. "That would get us barred from the Bazaar so fast it would make your head spin. Remember, the Merchants Association runs this dimension."

"Well, you said you wanted outside help," I pointed out.

"I didn't expect to go that far outside," he grimaced. "An Imp, a senile Archer, and a gargoyle."

"And a salamander," I added.

"Gus is still bumming around with Berfert?" Aahz asked, brightening slightly. "That's a plus."

"The only really uncertain factor," I said thoughtfully, "is the Gremlin."

"How do you figure that?" Aahz yawned.

"Well, he's been following Ajax. The question is, why? And will he follow us to Klah?"

"Kid," Aahz said solemnly, "I've told you before. There are no such things as Gremlins."

"But Aahz, I saw him."

"Don't let it bother you, kid," Aahz sympathized. "After a day like you've been through, I wouldn't be surprised if you saw a Jabberwocky."

"What's a—"

"Is everything set?" Tanda asked, joining our conversation.

"About as set as we'll ever be," Aahz sighed. "Though if you want my honest opinion, with a crew like this, we're set more for a zoo than a war."

"Aahz is a bit critical of my choice in recruits," I confided.

"What's your gripe, Aahz?" she asked, cocking her head. "I thought you and Gus were old foxhole buddies."

"I'm not worried about Gus," Aahz put in hastily. "Or Berfert either. That little lizard's terrific under fire."

"Well, I can vouch for Ajax," Tanda informed him. "Don't let his age fool you. I'd rather have him backing my move than a whole company of counterfeit archers."

"Is he really from Archiah?" Aahz asked skeptically.

"That's what he's said as long as I've known him," Tanda shrugged. "And after seeing him shoot, I've got no reason to doubt it. Why?"

"I've never met a genuine Archer before," Aahz said. "For a while I was willing to believe the whole dimension was a legend. Well, if he can shoot half as well as Archers are supposed to, I've got no gripes having him on the team."

I started to feel a little better. Unfortunately, Aahz noticed my smile.

"The Imp is another story," he said grimly. "I'm not wild about working with any Imp, but to hire one without powers is a waste of good money."

"Don't forget he's an Assassin," Tanda pointed out. "Powers or no powers, I'll bet we find a use for him. When we were talking with the Gremlin just now—"

"Now don't *you* start on that!" Aahz snarled.

"Start on what?" Tanda blinked.

"The Gremlin bit," Aahz scowled. "Any half-wit knows there are no such things as Gremlins."

"Do you want to tell him that?" Tanda smiled. "I'll call him over here and . . . oh, rats! He's gone again."

"If you're quite through," Aahz grumbled, rising from his chair, "we'd best get moving. There's a war waiting for us, you know."

"Oops! That reminds me!" Tanda exclaimed, fishing inside her tunic.

"I know I shouldn't ask," Aahz signed, "but what—"

"Here!" Tanda announced, flipping him a familiar object.

It was a metal rod about eight inches long and two inches in diameter with a button on one end of it.

"A D-Hopper!" I cried, recognizing the device instantly.

"It's the same one you gave Isstvan," Tanda smiled proudly. "I lifted it from him when we parted company. You'll probably want to undo whatever you did to the controls before you use it, though.''

"If I can remember for sure," Aahz scowled, staring at the device.

"I thought it might come in handy in case we get separated on this job and you need a fast exit," Tanda shrugged.

"The thought's appreciated," Aahz smiled, putting an arm around her.

"Does this mean you'll be able to teach me how to travel the dimensions?" I asked hopefully.

"Not now I won't," Aahz grimaced. "We've got a war to fight, remember?"

"Oh! Yes, of course."

"Well, get your troops together and let's go," Aahz ordered.

"Okay," I agreed, rising from my chair. "I'll get Gleep and . . . wait a minute! Did you say *my* troops?"

"You hired 'em, you lead 'em," my mentor smiled.

"But you're—"

"I'll be your military advisor, of course," Aahz continued casually. "But the job of Fearless Leader is all yours. You're the court magician, remember?"

I swallowed hard. Somehow this had never entered into my thinking.

"But what do I do?" I asked desperately.

"Well," Aahz drawled. "First, I'd advise you to move 'em outside so we can all head for Klah together . . . that is, unless you're willing to leave your dragon behind."

That didn't even deserve an answer. I turned to face the troops, sweeping them with what I hoped was a masterful gaze which would immediately command their attention.

No one noticed. They were all involved in a jovial conversation.

I cleared my throat noisily.

Nothing.

I considered going over to their table.

"Listen up!" Aahz barked suddenly, scaring me half to death.

The conversation stopped abruptly and all heads swiveled my way.

"Aah . . ." I began confidently. "We're ready to go now. Everybody outside. Wait for me by the dragon."

"Right, boss!" Brockhurst called, starting for the door.

"I'll be a minute, youngster," Ajax wheezed, struggling to rise.

"Here, Gramps," Gus said. "Let me give you a hand."

"Name's not Gramps, it's Ajax!" the Archer scowled.

"Just trying to be helpful," the gargoyle apologized.

"I kin' stand up by myself," Ajax insisted. "Just 'cause I'm old don't mean I'm helpless."

I glanced to Aahz for help, but he and Tanda were already headed out.

As I turned back to Ajax, I thought I caught a glimpse of a small, blue figure slipping out through the door ahead of us. If it was the Gremlin, he was nowhere in sight when I finally reached the street.

Chapter Sixteen:

"Myth-conceptions are the major cause of wars!"

—A. HITLER

FORTUNATELY, the army had not moved from the position it held when we left for Deva. I say fortunately because Aahz pointed out they might well have renewed their advance in our absence. If that had happened, we would have returned to find ourselves behind the enemy lines, if not actually in the middle of one of their encampments.

Of course, he pointed this out to me after we had arrived back on Klah. Aahz is full of helpful little tidbits of information, but his timing leaves a lot to be desired.

Ajax lost no time upon our arrival. Moving with a briskness that belied his years, he strung his bow and stood squinting at the distant encampments.

"Well, youngster," he asked, never taking his eyes from the enemy's formations, "what's my first batch of targets?"

His eagerness took me aback a bit, but Aahz covered for me neatly.

"First," he said loftily, "we'll have to hold a final planning session."

"We didn't expect to have you along, Ajax," Tanda added. "Having a genuine Archer on our side naturally calls for some drastic revisions of our battle plans."

"Don't bother me none," Ajax shrugged. "Just wanted ta let you know I was ready to earn my keep. Take yer time. Seen too many wars messed up 'cause nobody bothered to do any plannin'! If ya don't mind, though, think I'll take me a little nap. Jes' holler when ya want some shootin' done."

"Ah . . . go ahead, Ajax," I agreed.

Without further conversation, Ajax plopped down and pulled his cloak a bit closer about him. Within a few minutes, he was snoring lightly, but I noticed his bow was still in his grip.

"Now there's a seasoned soldier," Aahz observed. "Gets his sleep when and where he can."

"You want me to do a little scouting, boss?" Gus asked.

"Um . . ." I hesitated, glancing quickly at Aahz.

Aahz caught my look and gave a small nod.

"Sure, Gus," I finished. "We'll wait for you here."

"I'll scout in the other direction," Brockhurst volunteered.

"Okay," I nodded. "Aahz, can you give 'em a quick briefing?"

I was trying to drop the load in Aahz's lap, but he joined the conversation as smoothly as if we had rehearsed it this way.

"There are a couple of things we need specific information on," he said solemnly. "First, we need a battlefield, small with scattered cover. Gus, you check that out. You know what we're going to need. Brockhurst, see what details you can bring back on the three nearest encampments."

Both scouts nodded briskly.

"And both of you, stay out of sight," Aahz warned. "The information's no good to us if you don't come back."

"C'mon, Aahz," Gus admonished. "What have they got that can put a dent in the old rock?"

He demonstrated by smashing his forearm into a sapling. The tree went down, apparently without affecting the gargoyle's arm in the slightest.

"I don't know," Aahz admitted. "And I don't want to know, yet. You're one of our surprise weapons. No point in giving the enemy an advance warning. Get my meaning?"

"Got it, Aahz," Gus nodded, and lumbered off.

"Be back in a bit," Brockhurst said with a wave of his hand, heading off in the opposite direction.

"Now that we've got a minute," I murmured to Aahz as I returned Brockhurst's wave, "would you mind telling me what our final plan is? I don't even know what the preliminary plans were."

"That's easy," Aahz replied. "We don't have one . . . yet."

"Well, when are we going to form one?" I asked with forced patience.

"Probably on the battlefield," Aahz yawned. "Until then it's pointless. There're too many variables until then."

"Wouldn't it be a good idea to have at least a

general idea as to what we're going to do *before* we wander out on the battlefield?" I insisted. "It would do a lot for my peace of mind."

"Oh, I've already got a general idea as to what we'll be doing," Aahz admitted.

"Isn't he sweet?" Tanda grimaced. "Would you mind sharing it with us, Aahz? We've got a stake in this, too."

"Well," he began lazily, "the name of the game is delay and demoralize. The way I figure it, we aren't going to overpower them. We haven't got enough going for us to even try that."

I bit back a sarcastic observation and let him continue.

"Delay and demoralize we should be able to do, though," Aahz smiled. "Right off the bat, we've got two big weapons going for us in that kind of a fight."

"Ajax and Gus," I supplied helpfully.

"Fear and bureaucracy," Aahz corrected.

"How's that again?" Tanda frowned.

"Tanda, my girl," Aahz smiled, "you've been spoiled by your skylarking through the dimensions. You've forgotten how the man on the street thinks. The average person in any dimension doesn't know the first thing about magik, particularly about its limitations. If the kid here tells 'em he can make the sun stop or trees grow upside down, they'll believe him. Particularly if he's got a few strange characters parading around as proof of his power, and I think you'll have to admit, the crew he's got backing him this time around is pretty strange."

"What's bureaucracy?" I asked, finally getting a word in edgewise.

"Red tape . . . the system," Aahz informed me.

"The organization to get things done that keeps
things from getting done. In this case, it's called the
chain-of-command. An army the size of the one
we're facing has to function like a well-oiled machine
or it starts tripping over its own feet. I'm betting if
we toss a couple of handfuls of sand into its gears,
they'll spend more time fighting each other than
chasing us."

This was one of the first times Aahz had actually
clarified something he said. I wished he hadn't. I was
more confused than I had been before.

"Um . . . how are we going to do all this?" I
asked.

"We'll be able to tell better after you've had your
first war council," Aahz shrugged.

"Aren't we having it now?"

"I meant with the enemy," Aahz scowled. "Sometime in the near future, you're going to have to sit
down with one of their officers and decide how this
war's going to be fought."

"Me?" I blinked.

"You *are* the leader of the defenses, remember?"
Aahz grinned at me.

"It's part of the job, handsome," Tanda confirmed.

"Wait a minute," I interrupted. "It just came to
me. I think I have a better idea."

"This I've got to hear," Aahz grinned.

"Shut up, Aahz," Tanda ordered, poking him in
the ribs. "Whatcha got, handsome?"

"We've got a couple of trained Assassins on our
side, don't we?" I observed. "Why don't we just put
'em to work? If enough officers suddenly turn up
dead, odds are the army will fall apart. Right?"

"It won't work, kid," Aahz announced bluntly.

"Why not?"

"We can bend the rules, but we can't break 'em," Aahz explained. "Wars are fought between the troops. Killing off the officers without engaging their troops goes against tradition. I doubt if your own force would stand still for it. Old troopers like Ajax would have no part of a scheme like that."

"He's right," Tanda confirmed. "Assassins take contracts on individuals in personal feuds, but not against the general staff of an army."

"But it would be so easy," I insisted.

"Look at it this way, kid," Aahz put in. "If you could do it, they could do it. The way things are now, you're exempt from Assassins. Would you really want to change that?"

"What do I say in a war council?" I asked.

"I'll brief you on that when the time comes," Aahz reassured me. "Right now we have other things to plan."

"Such as what?" Tanda asked.

"Such as what to do about those signal towers," Aahz retorted, jerking his head at one of the distant structures.

"We probably won't have time to break their code, so the next best thing is to disrupt their signals somehow. Now, you said you picked up some special effects items back at the Bazaar. Have you got anything we could use on the signal towers?"

"I'm not sure," Tanda frowned thoughtfully. "I wish you had said something about that before I went shopping."

"What about Ajax?" I suggested.

"What about him?" Aahz countered.

"How close would he have to be to the towers to disrupt things with his archery?"

"I don't know," Aahz shrugged. "Why don't you ask him."

Eager to follow up on my own suggestion, I squatted down next to the dozing bowman.

"Um . . . Ajax," I called softly.

"Whatcha need, youngster?" the old man asked, coming instantly awake.

"Do you see those signal towers?" I asked, pointing at the distant structures.

Ajax rose to his feet and squinted in the indicated direction. "Sure can," he nodded.

"We . . . um . . . I was wondering," I explained, "can you use your bow to disrupt their signals?"

In response, Ajax drew an arrow from beneath his cloak, cocked it, and let fly before I could stop him.

The shaft disappeared in the direction of the nearest tower. With sinking heart, I strained my eyes trying to track its flight.

There was a man standing on the tower's platform, his standard leaning against the railing beside him. Suddenly, his standard toppled over, apparently breaking off a handspan from its crosspiece. The man bent and retrieved the bottom portion of the pole, staring with apparent confusion at the broken end.

"Any other targets?" Ajax asked.

He was leaning casually on his bow, his back to the tower. He hadn't even bothered watching to see if his missile struck its mark.

"Um . . . not just now, Ajax," I assured him. "Go back to sleep."

"Fine by me, sonny," Ajax smiled, resettling himself. "There'll be plenty of targets tomorrow."

"How do you figure that?" I asked.

"According to that signal I just cut down," he grinned, "the army's fixin' to move out tomorrow."

"You can read the signals?" I blinked.

"Sure," Ajax nodded. "There're only about eight different codes armies use, and I know 'em all. It's part of my trade."

"And they're moving out tomorrow?" I pressed.

"That's what I said." The bowman scowled. "What's the matter, are you deaf?"

"No," I assured him hastily. "It just changes our plans is all. Go back to sleep."

Returning to our little conference, I found Aahz and Tanda engrossed in a conversation with Brockhurst.

"Bad news, kid," Aahz informed me. "Brockhurst here says the army's going to move out tomorrow."

"I know," I said. "I just found out from Ajax. Can you read the signal flags too, Brockhurst?"

"Naw," the Imp admitted. "But the Gremlin can."

"What Gremlin?" Aahz bared his teeth.

"He was here a minute ago," Brockhurst scowled, looking around.

"Well, handsome," Tanda sighed, eyeing me, "I think we just ran out of planning time. Better call your dragon. I think we're going to need all the help we can get tomorrow."

Gleep had wandered off shortly after our arrival, though we could still hear him occasionally as he poked about in the underbrush.

"You go get the dragon, Tanda," Aahz ordered.

"Though it escapes me how he's supposed to be any help. The 'boss' here and I have to discuss his war council tomorrow."

Any confidence I might have built up listening to Aahz's grand plan earlier fled me. Tanda was right. We had run out of time.

Chapter Seventeen:

"Diplomacy is the delicate weapon of the civilized warrior."

—HUN, A.T.

WE waited patiently for our war council. The two of us, Aahz and me. Against an army.

This was, of course, Aahz's idea. Left to my own devices, I wouldn't be caught dead in this position.

Trying to ignore that unfortunate choice of words, I cleared my throat and spoke to Aahz out of the corner of my mouth.

"Aahz?"

"Yeah, kid?"

"How long are we going to stand here?"

"Until they notice us and do something about it."

Terrific. Either we'd rot where we stood, or someone would shoot us full of arrows.

We were standing about twenty yards from one of the encampments, with nothing between us and them but meadow. We could see clearly the bustle of activity within the encampment and, in theory, there was nothing keeping them from seeing us. This is why we were standing where we were, to draw attention to ourselves. Unfortunately, so far no one had noticed.

It had been decided that Aahz and I would work alone on this first sortie to hide the true strength of our force. It occurred to me that it also hid the true weakness of our force, but I felt it would be tactless to point this out.

At first, Brockhurst had argued in favor of his coming along with me instead of Aahz, claiming that as an Imp he had much more experience at bargaining than a demon. It was pointed out to him rather forcefully by Aahz that in this instance we weren't bargaining for glass beads or whoopie cushions, but for a war . . . and if the Imp wanted to prove to Aahz that he knew more about fighting. . . .

Needless to say, Brockhurst backed down at that point. This was good, as it saved me from having to openly reject his offer. I mean, I may not be the fastest learner around, but I could still distinctly remember Aahz getting the best of Brockhurst the last time the two of them had squared off for a bargaining session.

Besides, if this meeting went awry, I wanted my mentor close at hand to share the consequences with me.

So here we stood, blatantly exposed to the enemy without even a sword for our defense. That was another of Aahz's brainstorms. He argued that our being unarmed accomplished three things. First, it showed that we were here to talk, not to fight. Second, it demonstrated our faith in my magical abilities to defend us. Third, it encouraged our enemy to meet us similarly unarmed.

He also pointed out that Ajax would be hiding in

the tree line behind us with strung bow and cocked arrow, and would probably be better at defending us if anything went wrong than a couple of swords would.

He was right, of course, but it did nothing to settle my nerves as we waited.

"Heads up, kid," Aahz murmured. "We've got company."

Sure enough, a rather stocky individual was striding briskly across the meadow in our direction.

"Kid!" Aahz hissed suddenly. "Your disguise!"

"What about it?" I whispered back.

"It isn't!" came the reply.

He was right! I had carefully restored his "dubious character" appearance, but had forgotten completely about changing my own. Having our motley crew accept my leadership in my normal form had caused me to overlook the fact that Klahds are harder to impress than demons.

"Should I—" I began.

"Too late!" Aahz growled. "Fake it."

The soldier was almost upon us now, close enough for me to notice when he abandoned his bored expression and forced a smile.

"I'm sorry, folks," he called with practiced authority. "You'll have to clear the area. We'll be moving soon and you're blocking the path."

"Call your duty officer!" Aahz boomed back at him.

"My who?" the soldier scowled.

"Duty officer, officer of the day, commander, whatever you call whoever's currently in charge of your formation," Aahz clarified. "Somebody's got to be running things, and if you're officer material, I'm the Queen of the May."

Whether or not the soldier understood Aahz's allusion (I didn't), he caught the general implication.

"Yeah, there's someone in charge," he snarled, his complexion darkening slightly. "He's a very busy man right now, too busy to stand around talking to civilians. We're getting ready to move our troops, mister, so take your son and get out of the way. If you want to watch the soldiers, you'll have to follow along and watch us when we camp tonight."

"Do you have any idea who you're talking to?" I said in a surprisingly soft voice.

"I don't care who your father is, sonny," the soldier retorted. "We're trying to—"

"The name's not 'sonny,' it's *Skeeve!*" I hissed, drawing myself up. "Court magician to the kingdom of Possiltum, pledged to that kingdom's defense. Now I advise you to call your officer . . . or do you want to wake up tomorrow morning on a lily pad?"

The soldier recoiled a step and stood regarding me suspiciously.

"Is he for real?" he asked Aahz skeptically.

"How's your taste for flies?" Aahz smiled.

"You mean he can really—"

"Look," interrupted Aahz, "I'm not playing servant to the kid because of his terrific personality, if you know what I mean."

"I see . . . um. . . ." The soldier was cautiously backing toward the encampment. "I'll . . . um . . . I'll bring my commanding officer."

"We'll be here," Aahz assured him.

The soldier nodded and retreated with noticeably greater speed than he had displayed approaching us.

"So far, so good," my mentor said with a grin.

"What's wrong with my personality?" I asked bluntly.

Aahz sighed. "Later, kid. For the time being, concentrate on looking aloof and dignified, okay?"

Okay or not, there wasn't much else to do while we waited for the officer to put in his appearance.

Apparently, news of our presence spread through the encampment in record time, for a crowd of soldiers gathered at the edge of the camp long before we saw any sign of the officer. It seemed all preparations to move were suspended at least temporarily while the soldiers lined up and craned their necks to gawk at us.

It was kind of a nice feeling to have caused such a sensation, until I noticed several soldiers were taking time to strap on weapons and armor before joining the crowd.

"Aahz!" I whispered.

"Yeah, kid?"

"I thought this was supposed to be a peaceful meeting."

"It is," he assured me.

"But they're arming!" I pointed out.

"Relax, kid," he whispered back. "Remember, Ajax is covering us."

I tried to focus on that thought. Then I saw what was apparently the officer approaching us flanked by two soldiers, and I focused on the swords they were all wearing.

"Aahz!" I hissed.

"Relax, kid," Aahz advised me. "Remember Ajax."

I remembered. I also remembered we were vastly outnumbered.

"I understand you gentlemen are emissaries of Possiltum?" the officer asked, coming to a halt in front of us.

I nodded stiffly, hoping the abruptness of my motion would be interpreted as annoyance rather than fear.

"Fine," the officer smirked. "Then as the first representative of the Empire to contact a representative of Possiltum, I have the pleasure of formally declaring war on your kingdom."

"What is your name?" Aahz asked casually.

"Claude," the officer responded. "Why do you ask?"

"The historians like details," Aahz shrugged. "Well, Claude, as the first representative of Possiltum to meet with a representative of your Empire in times of war, it is our pleasure to demand your unconditional surrender."

That got a smile out of the officer.

"Surrender?" he chortled. "To a cripple and a child? You must be mad. Even if I had the authority to do such a thing, I wouldn't."

"That's right." Aahz shook his head in mock self-admonishment. "We should have realized. Someone in charge of a supply company wouldn't swing much weight in an army like this, would he?"

We had chosen this particular group of soldiers to approach specifically because they were a supply unit. That meant they were lightly armed and hopefully not an elite fighting group.

Aahz's barb struck home, however. The officer stopped smiling and dropped his hand to his sword hilt. I found myself thinking again of Ajax's protection.

"I have more than enough authority to deal with you two," he hissed.

"Authority, maybe," I yawned. "But I frankly doubt you have the power to stand against us."

As I mentioned, I did not feel as confident as I sounded. The officer's honor guard had mimicked his action, so that now all three of our adversaries were standing ready to draw their swords.

"Very well," Claude snarled. "You've been warned. Now we're going to bring our wagons across this spot, and if you're on it when we get here you've no one to blame but yourselves."

"Accepted!" Aahz leered. "Shall we say noon tomorrow?"

"Tomorrow?" the officer scowled. "What's wrong with right now?"

"Come, come, Claude," Aahz admonished. "We're talking about the first engagement of a new campaign. Surely you want some time to plan your tactics."

"Tactics?" Claude echoed thoughtfully.

". . . and to pass the word to your superiors that you're leading the opening gambit," Aahz continued casually.

"Hmm," the officer murmured.

". . . and to summon reinforcements," I supplied. "Unless, of course, you want to keep all the glory for yourself."

"Glory!"

That did it. Claude pounced on the word like a Deveel on a gold piece. Aahz had been right in assuming supply officers don't see combat often.

"I . . . uh . . . I don't believe we'll require reinforcements," he murmured cagily.

"Are you sure?" Aahz sneered. "The odds are only about a hundred to one in your favor."

"But he *is* a magician," Claude smiled. "A good officer can't be too careful. Still, it would be pointless to involve too many officers . : . er . . . I mean, soldiers in a minor skirmish.''

"Claude," Aahz said with grudging admiration, "I can see yours is a military mind without equal. Win or lose, I look forward to having you as an opponent."

"And you, sir," the officer returned with equal formality. "Shall we say noon then?"

"We'll be here," Aahz nodded.

With that, the officer turned and strode briskly back to his encampment, his bodyguard trudging dutifully beside him.

Our comrades were bristling with questions when we reentered the tree line.

"Is it set, boss?" Brockhurst asked.

"Any trouble?" Tanda pressed.

"Piece of cake," Aahz bragged. "Right, kid?"

"Well," I began modestly, "I was a little worried when they started to reach for their swords. I would have been terrified if I didn't know Ajax was . . . say, where is Ajax?"

"He's up in that clump of bushes," Gus informed me, jerking a massive thumb at a thicket of greenery on the edge of the tree line. "He should be back by now."

When we found Ajax, he was fast asleep curled around his bow. We had to shake him several times to wake him.

Chapter Eighteen:

"Just before the battle, Mother, I was thinking most of you . . . "

—SONNY BARKER

A LONG, slimy tongue assaulted me from the darkness, accompanied by a blast of bad breath which could have only one source.

"Gleep!"

I started to automatically cuff the dragon away, then had a sudden change of heart.

"Hi, fella," I smiled, scratching his ear. "Lonely?"

In response, my pet flopped on his side with a thud that shook the ground. His serpentine neck was long enough that he managed to perform this maneuver without moving his head from my grasp.

His loyal affection brought a smile to my face for the first time since I had taken up my lonely vigil. It was a welcome antidote to my nervous insomnia.

I was leaning against a tree, watching the pinpoints of light that marked the enemy's encampment. Even though the day's events had left me exhausted, I found myself unable to sleep, my mind awash with fears and anticipation of tomorrow's clash. Not wishing to draw attention to my discomfort, I had crept to this place to be alone.

As stealthy as I had attempted to be, however, apparently Gleep had noted my movement and come to keep me company.

"Oh, Gleep," I whispered. "What are we going to do?"

For his answer, he snuggled closer against me and laid his head in my lap for additional patting. He seemed to have unshakable faith in my ability to handle any crisis as it arose. I wished with all my heart I shared his confidence.

"Skeeve?" came a soft voice from my right.

I turned my head and found Tanda standing close beside me. The disquieting thing about having an Assassin for a friend is that they move so silently.

"Can I talk to you for a moment?"

"Sure, Tanda," I said, patting the ground next to me. "Have a seat."

Instead of sitting at the indicated spot, she sank to the ground where she stood and curled her legs up under her.

"It's about Ajax," she began hesitantly. "I hate to bother you, but I'm worried about him."

"What's wrong?" I asked.

"Well, the team's been riding him about falling asleep today when he was supposed to be covering you," she explained. "He's taking it pretty hard."

"I wasn't too wild about it myself," I commented bitterly. "It's a bad feeling to realize that we really were alone out there. If anything *had* gone wrong, we would have been cut to shreds while placidly waiting for our expert bowman to intercede!"

"I know." Tanda's voice was almost too soft to be heard. "And I don't blame you for feeling like that. In a way, I blame myself."

"Yourself?" I blinked. "Why?"

"I vouched for him, Skeeve," she whispered. "Don't you remember?"

"Well, sure," I admitted. "But you couldn't have known—"

"But I should have," she interrupted bitterly. "I should have realized how old he is now. He shouldn't be here, Skeeve. That's why I wanted to talk to you about doing something."

"Me?" I asked, genuinely startled. "What do you want me to do?"

"Send him back," Tanda urged. "It isn't fair to you to endanger your mission because of him, and it isn't fair to Ajax to put him in a spot like this."

"That isn't what I meant," I murmured, shaking my head. "I meant why are you talking to me? Aahz is the one you have to convince."

"That's where you're wrong, Skeeve," she corrected. "Aahz isn't leading this group, you are."

"Because of what he said back on Deva?" I smiled. "C'mon, Tanda. You know Aahz. He was just a little miffed. You noticed he's called all the shots so far."

The moonlight glistened in Tanda's hair as she shook her head.

"I do know Aahz, Skeeve. Better than you do," she said. "He's a stickler for chain of command. If he says you're the leader, you're the leader."

"But—"

"Besides," she continued over my protest, "Aahz is only one member of the team. What's important is all the others are counting on you, too. On you, not on Aahz. You hired 'em, and as far as they're concerned, you're the boss.''

The frightening thing was she was right. I hadn't really stopped to think about it, but everything she said was true. I had just been too busy with my own worries to reflect on it. Now that I realized the full extent of my responsibilities, a new wave of doubts assaulted me. I wasn't even that sure of myself as a magician, and as a leader of men. . . .

''I'll have to think about it,'' I stalled.

''You don't have much time,'' she pointed out. ''You've got a war scheduled to start tomorrow.''

There was a crackling in the brush to our left, interrupting our conversation.

''Boss?'' came Brockhurst's soft hail. ''Are you busy?''

''Sort of,'' I called back.

''Well, this will only take a minute.''

Before I could reply, two shadows detached themselves from the brush and drew closer. One was Brockhurst, the other was Gus. I should have known from the noise that the gargoyle was accompanying Brockhurst. Like Tanda, the Imp could move like a ghost.

''We were just talking about Ajax,'' Brockhurst informed me, squatting down to join our conference.

The gargoyle followed suit.

''Yeah,'' Gus confirmed. ''The three of us wanted to make a suggestion to you.''

''Right,'' Brockhurst nodded. ''Gus and me and the Gremlin.''

''The Gremlin?'' I asked.

The Imp craned his neck to peer around him.

''He must have stayed back at camp,'' he shrugged.

"About Ajax," Tanda prompted.

"We think you should pull him from the team," Gus announced. "Send him back to Deva and out of the line of fire."

"It's not for us," Brockhurst hastened to clarify. "It's for him. He's a nice old guy, and we'd hate to see anything happen to him."

"He is pretty old," I murmured.

"Old!" Gus exclaimed. "Boss, the Gremlin says he's tailed him for over two hundred years . . . two hundred! According to him, Ajax was old when their paths first crossed. It won't kill him to miss this one war, but it might kill him to fight in it."

"Why is the Gremlin tailing him, anyway?" I asked.

"I've told you before, kid," a voice boomed in my ear, "gremlins don't exist."

With that pronouncement, Aahz sank down at my side, between me and Tanda. As I attempted to restore my heartbeat to normal, it occurred to me I knew an awful lot of light-footed people.

"Hi, Aahz," I said, forcing a smile. "We were just talking about—"

"I know, I heard," Aahz interrupted. "And for a change I agree."

"You do?" I blinked.

"Sure," he yawned. "It's a clear-cut breach of contract. He hired out his services as a bowman, and the first assignment you give him, he literally lies down on the job."

Actually, it had been the second assignment. I had a sudden flash recollection of Ajax drawing and firing in a smooth, fluid motion, cutting down a signal standard so distant it was barely visible.

"My advice would be to send him back," Aahz

was saying. "If you want to soothe your conscience, give him partial payment and a good recommendation, but the way he is, he's no good to anybody."

Perhaps it was because of Tanda's lecture, but I was suddenly aware that Aahz had specifically stated his suggestion as "advice," not an order.

"Heads up, boss," Brockhurst murmured. "We've got company."

Following his gaze, I saw Ajax stumbling toward us, his ghostlike paleness flickering in the darkness like . . . well, like a ghost. It occurred to me that what had started out as a moment of solitude was becoming awfully crowded.

"Evenin', youngster," he saluted. "Didn't mean to interrupt nothin! Didn't know you folks was havin' a meetin'."

"We . . . ah . . . we were just talking," I explained, suddenly embarrassed.

"I kin guess about what, too," Ajax sighed. "Well, I was goin' to do this private-like, but I suppose the rest o' you might as well hear it, too."

"Do what, Ajax?" I asked.

"Resign," he said. "Seems to me to be the only decent thing to do after what happened today."

"It could have happened to anyone," I shrugged.

"Nice of you to say so, youngster," Ajax smiled, "but I kin see the handwriting on the wall. I'm just too old to be any good to anybody anymore. 'Bout time I admitted it to myself."

I found myself noticing the droop in his shoulders and a listlessness that hadn't been there when we first met on Deva.

"Don't fret about payin' me," Ajax continued. "I didn't do nothin', so I figger you don't owe me nothin'. If somebody'll just blip me back to Deva, I'll get outta your way and let you fight your war the way it should be fought.''

"Well, Ajax," Aahz sighed, rising to his feet and extending his hand. "We're going to miss you."

"Just a minute!" I found myself saying in a cold voice. "Are you trying to tell me you're breaking our contract?"

Ajax's head came up with a snap.

"I expected better from a genuine Archer," I concluded.

"I wouldn't call it a breach of contract, youngster," the old bowman corrected me carefully. "More like a termination by mutual consent. I'm jes' too old—"

"Old?" I interrupted. "I knew you were old when I hired you. I knew you were old when I planned my strategy for tomorrow's fight around that bow of yours. I knew you were old, Ajax, but I didn't know you were a coward!"

There was a sharp intake of breath somewhere nearby, but I didn't see who it was. My attention was focused on Ajax. It was no longer a defeated, drooping old man, but a proud, angry warrior who loomed suddenly over me.

"Sonny," he growled, "I know I'm old, 'cause in my younger days I would have killed you for sayin' that. I never ran from a fight in my life, and I never broke a contract. If you got some shootin' fer me to do tomorrow, I'll do it. Then maybe you'll see what havin' a genuine Archer on your side is all about!"

With that, he spun on his heel and stalked off into the darkness.

It had been a calculated risk, but I still found I was

covered with cold sweat from facing the old man's anger. I also realized the rest of the group was staring at me in silent expectation.

"I suppose you're all wondering why I did that," I said, smiling.

I had hoped for a response, but the silence continued.

"I appreciate all your advice, and hope you continue to give it in the future. But I'm leading this force, and the final decisions have to be mine."

Out of the corner of my eye, I saw Aahz cock his eyebrow, but I ignored him.

"Everyone, including Ajax, said if I let him go, if I sent him back to Deva, there would be no harm done. I disagree. It would have taken away the one thing the years have left untouched . . . his pride. It would have confirmed to him his worst fears, that he's become a useless old man."

I scanned my audience. Not one of them could meet my eye.

"So he might get killed. So what? He's accepted that risk in every war he's fought in. I'd rather order him into a fight knowing for certain he'd be killed than condemn him to a living death as a washed-up has-been. This way, he has a chance, and as his employer, I feel I owe him that chance."

I paused for breath. They were looking at me again, hanging on my next words.

"One more thing," I snarled. "I don't want to hear any more talk about him being useless. That old man still handles a bow better than anyone I've ever seen. If I can't find a way to use him effectively, then it's my fault as a tactician, not his! I've got my shortcomings, but I'm not going to blame them on Ajax any more than I'd blame them on any of you."

Silence reigned again, but I didn't care. I had spoken my piece, and felt no compulsion to blather on aimlessly just to fill the void.

"Well, boss"—Brockhurst cleared his throat getting to his feet—"I think I'll turn in now."

"Me, too," echoed Gus, also rising.

"Just one thing." The Imp paused and met my gaze squarely. "For the record, it's a real pleasure working for you."

The gargoyle nodded his agreement, and the two of them faded into the brush.

There was a soft kiss on my cheek, but by the time I turned my head, Tanda had disappeared.

"You know, kid," Aahz said, "you're going to make a pretty good leader someday."

"Thanks, Aahz," I blinked.

". . . if you live that long," my mentor concluded.

We sat side by side in silence for a while longer. Gleep had apparently dozed off, for he was snoring softly as I continued petting him.

"If it isn't prying," Aahz asked finally, "what is this master plan you have for tomorrow that's built around Ajax?"

I sighed and closed my eyes.

"I haven't got one," I admitted. "I was kind of hoping you'd have a few ideas."

"I was afraid you were going to say that," Aahz grumbled.

Chapter Nineteen:

"What if they gave a war and only one side came—"

—LUCIFER

"WAKE up, kid!"

I returned to consciousness as I was being forcefully propelled sideways along the forest floor, presumably assisted by the ready toe of my mentor.

After I had slid to a stop, I exerted most of my energy and raised my head.

"Aahz," I announced solemnly, "as leader of this team, I have reached another decision. In the future, I want Tanda to wake me up."

"Not a chance," Aahz leered. "She's off scouting our right flank. It's me or the dragon."

Great choice. I suddenly realized how bright it was.

"Hey!" I blinked. "How late is it?"

"Figure we've got about a minute before things start popping," Aahz said casually.

"How long?" I gasped.

Aahz's brow furrowed for a moment as he reflected on his words. Klahdish units of time still gave him a bit of trouble.

"An hour!" he smiled triumphantly. "That's it. An hour."

"That's better," I sighed, sinking back to a horizontal position.

"On your feet, kid!" Aahz ordered. "We let you sleep as late as we could, but now you're needed to review the troops."

"Have you briefed everybody?" I yawned, sitting up. "Is the plan clear?"

"As clear as it's going to be, all things considered," Aahz shrugged.

"Okay," I responded, rolling to my feet. "Let's go. You can fill me in on any new developments along the way."

Aahz and I had been up most of the night formulating today's plan, and I found I was actually eager to see it implemented.

"You should be thankful you aren't on the other side," Aahz chortled as we moved to join the others. "Old Claude's been making the most of the time we gave him."

"Keeping them busy, is he?" I smiled.

"Since sunup," Aahz confirmed smugly. "Drilling, sharpening swords, never a dull moment in the Empire's army, that's for sure."

I wasn't sure I shared Aahz's enthusiasm for the enemy's spending lots of time sharpening their swords. Fortunately, I was spared the discomfort of replying as Gus lumbered up to us.

"You just missed Brockhurst's report," he informed us. "Still nothing on the left flank."

"Wouldn't we be able to tell from their signals if they were moving up additional support?" I asked.

"If you believe their signals," Aahz countered. "It wouldn't be the first time an army figured out the enemy had broken their code and started sending misleading messages."

"Oh," I said wisely.

"Speaking of signals," Aahz said with a grin, "you know the messages they were sending yesterday? The ones that went 'encountered minor resistance'?"

"I remember," I nodded.

"Well, it seems Claude has decided he needs to up the ante if he's going to get a promotion out of this. Overnight we've become 'armed opposition . . . must be subdued forcefully!' Neat, huh?"

I swallowed hard.

"Does that mean they'll be moving in reinforcements?" I asked, trying to sound casual.

"Not a chance, kid." Aahz winked. "Claude there has turned down every offer of assistance that came down the line. He keeps insisting he can handle it with the company he's commanding."

"I'd say he's got his neck way, way out," Gus commented.

". . . and we're just the ones to chop it off for him," Aahz finished.

"Where's Ajax?" I asked, changing the subject.

"Down at the forest line picking out his firing point," Gus replied. "Don't worry, boss. He's awake."

Actually, that wasn't my worry concerning Ajax at all. In my mind's eye, I could still see his angry stance when I called him a coward the night before.

"Mornin', youngster," the bowman hailed, emerging from the bush. "Think I got us a place all picked out."

"Hi, Ajax," I replied. "Say . . . um . . . when you get a minute, I'd like to talk to you about last night."

"Think nothin' of it," Ajax assured me with a grin. "I've plum fergot about it already."

There was a glint in his eye that contradicted his words, but if he was willing to pretend nothing had happened, I'd go along with it for now.

"I hate to interrupt," Aahz interrupted, "but I think friend Claude's just about ready to make his move."

Sure enough, the distant encampment was lining up in a marching formation. The hand-drawn wagons were packed and aligned, with the escort troops arrayed to the front and sides. The signal tower, despite its appearance, was apparently also portable and was being pushed along at the rear of the formation by several sweating soldiers.

"Late!" Ajax sneered. "I tell ya, youngster, armies are the same in any dimension."

"Okay, kid," Aahz said briskly. "Do your stuff. It's about time we got into position."

I nodded and closed my eyes for concentration. With a few strokes of my mental paintbrush, I altered Gus's features until the gargoyle was the mirror image of myself.

"Pretty good," Ajax commented critically, looking from Gus to me and back again.

I repeated the process, returning Aahz to his "dubious character" disguise.

"Well, we're off," Aahz waved. "Confusion to the enemy!"

Today's plan called for Gus substituting for me. The logic was that should anything go wrong, his stone flesh would not only keep him from harm, but also serve as a shield to defend Aahz.

Somehow it didn't seem right to me, to remain behind in relative safety while sending someone else to take my risks for me. It occurred to me that perhaps I had called the wrong person "coward" last night when speaking with Ajax.

The bowman seemed to accept the arrangement without question, however.

"Follow me, youngster," he cackled. "I don't want to miss any of this!"

With that, he turned and plunged into the brush, leaving me little choice but to trail along behind.

Fortunately, Ajax's chosen vantage point wasn't far. Old or not, I found he set a wicked pace.

Stringing his bow, he crouched and waited, chuckling softly in anticipation.

Settling in beside him, I took a moment to check the energy lines, the invisible streams of energy magicians draw their power from. There were two strong lines nearby, one air, one ground, which was good. While Aahz had taught me how to store the energies internally, with the amount of action scheduled for the day, I wanted all the power I could get.

We could see Aahz and Gus striding with great dignity toward the selected combat point. The opposing force watched them in frozen silence as they took their places.

For a moment, everyone stood in tableau.

Then Claude turned to his force and barked out an order. Immediately a half dozen archers broke from the formation and fanned out on either side of the wagons. Moving with slow deliberation, they each drew and cocked an arrow, then leveled the bows at the two figures blocking the company's progress.

I concentrated my energies.

Claude shouted something at our comrades. They remained motionless.

I concentrated.

The bowmen loosed their missiles. Gus threw up one hand dramatically.

The arrows stopped in mid-air and fell to the ground.

The bowmen looked at each other in amazement. Claude barked another order at them. They shakily drew and fired another barrage.

This one was more ragged than the first, but I managed to stop it as well.

"Nice work, youngster," Ajax exclaimed gleefully. "That's got 'em going."

Sure enough, the neat ranks of soldiers were rippling as the men muttered back and forth among themselves. Claude noted it, too, and ordered his bowmen back into the ranks.

Round one to us!

My elation was short-lived, though. The soldiers were drawing their swords now. The two groups assigned to guarding the sides of the wagon pivoted forward, forming two wings ready to engulf our teammates. As further evidence of Claude's nervousness, he even had the troops assigned to pulling the wagons leave their posts and move up to reinforce the center of his line.

That's what we were waiting for.

"Now, Ajax!" I hissed. "Arch 'em high."

"I remember, youngster," the archer grinned. "I'm ready when you are."

I waited until he raised his bow, then concentrated an intense beam of energy at a point a few inches in front of his bow.

It was like the candle-lighting exercise, and it worked as well now as it had when we had tried it last night.

As each shaft sped from Ajax's bow, it burst into flames and continued on its flight.

Again and again with incredible speed the bowman sent his missiles hissing through my ignition point. It required all my concentration to maintain the necessary stream of energy, moving it occasionally as his point of aim changed.

Finally, he dropped his bow back to his side.

"That oughta do it, youngster," he grinned. "Take a look."

I did. There in the distance, behind the soldiers' lines, thin plumes of smoke were rising from the wagons. In a few moments, Claude's supply company would be without supplies.

If we had a few moments! As we watched, the men began to advance on Aahz and Gus, their swords gleaming in the sun.

"Think we'd better do something about that!" Ajax muttered, raising his bow again.

"Wait a second, Ajax!" I ordered, squinting at the distant figures.

There had been a brief consultation between Aahz and Gus, then the gargoyle stepped back and began gesturing wildly at his companion.

It took me a moment, but I finally got the message. With a smile, I closed my eyes and removed Aahz's disguise.

Pandemonium reigned. The soldiers in the front ranks took one look at the demon opposing them and stampeded for the rear, half trampling the men behind them. As word spread through the formation, it became a rout, though I seriously doubt those in the rear knew what they were running from.

If anyone noticed the burning wagons, they didn't slow once.

"Whooee!" Ajax exclaimed, thumping me on the back. "That did it. Look at 'em run. You'd think those fellers never seed a Pervert before."

"They probably haven't," I commented, trying to massage some feeling back into my shoulder.

"You know," the bowman drawled, squinting at the scene below, "I got me an idea. Them fellers ran off so fast they fergot to signal to anybody. Think we should do it for 'em?"

"How?" I asked.

"Well," he grinned. "I know the signals, and you're a magician. If I told you what signal to run up, could you do it? Without anybody holdin' it?"

"Sure could," I agreed. "What'll we need for the signal?"

"Lemme think," he frowned. "We'll have to get a skull, and a couple of pieces of red cloth, and a black ball, an—"

"Wait a minute, Ajax," I said, holding up a hand. "I think there's an easier signal they'll understand. Watch this."

I sent one more blast of energy out, and the tower platform burst into flames.

"Think they'll get the message?" I smiled.

Ajax stared at the burning tower for a moment.

"Yer pretty good at that, youngster," he murmured finally. "Throwin' fire that far."

"Well," I began modestly, "we magicians can—"

" 'Course," he continued. "If you can do that, then you didn't really need me and Blackie to handle those wagons, did you?"

Too late I realized my mistake.

"Ajax, I—"

"Kinda strange, you goin' to all that trouble jes' to convince me I'm not useless."

"You're not useless," I barked. "Just because sometimes you're not necessary doesn't mean you're useless. I may be young, but I'm old enough to know that."

Ajax regarded me for a moment, then he suddenly smiled.

"Danged if you aren't right, youngst . . . Skeeve," he laughed. "Guess I knew it, but plum fergot it there fer a while. Let's go get some wine from that cask strapped to your dragon. I'd like to thank you proper fer remindin' me."

We headed back to camp together.

Chapter Twenty:

"Chain of command is the backbone of military structure and must be strictly obeyed."

—F. CHRISTIAN

THE mood back at the camp was understandably celebratory. If I had had any hopes for joining in the festivities, however, they were dashed when Aahz hailed me.

"Over here, kid!" he waved. "We've got some planning to do!"

"That's the other side o' bein' a general, youngster," Ajax murmured sympathetically. " 'T'aint all speeches and glory. You go on ahead. I'll do my drinkin' with the boys."

With a jerk of his head, he indicated Gus and Brockhurst who were already at the wine. Tanda was waiting for me with Aahz. That made my choice a little easier.

"Okay, Ajax," I smiled. "I'll catch up with you in a little bit."

"Congratulations, handsome!" Tanda winked as I

joined them. "That was as neat a bit of work as I've seen in a long time."

"Thanks, Tanda," I blushed.

"I see you and Ajax are on speaking terms again," Aahz said, regarding me with cocked eyebrows. "That's not a bad trick in itself. How did you do it?"

"We . . . um . . . we had a long talk," I replied vaguely. "You said we had some planning to do?"

"More like a briefing," Aahz admitted. "Tanda here brought along a few special effects items I think you should know about."

I had completely forgotten about Tanda's errand which had left me alone at the Bazaar. Now that I had been reminded, my curiosity soared.

"Whatcha got, Tanda?" I asked eagerly.

"Nothing spectacular," she shrugged. "Knowing Aahz was involved, I figured we'd be on a tight budget so I stuck to the basics."

"Just show him, huh?" Aahz growled. "Spare us the editorial comments."

She stuck her tongue out at him but produced a small cloth sack from her belt.

"First off," she began, "I thought we could use a little flash powder. It never fails to impress the yokels."

"Flash powder," I said carefully.

"You set fire to it," Aahz supplied. "It burns fast and gives you a cloud of smoke."

"I've got about a dozen small bags of it here," Tanda continued, showing me the contents of her sack. "Various colors and sizes."

"Can I try one?" I asked. "I've never worked with this stuff before."

"Sure," Tanda said. She grinned, extending the

sack. "They're yours to use as you see fit. You might as well know what you've got."

I took the sack and carefully selected one of the small bags from its interior.

"Better toss it to the ground, kid," Aahz cautioned. "Some folks can set it off in their hand, but that takes practice. If you tried it that way now, you'd probably lose a few fingers."

I obediently tossed the bag on the ground a few feet away. Watching it curiously, I focused a quick burst of energy on it.

There was a bright flash of light accompanied by a soft *pop*. Blinking my eyes, I looked at where the bag had been. A small cloud of green smoke hung in the air, slowly dissipating in the breeze.

"That's neat!" I exclaimed, reaching into the sack again.

"Take it easy," Aahz warned. "We don't have that much of the stuff."

"Oh! Right, Aahz," I replied, feeling a little sheepish. "What else do you have, Tanda?"

"Well," she said, smiling, "I guess this would be a pièce-de-résistance."

As she spoke, she seemed to draw something from behind her back. I say "seemed" because I couldn't see anything. From her movements, she looked to be holding a rod about three feet long, but there was nothing in her grasp.

"What is it?" I asked politely.

For a response, she grinned and held whatever it was in front of her. Then she opened her grip and disappeared into thin air.

"Invisibility," Aahz exclaimed. "A cloak of invisibility!"

"Couldn't afford one," came Tanda's voice from somewhere in front of us. "I had to settle for one of these."

What "one of these" was, it turned out, was a sheet of invisibility. It was a sheet of stiff material about three feet by seven feet. Tanda had been carrying it rolled up in a tube, and her disappearance had been caused by the sheet unrolling to its full size.

As she and Aahz chatted excitedly about her new find, I had an opportunity to further my knowledge in the field of invisibility.

Invisible sheets, it seems, were made of roughly the same material as invisible cloaks. Since the sheets were carried, not worn, they did not require the flexibility and softness necessary for a cloak. Consequently, they were considerably cheaper than the cloaks.

The effect was sort of like one-way glass. When you were on the right side of an invisible sheet, you could see through it perfectly well to observe whatever or whoever was on the other side. They, however, could not see you.

We were still discussing the potential uses of the new tool when Brockhurst hastened up to our group.

"Hey, boss!" he called. "We've got company!"

"Who? Where?" I asked calmly.

"Down on the meadow," the Imp responded, pointing. "The Gremlin says there's some kind of group forming out there."

"What Gremlin?" Aahz snarled.

"C'mon, Aahz," Tanda called, starting off. "Let's check this out."

There was indeed a group on the meadow, Empire soldiers all. The puzzling thing was their activity, or specifically their lack of it. They seemed to be simply standing and waiting for something.

"What are they doing, Aahz?" I whispered as we studied the group form the concealment of the tree line.

"They're standing and waiting," Aahz supplied.

"I can see that," I said. "But what are they waiting for?"

"Probably for us," my mentor replied.

"For us?" I blinked. "Why?"

"For a war council," Aahz grinned. "Look at it, kid. Aren't they doing the same thing we did when we wanted to talk? They're even standing in the same spot."

I restudied the group in this light. Aahz was right! The enemy was calling for a war council!

"Do you think we should go out there?" I asked nervously.

"Sure," Aahz replied. "But not right away. Let 'em sweat a little. They kept us waiting the first time, remember?"

It was nearly half an hour before we stepped from the tree line and advanced across the meadow to where the soldiers stood waiting. I had taken the precaution of outfitting Aahz in his "dubious character" disguise for the conference. Myself, I was bearing the invisibility sheet before me, so that though I was walking along beside Aahz, to the soldiers it appeared he was alone.

There were more soldiers at the meeting point than there had been at our first meeting with Claude. Even to my untrained eye, it was apparent that there were more than half a dozen officers present among the honor guard.

"You wish a meeting?" Aahz asked haughtily, drawing to a halt before the group.

There was a ripple of quick consultation among the soldiers. Finally one of them, apparently the leader, stepped forward.

"We wish to speak with your master!" he announced formally.

"He's kinda busy right now," Aahz yawned. "Anything I can help you with?"

The leader reddened slightly.

"I am the commander of this sector!" he barked. "I demand to see Skeeve, commander of the defense, not his lacky!"

I dropped one of the bags of flash powder on the ground at my feet.

"If you insist," Aahz growled, "I'll get him. But he won't be happy."

"I'm not here to make him happy," the leader shouted. "Now be off with you."

"That won't be necessary," Aahz leered. "He's a magician. He hears and sees what his servants hear and see. He'll be along."

That was my cue. I let drop the sheet of invisibility and simultaneously ignited the bag of flash powder.

The results were spectacular.

The soldiers, with the exception of the leader, fell back several steps. To them, it looked as if I had suddenly appeared from thin air, materializing in a cloud of red smoke.

For me, the effect was less impressive. As the bag of flash powder went off, it was made apparent to me that watching a cloud of smoke from a distance was markedly different from standing at ground zero.

As I was enveloped in the scarlet billows, my feeling was not of elated triumph but rather a nearly overwhelming desire to cough and sneeze.

My efforts to suppress my reactions caused me to contort my features to the point where I must have borne more than a faint resemblance to Gus.

"Steady, Master!" Aahz cautioned.

"Aahz. Ah!" I gasped.

"Do not let your anger overcome your reason," my mentor continued hastily. "They don't know the powers they trifle with."

"I . . . I did not wish to be disturbed," I managed at last, regaining my breath as the smoke dissipated.

The leader of the group had held his ground through the entire proceedings, though he looked a bit paler and less sure of himself than when he had been dealing with just Aahz.

"We . . . um . . . apologize for bothering you," he began uncertainly. "But there are certain matters requiring your immediate attention . . . specifically the war we are currently engaged in."

I eyed him carefully. He seemed to be of a different cut than Claude had been.

"I'm afraid you have me at a disadvantage, sir," I said cagily. "You seem to know me, but I don't recall having met you before."

"We have not met before," the officer replied grimly. "If we had, be assured one of us would not be here currently. I know you by reputation, specifically for your recent efforts to resist the advance of our army. For myself, I am Antonio, commander of the right wing of the left flank of the Empire's army. These are my officers."

He indicated the soldiers behind him with a vague wave of his hand. The men responded by drawing themselves more erect and thrusting out their chins arrogantly.

I acknowledged them with a slight nod.

"Where is Claude?" I asked casually. "I was under the impression he was an officer of this sector."

"You are correct," Antonio smirked. "He *was*. He is currently being detained until he can be properly court-martialed . . . for incompetence!"

"Incompetence?" I echoed. "Come now, sir. Aren't you being a little harsh? While Claude may have overstepped his abilities a bit, I wouldn't say he's incompetent. I mean, after all, he *was* dealing with supernatural powers, if you know what I mean."

As I spoke, I wiggled my fingers dramatically at Aahz and removed his disguise.

The jaws of the attending officers dropped, ruining their arrogant jut. Then Aahz grinned at them, and their mouths clicked shut in unison as they swallowed hard.

Antonio was unimpressed.

"Yes, yes," he said briskly, waving a hand as if at an annoying fly. "We have had reports, many reports, as to your rapport with demons. Claude's incompetence is in his disastrous underestimation of the forces opposing him. Be assured, I will not be guilty of the same error."

"Don't count on it, Tony," Aahz leered. "We demons can be a pretty tricky lot.

The officer ignored him.

"However, we are not here for idle pleasantries," he said, fixing me with a stern gaze. "I believe we have a dispute to settle concerning right of passage over this particular piece of terrain.''

"We have a dispute concerning your right of passage over the kingdom of Possiltum," I corrected.

"Yes, yes," Antonio yawned. "Of course, if you want to stop us from gaining Possiltum, you had best stop us here."

"That's about how we had it figured," Aahz agreed.

"Not to belabor the point, Antonio," I smiled, "but I believe we *do* have you stopped."

"Temporarily," the officer smiled. "I expect that situation to change shortly . . . shall we say, a few hours after dawn? Tomorrow?"

"We'll be here," Aahz nodded.

"Just a moment," I interrupted. "Antonio, you strike me as being a sporting man. Would you like to make our encounter tomorrow a little more interesting? Say, with a little side wager?"

"Such as what?" the officer scowled.

"If you lose tomorrow," I said carefully, "will you admit Claude's defeat had nothing to do with incompetence and drop the charges against him?"

Antonio thought for a moment, then nodded.

"Done," he said. "Normally I would fear what the reaction of my superiors would be, but I am confident of my victory. There are things even a demon cannot stand against."

"Such as?" Aahz drawled.

"You will see," the officer smiled. "Tomorrow."

With that, he spun on his heel and marched off, his officers trailing behind him.

"What do you think, Aahz?" I murmured.

"Think?" my mentor scowled. "I think you're

going soft, kid. First Brockhurst, now Claude. What is this 'be kind to enemies' kick you're on?"

"I meant about tomorrow," I clarified quickly.

"I dunno, kid," Aahz admitted. "He sounded too confident for comfort. I wish I knew what he's got up his sleeve that's supposed to stop demons."

"Well," I sighed, "I guess we'll see tomorrow."

Chapter Twenty-One:

"It takes a giant to fight a giant."
—H. PRYM

OUR pensiveness was still with us the next day.

Our opponents were definitely up to something, but we couldn't tell exactly what it was. Tanda and Brockhurst had headed out on a scouting trip during the night and had brought back puzzling news. The Empire's soldiers had brought up some kind of heavy equipment, but it was hidden from sight by a huge box. All our scouts could say for sure was that whatever the secret weapon was, it was big and it was heavy.

Gus offered to fly over the box to take a quick peek inside, but we vetoed the idea. With the box constantly in the center of a mass of soldiers, there was no way the gargoyle could carry out his mission unobserved. Even if he used the invisibility sheet, the army was so far flung that someone would see him. So far we had kept the gargoyle's presence on our team as a secret, and we preferred to keep it that way. Even if we disguised him as Aahz or myself, it would betray the fact that someone in our party was able to fly. As Aahz pointed out, it looked as if this campaign would be rough enough without giving the opposition advance warning of the extent of our abilities.

This was all tactically sound and irrefutably logical. Nonetheless, it did nothing to reassure me as Aahz and I stood waiting for Antonio to make his opening gambit.

"Relax, kid," Aahz murmured. "You look nervous."

"I *am* nervous," I snapped back. "We're standing out here waiting to fight, and we don't know who or what we're supposed to be fighting. You'll forgive me if that makes me a trifle edgy."

I was aware I was being unnecessarily harsh on my mentor. Ajax and Gus were standing by, and Brockhurst and Tanda were watching for any new developments. The only team member unaccounted for this morning was the Gremlin, but I thought it wisest not to bring this to Aahz's attention. I assumed our elusive blue friend was off somewhere with Gleep, as my pet was also missing.

Everything that could have been done in preparation had been done. However, I still felt uneasy.

"Look at it this way, kid," Aahz tried again. "At least we know what we *aren't* up against."

What we weren't dealing with was soldiers. Though a large number of them were gathered in the near vicinity, there seemed to be no effort being made to organize or arm them for battle. As the appointed time drew near, it became more and more apparent that they were to be spectators only in the upcoming fray.

"I think I'd rather deal with soldiers," I said glumly.

"Heads up, kid," Aahz retorted, nudging me with his elbow. "Whatever's going to happen is about to."

I knew what he meant, which bothered me. There was no time to ponder it, however. Antonio had just put in his appearance.

He strolled around one corner of the mammoth box deep in conversation with a suspicious-looking character in a hooded cloak. He shot a glance in our direction, smiled, and waved merrily.

We didn't wave back.

"I don't like the looks of this, kid," Aahz growled.

I didn't either, but there wasn't much we could do except wait. Antonio finished his conversation with the stranger and stepped back, folding his arms across his chest. The stranger waved some of the onlooking soldiers aside, then stepped back himself. Drawing himself up, he began weaving his hands back and forth in a puzzling manner. Then the wind carried the sound to me and I realized he was chanting.

"Aahz!" I gasped. "They've got their own magician."

"I know," Aahz grinned back. "But from what I can hear he's bluffing them the same way you bluffed the court back at Possiltum. He probably doesn't have any more powers than I do."

No sooner had my mentor made his observation than the side of the huge box which was facing us slowly lowered itself to the ground. Revealed inside the massive container was a dragon.

The box had been big, better than thirty feet long and twenty feet high, but from the look of the dragon he must have been cramped for space inside.

He was big! I mean, really big!

Now I've never kidded myself about Gleep's size. Though his ten-foot length might look big here on Klah, I had seen dragons on Deva that made him look small. The dragon currently facing us, however, dwarfed everything I had seen before.

He was an iridescent bluish-green his entire length, which was far more serpentine than I was accustomed to seeing in a dragon. He had massive bat wings that he stretched and flexed as he clawed his way out of the confining box. There was a silver glint from his eye sockets which would have made him look machinelike were it not for the fluid grace of his powerful limbs.

For a moment, I was almost overcome by the beautiful spectacle he presented, emerging onto the battlefield. Then he threw his head back and roared, and my admiration turned icy cold within me.

The great head turned until its eyes were focused directly on us. Then he began to stalk forward.

"Time for the better part of valor, kid," Aahz whispered, tugging at my sleeve. "Let's get out of here."

"Wait a minute, Aahz!" I shot back. "Do you see that? What the keeper's holding?"

A glint of gold in the sunlight had caught my eye. The dragon's keeper had a gold pendant clasped in his fist as he urged his beast forward.

"Yeah!" Aahz answered. "So?"

"I've seen a pendant like that before!" I explained excitedly. "That's how he's controlling the dragon!"

The Deveel who had been running the Dragon stall where I acquired Gleep had worn a pendant like that. The pendant was used to control dragons . . . unattached dragons, that is. Attached dragons can be controlled by their owner without other assistance. A dragon becomes attached to you when you feed it. That's how I got Gleep. I fed him, sort of. Actually, he helped himself to a hefty bit of my sleeve.

"Well, don't just stand there, kid," Aahz barked, interrupting my reverie. "Get it!"

I reached out with my mind and took a grab at the pendant. The keeper felt it start to go and tightened his grip on it, fighting me for its possession.

"I . . . I can't get it, Aahz," I cried. "He won't let go."

"Then hightail it outta here, kid," my mentor ordered. "Tell Ajax to bag us that keeper. Better tell Gus to stand by with Berfert just in case. I'll try to keep the dragon busy."

An image flashed in my mind. It was a view of me, Skeeve, court magician, bolting for safety while Aahz faced the dragon alone. Something snapped in my mind.

"You go!" I snapped.

"Kid, are you—"

"It's my war and my job," I shouted. "Now get going."

With that I turned to face the oncoming dragon, not knowing or caring if Aahz followed my orders. I was Skeeve!

But it was an awfully big dragon!

I tried again for the pendant, nearly lifting the

keeper from his feet with my effort, but the man clung firmly to his possession, screaming orders at the dragon as he did.

I shot a nervous glance at the grim behemoth bearing down on me. If I tried to levitate out of the way, he could just. . . .

"Look out, kid!" came Aahz's voice from behind me.

I half turned, then something barreled past me, positioning itself between me and the oncoming menace.

It was Gleep!

"Gleep!" I shouted. "Get back here!"

My pet paid me no mind. His master was being threatened, and he meant to have a hand in this no matter what I said.

No longer a docile, playful companion, he planted himself between me and the monster, lowered his head to the ground, and hissed savagely, a six-foot tongue of flame leaping from his mouth as he did.

The effect on the big dragon was astonishing. He lurched to a stop and sat back on his haunches, cocking his head curiously at the mini-dragon blocking his path.

Gleep was not content with stopping his opponent, however. Heedless of the fact that the other dragon was over four times his size he began to advance stiffly, challenging his rival's right to the field.

The large dragon blinked, then shot a look behind him. Then he looked down on Gleep again, drawing his head back until his long neck formed a huge question mark.

Gleep continued to advance.

I couldn't understand it. Even if the monster

couldn't flame, which was doubtful, it was obvious he had the sheer physical power to crush my pet with minimal effort. Still he did nothing, looking desperately about him almost as if he were embarrassed.

I watched in spellbound horror. It couldn't last. If nothing else, Gleep was getting too close to the giant to be ignored. Any minute now, the monster would have to react.

Finally, after a final glance at his frantic keeper, the big dragon did react. With a sigh, one of his taloned front paws lashed out horizontally in a cuff that would have caved in a building. It struck Gleep on the side of his head and sent him sprawling.

My pet was game, though, and struggled painfully to his feet, shaking his head as if to clear it.

Before he could assume his aggressive stance, however, the big dragon stretched his neck down until their heads were side by side, and he began to mutter and grumble in Gleep's ear. My dragon cocked his head as if listening, then "whuffed" in response.

As the stunned humans and nonhumans watched, the two dragons conversed in the center of the battlefield punctuating their mutterings with occasional puffs of smoke.

I tried to edge forward to get a better idea of exactly what was going on, but the big dragon turned a baleful eye on me and let loose a blast of flame which kept me at a respectful distance. Not that I was afraid, mind you; Gleep seemed to have the situation well in hand . . . or talon as the case might be. Well, I had always told Aahz that Gleep was a very talon-ted dragon.

Finally, the big dragon drew himself up, turned, and majestically left the field without a backward glance, his head impressively high. Ignoring the angry shouts of the soldiers, he returned to his box and dropped his haunches, sitting with his back to the entire proceeding.

His keeper's rage was surpassed only by Antonio's. He screamed at the keeper with purpled face and frantic gestures until the keeper angrily pulled the control pendant from around his neck, handed it to the officer, and stalked off. Antonio blinked at the pendant, then flung it to the ground and started off after the keeper.

That was all the opening I needed. Reaching out with my mind, I brought the pendant winging to my hand.

"Aahz!" I began.

"I don't believe it," my mentor mumbled to himself. "I saw it, but I still don't believe it."

"Gleep!"

My pet came racing up to my side, understandably pleased with himself.

"Hi, fella!" I cried, ignoring his breath and throwing my arms around his neck in a hug. "What happened out there, anyway?"

"Gleep!" my pet said evasively, carefully studying a cloud.

If I had expected an answer, it was clear I wasn't going to get one.

"I still don't believe it," Aahz repeated.

"Look, Aahz," I said, holding the pendant aloft. "Now we don't have to worry about that or any other dragon. We've shown a profit!"

"So we did," Aahz scowled. "But do me a favor, huh, kid?"

"What's that, Aahz?" I asked.

"If that dragon, or any dragon, wanders into our camp, don't feed it! We already have one, and that's about all my nerves can stand. Okay?"

"Sure, Aahz," I smiled.

"Gleep!" said my pet, rubbing against me for more petting, which he got.

Chapter
Twenty-Two:

"Hell hath no fury like a demon scorched."
—C. MATHER

OUR next war council made the previous ones look small. This was only to be expected, as we were dealing with the commander of the entire left flank of the Empire's army.

Our meeting was taking place in a pavilion constructed specifically for that purpose, and the structure was packed with officers, including Claude. It seemed Antonio was true to his word, even though he himself was not currently present.

In the face of such a gathering, we had decided to show a bit more force ourselves. To that end, Tanda and Brockhurst were accompanying us, while Gleep snuffled around outside. Gus and Ajax we were still holding in reserve, while the Gremlin had not reappeared since the confrontation of dragons.

I didn't like the officer we were currently dealing with. There was something about his easy, oily manner that set me on edge. I strongly suspected he had ascended to his current position by poisoning his rivals.

"So you'd like us to surrender," he was saying thoughtfully, drumming his fingers on the table before him.

". . . or withdraw, or turn aside," I corrected. "Frankly, we don't care what you do, as long as you leave Possiltum alone."

"We've actually been considering doing just that," the commander said, leaning back in his chair to study the pavilion's canopy.

"Is that why you've been moving up additional troops all day long?" Brockhurst asked sarcastically.

"Merely an internal matter, I assure you," the commander purred. "All my officers are assembled here, and they're afraid their troops will fall to mischief if left to their own devices."

"What my colleague means," Aahz interjected, "is we find it hard to believe you're actually planning to accede to our demands."

"Why not?" the commander shrugged. "That *is* what you've been fighting for, isn't it? There comes a point when a commander must ask himself if it won't cost him more dearly to fight a battle than to pass it by. So far, your resistance utilizing demons and dragons has shown us this battle could be difficult indeed."

"There are more where they come from," I interjected, "should the need arise."

"So you've demonstrated," the commander smiled, waving a casual hand at Tanda and Brockhurst. "Witches and devils made an impressive addition to your force."

I deemed it unwise to point out to him that Brockhurst was an Imp, not a Deveel.

"Then you agree to bypass Possiltum?" Aahz asked bluntly.

"I agree to discuss it with my officers," the commander clarified. "All I ask is that you leave one of your . . . ah . . . assistants behind."

"What for?" I asked. I didn't like the way he was eyeing Tanda.

"To bring you word of our decision, of course," the commander shrugged. "None of my men would dare enter your camp, even granted a messenger's immunity."

There was a mocking tone to his voice I didn't like.

"I'll stay, Skeeve," Aahz volunteered.

I considered it. Aahz had demonstrated his ability to take care of himself time and time again. Still I didn't trust the commander.

"Only if you are willing to give us one of your officers in return as a hostage," I replied.

"I've already said none of—" the commander began.

"He need not enter our camp," I explained. "He can remain well outside our force, on the edge of the tree line in full view of your force. I will personally guarantee his safety."

The commander chewed his lip thoughtfully.

"Very well," he said. "Since you have shown an interest in his career, I will give you Claude to hold as a hostage."

The young officer paled but remained silent.

"Agreed," I said. "We will await your decision."

I nodded to my comrades, and they obediently began filing out of the pavilion. Claude hesitated, then joined the procession.

I wanted to tell Aahz to be careful but decided

against it. It wouldn't do to admit my partner's vulnerability in front of the commander. Instead, I nodded curtly to the officers and followed my comrades.

Tanda and Brockhurst were well on their way back to the treeline. Claude, on the other hand, was waiting for me as I emerged and fell in step beside me.

"While we have a moment," he said stiffly, "I would like to thank you for interceding in my behalf with my superiors."

"Don't mention it," I mumbled absently.

"No, really," he persisted. "Chivalry to an opponent is rarely seen these days. I think—"

"Look, Claude," I growled, "credit it to my warped sense of justice. I don't like you, and didn't when we first met, but that doesn't make you incompetent. Unpleasant, perhaps, but not incompetent."

I was harsher with him than I had intended to be, but I was worried about Aahz.

Finding himself thus rebuked, he sank into an uncomfortable silence which lasted almost until we reached the trees. Then he cleared his throat and tried again.

"Um . . . Skeeve?"

"Yeah?" I retorted curtly.

"I . . . um . . . what I was trying to say was that I am grateful and would repay your favor by any reasonable means at my disposal."

Despite my concern, his offer penetrated my mind as a potential opportunity.

"Would answering a few questions fall under the heading of 'reasonable'?" I asked casually.

"Depending upon the questions," he replied carefully. "I am still a soldier, and my code of conduct clearly states—"

"Tell you what," I interrupted. "I'll ask the questions, and you decide which ones are okay to answer. Fair enough?"

"So it would seem," he admitted.

"Okay," I began. "First question. Do you think the commander will actually bypass Possiltum?"

The officer avoided my eyes for a moment, then shook his head briskly.

"I should not answer that," he said, "but I will. I do not feel the commander is even considering it as a serious possibility, nor does any officer in that tent. He is known as 'the Brute,' even among his most loyal and seasoned troops. May I assure you he did not acquire that nickname by surrendering or capitulating while his force was still intact."

"Then why did he go through the motions of the meeting just now?" I queried.

"To gain time," Claude shrugged. "As your assistants noted, he is using the delay to mass his troops. The only code he adheres to is 'Victory at all costs.' In this case, it seems it is costing him his honor."

I thought about this for a moment before asking my next question.

"Claude," I said carefully, "you've faced us in battle, and you know your own army. If your prediction is correct and the Brute attacks in force, in your opinion, what are our chances of victory?"

"Nil," the officer replied quietly. "I know it may sound like enemy propaganda, but I ask you to believe my sincerity. Even with the additional forces you displayed this evening, if the Brute sets the legions in motion, they'll roll right over you. Were I in your position, I would take advantage of the cover of night to slip away, and not fear the stigma of cowardice. You're facing the mightiest army ever assembled. Against such a force there is no cowardice, only self-preservation.''

I believed him. The only question was what should I do with the advice.

"I thank you for your counsel," I said formally. "And will consider your words carefully. For now, if you will please remain here in the open as promised, I must consult with my troops."

"One more thing," Claude said, laying a restraining hand on my arm. "If any harm befalls your assistant, the one you left at the meeting, I would ask that you remember I was here with you and had no part in it."

"I will remember," I nodded, withdrawing my arm. "But if the Brute tries to lay a hand on Aahz, I'll wager he'll wish he hadn't."

As I turned to seek out my team, I wished I felt as confident as I sounded.

Tanda came to me readily when I caught her eye and beckoned her away from the others.

"What is it, Skeeve?" she asked as we moved away into the shadows. "Are you worried about Aahz?"

I was, though I didn't want to admit it just yet. The night was almost gone with no signs of movement or activity from the pavilion. Still, I clung to my faith in Aahz. When that failed, I turned my mind to other exercises to distract it from fruitless worry.

"Aahz can take care of himself," I said gruffly.

"There's something else I wanted your opinion on."

"What's that?" she asked, cocking her head.

"As you know," I began pompously, "I am unable to see the disguise spells I cast. Though everyone else is fooled, as the originator of the spell, I still continue to see things in their true form."

"I didn't know that," she commented. "But continue."

"Well," I explained, "I was thinking that if we actually have to fight the army, we could use additional troops. I've got an idea, but I need you to tell me if it actually works."

"Okay," she nodded. "What is it?"

I started to resume my oration, then realized I was merely stalling. Instead, I closed my eyes and focused my mind on the small grove of trees ahead.

"Hey!" cried Tanda. "That's terrific."

I opened my eyes, being careful to maintain the spell.

"What do you see?" I asked nervously.

"A whole pack of demons . . . oops . . . I mean Perverts," she reported gaily. "Bristling with swords and spears. That's wild!"

It worked. I was correct when I guessed that my disguise spell could work on any living thing, not just men and beasts.

"I've never seen anything like it," Tanda marveled. "Can you make them move?"

"I don't know," I admitted. "I just—"

"Boss! Hey, Boss!" Brockhurst shouted, sprinting up to us. "Come quick! You'd better see this!"

"What is it?" I called, but the Imp had reversed his course and was headed for the tree line.

A sudden fear clutched at my heart.

"C'mon, Tanda," I growled and started off.

By the time we reached the tree line the whole team was assembled there, talking excitedly among themselves.

"What is it?" I barked, joining them.

The group fell silent, avoiding my eyes. Brockhurst lifted a hand and pointed across the meadow.

There, silhouetted against a huge bonfire was Aahz, hanging by his neck from a crude gallows. His body was limp and lifeless as he rotated slowly at the end of the rope. At his feet, a group of soldiers were gathered to witness the spectacle.

Relief flooded over me, and I began to giggle hysterically. Hanging! If only they know!

Alarm showed in the faces of my team as they studied my reaction in shocked silence.

"Don't worry!" I gasped. "He's okay!"

Early in my career with Aahz, I had learned that one doesn't kill demons by hanging them. Their neck muscles are too strong! They can hang all day without being any the worse for wear. I had, of course, learned this the hard way one day when we. . . .

"At least they have the decency to burn the body," Claude murmured from close beside me.

My laughter died in my throat.

"What?" I cried, spinning around.

Sure enough, the soldiers had cut down Aahz's "body" and were carrying it toward the bonfire with the obvious intention of throwing it in.

Fire! That was a different story. Fire was one of the things that could kill Aahz deader than. . . .

"Ajax!" I cried. "Quick! Stop them from—"

It was too late.

With a heave from the soldiers, Aahz arched into the roaring flames. There was a quick burst of light, then nothing.

Gone! Aahz!

I stood staring at the bonfire in disbelief. Shock numbed me to everything else as my mind reeled at the impact of my loss.

"Skeeve!" Tanda said in my ear, laying a hand on my shoulder.

"Leave me alone!" I croaked.

"But the army . . ."

She let the word trail off, but it made its impact. Slowly I became conscious of the world around me.

The legions, having given us our answer, were massing for battle. Drums boomed, heralding the rising sun as it reflected off the polished weapons arrayed to face us.

The army. They had done this!

With deliberate slowness I turned to face Claude. He recoiled in fear from my gaze.

"Remember!" he cried desperately. "I had nothing to—"

"I remember," I replied coldly. "And for that reason only I am letting you go. I would advise, however, that you choose a path to follow other than rejoining the army. I have tried to be gentle with them, but if they insist on having war, as I am Skeeve, we shall give it to them!"

Chapter
Twenty-Three:

"What is this, a Chinese fire drill?"
—SUN TZU

I DIDN'T see where Claude went after I finished speaking with him, nor did I care. I was studying the opposing army with a new eye. Up to now I had been thinking defensively, planning for survival. Now I was thinking as the aggressor.

The legions were in tight block formations, arrayed some three or four blocks deep and perhaps fifteen blocks wide. Together they presented an awesome impression of power, an irresistible force that would never retreat.

That suited me fine. In fact, I wanted a little insurance that they would not retreat.

"Ajax!" I called without turning my head.

"Here, youngster!" the bowman replied from close beside me.

"Can Blackie send your arrows out beyond those formations?"

"I reckon so," he drawled.

"Very well," I said grimly. "The same drill as the first battle, only this time don't go for the wagons. I want a half circle of fire around their rear."

As before, the bowstring set up a rhythmic "thung" as the bowman began to lose shaft after shaft. This time, however, it seemed the arrows burst into flame more readily.

"Ease off, youngster," Ajax called. "Yer burnin' em up before they reach the ground."

He was right. Either I was standing directly on a force line, or my anger had intensified my energies. Whatever the reason, I found myself with an incredible amount of power at my disposal.

"Sorry, Ajax," I shouted, and diverted a portion of my mind away from the ignition point.

"Tanda!" I called. "Run back and get Gleep!"

"Right, Skeeve," came the reply.

I had a hunch my pet might come in handy before this brawl was done.

The front row of the army's formation was beginning to advance to the rhythmic pounding of drums. I ignored them.

"Brockhurst!"

"Here, boss!" the Imp responded, stepping to my side.

"Have you spotted the commander yet?"

"Not yet," came the bitter reply. "He's probably buried back in the middle of the formation somewhere."

"Well, climb a tree or something and see if you can pinpoint him," I ordered.

"Right, boss! When I see him, do you want me to go after him?"

"No!" I replied grimly. "Report back to me. I

want to handle him myself."

The front line was still advancing. I decided I'd better do something about it. With a sweep of my mind, I set fire to the meadow in front of the line's center. The blocks confronted by this barrier ground to a halt while the right and left wings continued their forward movement.

"Gleep!" came a familiar voice accompanied by an even more familiar blast of bad breath.

"We're back!" Tanda announced unnecessarily.

I ignored them and studied the situation. Plumes of white smoke rising from behind the Empire's formation indicated that Ajax was almost finished with his task. Soon, the army would find itself cut off from any retreat. It was time to start thinking about our attack. The first thing I needed was more information.

"Gus!" I said thoughtfully, "I want you to take a quick flight over their formations. See if you can find a spot to drop Berfert where he can do some proper damage."

"Right, boss," the gargoyle grunted, lumbering forward.

"Wait a minute," I said, a thought occurring to me. "Tanda, have you still got the invisibility sheet with you?"

"Right here!" she grinned.

"Good," I nodded. "Gus, take the sheet with you. Keep it in front of you as long as you can while you're checking them out. There's no sense drawing fire until you have to."

The gargoyle accepted the sheet with a shrug.

"If you say so, boss," he muttered. "But they can't do much to me."

"Use it anyway," I ordered. "Now get moving."

The gargoyle sprang heavily into the air and started across the meadow with slow sweeps of his massive wings. I found it hard to believe anything that big and made of stone could fly, but I was seeing it. Maybe he used levitation.

"All set, youngster," Ajax chortled, interrupting my thoughts. "Anything else I can do for ya?"

"Not just now, Ajax," I replied. "But stand by."

I was glad that portion of my concentration was free now. This next stunt was going to take all the energy I could muster.

I focused my mind on the grass in front of the advancing left wing. As testimony to the effectiveness of my efforts, that portion of the line ground to an immediate halt.

"Say!" Tanda breathed in genuine admiration. "That's neat."

The effect I was striving for was to have the grass form itself into an army of Imps, rising from the ground to confront the Empire's troops. I chose Imps this time instead of demons because Imps are shorter, therefore requiring less energy to maintain the illusion.

Whatever my efforts actually achieved, it was enough to have the soldiers react. After several shouted orders from their officers, the troops let fly a ragged barrage of javelins at the grass in front of them. The weapons, of course, had no effect on their phantom foe.

"Say, youngster," Ajax said, nudging me lightly. "You want me to do something about those jokers shootin' at our gargoyle?"

I turned slightly to check Gus's progress. The flying figure had passed over the center line troops, the ones my fire was holding in check. The soldiers could now see the figure behind the invisible sheet, and were reacting with enviable competence.

The archers in their formation were busy loosing their shafts at this strange figure that had suddenly appeared overhead, while their comrades did their best to reach the gargoyle with hurled javelins.

I saw all this at a glance. I also saw something else.

"Wait a minute, Ajax," I ordered. "Look at that!"

The various missiles loosed by the center line were falling to earth in the massed formations of the troops still awaiting commands. Needless to say, this was not well received, particularly as they were still unable to see the actual target of their advance force. To them, it must have appeared that by some magik or demonic possession, their allies had suddenly turned and fired on them.

Now a few blocks began to return the fire, ordering their own archers into action. Others responded by raising their shields and starting forward with drawn swords.

The result was utter chaos, as the center line troops tried to defend themselves from the attacks of their own reinforcements.

Mind you, I hadn't planned it this way, but I was quick to capitalize on the situation. If the presence of a gargoyle could cause this kind of turmoil, I thought it would be a good idea to up the ante a little.

With a quick brush of my mind, I altered Gus's appearance. Now they had a full-grown dragon hovering over their midst. The effect was spectacular.

I, however, did not allow myself the luxury of watching. I had learned something in this brief exchange, and I wanted to try it out.

I dissolved my Imp army, then reformed them, not in front of the troops, but in their midst!

This threw the formations into total disorder. As the soldiers struck or threw at the phantom figures, more often than not they struck their comrades instead.

If this kept up, they would be too busy fighting each other to bother with us.

"Boss!" Brockhurst called, darting up to my side. "I've got the commander spotted!"

"Where?" I asked grimly, trying not to take my concentration from the battle raging in the meadow.

The Imp pointed.

Sure enough! There was the Brute, striding angrily from formation to formation, trying to restore order to his force.

I heard the telltale whisper of an arrow being drawn.

"Ajax!" I barked. "Hold your fire. He's mine . . . all mine!"

As I said this, I dissolved all the Imps in the Brute's vicinity, and instead changed the commander's features until he took on the appearance of Aahz.

The dazed soldiers saw a demon appear in their midst brandishing a sword, a demon of a type they knew could be killed. They needed no further prompting.

I had one brief glimpse of the Brute's startled face before his troops closed on him, then a forest of uniforms blotted him from my view.

"Mission accomplished, boss!" Gus announced, appearing beside me. "What next?"

"What . . . did you . . . ?" I stammered.

I had forgotten that on his return trip, the invisibility sheet would shield the gargoyle from our view. His sudden appearance had startled me.

"Berfert'll be along when he gets done with their siege equipment," Gus continued, waving toward the enemy.

I looked across the meadow. He was right! The heavy equipment which had been lined up behind the army was now in flames.

Then I noticed something else.

The army wasn't fighting each other anymore. I realized with a start that between settling accounts with the Brute and Gus's reappearance, I had forgotten to maintain the Imp army!

In the absence of any visible foe, the Empire troops had apparently come to their senses and were now milling about trying to reestablish their formations.

Soon now, they would be ready to attack again.

"What do we do next, boss?" Brockhurst asked eagerly.

That was a good question. I decided to stall while I tried to work out an answer.

"I'll draw you a diagram," I said confidently. "Somebody give me a sword."

"Here, kid. Use mine," Aahz replied, passing me the weapon.

"Thanks," I said absently. "Now, this line is their main formation. If we . . . *Aahz!?*"

"Ready and able," my mentor grinned. "Sorry I'm late."

It *was* Aahz! He was standing there calmly with his arms folded as if he had been part of our group all along. The reactions of the others, however, showed that they were as surprised as I was at his appearance.

"But you . . ." I stammered. "The fire . . ."

"Oh, that," Aahz shrugged. "About the time I figured what they were doing, I used the D-Hopper to blink out to another dimension. The only trouble was I hadn't gotten around to relabeling the controls yet, and I had a heck of a time finding my way back to Klah."

Relief flooded over me like a cool wave. Aahz was alive! More important, he was here! The prospects for the battle suddenly looked much better.

"What should we do next, Aahz?" I asked eagerly.

"I don't know why you're asking me," my mentor blinked innocently. "It looks like you've been doing a fine job so far all by yourself."

Terrific! Now that I need advice, I get compliments.

"Look, Aahz," I began sternly. "We've got a battle coming up that—"

"Boss!" Brockhurst interrupted. "Something's going on out there!"

With a sinking heart, I turned and surveyed the situation again.

A new figure had appeared on the scene, an officer from the look of him. He was striding briskly along the front of the formation alternately shouting and waving his hands. Trailing along in his wake was a cluster of officers, mumbling together and shaking their hands.

"What in the world is that all about?" I murmured half to myself.

"Brace yourself, kid," Aahz advised. "If I'm hearing correctly, it's bad news."

"C'mon, Aahz," I sighed. "How could things get worse than they already are?"

"Easy," Aahz retorted. "*That* is the supreme commander of the Empire's army. He's here to find out what's holding up his left flank's advance."

Chapter
Twenty-Four:

*" . . . and then I said to myself, 'Why
should I split it two ways—'"*
—G. MOUSER

THE supreme commander's name was Big Julie, and
he was completely different from what I had expected.

For one thing, when he called for a war council,
he came to us. Flanked by his entire entourage of
officers, he came all the way across the meadow
to stand just short of the tree line, and he came unarmed. What was more, all of his officers were
unarmed, presumably at his insistence.

He seemed utterly lacking in the arrogance so
prevalent in the other officers we had dealt with, in-
viting us into the large tent he had had erected in the
meadow for the meeting. Introducing him to the
members of my force, I noticed he treated them with
great respect and seemed genuinely pleased to meet
each of them, even Gleep.

Our whole team was present for the meeting. We

figured that if there was ever a time to display our power, this was it.

In a surprising show of generosity, Aahz broke out the wine and served drinks to the assemblage. I was a little suspicious of this. Aahz isn't above doctoring drinks to win a fight, but when I caught his eye and raised an eyebrow, he responded with a small shake of his head. Apparently he was playing this round straight.

Then we got down to business.

Big Julie heard us out, listening with rapt attention. When we finished, he sighed and shook his head.

"Ah'm sorry," he announced. "But I can't do it. We've got to keep advancing, you know? That's what armies do!"

"Couldn't you advance in another direction for a while?" I suggested hopefully.

"Aie!" he exclaimed, spreading his hands defensively. "What do you think I got here, geniuses? These are soldiers. They move in straight lines, know what I mean?"

"Do they have to move so vigorously?" Aahz muttered. "They don't leave much behind."

"What can I say?" Big Julie shrugged. "They're good boys. They do their job. Sometimes they get a little carried away . . . like the Brute."

I had hoped to avoid the subject of the Brute, but since it had come up, I decided to face it head on.

"Say . . . um . . . Julie," I began.

"Big Julie!" one of the officers growled out of the corner of his mouth.

"Big Julie!" I amended hastily. "About the Brute. Um . . . he was . . . well . . . I wanted . . ."

"Don't mention it," Julie waved. "You want to

know the truth? You did me a favor."

"I did?" I blinked.

"I was getting a little worried about the Brute, you know what I mean?" the commander raised his eyebrows. "He was getting a little too ambitious."

"In that case. . . ." I smiled.

"Still . . ." Julie continued, "that's a bad way to go. Hacked apart by your own men. I wouldn't want that to happen to me."

"You should have fed him to the dragons," Aahz said bluntly.

"The Brute?" Julie frowned. "Fed to the dragons? Why?"

"Because then he could have been 'et, too'!"

Apparently this was supposed to be funny, as Aahz erupted into sudden laughter as he frequently does at his own jokes. Tanda rolled her eyes in exasperation.

Big Julie looked vaguely puzzled. He glanced at me, and I shrugged to show I didn't know what was going on either.

"He's strange," Julie announced, stabbing an accusing finger at Aahz. "What's a nice boy like you doing hanging around with strange people? Hey?"

"It's the war," I said apologetically. "You know what they say about strange bedfellows."

"You seem to be doin' all right for yourself!" Julie winked, then leered at Tanda.

"You want I should clean up his act, Boss?" Brockhurst asked grimly, stepping forward.

"See!" Julie exploded. "That's what I mean. This is no way to learn warfare. Tell you what. Why don't you let me fix you up with a job, hey? What do you say to that?"

"What pay scale?" Aahz asked.

"Aahz!" I scowled, then turned back to Julie. "Sorry, but we've already got a job . . . defending Possiltum. I appreciate your offer, but I don't want to leave a job unfinished."

"What have I been telling you?" Julie appealed to his officers. "All the good material has been taken already. Why can't you bring me recruits like this, eh?"

This was all very flattering, but I clung tenaciously to the purpose of our meeting.

"Um . . . Jul . . . I mean, Big Julie," I continued. "About defending Possiltum. Couldn't you find another kingdom somewhere to attack? We really don't want to have to fight you."

"*You* don't want to fight?" Julie erupted sarcastically. "You think *I* want to fight? You think I *like* doing this for a living? You think my boys like killing and conquering all the time?"

"Well . . ." I began tactfully.

Big Julie wasn't listening. He was out of his seat and pacing up and down, gesturing violently to emphasize his words.

"What kind of ding-bat *wants* to fight?" he asked rhetorically. "Do I look crazy? Do my boys look crazy? Everybody thinks we got some kind of weird drive that keeps us going. They think that all we want to do in the whole world is march around in sweaty armor and sharpen swords on other people's helmets. That's what you think too, isn't it? Eh? Isn't it?"

This last was shouted directly at me. By now I was pretty fed up with being shouted at.

"Yes!" I roared angrily. "That's what I think!"

"Well," Julie scowled. "You're wrong because—"

"That's what I think because if you didn't like doing it, you wouldn't do it!" I continued, rising to my own feet.

"Just like that!" Julie shouted sarcastically. "Just stop and walk away."

He turned and addressed his officers.

"He thinks it's easy! Do you hear *that?* Any of you who don't like to fight, just stop. Eh? Just like that."

A low chorus of chuckles rose from his assembled men. Despite my earlier burst of anger, I found myself starting to believe him. Incredible as it seemed, Julie and his men didn't like being soldiers!

"You think we wouldn't quit if we could?" Julie was saying to me again. "I bet there isn't a man in my whole army who wouldn't take a walk if he thought he could get away with it."

Again there was a murmur of assent from his officers.

"I don't understand," I said, shaking my head. "If you don't want to fight, and we don't want to fight, what are we doing here?"

"Did you ever hear of loan sharks?" Julie asked. "You know about organized crime?"

"Organized crime?" I blinked.

"It's like government, kid," Aahz supplied. "Only more effective."

"You'd better believe 'more effective,' " Julie nodded. "That's what we're doing here! Me and the boys, we got a list of gambling debts like you wouldn't believe. We're kinda working it off, paying 'em back in land, you know what I mean?"

"You haven't answered my question," I pointed out. "Why don't you just quit?"

"Quit?" Julie seemed genuinely astonished. "You

gotta be kidding. If I quit before I'm paid up, they break my leg. You know?" His wolfish grin left no doubt the thugs in question would do something a great deal more fatal and painful than just breaking a leg.

"It's the same with the boys here. Right, boys?" He indicated his officers with a wave of his hand.

Vigorous nods answered his wave.

"And you ought to see the collection agent they use. Kid, you might be a fair magician where you come from. But"—he shuddered—"this, believe me, you don't want to see."

Knowing how tough Big Julie was, I believed him.

Giving me a warm smile, he draped his arm around my shoulders.

"That's why it's really gonna break my heart to kill you. Ya know?"

"Well," I began, "you don't have to . . . KILL ME?"

"That's right," he nodded vigorously. "I knew you'd understand. A job's a job, even when you hate it."

"Whoa!" Aahz interrupted, holding one flattened hand across the top of the other to form a crude T. "Hold it! Aren't you overlooking something, Jules?"

"That's 'Big Julie.' " one of the guards admonished.

"I don't care if he calls himself the Easter Bunny!" my mentor snarled. "He's still overlooking something."

"What's that?" Julie asked.

"Us." Aahz smiled, gesturing to the team. "Aside from the minor detail that Skeeve here's a magician and not that easy to kill, he's got friends. What do you think we'll be doing while you make a try for our leader?''

The whole team edged forward a little. None of them were smiling, not even Gus. Even though they were my friends who I knew and loved, I had to admit they looked mean. I was suddenly very glad they were on my side.

Big Julie, on the other hand, seemed unimpressed.

"As a matter of fact," he smiled, "I expect you to be dying right along with your leader. That is, unless you're really good at running.''

"Running from what?" Gus growled. "I still think you're overlooking something. By my count, we've got you outnumbered. Even if you were armed—''

The supreme commander cut him short with a laugh. It was a relaxed, confident laugh which no one else joined in on. Then the laugh disappeared, and he leaned forward with a fierce scowl.

"Now, I'm only gonna say this once, so alla you listen close. Big Julie didn't get where he is today by overlooking nothin'. You think I'm outnumbered? Well, maybe you'd just better count again.''

Without taking his eyes from us, he waved his hand in a short, abrupt motion. At the signal, one of his guards pulled a cord and the sides of the tent fell away.

There were soldiers outside. They hadn't been there when we entered the tent, but they were there now. Hoo boy were they. Ranks and ranks of them completely surrounding the tent, the nearest barely an arm's length away. The front three rows were archers, with arrows nocked and drawn, leveled at our team.

I realized with a sudden calm clarity that I was

about to die. The whole meeting had been a trap, and it was a good one. Good enough that we would all be dead if we so much as twitched. I couldn't even kid myself that I could stop that many arrows if they were all loosed at once. Gus might survive the barrage, and maybe the others could blip away to another dimension in time to save themselves, but I was too far away from Aahz and the D-Hopper to escape.

"I . . . um . . . thought war councils were supposed to be off limits for combat." I said carefully.

"I also didn't get where I am today by playing fair," Big Julie shrugged.

"You know," Aahz drawled, "for a guy who doesn't want to fight, you run a pretty nasty war."

"What can I say?" the supreme commander asked, spreading his hands in helpless appeal. "It's a job. Believe me, if there was any other way, I'd take it. But as it is . . ."

His voice trailed off, and he began to raise his arm. I realized with horror that when his hand came down, so would the curtain.

"How much time do we have to find another way?" I asked desperately.

"You don't," Big Julie sighed.

"AND WE DON'T NEED ANY!" Aahz roared with sudden glee.

All eyes turned toward him, including my own. He was grinning broadly while listening to something the Gremlin was whispering in his ear.

"What's that supposed to mean?" the supreme commander demanded. "And where did this little blue fella come from? Eh?"

He glared at the encircling troops, who looked at

each other in embarrassed confusion.

"This is a Gremlin," Aahz informed him, slipping a comradely arm around the shoulders of his confidant, "And I think he's got the answer to our problems. *All* our problems. You know what I mean?"

"What does he mean?" Julie scowled at me. "Do you understand what he's sayin'?"

"Tell him, Aahz," I ordered confidently, wondering all the while what possible solution my mentor could have found to this mess.

"Big Julie," Aahz smiled, "what could those loan sharks of yours do if you and your army simply disappeared?"

And so, incredibly, it was ended.

Not with fireworks or an explosion or a battle. But like a lot of things in my life, in as crazy and off-hand a way as it had started.

And when it had ended, I almost wished it hadn't.

Because then I had to say good-bye to the team.

Saying good-bye to the team was harder than I would have imagined. Somehow, in all my planning, I had never stopped to consider the possibility of emerging victorious from the war.

Despite my original worries about the team, I found I had grown quite close to each of them. I would have liked to keep them around a little longer, but that would have been impossible. Our next stop was the capital, and they would be a little too much to explain away.

Besides, as Aahz pointed out, it was bad for morale to let the troops find out how much their commander was being paid, particularly when it was extremely disproportionate to their own wages.

Following his advice, I paid each of them personally. When I was done, however, I found myself strangely at a loss for words. Once again, the team came to my aid.

"Well, boss," Brockhurst sighed. "I guess this is it. Thanks for everything."

"It's been a real pleasure working for you," Gus echoed. "The money's nice, but the way I figure it, Berfert and I owe you a little extra for getting us out of that slop chute. Anytime you need a favor, look us up."

"Youngster," Ajax said, clearing his throat, "I move around a lot, so I'm not that easy to track. If you ever find yourself in a spot where you think I can lend a hand, jes' send a message to the Bazaar and I'll be along shortly."

"I didn't think you visited the Bazaar that often," I asked, surprised.

"Normally I don't," the bowman admitted. "But I will now . . . jest in case."

Tanda was tossing her coin in the air and catching it with practiced ease.

"I shouldn't take this," she sighed. "But a girl's gotta eat."

"You earned it," I insisted.

"Yea, well, I guess we'll be going," she said, beckoning to the others. "Take care of yourself, handsome."

"You will be coming back?" I asked hurriedly.

She made a face.

"I don't think so," she said wryly, "If Grimble saw us together . . ."

"I meant, ever," I clarified.

She brightened immediately.

"Sure," she winked. "You won't get rid of me that easily. Say good-bye to Aahz for me."

"Say good-bye to him yourself," Aahz growled, stepping out of the shadows.

"There you are!" Tanda grinned. "Where's the Gremlin? I thought you two were talking."

"We were," Aahz confirmed, looking around him. "I don't understand. He was here a minute ago."

"It's as if he didn't exist, isn't it, Aahz?" I suggested innocently.

"Now look, kid!" my mentor began angrily.

A chorus of laughter erupted from the team. He spun in that direction to deliver a scathing reply, but there was a blip of light and they were gone.

We stood silently together for several moments staring at the vacant space. Then Aahz slipped an arm around my shoulder.

"They were a good team, kid," he sighed. "Now pull yourself together. Triumphant generals don't have slow leaks in the vicinity of their eyes. It's bad for the image."

Chapter
Twenty-Five:

"Is everybody happy?"

—MACHIAVELLI

AAHZ and I entered the capital at the head of a jubilant mob of Possiltum citizens.

We were practically herded to the front of the palace by the crowd pressing us forward. The cheering was incredible. Flowers and other less identifiable objects were thrown at us or strewn in our path, making the footing uncertain enough that more than once I was afraid of falling and being trampled. The people, at least, seemed thoroughly delighted to see us. All in all, though, our triumphal procession was almost as potentially injurious to our life and limb as the war had been.

I was loving it.

I had never had a large crowd make a fuss over me before. It was nice.

"Heads up, kid," Aahz murmured, nudging me in the ribs. "Here comes the reception committee."

Sure enough, there was another procession emerging from the main gates of the palace. It was smaller

203

than ours, but made up for what it lacked in numbers with the prestige of its members.

The king was front and center, flanked closely by Grimble and Badaxe. The chancellor was beaming with undisguised delight. The general, on the other hand, looked positively grim.

Sweeping the crowd with his eyes, Badaxe spotted several of his soldiers in our entourage. His dark expression grew even darker, boding ill for those men. I guessed he was curious as to why they had failed to carry out his orders to stop our return.

Whatever he had in mind, it would have to wait. The king was raising his arms, and the assemblage obediently fell silent to hear what he had to say.

"Lord Magician," he began, "know that the cheers of the grateful citizens of Possiltum only echo my feelings for this service you have done us."

A fresh wave of applause answered him.

"News of your victory has spread before you," he continued. "And already our historians are recording the details of your triumph . . . as much as is known, that is."

An appreciative ripple of laughter surged through the crowd.

"While we do not pretend to comprehend the workings of your powers," the king announced, "the results speak for themselves. A mighty army of invincible warriors vanished into thin air, weapons and all. Only their armor and siege machines littering the empty battlefield mark their passing. The war is won! The threat to Possiltum is ended forever!"

At this, the crowd exploded. The air again filled with flowers and shouting shook the very walls of the palace.

The king tried to shout something more, but it was lost in the jubilant noise. Finally he shrugged and reentered the palace, pausing only for a final wave at the crowd.

I thought it was a rather cheap ploy, allowing him to cash in on our applause as if it were intended for him, but I let it go. Right now we had bigger fish to fry.

Catching the eyes of Grimble and Badaxe, I beckoned them forward.

"I've got to talk to you two," I shouted over the din.

"Shouldn't we go inside where it's quieter?" Grimble shouted back.

"We'll talk here!" I insisted.

"But the crowd . . ." the chancellor gestured.

I turned and nodded to a figure in the front row of the mob. He responded by raising his right arm in a signal. In response, the men in the forefront of the crowd locked arms and formed a circle around us, moving with near military precision. In a twinkling, there was a space cleared in the teeming populace, with the advisors, Aahz, Gleep, myself, and the man who had given the signal standing alone at its center.

"Just a moment," Badaxe rumbled, peering suspiciously at the circle. "What's going on—"

"General!" I beamed, flashing my biggest smile. "I'd like you to meet the newest citizen of Possiltum."

Holding my smile, I beckoned the mob leader forward.

"General Badaxe," I announced formally, "meet Big Julie. Big Julie, Hugh Badaxe!"

"Nice to meet you!" Julie smiled. "The boy here, he's been tellin' me all about you!"

The general blanched as he recognized the Empire's top commander.

"You!" he stammered. "But you . . . you're—"

"I hope you don't mind, General," I said smoothly. "But I've taken the liberty of offering Big Julie a job . . . as your military consultant."

"Military consultant?" Badaxe echoed suspiciously.

"What's the matter," Julie scowled. "Don't you think I can do it?"

"It's not that," the general clarified hastily. "It's just that . . . well—"

"One thing we neglected to mention, General," Aahz interrupted. "Big Julie here is retiring from active duty. He's more than willing to leave the running of Possiltum's army to you, and agrees to give advice only when asked."

"That's right!" Julie beamed. "I just wanna sit in the sun, drink a little wine, maybe pat a few bottoms, you know what I mean?"

"But the king . . ." Badaxe stammered.

". . . . doesn't have to be bothered with it at all," Aahz purred. "Unless, of course, you deem it necessary to tell him where your new battle plans are coming from."

"Hmm," the general said thoughtfully. "You sure you'd be happy with things that way, Julie?"

"Positive!" Julie nodded firmly. "I don't want any glory, no responsibility, and no credit. I had too much of that when I was workin' for the Empire, you know what I mean? Me and the boys talked it over, and we decided—"

"The boys?" Badaxe interrupted, frowning.

"Um . . . that's another thing we forgot to mention, General," I smiled. "Big Julie isn't the only new addition to Possiltum's citizenry."

I jerked my head at the circle of men holding back the crowd.

The general blinked at the men, then swiveled his

head around noting how many more like them were scattered through the crowd. He blanched as it became clear to him both where the Empire's army had disappeared to, and why his men had been unsuccessful in stopping our return to the capital.

"You mean to tell me you—" Badaxe began.

"Happy Possiltum citizens all, General!" Aahz proclaimed, then dropped his voice to a more confidential level. "I think you'll find that if you should ever have to draft an army, these new citizens will train a lot faster than your average plow pusher."

Apparently the general did. His eyes glittered at the thought of the new force we had placed at his command. I could see him mentally licking his chops in anticipation of the next war.

"Big Julie!" he declared with a broad smile. "You and your . . . er . . . boys are more than welcome to settle here in Possiltum. Let me be one of the first to congratulate you on your new citizenship."

He extended his hand, but there was an obstruction in his way. The obstruction's name was J.R. Grimble.

"Just a moment!" the chancellor snarled. "There's one minor flaw in your plans. It is my intention to advise the king to disband Possiltum's army."

"What?" roared Badaxe.

"Let me handle this, General," Aahz said soothingly. "Grimble, what would you want to do a fool thing like that for?"

"Why, because of the magician, of course," the chancellor blinked. "You've demonstrated he is quite capable of defending the kingdom without the aid of an army, so I see no reason why we should continue to bear the cost of maintaining one."

"Nonsense!" Aahz scolded. "Do you think the

great Skeeve has nothing to do with his time but guard your borders? Do you want to tie up your high-cost magician doing the job a low-cost soldier could do?''

"Well . . ." Grimble scowled.

"Besides," Aahz continued. "Skeeve will be spending considerable time on the road furthering his studies . . . which will of course increase his value to Possiltum. Who will guard your kingdom while he's away, if not the army?"

"But the cost is . . ." Grimble whined.

"If anything," Aahz continued ignoring the chancellor's protests. "I should think you'd want to expand your army now that your borders have increased in size."

"What's that?" Grimble blinked, "What about our borders?"

"I thought it was obvious," Aahz said innocently. "All these new citizens have to settle somewhere . . . and there is a lot of land up for grabs just north of here. As I understand it, it's completely unguarded at the moment. Possiltum wouldn't even have to fight for it, just move in and settle. That is, of course, provided you have a strong army to hold it once you've got it."

"Hmm," the chancellor said thoughtfully, stroking his chin with his hand.

"Then again," Aahz murmured quietly, "there's all the extra tax money the new citizens and land will contribute to the kingdom's coffers."

"Big Julie!" Grimble beamed. "I'd like to welcome you and your men to Possiltum."

"I'm welcoming him first!" Badaxe growled. "He's *my* advisor."

As he spoke, the general dropped his hand to the

hilt of his axe, a move which was not lost on the chancellor.

"Of course, General," Grimble acknowledged, forcing a grin. "I'll just wait here until you're through. There are a few things I want to discuss with our new citizens."

"While you're waiting, Grimble," Aahz smiled, "there are a few things we have to discuss with you."

"Such as what?" the chancellor scowled.

"Such as the Court Magician's pay!" my mentor retorted.

"Of course," Grimble laughed. "As soon as we're done here we'll go inside and I'll pay him his first month's wages."

"Actually," Aahz drawled. "What we wanted to discuss was an increase."

The chancellor stopped laughing.

"You mean a bonus, don't you?" he asked hopefully. "I'm sure we can work something out, considering—"

"I mean an increase!" Aahz corrected firmly. "C'mon, Grimble. The kingdom's bigger now. That means the magician's job is bigger and deserves more pay."

"I'm not sure I can approve that," the chancellor responded cagily.

"With the increase of your tax base," Aahz pressed, "I figure you can afford—"

"Now let's be careful," Grimble countered. "Our overhead has gone up right along with that increase. In fact, I wouldn't be surprised if . . ."

"C'mon, Gleep," I murmured to my pet. "Let's go see Buttercup."

I had a feeling the wage debate was going to last for a while.

Chapter Twenty-Six:

"All's well that ends well."

—E. A. POE

I WAS spending a leisurely afternoon killing time in my immense room in the palace.

The bargaining session between Aahz and Grimble had gone well for us. Not only had I gotten a substantial wage increase, I was also now housed in a room which was only a little smaller than Grimble's, which in turn was second only to the king's in size. What was more, the room had a large window, which was nice even if it did look out over the stables. Aahz had insisted on this, hinting darkly that I might be receiving winged visitors in the night. I think this scared me more than it did Grimble, but I got my window.

When I chose, I could look down from my perch and keep an eye on Gleep and Buttercup in the stables. I could also watch the hapless stable boy who had been assigned to catering to their every need. That had been part of the deal, too, though I had

210

pushed for it a lot harder than Aahz.

Aahz was housed in the adjoining room, which was nice, though smaller than mine. The royal architects were scheduled to open a door in our shared wall, and I had a hunch that when they did, the room arrangement would change drastically. For the moment, at least, I had a bit of unaccustomed privacy.

The room itself, however, was not what was currently commanding my attention. My mind was focused on Garkin's old brazier. I had been trying all afternoon to unlock its secrets, thus far without success. It stood firmly in the center of the floor where I had first placed it, stubbornly resisting my efforts.

I perched on my windowsill and studied the object glumly. I could levitate it easily enough, but that wasn't what I wanted. I wanted it to come alive and follow me around the way it used to follow Garkin.

That triggered an idea in my mind. It seemed silly, but nothing else had worked.

Drawing my eyebrows together, I addressed the brazier without focusing my energies on it.

"Come here!" I thought.

The brazier seemed to waiver for a moment, then it trotted to my side, clacking across the floor on its spindly legs.

It worked! Even though it was a silly little detail, the brazier's obedience somehow made me feel more like a magician.

"Hey, kid!" Aahz called, barging through my door without knocking. "Have you got a corkscrew?"

"What's a corkscrew?" I asked reflexively.

"Never mind," my mentor sighed. "I'll do it myself."

With that, he shifted the bottle of wine he was

holding to his left hand, and inserted the claw on his right forefinger into the cork. The cork made a soft pop as he gently eased it from the neck of the bottle, whereupon the cork was casually tossed into a corner as Aahz drank deeply of the wine.

"Ahh!" he gasped, coming up for air. "Terrific bouquet!"

"Um . . . Aahz?" I said shyly, leaving my window perch and moving to the table. "I have something to show you."

"First, could you answer a question?" Aahz asked.

"What?" I frowned.

"Why is that brazier following you around the room?"

I looked, and was startled to find he was right! The brazier had scuttled from the window to the table to remain by my side. The strange part was that I hadn't summoned it.

"Um . . . that's what I was going to show you," I admitted. "I've figured out how to get the brazier to come to me all by itself . . . no levitation or anything."

"Swell," Aahz grunted. "Now, can you make it stop?"

"Um . . . I don't know," I said, sitting down quickly in one of the chairs.

I didn't want to admit it, but while we were talking I had tried several mental commands to get the brazier to go away, all without noticeable effect. I'd have to work this out on my own once Aahz had left.

"Say, Aahz," I said casually, propping my feet on the table. "Could you pour me some of that wine?"

Aahz cocked an eyebrow at me, then crossed the

room slowly to stand by my side.

"Kid," he said gently, "I want you to look around real carefully. Do you see anybody here except you and me?"

"No," I admitted.

"Then we're in private, not in public . . . right?" he smiled.

"That's right," I agreed.

"Then get your own wine, apprentice!" he roared, kicking my chair out from under me.

Actually, it wasn't as bad as it sounds. I exerted my mind before I hit the floor and hovered safely in thin air. From that position, I reached out with my mind and lifted the bottle from Aahz's hand, transferring it to my own.

"If you insist," I said casually, taking a long pull on the bottle.

"Think you're pretty smart, don't you!" Aahz snarled, then he grinned. "Well, I guess you are at that. You've done pretty well . . . for an amateur."

"A professional," I corrected with a grin. "A salaried professional."

"I know." Aahz grinned back. "For an amateur, you're pretty smart. For a professional you've got a lot to learn."

"C'mon, Aahz!" I protested.

"But that can wait for another day," Aahz conceded. "You might as well relax for a while and enjoy yourself . . . while you can."

"What's that supposed to mean?" I frowned.

"Nothing!" Aahz shrugged innocently. "Nothing at all."

"Wait a minute, Aahz," I said sharply, regaining my feet. "I'm Court Magician now, right?"

"That's right, Skeeve," my mentor nodded.

"Court Magician is the job you pushed me into because it's so easy, right?" I pressed.

"Right again, kid." He smiled, his nodding becoming even more vigorous.

"Then nothing can go wrong? Nothing serious?" I asked anxiously.

Aahz retrieved his wine bottle and took a long swallow before answering.

"Just keep thinking that, kid." He grinned. "It'll help you sleep nights."

"C'mon, Aahz!" I whined. "You're supposed to be my teacher. If there's something I'm missing, you've got to tell me. Otherwise I won't learn."

"Very well, *apprentice*." Aahz smiled, evilly emphasizing the word. "There are a few things you've overlooked."

"Such as?" I asked, writhing under his smile.

"Such as Gus, Ajax, and Brockhurst, who you just sent back to Deva without instructions."

"Instructions?" I blinked.

"Tanda we don't have to worry about, but the other three—"

"Wait a minute, Aahz," I interrupted before he got too far from the subject. "What instructions?"

"Instructions not to talk about our little skirmish here," Aahz clarified absently. "Tanda will know enough to keep her mouth shut, but the others won't."

"You think they'll talk?"

"Is a frog's behind watertight?" Aahz retorted.

"What's a frog?" I countered.

"Money in their pockets, fresh from a successful campaign against overwhelming odds . . . of course

they'll talk!" Aahz thundered. "They'll talk their
fool heads off to anyone who'll listen. What's more,
they'll embellish it a little more with each telling until
it sounds like they're the greatest fighters ever to spit
teeth and you're the greatest tactician since Gronk!"

"What's wrong with that?" I inquired, secretly
pleased. I didn't know who Gronk was, but what
Aahz was saying had a nice ring to it.

"Nothing at all." Aahz responded innocently.
"Except now the word will be out as to who you are,
where you are, and what you are . . . also that you're
for hire and that you subcontract. If there's any place
in all the dimensions that folks will take note of information like that, it's the Bazaar."

Regardless of what my mentor may think, I'm not
slow. I realized in a flash the implications of what he
was saying . . . realized them and formulated an
answer.

"So we suddenly get a lot of strange people dropping in on us to offer jobs, or looking for work," I
acknowledged. "So what? All that means is I get a
lot of practice saying 'No.' Who knows, it might improve my status around here a little if it's known that
I regularly consult with strange beings from other
worlds."

"Of course," Aahz commented darkly, "there's
always the chance that someone at the Bazaar will
hear that the other side is thinking of hiring you and
decide to forcibly remove you from the roster. Either
that, or some young hotshot will want to make a
name for himself by taking on this unbeatable magician everyone's talking about."

I tried not to show how much his grim prophecy
had unnerved me. Then I realized he would probably

keep heaping it on until he saw me sweat. Consequently, I sweated . . . visibly.

"I hadn't thought of that, Aahz," I admitted. "I guess I did overlook something there."

"Then again there's Grimble and Badaxe," Aahz continued as if he hadn't heard me.

"What about Grimble and Badaxe?" I asked nervously.

"In my estimation," Aahz yawned, "the only way those two would ever work together would be against a common foe. In my further estimation, the best candidate for that 'common foe' position is you!"

"Me?" I asked in a very small voice.

"You work it out, kid," my mentor shrugged. "Until you hit the scene there was a two-way power struggle going as to who had the king's ear. Then you came along and not only saved the kingdom, you increased the population, expanded the borders, and added to the tax base. That makes you the most popular and therefore the most influential person in the king's court. Maybe I'm wrong, but I don't think Grimble and Badaxe are going to just sigh and accept that. It's my guess they'll 'double team' you and attack anything you say or do militarily and monetarily, and that's a tough one-two punch to counter."

"Okay. Okay. So there were two things I overlooked," I said. "Except for that—"

"And of course there's the people Big Julie and his men owe money to," Aahz commented thoughtfully. "I wonder how long it will be before they start nosing around looking for an explanation as to what happened to an entire army? More important, I wonder who they'll be looking for by name to provide them with that explanation?"

"Aahz?"

"Yeah, kid?"

"Do you mind if I have a little more of that wine?"

"Help yourself, kid. There's lots."

I had a hunch that was going to be the best news I would hear for a long time.

MYTH DIRECTIONS

Robert Asprin

Chapter One:

"Dragons and Demons and Kings, Oh my!"

— THE COWARDLY KLAHD

"THIS place stinks!" my scaly mentor snarled, glaring out the window at the rain.

"Yes, Aahz," I agreed meekly.

"What's that supposed to mean?" he snapped, turning his demon's speckled gold eyes on me.

"It means," I gulped, "that I agree with you. The Kingdom of Possiltum, and the palace specifically, stink to high heaven—both figuratively and literally."

"Ingratitude!" Aahz made his appeal to the ceiling. "I lose my powers to a stupid practical joker, and instead of concentrating on getting them back, I take on some twit of an apprentice who doesn't have any aspirations higher than being a thief, train him, groom him, and get him a job paying more than he could spend in two lifetimes, and what happens? He complains! I suppose you think you could have done better on your own?"

1

It occurred to me that Aahz's guidance had also gotten me hung, embroiled in a magik duel with a master magician, and recently, placed in the unenviable position of trying to stop the world's largest army with a handful of down-at-the-heels demons. It also occurred to me that this was not the most tactful time to point out these minor nerve-jangling incidents.

"I'm sorry, Aahz," I grovelled. "Possiltum *is* a pretty nice kingdom to work for."

"It stinks!" he declared, turning to the window again.

I stifled a sigh. A magician's lot is not a happy one. I stole that saying from a tune Aahz sings off and on . . . key. More and more, I was realizing the truth of the jingle. As the court magician to my king I had already endured a great deal more than I had ever bargained for.

Actually the king of Possiltum isn't my king. I'm *his* royal magician, an employee at best.

Aahz isn't *my* demon, either. I'm his apprentice, trying desperately to learn enough magik to warrant my aforementioned lofty title.

Gleep is definitely my dragon, though. Just ask Aahz. Better still, ask anyone in the court of Possiltum. Anytime my pet wreaks havoc with his playful romping, I get the blame and J.R. Grimble, the king's chancellor, deducts the damages from my wages.

Naturally, this gets Aahz upset. In addition to managing my magik career, Aahz also oversees our finances. Well, that's something of an understatement. He shamelessly bleeds the kingdom for every monetary consideration he can get for us (which is considerable) and watches over our expenses. When it comes to spending our ill-gotten wealth, Aahz would rather part with my blood. As you might guess, we argue a lot over this.

Gleep is understanding though; which is part of the reason I keep him around. He's quite intelligent and understanding for a baby dragon with a one word vocabulary. I spend a considerable amount of time telling him my troubles, and he always listens attentively without interrupting or arguing or shouting about how stupid I am. This makes him better company than Aahz.

It says something about one's lifestyle when the only one you can get sympathy from is a dragon.

Unfortunately, on this particular day I was cut off from my pet's company. It was raining, and when it rains in Possiltum, it doesn't kid around. Gleep is to big to live indoors with us, and the rain made the courtyard impassable, so I couldn't reach the stables where he was quartered. What was more, I couldn't risk roaming the halls of the castle for fear of running into the king. If that happened, he would doubtless ask when I was going to do something about the miserable weather. Weather control was not one of my current skills, and I was under strict orders from Aahz to avoid the subject at all costs. As such, I was stuck waiting out the rain in my own quarters. That in itself wouldn't be so bad, if it wasn't for the fact that I shared those quarters with Aahz.

Rain made Aahz grouchy, or I should say grouchier than usual. I'd rather be locked in a small cage with an angry spider-bear than be alone in a room with Aahz when he's in a bad mood.

"There must be *something* to do," Aahz grumbled, begging to pace the floor. "I haven't been this bored since the Two Hundred Year Siege."

"You could teach me about dimension travel," I suggested hopefully.

This was one area of magik Aahz had steadfastly refused to teach me. As I mentioned earlier, Aahz is a demon, short for "dimension traveler." Most of my close friends these days were demons, and I was eager to add dimension traveling to my meager list of skills.

"Don't make me laugh, kid." Aahz laughed harshly. "At the rate you're learning, it would take more than two hundred years to teach it to you."

"Oh," I said, crestfallen. "Well—you could tell me about the Two Hundred Year Siege."

"The Two Hundred Year Siege," Aahz murmured dreamily, smiling slightly to himself. Large groups of armed men have been known to turn pale and tremble visibly before Aahz's smile.

"There isn't much to tell," he began, leaning against a table and hefting a large pitcher of wine. "It was me and another magician, Diz-Ne. He was a snotty little upstart . . . you remind me a bit of him."

"What happened?" I urged, anxious to get the conversation away from me.

"Well, once he figured out he couldn't beat me flat out, he went defensive," Aahz reminisced. "He was a real nothing magikally, but he knew his defense spells. Kept me off his back for a full two hundred years, even though we drained most of the magik energies of that dimension in the process."

"Who won?" I pressed eagerly.

Aahz cocked an eyebrow at me over the lip of the wine pitcher.

"I'm telling the story, kid," he pointed out. "You figure it out."

I did, and swallowed hard.

"Did you kill him?"

"Nothing that pleasant," Aahz smiled. "What I did to him once I got through his defenses will last a lot longer than two hundred years—but I guarantee you, he won't get bored."

"Why were you fighting?" I asked in a desperate

effort to forestall the images my mind was manufacturing.

"He welshed on a bet," my mentor shrugged, hefting the wine again.

"That's all?"

"That's enough," Aahz insisted grimly. "Betting's a serious matter—in any dimension."

"Um—Aahz?" I frowned. "Weren't Big Julie and his men running from gambling debts when we met them?"

That's the army I mentioned earlier. Big Julie and his men were currently disguised as happy citizens of Possiltum.

"That's right, kid," Aahz nodded.

"Then that's why you said the loansharks would probably come looking for them," I declared triumphantly.

"Wrong," Aahz said firmly.

"Wrong?" I blinked.

"I didn't say they'd probably come looking," he corrected. "I said they *would* come looking. Bank on it. There are only two questions involved here: When are they coming, and what are you going to do about it?"

"I don't know about the 'when,' " I commented with careful deliberation, "but I've given some thought to what I'm going to do."

"And you've decided—" Aahz prompted.

"To grab our money and run!" I declared. "That's why I want to learn dimension travel. I figure there won't be anywhere in this dimension we could hide, and that means leaving Klah for greener, safer pastures."

Aahz was unmoved.

"If push comes to shove," he yawned, "we can use the D-Hopper. As long as we've got a mechanical means of traveling to other dimensions, there's no need for you to learn how to do it magically."

"C'mon, Aahz!" I exploded. "Why won't you teach me? What makes dimension traveling so hard to learn?"

Aahz studied me for a long moment, then heaved a big sigh. "All right, Skeeve," he said. "If you listen up, I'll try to sketch it out for you."

I listened. With every pore, I listened. Aahz didn't call me by my given name often, and when he did, it was serious.

"The problem is that to travel the dimensions, even using pentacles for beacons—gateways—requires knowing your destination dimension . . . knowing it almost as well as your home dimension. If you don't, then you can get routed into a dimension you aren't even aware of, and be trapped there with no way out."

He paused to take another drink from the wine pitcher.

"Now, you've only been in one dimension besides Klah," he continued. "That was Deva, and you only saw the Bazaar. You know the Bazaar well enough to know it's constantly changing and rearranging. You *don't* know it well enough to have zeroed in on the few permanent fixtures you could use to home in on for a return trip, so effectively, you don't know any other dimensions well enough to be sure of your destination if you tried to jump magikally. That's why you can't travel the dimensions without using the D-Hopper! End of lecture."

I blinked.

"You mean the only reason I can't do it magikally is because I don't know the other dimensions?" I asked.

"That's the *main* reason," Aahz corrected.

"Then let's go!" I cried, leaping to my feet. "I'll get the D-Hopper and you can show me a couple new dimensions while we're waiting for the rain to stop."

"Not so fast, kid!" Aahz interrupted, holding up a

restraining hand. "Sit down."

"What's wrong?" I challenged.

"Do you *really* think that possibility hadn't occurred to me?" he asked, an edge of irritation creeping into his voice.

I thought about it, and sat down again.

"Why don't you think it's a good idea?" I queried in a more humble tone.

"There are a few things you've overlooked in your enthusiasm," he intoned dryly. "First of all, remember that in another dimension, you'll be a demon. Now, except for Deva which makes its money on cross-dimension trade, most dimensions don't greet demons with flowers and red carpets. The fact is, a demon is likely to be attacked on sight by whoever's around with whatever's handy."

He leaned forward to emphasize his words. "What I'm trying to say is, it's dangerous! Now, if we went touring and ran into trouble, what do we have to defend ourselves? I've lost my powers and yours are still so undeveloped as to be practically non-existent. Who's going to handle the natives?"

"How dangerous is it?" I asked hesitantly.

"Let me put it to you this way, kid," Aahz sighed. "You spend a lot of time griping about how I keep putting your life in jeopardy with my blatant disregard for danger. Right?"

"Right." I nodded vigorously.

"Well, now I'm saying the trip you're proposing is dangerous. Does that give you a clue as to what you'll be up against?"

I leaned back in my chair and stretched, trying to make it look nonchalant.

"How abut sharing some of that wine?" I suggested casually.

For a change, Aahz didn't ignore the request. He tossed the pitcher into the air as he rose and strode to the window again. Reaching out with my mind, I gently grabbed the pitcher and brought it floating to my outstretched hand without spilling a drop.

As I said, I *am* the court magician of Possiltum. I'm not without powers.

"Don't let it get you down, kid," Aahz called from the window. "If you keep practicing, someday we can take that tour under your protection. But until you reach that level, or until we find you a magikal bodyguard, it'll just have to wait."

"I suppose you're right, Aahz," I conceded. "It's just that sometimes . . ."

There was a soft BAMF! as the ether was rent asunder and a demon appeared in the room. Right there! In my private quarters in the Possiltum royal palace!

Before I could recover from my surprise or Aahz could move to intervene, the demon plopped itself onto my lap and planted a big, warm kiss full on my mouth.

"Hi, handsome!" it purred. "How's tricks?"

Chapter Two:

"When old friends get together, everything else fades to insignificance."

—WAR, FAMINE, PESTILENCE, AND DEATH

"TANDA!" I exclaimed, recovering from shock sufficiently to fasten my arms around her waist in an energetic hug.

"In the flesh!" she winked, pressing hard against me.

My temperature went up several degrees, or maybe it was the room. Tananda has that effect on me—and rooms. Lusciously curvaceous, with a mane of light green hair accenting her lovely olive complexion and features, she could stop a twenty-man brawl with a smile and a deep sigh.

"He isn't the only one in the room, you know," Aahz commented dryly.

"Hi, Aahz!" my adorable companion cried, untangling herself from my lap and throwing herself into Aahz's arms.

The volume of Tananda's affections is exceeded only by her willingness to share them. I had a secret belief, though, that Tananda liked me better than she liked Aahz. This belief was tested for strength as their greeting grew longer and longer.

"Um . . . what brings you to these parts?" I interrupted at last.

That earned me a dark look from Aahz, but Tananda didn't bat an eye.

"Well," she dimpled, "I could say I was just in the neighborhood and felt like dropping by, but that wouldn't be true. The fact is, I need a little favor."

"Name it," Aahz and I declared simultaneously.

Aahz is tight-fisted and I'm chicken, but all bets are off when it comes to Tananda. She had helped us out of a couple of tight spots in the past, and we both figured we owed her. The fact she had helped us *into* as many tight spots as she had helped us out of never entered our minds. Besides—she was *awfully* nice to have around.

"It's nothing really," she sighed. "I have a little shopping to do and was hoping I could borrow one of you two to help me carry things."

"You mean today?" Aahz frowned.

"Actually, for the next couple days," Tananda informed him. "Maybe as long as a week."

"Can't do it," Aahz sighed. "I have to referee a meeting between Big Julie and General Badaxe tomorrow. Any chance you could postpone it until next week?"

"Ummm . . . you weren't the one I was thinking of, Aahz," Tananda said, giving the ceiling a casual survey. "I was thinking Skeeve and I could handle it."

"Me?" I blinked.

Aahz scowled.

"Not a chance," he declared. "The kid can't play step-and-fetch-it for you. It's beneath his dignity."

"No, it isn't!" I cried. "I mean, if it wouldn't be beneath *you*, Aahz, how could it be beneath me?"

"I'm not the court magician of Possiltum!" he argued.

"I can disguise myself!" I countered. "That's one of my best spells. You've said so yourself."

"I think your scaly green mentor is just a lee-tle bit jealous," Tananda observed, winking at me covertly.

"Jealous?" Aahz exploded. "Me? Jealous of a little . . . " He broke off and looked back and forth between Tananda and myself as he realized he was being baited.

"Oh—I suppose it would be okay," he grumbled at last. "Go ahead and take him—even though it's beyond me what you expect to find in this backwater dimension worth shopping for."

"Oh, Aahz!" Tananda laughed. "You're a card. Shopping in Klah? I may be a little flighty from time to time, but I'm not crazy."

"You mean we're headed for other dimensions?" I asked eagerly.

"Of course," she nodded. "We have quite an itinerary ahead of us. First, we'll hop over to—"

"What's an itinerary?" I asked.

"Stop!" Aahz shouted, holding up a hand for silence.

"But I was just—"

"Stop!"

"We were—"

"Stop!"

Our conversation effectively halted, we turned our attention to Aahz. With melodramatic slowness, he folded his arms across his chest.

"No," he said.

"No?" I shrieked. "But, Aahz . . . "

" 'But, Aahz' nothing," he barked back. "I said 'No' and I meant it."

"Wait a minute," Tananda interceded, stepping between us. "What's the problem, Aahz?"

"If you think I'm going to let my apprentice go

traipsing around the dimensions alone and unprotected—"

"I won't be alone," I protested. "Tananda will be there."

"—a prime target for any idiot who wants to bag a demon," Aahz continued, ignoring my outburst, "just so you can have a beast of burden for your shopping jaunt, well, you'd better think again."

"Are you through?" Tananda asked testily.

"For the moment," Aahz nodded, matching her glare for glare.

"First of all," she began, "as Skeeve pointed out, if you'd bothered to listen, he won't be alone. I'll be with him. That means, second of all, he won't be unprotected. Just because I let my membership with the Assassins Guild expire doesn't mean I've forgotten everything."

"Yeah, Aahz," I interjected.

"Shut up, kid," he snapped.

"Third of all," Tananda continued, "you've got to stop thinking of Skeeve here as a kid. He stopped Big Julie's army, didn't he? And besides, he *is* your apprentice. I assume you've taught him *something* over the last couple of years."

That hit Aahz in his second most sensitive spot. His vanity. His most sensitive spot is his money pouch.

"Well . . . " he waivered.

"C'mon, Aahz," I pleaded. "What could go wrong?"

"The mind boggles," he retorted grimly.

"Don't exaggerate, Aahz," Tananda reprimanded.

"Exaggerate!" my mentor exploded anew. "The first time I took Mr. Wonderful here off-dimension, he bought a dragon we neither need nor want and nearly got killed in a brawl with a pack of cutthroats."

"A fight which he won, as I recall," Tananda observed.

"The second time we went out," Aahz continued undaunted, "I left him at a fast-food joint where he promptly recruited half the deadbeats at the Bazaar for a fighting force."

"They won the war!" I argued.

"That's not the point," Aahz growled. "The point is, every time the kid here hits another dimension, he ends up in trouble. He draws it like a magnet."

"This time I'll be there to keep an eye on him," Tananda soothed.

"You were there the first two times," Aahz pointed out grimly.

"So were you!" she countered.

"That's right!" Aahz agreed. "And both of us together couldn't keep him out of trouble. Now do you see why I want to keep him right here in Klah?"

"Hmm," Tananda said thoughtfully. "I see your point, Aahz."

My heart sank.

"I just don't agree with it," she concluded.

"Damn it, Tananda . . . " Aahz began, but she waved him to silence.

"Let me tell you a story," she smiled. "There was this couple see, who had a kid they thought the world of. They thought so much of him, in fact, that when he was born they sealed him in a special room. Just to be sure nothing would happen to him, they screened everything that went into the room; furniture, books, food, toys, *everything*. They even filtered the air to be sure he didn't get any diseases."

"So?" Aahz asked suspiciously.

"So—on his eighteenth birthday, they opened the room and let him out," Tanda explained. "The kid took two steps and died of excitement."

"Really?" I asked, horrified.

"It's exaggerated a bit," she admitted, "but I

think Aahz gets the point."

"I haven't been keeping him sealed in," Aahz mumbled. "There've been some real touch-and-go moments, you know. You've been there for some of them."

"But you *have* been a little overprotective, haven't you, Aahz?" Tananda urged gently.

Aahz was silent for several moments, avoiding our eyes. "All right," he sighed at last. "Go ahead, kid. Just don't come crying to me if you get yourself killed."

"How could I do that?" I frowned.

Tananda nudged me in the ribs and I took the hint.

"There are a few things I want settled before you go," Aahz declared brusquely, a bit of his normal spirit returning.

He began moving back and forth through the room, gathering items from our possessions.

"First," he announced, "here's some money of your own for the trip. You probably won't need it, but you always walk a little taller with money in your pouch."

So saying, he counted out twenty gold pieces into my hands. Realizing I had hired a team of demons to fight a war for five gold pieces, he was giving me a veritable fortune!

"Gee, Aahz . . . " I began, but he hurried on.

"Second, here's the D-Hopper." He tucked the small metal cylinder into my belt. "I've set it to bring you back here. If you get into trouble, if you *think* you're getting into trouble, hit the button and come home *right then*. No heroics, no jazzy speeches. Just hit and get. You understand me?"

"Yes, Aahz," I promised dutifully.

"And finally," he announced, drawing himself up to his full height, "the dragon stays here. You aren't going to drag your stupid pet along with you and that's final. I know you'd like to have him with you, but he'd only cause problems."

"Okay, Aahz," I shrugged.

Actually, I had figured on leaving Gleep behind, but it didn't seem tactful to point that out.

"Well," my mentor sighed, sweeping us both with a hard gaze, "I guess that's that. Sorry I can't hang around to see you off, but I've got more pressing things to do."

With that he turned on his heels and left, shutting the door behind him more forcefully than was necessary.

"That's funny," I said, staring after him. "I didn't think he had anything important to do. In fact, just before you showed up, he was complaining about being bored."

"You know, Skeeve," Tananda said softly, giving me a strange look, "Aahz is really quite attached to you."

"Really?" I frowned. "What makes you say that?"

"Nothing," she smiled. "It was just a thought. Well, are you ready to go?"

"As ready as I'll ever be," I declared confidently. "What's our first stop? The Bazaar at Deva?"

"Goodness, no!" she retorted, wrinkling her nose. "We're after something really unique, not the common stuff they have at the Bazaar. I figure we're going to have to hit some out-of-the-way dimensions, the more out-of-the-way the better."

Despite my confidence, an alarm gong went off in the back of my mind at this declaration.

"What are we looking for, anyway?" I asked casually.

Tananda shot a quick glance at the door, then leaned forward to whisper in my ear.

"I couldn't tell you before," she murmured conspiratorially, "but we're after a birthday present. A birthday present for Aahz!"

Chapter Three:

"That's funny, I never have any trouble with service when I'm shopping."

—K. KONG

EVER since he took me on as an apprentice, Aahz has complained that I don't practice enough. He should have seen me on the shopping trip! In the first three days after our departure from Klah I spent more time practicing magik than I had in the previous year.

Tananda had the foresight to bring along a couple of translator pendants which enabled us to understand and be understood by the natives in the dimensions we visited. That was fine for communications, but there remained the minor detail of our physical appearance. Disguises were my job.

Besides flying Aahz had taught me one other spell which had greatly enhanced my ability to survive dubious situations; that was the ability to change the outward appearance of my own, or anyone else's, physical features. Tagging along with Tananda, this skill got a real workout.

The procedure was simple enough. We would ar-

16

rive at some secluded point, then creep to a spot where I would observe a few members of the local population. Once I had laid eyes on them I could duplicate their physical form for our disguises and we could blend with the crowd. Of course, my nerves had to be calmed so I wouldn't jump out of my skin when catching a passing glance of the being standing next to me.

If from this you conclude that the dimensions we visited were inhabited by people who looked a little strange . . . you're wrong. The dimensions we visited were peopled by beings who looked *very* strange.

When Tananda decides to tour out-of-the-way dimensions, she doesn't kid around. None of the places we visited looked normal to my untraveled eyes but a few in particular stand out in my memory as being exceptionally weird.

Despite Tananda's jokes about rental agencies, Avis turned out to be populated with bird-like creatures with wings and feathers. In that dimension I not only had to maintain our disguises, I had to fly us from perch to perch as per the local method of transportation. Instead of traversing their market center as I had expected, we spent considerable time viewing their national treasures. These treasures turned out to be a collection of broken pieces of colored glass and bits of shiny metal which to my eye were worthless—but Tananda studied them with quiet intensity.

To maintain our disguises, we had to eat and drink without hands—which proved to be harder than it sounded. Since the food consisted of live grubs and worms, I passed on any opportunity to sample the local cuisine. Tananda, however, literally dove into (remember—no hands!) a bowlful. Whether she licked her lips because she found the fare exceptionally tasty or if she was attempting to catch a few of the wriggly morsels that were trying to escape their fate was not important; I found the sight utterly revolting. To avoid having to watch her, I tried the local wine.

The unusual drinking style meant that I ended up taking larger swallows than I normally would, but that was okay as the wine was light and flavorful. Unfortunately, it also proved to be much stronger than anything I had previously sampled. After I had nearly flown us into a rather large tree Tananda decided it was time for us to move to another dimension.

As a footnote to that particular adventure, the wine had two side effects: first, I developed a colossal headache, and, second, I became violently nauseous. The latter was because Tananda gleefully told me how they make wine on Avis. To this day I can't hear the name Avis without having visions of flying through the air and a vague tinge of air-sickness. As far as I'm concerned, when rating dimensions on a scale of ten, Avis will always be a number two.

Another rather dubious dimension we spent considerable time in was Gastropo. The length of our stay there had nothing to do with our quest. Tananda decided, after relatively few stops, that the dimension had nothing to offer of a quality suitable for Aahz's present. What delayed us was our disguises.

Let me clarify that before aspersions are cast on my admittedly limited abilities, the physical appearance part was easy. As I've said, I'm getting quite good at disguise spells. What hung us up was the manner of locomotion. After flying from tree to tree in Avis, I would have thought I was ready to get from point A to point B in any conceivable way. Well, as Aahz has warned me, the dimensions are an endless source of surprises.

The Gastropods were snails—large snails, but snails none the less. Spiral shells, eyes on stalks—the whole bit. I could handle that. What I couldn't get used to was inching my way along with the rest of the local pedestrians—excuse me, *pod*-estrians.

"Tanda," I growled under my breath. "How long are we going to stay in this god-awful dimension?"

"Relax, handsome," she chided, easing forward another inch. "Enjoy the scenery."

"I've been enjoying this particular hunk of scenery for half a day," I complained. "I'm enjoying it so much I've memorized it."

"Don't exaggerate," my guide scolded. "This morning we were on the other side of that tree."

I closed my eyes and bit back my first five or six responses to her correction. "How long?" I repeated.

"I figure we can split after we turn that corner."

"But that corner's a good twenty-five feet away!" I protested.

"That's right," she confirmed. "I figure we'll be there by sundown."

"Can't we just walk over there at normal speed?"

"Not a chance; we'd be noticed."

"By who?"

"Whom. Well, by your admirer, for one."

"My what?" I blinked.

Sure enough, there was a Gastropod chugging heroically along behind us. When it realized I was looking at it, it began to wave its eye-stalks in slow, but enthusiastic, motions.

"It's been after you for about an hour," Tananda confided. "That's why I've been hurrying."

"That does it!" I declared, starting off at a normal pace. "C'mon, Tanda, we're getting out of here."

Shrill cries of alarm were being sounded by the Gastropods as I rounded the corner, followed, shortly, by my guide.

"What's the matter with you?" she demanded. "We could—"

"Get us out—now!" I ordered.

"But—"

"Remember how I got my dragon?" I barked. "If

I let an amorous snail follow me home, Aahz will disown me as his apprentice. Now, are you going to get us out of here, or do I use the D-Hopper and head for home?''

"Don't get your back up," she soothed, beginning her ritual to change dimensions. "You shouldn't have worried though, we're looking for cargo—not S-cargo."

We were in another dimension before I could ask her to explain why she was giggling. So it went, dimension after dimension until I gave up trying to predict the unpredictable and settled for coping with the constants. Even this turned out to be a chore. For one thing, I had some unexpected problems with Tananda. I had never noticed it before, but she's really quite vain. She didn't just want to look like a native—she wanted to look like an *attractive* native.

Anyone who thinks beauty is a universal concept should visit some of the places we did. Whatever grotesque form I was asked to duplicate Tananda always had a few polite requests for improving her appearance. After a few days of "the hair should be more matted," or "shouldn't my eye be a bit more bloodshot?" or "a little more slime under the armpits," I was ready to scream. It probably wouldn't have been so annoying if her attention to detail had extended just a little bit to my appearance. All I'd get was—"You? You look fine." That how I know she's vain; she was more interested in her own appearance than mine.

That wasn't the only thing puzzling about Tananda's behavior. Despite her claim that we were on a shopping trip, she steadfastly avoided the retail sections of the dimensions we visited. Bazaars, farmers' markets, flea markets and all the rest were met with the same wrinkled nose (when there was a nose) and "we don't want to go *there*." Instead she seemed to be content as a tourist. Her inquiries would invar-

iably lead us to national shrines or the public displays
of royal treasures. After viewing several of these we
would retire to a secluded spot and head off for the
next dimension.

In a way this suited me fine. Not only was I getting
a running, flying, and crawling tour of the dimensions, I was doing it with Tananda. Tananda is
familiar with the social customs of over a hundred
dimensions and in every dimension she was just
that—familiar. I rapidly learned that in addition to
beauty, morality varied from dimension to dimension. The methods of expressing affection in some of
the dimensions we visited defy description but in-
variably make me blush at the memory. Needless to
say, after three days of this I was seriously trying to
progress beyond the casual friendship level with my
shapely guide. I mean, Tananda's interpretation of
casual friendship was already seriously threatening
the continued smooth operation of my heart—not to
mention other organs.

There was a more pressing problem on my mind,
however. After three days of visiting strange worlds,
I was hungry enough to bite my own arm for the
blood. They say if you're hungry enough you'll eat
anything. Don't you believe it. The things placed
before me and called food were unstomachable
despite starvation. I know; I tried occasionally, out
of desperation, only to lose everything else in my
stomach along with the latest offering. Having
Tananda sitting across from me, joyfully chewing
tentacled things that oozed out of her mouth and
wriggled didn't help.

Finally I expressed my distress and needs to Tananda.

"I wondered why you hadn't been eating much,"
she frowned. "But I thought maybe you were on a
diet, or something. I wish you'd spoken up sooner."

"I didn't want to be a bother," I explained lamely.

"It isn't that," she waved. "It's just that if I had known two dimensions ago there were half a dozen humanoid dimensions nearby that we could have hopped over to. Right now, there's only one that would fit the bill without us having to go through a couple of extra dimensions along the way."

"Then let's head for that one," I urged. "The sooner I eat the better off we'll be." I wasn't exaggerating. My stomach was beginning to growl so loudly it was a serious threat to our disguises.

"Suit yourself," she shrugged, pulling me behind a row of hedges that tinkled musically in the breeze. "Personally, though, it's not a dimension I normally stop in."

Again the alarm sounded in the back of my head, despite my hunger. "Why not?" I asked suspiciously.

"Because they're weird there—I mean, *really* weird," she confided.

Images flashed across my mind of the beings we'd already encountered. "Weirder than the natives we've been imitating?" I gulped. "I thought you said they'd be humanoid?"

"Not weird physically," Tananda chided, taking my hand. "Weird mentally. You'll see."

"What's the name of the dimension?" I called desperately as she closed her eyes to begin our travels. The scenery around us faded, there was a rush of darkness, then a new scene burst brightly and noisily into view.

"Jahk," she answered, opening her eyes since we were there.

Chapter Four:

> *"'Weird' is a relative, not an absolute
> term."*
>
> —BARON FRANK N. FURTER

YOU recall my account of our usual modus operandi
on hitting a new dimension? How we would arrive inconspicuously and disguise ourselves before mingling
with the natives? Well, however secluded Tananda's
landing point in Jahk might be normally—it wasn't
when we arrived.

As the dimension came into focus it was apparent
that we were in a small park, heavily overgrown with
trees and shrubs. It was not the flora of the place
which caught and held my attention, however, it was
the crowd. What crowd? you might ask. Why, the
one carrying blazing torches and surrounding us, of
course. Oh—that crowd!

Well, to be completely honest, they weren't actually surrounding us. They were surrounding the contraption we were standing on. I had never really
known what a contraption was when Aahz had used

the word in conversation, and being Aahz he wouldn't define the word when I asked him to. Now that I was here, however, I recognized one on sight. The thing we were standing on had to be a contraption.

It was some sort of wagon—in that it was large and had four wheels. Beyond that I couldn't tell much about it, because it was completely covered by tufts of colored paper. That's right, I said paper—light fluffy stuff that would be nice if you had a cold, runny nose. But this paper was mostly yellow and blue. Looming over us was some kind of monstrous, dummy warrior complete with helmet—also covered with tufts of blue and yellow paper.

Of all the things that had flashed across my mind when Tananda warned me that the Jahks were weird, the one thing that had not occurred to me was that they were blue-and-yellow-paper freaks.

"Get off the float!"

This last was shouted at us from someone in the crowd.

"I beg your pardon," I shouted back.

"The float! Get off of it!"

"C'mon, handsome," Tananda hissed, hooking my elbow in hers.

Together we leaped to the ground. As it turned out we were barely in time. With a bloodthirsty howl, the crowd surged forward and tossed their torches onto the contraption we had so recently abandoned. In moments it was a mass of flames the heat of which warmed the already overheated crowd. They danced and sang, joyfully oblivious to the destruction of the contraption.

Edging away from the scene, I realized with horror that it was being duplicated throughout the park. Wherever I looked there were bonfires set on contraptions, and jubilant crowds.

"I think we arrived at a bad time," I observed.

"What makes you say that?" Tananda asked.

"Little things," I explained, "like the fact they're in the middle of torching the town."

"I don't think so," my companions shrugged. "When you torch a town you don't usually start with the parks."

"Okay, then you tell me just what they're doing."

"As far as I can tell, they're celebrating."

"Celebrating what?"

"Some kind of victory. As near as I can tell, everyone's shouting—we won! we won!"

I surveyed the blazes again. "I wonder what they'd do if they lost?"

Just then a harried-looking individual strode up to us. His no-nonsense, business-like manner was an island of sanity in a sea of madness. I didn't like it. Not that I have anything against sanity, mind you. It's just that up 'til now we had been pretty much ignored. I feared that was about to change.

"Here's your pay," he said brusquely, handing us each a pouch. "Turn in your costume at the Trophy Building." With that he was gone, leaving us openmouthed and holding the bags.

"What was that all about?" I managed to say.

"Beats me," Tananda admitted. "They lost me when they called that contraption a float."

"Then I'm right! It is a contraption," I exclaimed with delight. "I knew they had to be wrong; a float is airtight and won't sink in water."

"I thought it was made with ice cream and gingerale?" Tananda frowned.

"With what and what?" I blinked.

"Great costumes—really great!" someone shouted to us as they staggered by.

"Time to do something about our disguises," Tananda murmured as she waved to the drunk.

"Right," I nodded, glad we could agree on something.

The disguises should have been easy after my recent experience in other dimensions. I mean the Jahks were humanoid and I had lots of ready models to work from. Unfortunately I encountered problems.

The first was pride. Despite the teeming masses around us, I couldn't settle on two individuals whose appearance I wanted to duplicate. I never considered myself particularly vain; I've never considered myself as being in top physical condition—of course, that was before I arrived in Jahk.

Every being I could see was extremely off-weight—either over or under. If a specific individual wasn't ribs-protruding thin to the point of looking brittle, he was laboring along under vast folds of fat which bunched and bulged at waist, chin and all four cheeks. Try as I might, I couldn't bring myself to alter Tananda or myself to look like these wretched specimens.

My second problem was that I couldn't concentrate, anyway. Disguise spells, like any other magik, require a certain amount of concentration. In the past I've been able to cast spells in the heat of battle or embarrassment. In our current situation I couldn't seem to get my mind focused.

You see there was this song—well, I think it was a song. Anyway the crowd acted like it was singing a rhythmic chant; the chant was incredibly catchy. Even in the short time we'd been there I'd almost mastered the lyrics—which is a tribute to the infectious nature of the song rather than any indication of my ability to learn lyrics. The point is that every time I tried concentrating on our disguises, I found myself singing along with the chant instead. Terrific!

"Any time you're ready, handsome."

"What's that, Tananda?"

"The disguises," she prompted, glancing about

nervously. "The spell will work better when you aren't humming."

"I—er, um—I can't seem to find two good models," I alibi'd lamely.

"Are you having trouble counting up to two all of a sudden?" she scowled. "By my count you've got a whole parkful of models."

"But none I want to look like—want *us* to look like," I amended quickly.

"Check me on this," Tananda said, pursing her lips. "Two days ago you disguised us as a pair of slimy slugs, right?"

"Yes, but—"

"And before that as eight-legged dogs?"

"Well, yes, but—"

"And you never complained about how you looked in your disguise then, right?"

"That was different," I protested.

"How?" she challenged.

"Those were—well, things! These are humanoids and I know what humanoids should look like."

"What they *should* look like isn't important," my guide argued. "What matters is what they *do* look like. We've got to blend with the crowd—and the sooner the better."

"But—" I began.

"Because if we don't," she continued sternly, "we're going to run into someone who's both sober and unpreoccupied—which will give us the choice between being guest-of-honor at the next bonfire they light or skipping this dimension before you've had anything to eat."

"I'll try again," I sighed, scanning the crowd once more.

In a desperate effort to comply with Tananda's order, I studied the first two individuals my eyes fell on, then concentrated on duplicating their appearance without really considering how they looked.

"Not bad," Tananda commented dryly, surveying her new body. "Of course, I always thought I looked better as a woman."

"You want a disguise, you get a disguise," I grumbled.

"Hey, handsome," my once-curvaceous comrade breathed, laying a soft, but hairy, hand on my arm. "Relax, we're on the same side. Remember?"

My anger melted away at her touch—as always. Maybe someday I'll develop an immunity to Tananda's charms. Until then I'll just enjoy them. "Sorry, Tanda," I apologized. "Didn't mean to snap at you—log it off to hunger."

"That's right," she exclaimed, clicking her fingers, "we're supposed to be finding you some food. It completely slipped my mind again what with this racket going on. C'mon, let's see what the blue-plate special is today."

Finding a place to eat turned out to be more of a task than either of us anticipated. Most of the restaurants we came across were either closed or only serving drinks. I half-expected Tananda to suggest that we drink our meal, but mercifully that possibility wasn't mentioned.

We finally located a little sidewalk cafe down a narrow street and elbowed our way to a small table, ignoring the glares of our fellow diners. Service was slow, but my companion sped things up a bit by emptying the contents of one of our pouches onto the tabletop thus attracting the waiter's attention. In short order we were presented with two bowls of steaming whatever. I didn't even try to identify the various lumps and crunchies. It smelled good and tasted better and after several days of enforced fasting, that was all that mattered to me. I glutted myself and was well into my second bowl by the time Tananda finished her first. Pushing the empty dish

away she began to study the crowd on the street with
growing interest.

"Have you figured out yet what's going on?" she
asked.

"Murppg!" I replied through a mouthful of food.

"Hmmm?" she frowned.

"I can't tell for sure," I said, swallowing hard.
"Everybody's happy because they won something,
but darned if I can hear what they won."

"Well," Tananda shrugged. "I warned you they
were weird."

Just then the clamor in the streets soared to new
heights, drowning out any efforts at individual conversation. Craning our necks in an effort to locate
the source of the disturbance, we beheld a strange
phenomenon. A wall-to-wall mob of people was
marching down the street, chanting in unison and
sweeping along, or trampling, any smaller groups it
encountered. Rather than expressing anger or resent-
ment at this intrusion, the people around us were
jumping up and down and cheering, hugging each
other with tears of pure joy in their eyes. The focus
of everyone's attention seemed to be sitting on a litter
borne aloft by the stalwarts at the head of the crowd.
I was fortunate enough to get a look at it as it passed
by—fortunate in that I could see it without having to
move. The crowds were such that I couldn't move if
I'd wanted to, so it was just as well that it passed
close by.

To say they carried a statue would be insufficient.
It was the *ugliest* thing I had ever seen in my life and
that included everything I'd just seen on this trip with
Tananda. It was small, roughly twice the size of my
head, and depicted a large, four-legged toad holding
a huge eyeball in its mouth. Along its back, instead
of warts, were the torsos, heads and arms of tiny
Jahks intertwined in truly grotesque eroticism. These
figures were covered with the warty protrusions one

would expect to have found on the toad itself. As a crowning touch, the entire thing had a mottled gold finish which gave the illusion of splotches crawling back and forth on the surface.

I was totally repulsed by the statue, but it was obvious the crowd around me did not share these feelings. They swept forward in a single wave, joining the mob and adding their voices to the chant which could still be heard long after the procession had vanished from sight. Finally we were left in relative quiet on a street deserted save for a few random bodies of those not swift enough to either join or evade the mob.

"Well," I said casually, clearing my throat. "I guess we know what they won, now. Right?"

There was no immediate response. I shot a sharp glance at my companion and found her staring down the street after the procession.

"Tanda," I repeated, slightly concerned.

"That's it," she said with sudden, impish glee.

"That's what?" I blinked.

"Aahz's birthday present," she proclaimed.

I peered down the street, wondering what she was looking at. "What is?" I asked.

"That statue," she said firmly.

"*That* statue?" I cried, unable to hide my horror.

"Of course," she nodded, "it's perfect. Aahz will have never seen one, much less owned one."

"How do you figure that?" I pressed.

"It's obviously one-of-a-kind," she explained. "I mean, who could make something like that twice?"

She had me there, but I wasn't about to give up the fight. "There's just one little problem. I'm no expert on psychology, but if that pack we just saw is any decent sample, I don't think the folks around here are going to be willing to sell us their pretty statue."

"Of course not, silly," she laughed, turning to her

food again. "That's what makes it priceless. I never planned to *buy* Aahz's present."

"But if it isn't for sale, how do we get it?" I frowned, fearing the answer.

Tananda choked suddenly on her food. It took me a moment to realize she was laughing. "Oh, Skeeve," she gasped at last, "you're such a kidder."

"I am?" I blinked.

"Sure," she insisted, looking deep into my eyes. "Why do you think it was so important for you to come along on this trip. I mean, you've always said you wanted to be a thief."

Chapter Five:

"Nothing is impossible. Anything can be accomplished with proper preparation and planning."

—PONCE DE LEON

IT was roughly twelve hours later, the start of a new day. We were still in Jahk. I was still protesting. At the very least, I was sure this latest madcap project was *not* in line with Aahz's instructions to stay out of trouble.

Tananda, on the other hand, insisted that it would not be any trouble—or it *might* not be any trouble. We wouldn't know for sure until we saw what kind of security the locals had on the statue. In the meantime, why assume the worst?

I took her advice. I assumed the best. I assumed the security would be impenetrable and that we'd give the whole idea up as a lost cause.

So it was, with different but equally high hopes, we set out in search of the statue.

The town was deathly still in the early morning light. Apparently everyone was sleeping off the prior night's festivities—which seemed a reasonable pastime, all things considered.

We did manage to find one open restaurant, however. The owner was wearily shoveling out the rubble left by the celebrating crowds, and grudgingly agreed to serve us breakfast.

I had insisted on this before setting out. I mean, worried or not, it takes more than one solid meal to counterbalance the effects of a three-day stretch without food.

"So," I declared once we were settled at the table. "How do we go about locating the statue?"

"Easy," Tananda winked. "I'll ask our host a few subtle questions when he serves our food."

As if summoned by her words, the owner appeared with two steaming plates of food, which he plopped on the table in front of us with an unceremonious *klunk*.

"Thanks," I nodded, and was answered with an unenthusiastic grunt.

"Say, could we ask you a couple questions?" Tananda purred.

"Such as?" the man responded listlessly.

"Such as where do they keep the statue?" she asked bluntly.

I choked on my food. Tananda's idea of interrogation is about as subtle as a flogging. I keep forgetting she's a long standing drinking partner of Aahz's.

"The statue?" our host frowned.

"The one that was being carried up and down the streets yesterday," Tananda clarified easily.

"Oh! You mean the *Trophy*," the man laughed. "Statue. Hey, that's a good one. You two must be new in town."

"You might say that," I confirmed dryly. I had never been that fond of being laughed at—particularly early in the morning.

"Statue, trophy, what's the difference," Tananda shrugged. "Where is it kept?"

"It's on public display in the Trophy Building, of course," the owner informed us. "If you want to see it, you'd best get started early. After five years, everyone in the city's going to be showing up for a look-see."

"How far is it to—" Tananda began, but I interrupted her.

"You have a whole building for trophies?" I asked with forced casualness. "How many trophies are there?"

"Just the one," our host announced. "We put up a building especially for it. You two must *really* be new not to know that."

"Just got in yesterday," I confirmed. "Just to show you how new we are, we don't even know what the trophy's for."

"For?" the man gaped. "Why, it's for winning the Big Game, of course."

"What big game?"

The question slipped out before I thought. It burst upon the conversation like a bombshell, and our host actually gave ground a step in astonishment. Tananda nudged my foot warningly under the table, but I had already realized I had made a major blunder.

"I can see we have a lot to learn about your city, friend," I acknowledged smoothly. "If you have the time, we'd appreciate your joining us in a glass of wine. I'd like to hear more about this Big Game."

"Say, that's nice of you," our host declared, brightening noticeably. "Wait right here. I'll fetch the wine."

"What was that all about?" Tananda hissed as soon as he had moved out of earshot.

"I'm after some information," I retorted. "Specifically, about the Trophy."

"I know that," she snapped. "The question is 'Why?' "

"As a thief," I explained loftily, "I feel I should

know as much as possible about what I'm trying to steal."

"Who ever told you that?" Tananda frowned. "All you want to know about a target item is how big it is, how heavy it is, and what it will sell for. Then you study the security protecting it. Learning a lot about the item itself is a handicap, not an advantage."

"How do you figure that?" I asked, my curiosity aroused in spite of myself.

My companion rolled her eyes in exasperation.

"Because it'll make you feel guilty," she explained. "When you find out how emotionally attached the current owner is to the item, or that he'll be bankrupt without it, or that he'll be killed if it's stolen, then you'll be reluctant to take it. When you actually make your move, guilt can make you hesitate, and hesitant thieves either end up in jail or dead."

I was going to pursue the subject further, but our host chose that moment to rejoin us. Balancing a bottle and three glasses in his hands, he hooked an extra chair over to our table with his foot.

"Here we go," he announced, depositing his load in front of us. "The best in the house—or the best that's left after the celebrations. You know how that is. No matter how much you stock in advance, it's never enough."

"No, we don't know," I corrected. "I was hoping you could tell us."

"That's right," he nodded, filling the glasses. "You know I still can't believe how little you know about politics."

"Politics?" I blinked. "What does the Big Game have to do with politics?"

"It has everything to do with politics," our host proclaimed mightily. "That's the point. Don't you see?"

"No," I admitted bluntly.

The man sighed.

"Look," he said, "this land has two potential capitals. One is Veygus, and this one, as you know, is Ta-hoe."

I hadn't known it, but it seemed unwise to admit my ignorance. I'm slow, but not dumb.

"Since there can only be one capital at any given time," our host continued, "the two cities compete for the privilege each year. The winner is the capital and gets to be the center of government for the next year. The Trophy is the symbol of that power, and Veygus has had it for the last five years. Yesterday we finally won it back."

"You mean the Big Game decides who's going to run the land?" I exclaimed, realization dawning at last. "Excuse my asking, but isn't that a bit silly?"

"No sillier than any other means of selecting governmental leadership," the man countered, shrugging his bony shoulders. "It sure beats going to war. Do you think it's a coincidence that we've been playing the game for five hundred years and there hasn't been a civil war in that entire time?"

"But if the Big Game has replaced civil war, then what—" I began, but Tananda interrupted.

"I hate to interrupt," she interrupted, "but if we're going to beat the crowds, we'd better get going. Where did you say the Trophy Building was, again?"

"One block up and six blocks to the left," our host supplied. "You'll know it by the crowds. I'll set the rest of the bottle aside and we can finish it after you've seen the Trophy."

"We'd appreciate that," Tananda smiled, paying him for our meal.

Apparently she had succeeded in using the right currency, for the owner accepted it without batting an eye and waved a fond farewell as we started off.

"I was hoping to find out more about this Big

Game,'' I grumbled as we passed out of earshot.

"No, you weren't," my guide corrected.

"I wasn't?" I frowned.

"No. You were getting involved," she pointed out. "We're here to get a birthday present, not to get embroiled in local politics."

"I wasn't getting involved," I protested. "I was just trying to get a little information."

Tananda sighed heavily.

"Look, Skeeve," she said, "take some advice from an old dimension traveler. Too much information is poison. Every dimension has its problems, and if you start learning the gruesome details, it occurs to you how simple it would be to help out. Once you see a problem *and* a solution, you feel almost obligated to meddle. That always leads to trouble, and we're supposed to be avoiding trouble this trip, remember?"

I almost pointed out the irony of her advising me to avoid trouble while en route to engineer a theft. Then it occurred to me that if the theft didn't bother her, but local politics did, I might be wise to heed her advice. As I've said, I'm slow, but not dumb.

As predicted, the Trophy Building was crowded despite the early hour. As we approached, I marveled anew at the physique of the natives—or specifically, the lack thereof.

Tananda did not seem to share my fascination with the natives, and threaded her way nimbly through the throng, leaving me to follow behind. There was no organized line, and by the time we got through one of the numerous doors, the throng was thick enough to impede our progress. Tananda continued making her way closer to the Trophy, but I stopped just inside the door. My advantage of height gave me a clear view of the Trophy from where I was.

If anything, it was uglier seen plainly than it had been viewed from a distance.

"Isn't it magnificent?" the woman standing next to me sighed.

It took me a moment to realize she was speaking to me. My disguise made me look shorter, and she was talking to my chest.

"I've never seen anything like it," I agreed lamely.

"Of course not," she frowned. "It's the last work done by the great sculptor Watgit before he went mad."

It occurred to me that the statue might have been done *after* he went mad. Then it occurred to me that it might have driven him mad—especially if he had been working from a live model. I became so lost in the horrible thought that I started nervously when Tananda reappeared at my side and touched my arm.

"Let's go, handsome," she murmured. "I've seen enough."

The brevity of her inspection gave me hope.

"There's no hope, eh?" I sighed dramatically. "Gee, that's tough. I had really been looking forward to testing my skills."

"That's good," she purred, taking my arm. "Because I think I see a way we can pull this caper off."

I wasn't sure what a caper was, but I was certain that once I found out I wouldn't like it. I was right.

Chapter Six:

"Now you see it, now you don't."
—H. SHADOWSPAWN

"ARE you positive there was no lock on the door?" I
asked for the twenty-third time.

"Keep it down," Tananda hissed, laying a soft
hand on my lips, though none too gently. "Do you
want to wake everybody?"

She had a point. We were crouched in an alley
across from the Trophy Building, and as the whole
idea of our waiting was to be sure everyone was
asleep, it was counterproductive to make so much
noise we kept them awake. Still, I had questions I
wanted answered.

"You're sure?" I asked again in a whisper.

"Yes, I'm sure," Tananda sighed. "You could
have seen for yourself if you had looked."

"I was busy looking at the statue," I admitted.

"Uh-huh," my partner snorted. "Remember what
I said about getting over-involved with the target?
You were supposed to be checking security, not play-
ing art connoisseur."

39

"Well, I don't like it," I declared suspiciously, eager to get the conversation off my shortcomings. "It's too easy. I can't believe they'd leave something they prize as highly as that Trophy in an unlocked, unguarded building."

"There are a couple things you've overlooked," Tanda chided. "First of all, that statue's one of a kind. That means any thief who stole it would have some real problems trying to sell it again. If he even showed it to anyone here in Ta-hoe, they'd probably rip his arms off."

"He could hold it for ransom," I pointed out.

"Hey, that's pretty good," my guide exclaimed softly, nudging me in the ribs. "We'll make a thief of you yet! However, that brings us to the second thing you overlooked."

"Which is?"

"It's not unguarded," she smiled.

"But you said—" I began.

"Sshh!" she cautioned. "I said there would be no guards in the building with the Trophy."

I closed my eyes and regained control of my nerves, particularly those influenced by blind panic.

"Tanda," I said gently. "Don't you think it's about time you shared some of the details of your master plan with me?"

"Sure, handsome," she responded, slipping an arm around my waist. "I didn't think you were interested."

I resisted an impulse to throttle her.

"Just tell me," I urged. "First off, what *is* the security on the Trophy."

"Well," she said, tapping her chin with one finger, "as I said, there are no guards in the building. There is, however, a silent alarm that will summon guards. It's triggered by the nightingale floor."

"The what?" I interrupted.

"The nightingale floor," she repeated. "It's a

fairly common trick throughout the dimensions. The wooden floor around the Trophy is riddled with deliberately loosened boards that creak when you step on them. In this case, they not only creak, they trip an alarm."

"Wonderful!" I grimaced. "So we can't set foot in the room we're supposed to steal something out of. Anything else?"

I was speaking sarcastically, but Tananda took me seriously.

"Just the magikal wards around the statue itself," she shrugged.

"Magikal wards?" I gulped. "You mean there's magik in this dimension?"

"Of course there is," Tananda smiled. "You're here."

"I didn't set any wards," I exclaimed.

"That wasn't what I meant," Tanda chided. "Look, you tapped into the magikal force lines to disguise us. That means there's magik here for anyone trained to use it—not just us, anyone. Even if none of the locals are adept, there's nothing stopping someone from another dimension from dropping in and using what's here."

"Okay, okay," I sighed. "I guess I wasn't thinking. I guess the next question is, how are we supposed to beat the funny floor and the wards?"

"Easy," she grinned. "The wards are sloppy. Someone set up a fence instead of a dome when they cast the wards. All you have to do is levitate the Trophy over the wards and float it across the floor into our waiting arms. We never even have to set foot in the room."

"Whoa!" I cautioned, holding up a hand. "There's one problem with that. I can't do it."

"You can't?" she blinked. "I thought levitation was one of your strongest spells."

"It is," I conceded. "But that statue's heavy. I

couldn't levitate it from a distance. It has something to do with what Aahz calls leverage. I'd have to be close, practically standing on top of it."

"Okay," she said at last. "We'll just have to switch to Plan B."

"You have a Plan B?" I asked, genuinely impressed.

"Sure," she grinned. "I just made it up. You can fly us both across the floor and over the wards. Then we latch onto the Trophy and fly back to Klah from inside the wards."

"I don't know," I frowned.

"Now what's wrong?" my guide scowled.

"Well, flying's a form of levitation," I explained. "I've never tried flying myself and someone else, and even if I can do it, we'll be pushing down on the floor as hard as if we were walking on it. It might set the alarm off."

"If I understand flying," Tanda pondered, "our weight would be more dispersed than if we were walking, but you're right. There's no point in taking the extra risk of flying us both across the floor."

She snapped her fingers suddenly.

"Okay. Here's what we'll do," she exclaimed, leaning forward. "You fly across to the Trophy alone while I wait by the door. Then, when you're in place, you can use the D-Hopper to bring yourself and the Trophy back to Klah, while I blip back magikally."

For some reason, the thought of dividing our forces in the middle of a theft bothered me.

"Say . . . um, Tanda," I said, "it occurs to me that even if we set off the alarm, we would be long gone by the time the guards arrived. I mean, if they haven't had war for over five hundred years, they're bound to be a little sloppy turning out."

"No," Tananda countered firmly. "If we've got a way to completely avoid alerting the guards, we'll take it. I promised Aahz to keep you out of trouble, and that means—"

She broke off suddenly, staring across the street.

"What is it?" I hissed, craning my neck for a better look.

In response, she pointed silently at the darkened Trophy Building.

A group of a dozen cloaked figures had appeared from the shadows beside the building. They looked briefly up and down the street, then turned and disappeared into the building.

"I thought you said there wouldn't be any guards in the building!" I whispered frantically.

"I don't understand it," Tananda murmured, more to herself than to me. "It's not laid out for a guard force."

"But if there are guards, we can't—" I began, but Tananda silenced me with a hand on my arm.

The group had reemerged from the building. Moving more slowly than when we had first seen them, they edged their way back into the shadows and vanished from sight.

"That's a relief," Tananda declared, letting out a pent-up breath. "It's just a pack of drunks sneaking an after-hours look at the Trophy."

"They didn't act like drunks," I commented doubtfully.

"C'mon, handsome," my guide declared, clapping a hand on my shoulder. "It's time we got this show on the road. Follow me."

Needless to say, I didn't want to go, but I was even more reluctant to be left behind. This left me no choice but to follow as she headed across the street. As I went, though, I took the precaution of fumbling out my D-Hopper. I didn't like the feel of this, and wanted to be sure my exit route was at hand in case of trouble.

"In you go!" Tananda ordered, holding the door

open. "Be sure to sing out when you're in position. I want to be there to see Aahz's face when you give him the Trophy."

"I can't see anything," I protested, peering into the dark building.

"Of course not!" Tananda snapped. "It's dark. You know where the Trophy is, though, so get going."

At her insistence, I reached out with my mind and pushed gently against the floor. As had happened a hundred times in practice, I lifted free and began to float toward the estimated position of the statue.

As I went, it occurred to me I had neglected to ask Tananda how high the wards extended. I considered going back or calling to her, but decided against it. Noise would be dangerous, and time was precious. I wanted to get this over with as soon as possible. Instead, I freed part of my mind from the task of flying and cast about in front of me, seeking the tell-tale aura of the magikal wards. There were none.

"Tanda!" I hissed, speaking before I thought. "The wards are down!"

"Impossible," came her response from the door. "You must be in the wrong spot. Check again."

I tried again, casting about the full extent of the room. Nothing. As I peered about, I realized my eyes were acclimating to the darkness.

"There are no wards," I called softly. "I'm right over the pedestal and there are no wards."

Something was tugging at my consciousness. Something I had seen was terribly wrong, but my attention was occupied scanning for the wards.

"If you're over the pedestal," Tananda called, "then drop down and get the Trophy. And hurry! I think I hear someone coming."

I lowered myself to the floor, gently as I remembered the creaky boards, and turned to the pedestal. Then it burst upon me what was wrong.

"It's gone!" I cried.

"What?" Tananda gasped, her silhouette appearing in the doorway.

"The Trophy! It's gone!" I exclaimed, running my hands over the vacant pedestal.

"Get out, Skeeve," Tananda called, suddenly full volume.

I started for the door, but her voice stopped me.

"No! Use the D-Hopper. Now!"

My thumb went to the activator button on the device I had been clutching, but I hesitated.

"What about you?" I called. "Aren't you coming?"

"After you're gone," she insisted. "Now get go—"

Something came flying out of the dark and struck her silhouette. She went down in a boneless heap.

"Tanda!" I shouted, starting forward.

Suddenly the doorway was filled with short silhouettes swarming all over Tananda's prone form.

I wavered for a moment in indecision.

"There's another one inside!" someone called.

So much for indecision. I hit the button.

There was the now familiar rush of darkness . . . and I was back in my quarters on Klah.

Aahz was seated at a table with his back to me, but he must have heard the *BAMF* of my arrival.

"It's about time!" he growled. "Did you enjoy your little—"

He broke off as he turned and his eyes took in the expression on my face.

"Aahz," I cried, stumbling forward. "We're in trouble."

His fist came down in a crash which splintered the table.

"I knew it!" he snarled.

Chapter Seven:

"A friend in need is a pest."

—FAFHRD

"Now let's see if I've got this straight," Aahz grumbled, pacing the length of the room. "You got away without a scratch, but Tanda got caught. Right?"

"I couldn't help it!" I moaned, shaking my head. "They were all over her and you said—"

"I know, I know," my mentor waved. "You did the right thing. I'm just trying to get a clear picture of the situation. You're sure this was in Jahk? The weird dimension with the short, pale guys? Skinny or overweight?"

"That's right," I confirmed. "Do you know it?"

"I've heard of it," Aahz shrugged, "but I've never gotten around to visiting. It's talked around a bit on the gambling circuit."

"Must be because of the Big Game," I suggested brightly.

"What I can't figure," Aahz mused, ignoring my comments, "is what you two were doing there."

"Um . . . it was sort of because of me," I admitted in a small voice.

"You?" Aahz blinked, halting his pacing to stare at me. "Who told you about Jahk?"

"No one," I clarified hastily. "It wasn't that I asked to go to Jahk specifically. I was hungry, and Tanda said Jahk was the closest dimension where I could find something to eat."

"I know how that is," my mentor grimaced. "Eating is always a problem when you're traveling the dimensions—even the humanoid ones."

"It's even rougher when you aren't even visiting humanoid dimensions," I agreed.

"Is that a fact?" Aahz murmured, eyeing me suspiciously. "Which dimensions did you visit, anyway?"

"Um . . . I can't remember all the names," I evaded. "Tanda—um—felt there would be less chance of trouble in some of the out of the way dimensions."

"What did the natives look like?" Aahz pressed.

"Aren't we getting off the subject?" I asked desperately. "The real issue is Tanda."

Surprisingly, the ploy worked.

"You're right, kid," Aahz sighed. "Okay. I want you to think hard. You're sure you don't know who jumped her or why?"

My conversational gambit had backfired. The question placed me in a real dilemma. On the one hand, I couldn't expect Aahz to come up with a rescue plan unless he knew the full situation. On the other, I wasn't particularly eager to admit what we were doing when Tananda was captured.

"Um . . . " I said, avoiding his eyes. "I think I can remember a few things about those other dimensions after all. There was one where . . . "

"Wait a minute," Aahz interrupted. "You were the one who said we should focus on Tanda's problem. Now don't go straying off . . . "

He stopped in mid-sentence to examine me closely. "You're holding out on me, kid," he announced in a cold voice that allowed no room for argument. "Now give! What haven't you told me about this disaster?"

His words hung expectantly in the air, and it occurred to me I couldn't stall any longer.

"Well . . . " I began, clearing my throat. "I'm not sure, but I think the ones who grabbed Tanda were the city guardsmen."

"Guardsmen?" Aahz frowned. "Why would they want to put the grab on Tanda? All you were doing was getting a bite to eat and maybe a little shopping."

I didn't answer, taking a sudden interest in studying my feet in close detail.

"That *is* all you were doing, wasn't it?"

I tried to speak, but the words wouldn't come.

"What *were* you doing?" Aahz growled. "Come on. Out with it. I should have known it wasn't just . . . Hey! You didn't kill anyone, did you?"

Strong hands closed on my shoulders and my head was tossed about by a none too gentle shaking.

"We didn't kill anyone!" I shouted, the process difficult because my jaw was moving in a different direction than my tongue. "We were just stealing . . . "

"Stealing!?!"

The hands on my shoulders released their grip so fast I fell to the floor. Fortunately, I had the presence of mind to break my fall with my rump.

"I don't believe it! Stealing!" Aahz made his appeal to the ceiling. "All this because you tried to steal something."

My rump hurt, but I had other more pressing matters to deal with. I was desperately trying to phrase my explanation when I realized with some astonishment that Aahz was laughing.

"Stealing!" he repeated. "You know, you really had me going for a minute there, kid. Stealing! And I thought it was something important."

"You mean, you aren't mad?" I asked incredulously.

"Mad? Naw!" he proclaimed. "Like the old saying goes, 'you can take the boy out of thieving' . . . Heck! Most demons are thieves. It's the only way to get something if you don't have any native coinage."

"I thought you'd really be upset," I stammered, still unwilling to believe my good fortune.

"Now, don't get me wrong, kid," my mentor amended sternly, "I'm not overjoyed with your venture into thievery. You're supposed to be studying magik . . . the kind that will get you a raise as a court magician, not the kind that ends up with you running down a dark alley. Still, all things considered, you could have done a lot worse on your first solo trip through the dimension."

"Gee, thanks, Aahz," I beamed.

"So, let's see it," he smiled, extending a palm.

"See what?" I blinked.

"What you stole," he insisted. "If you came here direct from the scene of the crime, I assume you still have it with you."

"Umm . . . actually," I gulped, avoiding his eyes again. "I—that is, *we* didn't get it. It's still back in Jahk somewhere."

"You mean to say you went through all this hassle, got Tanda captured, and came running back here with your tail between your legs, and you didn't even bother to pick up what you were trying to steal?"

The storm clouds were back in Aahz's face. I realized I was on the brink of being in trouble again.

"But you said . . . " I protested.

"I know you aren't supposed to be a thief!" my mentor roared. "But once you set your hand to it, I expect you to at least be a successful thief! To think an apprentice of mine can't even put together a workable plan . . . "

"It was Tanda's plan," I offered weakly.

"It was?" Aahz seemed slightly mollified. "Well, you should have checked it over yourself before you joined in."

"I did," I protested. "As far as I can tell it should have worked."

"Oh, really?" came the sarcastic reply. "All right. Why don't you tell me all about this plan that didn't work after you okayed it."

He dragged up a chair and sat in front of me, leaving me little option but to narrate the whole story. I went over the whole thing for him; the plan, the nightingale floor, the magik wards, everything—except what we were trying to steal, and why. By the time I had finished, his jeering smile had faded to a thoughtful frown.

"You're right, kid," he admitted at last. "It should have worked. The only thing I can figure is that they moved your target somewhere else for safekeeping—but that doesn't make sense. I mean, why would they set up all the security arrangements if the target was going to be kept somewhere else? And that group hanging around the building before you went in sounds a bit suspicious."

He thought for a few more minutes, then sighed and shrugged his shoulders. "Oh, well," he proclaimed. "Nobody wins *all* the time. It didn't work and that's that. C'mon, kid. Let's get some sleep."

"Sleep?" I gasped. "What about Tanda?"

"What about her?" Aahz frowned.

"They're holding her prisoner in Jahk!" I exclaimed. "Aren't we going to try to rescue her?"

"Oh, that!" my mentor laughed. "Don't worry

about her. She'll be along on her own in a little while.''

"But they're holding her prisoner!" I insisted.

"You think so?" Aahz grinned. "Stop and think a minute, kid. How are they going to hold her? Remember, she can hop dimensions any time she wants. The only reason she didn't come back at the same time you did is that she got knocked cold. As soon as she wakes up, she'll be back. Mark my words.''

Something about his logic didn't ring true, but I couldn't put my finger on it.

"What if they execute her before she wakes up?" I asked.

"Execute her?" Aahz frowned. "For what? The heist didn't work, so they've still got their whatever. I can't see anyone getting upset enough to have her executed.''

"I dunno, Aahz," I said. "The whole city seemed pretty worked up over the Trophy, and . . . ''

"Trophy?" Aahz interrupted. "You mean the Trophy from the Big Game? What does that have to do with anything?''

"That's . . . um, that's what we were trying to steal," I explained.

"The Trophy?" Aahz exclaimed. "You two didn't aim small, did you? What did you want with—no, on second thought don't tell me. That woman's logic always makes my head hurt.''

"But now you see why I'm afraid they might execute her," I pressed, secretly relieved at not having to disclose the motive for our theft.

"It's a possibility," Aahz admitted, "but I still think they'd let her wake up first. Public trials are dramatic, especially for something as big as trying to steal the Big Game Trophy. Heck, Tanda's enough of a sport that she might even stick around for the trial before popping back here.''

"You really think so?" I pressed.

"I'm sure of it," Aahz declared confidently. "Now let's get some sleep. It sounds like it's been a long day for you."

I grudgingly retired to my bed, but I didn't go to sleep immediately. There was still something eluding my mental grasp—something important. As I lay there, my mind began wandering back over my trip—the sights, the smells, the strange beings . . .

"Aahz!" I shouted, bolting upright. "Aahz! Wake up!"

"What is it?" my mentor growled sleepily, struggling to rise.

"I just remembered! I was handling our disguises for the whole trip."

"So what?" Aahz growled. "It's good practice for you, but . . ."

"Don't you see?" I insisted. "If I'm here and Tanda's unconscious in Jahk, then she hasn't got a disguise! They'll be able to see she isn't one of them —that she's a demon!"

There was a frozen moment of silence, then Aahz was on his feet, looming over me.

"Don't just sit there, kid," he growled. "Get the D-Hopper. We're going to Jahk!"

Chapter Eight:

"Once more into the breach . . ."
—ZARNA, THE HUMAN CANNONBALL

FORTUNATELY, there *was* a setting for Jahk on our
D-Hopper though Aahz had to search a bit to find it.

I wanted to go armed to the teeth, but my mentor
vetoed the plan. Under cross-examination I had had
to admit that I hadn't seen anyone in that dimension
wearing arms openly except the city guards, and that
was that. My ability to disguise things was weak
when it came to metal objects, and swords and knives
would have made us awfully conspicuous walking
down the street. As Aahz pointed out, the one time
you don't want to wear weapons is when they're
more likely to get you into trouble than out of it.

I hate it when Aahz makes sense.

Anyway, aside from a few such minor squabbles
and disputes, our departure from Klah and our sub-
sequent arrival at Jahk was smooth and uneventful.
In hindsight, I realize that was the last thing to go
right for some time.

"Well, kid," Aahz exclaimed, looking about him eagerly, "where do we go?"

"I don't know," I admitted, scanning the horizon.

Aahz frowned. "Let me run this by you slowly," he sighed. "You've been here before, and I haven't. Now, even your limited brain should realize that that makes you the logical guide. Got it?"

"But I *haven't* been here before," I protested. "Not *here!* When Tanda and I arrived, we were in a park in Ta-hoe!"

At the moment, Aahz and I were standing beside a dirt road, surrounded by gently rolling meadows and a scattering of very strange trees. There wasn't even an outhouse in sight, much less the booming metropolis I had visited.

"Don't tell me, let me guess," Aahz whispered, shutting his eyes as if in pain. "Tanda handled your transport on the way in the first time. Right?"

"That's right," I nodded. "You made me promise to keep the D-Hopper set for Klah, and. . . ."

"I know, I know," my mentor waved impatiently. "I must say, though, you pick the damnedest times to be obedient. Okay! So the D-Hopper's set for a different drop zone than the one Tanda uses. We'll just have to dig up a native guide to get us oriented."

"Terrific!" I grimaced. "And where are we supposed to find a native guide?"

"How about right over there?" Aahz smirked, pointing.

I followed the line of his extended talon. Sure enough, not a stone's throw away was a small pond huddled in the shade of a medium sized tree. Seated, leaning against the tree, was a young native. The only thing that puzzled me was that he was holding one end of a short stick, and there was a string which ran from the stick's other end to the pond.

"What's he doing?" I asked suspiciously.

"From here, I'd say he's fishing," Aahz proclaimed.

"Fishing? Like that?" I frowned. "Why doesn't he just . . ."

"I'll explain later," my mentor interrupted. "Right now we're trying to get directions to Ta-hoe. Remember?"

"That's right!" I nodded. "Let's go."

I started forward, only to be stopped short by Aahz's heavy hand on my shoulder.

"Kid," he sighed, "aren't you forgetting something?"

"What?" I blinked.

"Our disguises, dummy," he snarled. "Your lazy old teacher would like to be able to ask our questions without chasing him all around the landscape for the answers."

"Oh! Right, Aahz."

Embarrassed by the oversight, I hastily did my disguise bit, and together we approached the dozing native.

"Excuse me, sir," I began, clearing my throat, "can you tell us the way to Ta-hoe?"

"What are you doing out here?" the youth demanded, without opening his eyes. "Don't you know the land between Veygus and Ta-hoe is a no-man's-land until the war's over?"

"What did he say?" Aahz scowled.

"What was that?" the youth asked, his eyes snapping open.

For a change, my mind grasped the situation instantly. I was still wearing my translator pendant from my travels with Tananda, but Aahz didn't have one. That meant that while I could understand and be understood by both Aahz and the native, neither of them could decipher what the other was saying. Our disguise was in danger of being discovered by the first native we'd met on our rescue mission. Terrific.

"Umm. Excuse me a moment, sir," I stammered at the youth.

Thinking fast, I removed the pendant from around

my neck and looped it over my arm. Aahz understood at once, and thrust his hand through the pendant, grasping my forearm with an iron grip. Thus, we were both able to utilize the power of the pendant.

Unfortunately, the native noticed this by-play. His eyes, which had opened at the sound of Aahz's voice, now widened to the point of popping out as he looked from one of us to the other.

"Fraternity initiation," Aahz explained conspiratorially, winking at him.

"A what?" I blinked.

"Later, kid," my mentor mumbled tensely. "Get the conversation going again."

"Right. Ummm . . . what was that you were saying about a war?"

"I was saying you shouldn't be here," the youth replied, regaining some of his bluster, but still eyeing the pendant suspiciously. "Both sides have declared this area off-limits to civilians until after the war's over."

"When did this war start?" I asked.

"Oh, it won't actually start for a week or so," the native shrugged. "We haven't had a war for over five hundred years and everyone's out of practice. It'll take them a while to get ready—but you still shouldn't be here."

"Well, what are *you* doing here?" Aahz challenged. "You don't look like a soldier to me."

"My dad's an officer," the youth yawned. "If a Ta-hoer patrol finds me out here, I'll just tell 'em who my father is and they'll keep their mouths shut."

"What if a patrol from Veygus finds you?" I asked curiously.

"The Veygans?" he laughed incredulously. "They're even more unprepared than Ta-hoe is. They haven't even got their uniforms designed yet, much less organized enough to send out patrols."

"Well, we appreciate the information," Aahz announced. "Now if you'll just point out the way to Ta-hoe, we'll get ourselves off your battlefield."

"The way to Ta-hoe?" the youth frowned. "You don't know the way to Ta-hoe? That's strange."

"What's strange?" my mentor challenged. "So we're new around here. So what?"

The youth eyed him passively.

"It's strange," he observed calmly, "because that road only runs between Veygus and Ta-hoe. Perhaps you can explain how it is that you're traveling a road without knowing either where you're going or where you're coming from?"

There was a moment of awkward silence, then I withdrew my arm from the translator pendant.

"Well, Aahz," I sighed, "how do we talk our way out of this one?"

"Put your arm back in the pendant," Aahz hissed. "He's getting suspicious."

"He's *already* suspicious," I pointed out. "The question is what do we do now?"

"Nothing to it," my mentor winked. "Just watch how I handle this."

In spite of my worries, I found myself smiling in eager anticipation. Nobody can spin a lie like Aahz once he gets rolling.

"The explanation is really quite simple," Aahz smiled, turning to the youth. "You see, we're magicians who just dropped in from another world. Having just arrived here, we are naturally disoriented."

"My, what a clever alibi," I commented dryly.

Aahz favored me with a dirty look.

"As I was saying," he continued, "we have come to offer our services to the glorious city of Ta-hoe for the upcoming war."

It occurred to me that that last statement was a little suspicious. I mean, we had clearly not known about the war at the beginning of this conversation.

Fortunately, the youth overlooked this minor detail.

"Magicians?" he smiled skeptically. "You don't look like magicians to me."

"Show him, kid," Aahz instructed.

"Show him?" I blinked.

"That's right," my mentor nodded. "Drop the disguises, one at a time."

With a shrug, I slipped my arm back into the translator pendant and let my disguise fall away.

"I am Skeeve," I announced, "and this"—I dropped Aahz's disguise—"is my friend and fellow magician, Aahz."

The effect on the youth couldn't have been greater if we had lit a fire under him. Dropping his pole, he sprang to his feet and began backing away until I was afraid he'd topple into the pond. His eyes were wide with fright, and his mouth kept opening and shutting, though no sounds came forth.

"That's enough, kid," Aahz winked. "He's convinced."

I hastily reassembled the disguises, but it did little to calm the youth.

"Not a bad illusion, eh, sport?" my mentor leered at him.

"I . . . I . . . " the youth stammered. Then he paused and set his lips. "Ta-hoe's that way."

"Thanks," I smiled. "We'll be on our way now."

"Not so fast, kid," Aahz waved. "What's your name, son?"

"Griffin . . . sir," the youth replied uneasily.

"Well, Griffin," Aahz smiled, "how would you like to show us the way?"

"Why?" I asked bluntly.

"Wake up, kid," my mentor scowled. "We can't just leave him here. He knows who and what we are."

"I know," I commented archly. "You told him."

" . . . and besides," he continued as if I hadn't

spoken, "he's our passport if we meet any Army patrols."

"I'd rather not . . . " Griffin began.

"Of course," Aahz interrupted. "There is another possibility. We could kill him here and now."

"I *insist* you let me escort you!" the youth proclaimed.

"Welcome, comrade!" I beamed.

"See, kid?" my mentor smiled, clapping me on the shoulder. "I told you you could settle things without my help."

"Ummm . . . there is one thing, though," Griffin commented hesitantly.

"And that is . . . " Aahz prompted.

"I hope you won't hold it against me if your services aren't accepted," the youth frowned.

"You doubt our powers?" my mentor scowled in his most menacing manner.

"Oh, it's not that," Griffin explained quickly. "It's just that . . . you see . . . well, we already have a magician."

"Is that all?" Aahz laughed. "Just leave him to us."

When Aahz says "us" in regard to magik, he means me. However bad things had gone so far, I had an uncomfortable foreboding they were going to get worse.

Chapter Nine:

"War may be Hell . . . but it's good for business!"
—THE ASSOCIATION FOR
MERCHANTS, MANUFACTURERS,
AND MORTICIANS

TA-HOE was a beehive of activity when we arrived. Preparations for the upcoming war were in full swing, and everybody was doing something. Surprisingly enough, most of the preparations were of a non-military nature.

"What *is* all this?" I asked our native guide.

"I told you," he explained. "We're getting ready for a war with Veygus."

"*This* is getting ready for a war?" I said, gazing incredulously about.

"Sure," Griffin nodded. "Souvenirs don't make themselves, you know."

There wasn't a spear or uniform in sight. Instead, the citizens were busily producing pennants, posters, and lightweight shirts with "Win the War" emblazoned across them.

"It's the biggest thing to hit Ta-hoe in my lifetime," our guide confided. "I mean, Big Game souvenirs are a stock item. If you design it right, you can even hang on to any overstock and sell it the following year. This war thing caught everybody flat-footed. A lot of people are complaining that they weren't given sufficient warning to cash in on it. There's a resolution before the council right now to postpone hostilities for another month. The folks who deal in knitted hats and stadium blankets are behind it. They claim that declaring war on such short notice will hurt their businesses by giving unfair advantage to the merchants who handle stuff like bumper stickers and posters that can be cranked out in a hurry."

I couldn't understand most of what he was talking about, but Aahz was enthralled.

"These folks really know how to run a war!" he declared with undisguised enthusiasm. "Most dimensions make their war profits off munitions and weapons contracts. I'll tell you, kid, if we weren't in such a hurry, I'd take notes."

It's a rare thing for Aahz to show admiration for anyone, much less a whole dimension, and I'd never before heard him admit there was anything he could learn about making money. I found the phenomenon unnerving.

"Speaking of being in a hurry," I interjected, "would you mind telling me *why* we're on our way to talk to Ta-hoe's magician?"

"That's easy," my mentor smiled. "For the most part, magicians stick together. There's a loyalty to others in the same line of work that transcends any national or dimensional ties. With any luck, we can enlist his aid in springing Tanda loose."

"That's funny," I observed dryly. "The magicians I've seen so far were usually at each other's throats. I got the definite impression they'd like nothing better than to see competing magicians, and us specifically, expire on the spot."

"There is that possibility," Aahz admitted, "but look at it this way. If he won't help us, then he'll probably be our major opponent and we'll want to get a fix on what he can and can't do before we make our plans. Either way, we want to see him as soon as possible."

You may have noticed Aahz's appraisals of a situation are usually far from reassuring. Some day I might get used to that, but in the meantime I'm learning to operate in a constant state of blind panic.

For a moment, our path was blocked by a crowd listening to a young rabble-rouser who spoke to them from atop a jury-rigged platform. As near as I could make out, they were protesting the war.

"I tell you, the council is withholding information from us!"

A growl arose from the assemblage.

"As citizens of Ta-hoe, we have the right to know the facts about this war!"

The response was louder and more fevered.

"How are we supposed to set the odds for this war, much less bet intelligently, if we don't know the facts?"

The crowd was nearing frenzied hysterics as we finally edged past.

"Who are these people?" I asked.

"Bookies," Griffin shrugged. "The council'd better watch its step. They're one of the strongest lobbies in Ta-hoe."

"I tell you, it's awe-inspiring," Aahz murmured dreamily.

"We've got to stand up for our rights! Demand the facts!" the rabble-rouser was screaming. "We've got to know the lineups, the battle plans, the . . . "

"They're barking up the wrong tree," Griffin commented. "They haven't gotten the information because the military hasn't devised a plan yet."

"Why don't you tell them?" I suggested.

Our guide cocked an eyebrow at me. "I thought you were in a hurry to see the magician," he countered.

"Oh, that's right," I returned, a little embarrassed by the oversight.

"Say, Griffin," Aahz called. "I've been meaning to ask. What started the war, anyway?"

For the first time since we'd met him, our youthful guide showed an emotion other than boredom or fear.

"Those bastards from Veygus stole our Trophy," he snarled angrily. "Now we're going to get it back or know the reason why."

For a change, I didn't need an elbow in the ribs from Aahz to remember to keep quiet. I got one anyway.

"Stole your Trophy, eh?" my mentor commented innocently. "Know how they did it?"

"A pack of 'em pulled a hit-and-run raid the day after the Big Game," Griffin proclaimed bitterly. "They struck just after sundown and got away before the guardsmen could respond to the alarm."

The memory of the group entering and leaving the Trophy Building while Tananda and I waited flashed across my mind. That explained a couple questions that had been bothering me, like "where did the statue go?" and "how did the guards arrive so fast?" We hadn't triggered any alarms! The group from Veygus had—inadvertently setting us up for the guards!

"I'd think you'd take better care of the Trophy, if it means so much to you," Aahz suggested.

Griffin spun on him, and I thought for a minute he was actually going to throw a punch. Then, at the last moment, he remembered that Aahz was a magician and dropped his arms to his side. I heaved a quiet sigh of relief. I mean, Aahz is strong! I was impressed with his strength in my own dimension of

Klah, and here on Jahk, *I* looked strong compared to the natives. If Griffin had thrown a punch, Aahz would have ripped him apart . . . literally!

"Our security precautions on the Trophy were more than adequate," our guide announced levelly, "under normal circumstances. The thieves had magikal assistance."

"Magikal assistance?" I said, finally drawn from my silence.

"That's right." Griffin nodded vigorously. "How else could they have moved such a heavy statue before the guards arrived?"

"They could have done it without magik," Aahz offered. "Say, if they had a lot of strong men on the job."

"Normally, I'd agree with you," our guide admitted, "but in this case, we actually captured the demon that helped them."

For a long moment there was silence. Neither Aahz nor I wanted to ask the next question. We were afraid of what the answer might be. Finally, Aahz spoke. "A demon, you say?" he asked, smiling his broadest. "What happened to it?"

His tone was light and casual, but there was a glint in his eye I didn't like. I found myself in the unique position of worrying about the fate of an entire dimension.

"The demon?" Griffin frowned. "Oh, the magician's holding it captive. Maybe he'll let you see it when you meet him."

"The magician? The one we're going to see?" Aahz pressed. "He's got the demon?"

"That's right," our guide answered. "Why do you ask?"

"Is she still unconscious?" I blurted.

The elbow from Aahz almost doubled me over this time, but it was too late. Griffin had stopped in his tracks and was studying me with a new intensity.

"How did you know it was unconscious?" he asked suspiciously. "And why do you refer to it as 'she'?"

"I don't know," I covered smoothly. "Must have been something you said."

"I said we'd captured a demon," he argued, "not how, and as far as its sex goes . . . "

"Look," Aahz interrupted harshly, "are we going to stand around arguing all day, or are you going to take us to the magician?"

Griffin stared at us hard for a moment, then shrugged his shoulders.

"We're here," he announced, pointing at a door in the wall. "The magician lives there."

"Well, don't just stand there, son," Aahz barked. "Knock on the door and announce us."

Our guide heaved a sigh of disgust, but obediently walked over and hammered on the indicated door.

"Aahz!" I hissed. "What are we going to say?"

"Leave it to me, kid," he murmured back. "I'll try to feel him out a little, then we'll play it by ear from there."

"What are we supposed to do with our ears?" I frowned.

Aahz rolled his eyes. "Kid . . . " he began.

Just then, the door opened, exposing a wizened old man who blinked at the sunlight.

"Griffin!" he exclaimed. "What brings you here?"

"Well, sir," our guide stammered, "I—that is, there are two gentlemen who want to speak with you. They say . . . Well, they're magicians."

The old man started at this and shot a sharp glance in our direction before he covered his reaction with a friendly smile.

"Magicians, you say! Well, come right in, gentlemen. Lad, I think you'd better wait outside here. Professional secrets and all that, you know."

"Um . . . actually, I thought I'd be on my way now," Griffin murmured uneasily.

"Wait here." There was steel in the old man's voice now.

"Yes, sir," our guide gulped, licking his lips.

I tried to hide my nervousness as we followed the magician into his abode. I mean, aside from the fact that we didn't have the vaguest idea of this man's power, and that we had no guarantee we'd ever get out of this place alive, I had nothing to worry about. Right?

"Aahz," I whispered. "Have you got a fix on this guy yet?"

"It's a little early to say," my mentor replied sarcastically. "In the meantime, I've got a little assignment for you."

"Like what?" I asked.

"Like, check his aura. Now."

One of the first things I had learned from Aahz was how to check auras, the field of magik around people or things. It seemed a strange thing to do just now, but I complied, viewing our host with unfocused eyes.

"Aahz," I gasped. "He's got an aura! The man's actually radiating magik. I can't do anything against someone that powerful."

"It's possible there is another explanation, kid," Aahz murmured. "He could be wearing a disguise spell like we are."

"Do you think so?" I asked hopefully.

"Well," my mentor drawled, "he's wearing a translator pendant, the same as we are. That makes it a good bet that he's not from this dimension. Besides, there's something familiar about his voice."

Our conversation ground to a halt as we reached our destination, a small room sparsely furnished with a large table surrounded by several chairs.

"If you'll be seated, gentlemen," our host said,

gesturing to the chairs, "perhaps you'll be good enough to tell me what it is you wish to speak to me about."

"Not so fast," Aahz challenged, holding up a hand. "We're used to knowing who we're dealing with. Could you do us the courtesy of removing your disguise before we start?"

The magician averted his eyes and began to fidget nervously. "You spotted it, eh?" he grumbled. "It figures. As you've probably guessed already, I'm relatively new to this profession. Not in your class at all, if you know what I mean."

An immense wave of relief washed over me, but Aahz remained skeptical.

"Just take off the disguise, huh?" he insisted.

"Oh, very well," our host sighed and began fumbling in his pocket.

We waited patiently until he found what he was looking for. Then the lines of his features began to waver . . . his body grew taller and fuller . . . until at last we saw . . .

"I thought so!" Aahz crowed triumphantly.

"Quigley!" I gasped.

"This *is* embarrassing," the demon hunter grumbled, slouching down into his chair.

Chapter Ten:

"Old heroes never die; they reappear in sequels"

—M. MOORCOCK

PHYSICALLY, Quigley was unchanged from when we first met him. Tall, long-boned and muscular, he still looked as if he'd be more at home in armor swinging a sword than sitting around in magician robes sipping wine with us. However, here we were, gathered in a conference which bore little resemblance to the formal interview I had originally anticipated.

"I was afraid you two would be along when I realized it was Tanda the guards captured," the ex-demon hunter grumbled.

"Afraid?" I frowned, genuinely puzzled. "Why should you be afraid of us?"

"Oh, come now, lad," Quigley smiled bitterly. "I appreciate your efforts to spare my feelings, but the truth of the matter is plain. My magikal powers don't hold a candle next to yours. I know full well that now that you're here you'll be able to take my job away from me without much difficulty. Either that, or make me look silly in front of my employers so that they'll fire me outright."

"That's ridiculous," I cried, more than slightly offended. "Look Quigley, I promise you we'll neither steal your job nor make you look silly while we're here."

"Really?" Quigley asked, brightening noticeably.

"You're being a little hasty with your promises, aren't you, kid?" Aahz interrupted in a warning tone.

"C'mon, Aahz," I grimaced. "You know that isn't why we're here."

"But, kid . . ."

I ignored him, turning back to Quigley.

"I promise you, Quigley. No job stealing, and nothing that will endanger your position. The truth is, I've already got a magician's job of my own. I'm surprised Tanda hasn't told you."

Strangely enough, instead of relaxing, Quigley seemed even more ill at ease and avoided my gaze.

"Well, actually, lad," he murmured uncomfortably, "Tanda hasn't said anything since she was turned over to my custody."

"She hasn't?" I asked, surprised. "That's funny. Usually the trouble is getting her to stop talking."

"Quite right," Quigley laughed uneasily. "Except this time—well—she hasn't regained consciousness yet."

"You mean she's still out cold?" Aahz exclaimed, surging to his feet. "Why didn't you say so? Come on, Quigley, wheel her out here. This might be serious."

"No, no. You misunderstand," Quigley waved. "She hasn't regained consciousness because I've kept a sleep spell on her."

"A sleep spell?" I frowned.

"That's right," Quigley nodded. "Tanda taught it to me herself. It's the first spell I learned, actually. Really very simple. As I understand it, all members of the Assassins Guild are required to learn it."

"Why?" Aahz interrupted.

"I never really gave it much thought," Quigley blinked. "I suppose it would help them in their work. You know, if you came on a sleeping victim, the spell would keep him from waking up until after you'd finished the job. Something like that."

"Not that!" Aahz moaned. "I know how assassins operate better than you do. I meant, why are you using a sleep spell on Tanda?"

"Why, to keep her from waking up, of course," Quigley shrugged.

"Brilliant," I muttered. "Why didn't we think of that?"

"Shut up, kid," my mentor snarled. "Okay, Quigley, let's try this one more time. Why don't you want to wake her up? I thought you two got along pretty well last time I saw you."

"We did," Quigley admitted, blushing. "But I'm a working magician now. If I let her wake up . . . well, I don't flatter myself about my powers. There would be nothing I could do to keep her from escaping."

"You don't want her to escape?" I blinked.

"Of course not. It would mean my job," Quigley smiled. "That's why I'm so glad you promised not to do anything that would jeopardize my position."

My stomach sank.

"Smooth move, kid," Aahz commented dryly. "Maybe next time you'll listen when I try to advise you."

I tried to say something in my own defense, but nothing came to mind, so I shut my mouth and used the time to feel miserable.

"Well, gentlemen," Quigley beamed, rubbing his hands together. "Now that that's settled, I suppose you'll be wanting to get on your way to wherever you're going."

"Not so fast, Quigley," Aahz declared, sinking

back into his chair and propping his feet up on the table. "If nothing else, I think you owe us an explanation. The last time we saw you, you were a demon hunter, heading off through the dimensions with Tanda to learn more about magik. Now, I was under the distinct impression you intended to use that knowledge to further your old career. What brought you over to our side of the fence?"

Quigley thought for a moment, then shrugged and settled back in his own chair.

"Very well," he said. "I suppose I can do that, seeing as how we were comrades-in-arms at one point."

He paused to take a sip of wine before continuing.

"Tanda and I parted company with the others shortly after we discovered your little joke. We thought it was quite amusing, particularly Tanda, but the others seemed quite upset, especially Isstvan, so we left them and headed off on our own."

The demon hunter's eyes went slightly out of focus as he sank back into his memories. "We traveled the dimensions for some time. Quite a pleasant time, I might add. I learned a lot about demons and a little about magik, and it set me to thinking about my chosen line of work as a demon hunter. I mean, demons aren't such a bad lot once you get to know them, and magik pays considerably better than swinging a sword."

"I hope you're paying attention, kid," Aahz grinned, prodding my shoulder.

I nodded, but kept my attention on Quigley.

"Then," the demon hunter continued, "circumstances arose that prompted Tanda to abandon me without money or a way back to my own dimension."

"Wait a minute," Aahz interrupted. "That doesn't sound like Tanda. What were these 'circumstances' you're referring to?"

"It was a misunderstanding, really," Quigley explained, flushing slightly. "Without going into lurid details, the end result involved my spending a night with a female other than Tanda."

"I can see why she'd move on without you," Aahz frowned, "but not why she'd take your money."

"Well, actually, it was the young lady I was with at the time who relieved me of my coinage," the demon hunter admitted, blushing a deeper shade of red.

"Got it," Aahz nodded. "Sounds like along with magik and demons, there are a few things you have to learn about women."

I wouldn't have minded a few lessons in that department myself, but I didn't think this was the time to bring it up.

"Anyway," Quigley continued hastily, "there I was, stranded and penniless. It seemed the only thing for me to do was to go to a placement service."

"A placement service?" Aahz blinked. "Just where was this that you were stranded?"

"Why, the Bazaar at Deva, of course," the demon hunter replied. "Didn't I mention that?"

"The Bazaar at Deva," my mentor sighed. "I should have known. Oh, well, keep going."

"There's really not that much more to tell." Quigley shrugged. "There were no openings for a demon hunter, but they managed to find me this position here in Jahk by lying about how much magik I knew. Since then, things have been pretty quiet—or they were before the guards appeared at my door carrying Tanda."

I was starting to wonder if *any* court magician was really qualified for his position.

"And you aren't about to let Tanda go. Right?" Aahz finished.

"Don't misunderstand," Quigley insisted, gnawing his lip. "I'd *like* to let her go. If nothing else it would do a lot for patching up the misunderstanding between Tanda and myself. Unfortunately, I just don't see any way I could let her escape without losing my job on grounds of incompetence."

"Say, maybe we could get you a job in Possiltum!" I suggested brightly.

"Kid," Aahz smiled, "are you going to stop that tongue of yours all by yourself, or do I have to tear it out by the roots?"

I took the hint and shut up.

"Thank you, lad," Quigley said, "but I couldn't do that. Unlike yourself, I'm still trying to build a reputation as a magician. How would it look if I left my first job in defeat with my tail between my legs?"

"You haven't got a tail," Aahz pointed out.

"Figure of speech," Quigley shrugged.

"Oh," my mentor nodded. "Well, if you think a hasty retreat from one's first job is unusual, my friend, you still have a lot to learn about the magik profession."

"Haven't I been saying that?" Quigley frowned.

I listened to their banter with only half an ear. The rest of me was floating on Quigley's implied compliment. I'm getting quite good at hearing indirect compliments. The direct ones are few and far between.

Come to think of it, I *was* getting a reputation as a magician. No one could deny we beat Isstvan at his own game—and I had actually recruited and commanded the team that stopped Big Julie's army. Why, in certain circles, my name must be . . .

"Bullshit!" Aahz roared, slapping his hand down on the table hard enough to make the chairs jump. "I tell you she didn't steal the damn Trophy!"

I collected my shattered nerves and turned my attention to the conversation once more.

"Oh, come now, Aahz," Quigley grimaced. "I traveled with Tanda long enough to know she's not above stealing something that caught her eye—nor are you two, I'd imagine."

"True enough," Aahz admitted easily, "but you can bet your last baseball card that if any of us went after your Trophy, we wouldn't be caught afterward."

"My last what?" Quigley frowned. "Oh, no matter. Look, even if I believed you I couldn't do anything. What's important is the *council* believes Tanda was involved, and they wouldn't even consider releasing her unless they got the Trophy back first."

"Oh, yeah?" Aahz smiled, showing all his teeth. "How many council members are there and how are they guarded?"

"Aahz!" Quigley said sternly. "If anything happened to the council, I'm afraid I'd see it as a threat to my job and therefore a direct violation of Master Skeeve's promise."

My mentor leaned back in his chair and stared at the ceiling. The heavy metal wine goblet in his hand crumpled suddenly, but aside from that there was no outward display of his feelings.

"Um . . . Quigley?" I ventured cautiously. I still had a vivid image in my mind of my tongue in Aahz's grasp instead of the wine goblet.

"Yes, lad?" Quigley asked, cocking an eyebrow at me.

"What did you say would happen if the Trophy were returned?"

Aahz's head swiveled around slowly until our gazes met, but his gold speckled eyes were thoughtful now.

"Well, I didn't say, actually," Quigley grumphed, "but that would change everything. With the Trophy back, the council would be ecstatic and definitely better disposed toward Tanda. . . . Yes, if the Trophy were returned, I think I could find an excuse to release her."

"Is that a promise?"

I may be ignorant, but I'm a fast learner.

Quigley studied me for a moment before answering. "Very well," he said at last. "Why do you ask?"

I shot a glance at Aahz. One eyelid slowly closed in a wink, then he went back to studying the ceiling.

"Because," I announced, relief flooding over me, "I think I've come up with a way we can free Tanda, protect your job, and stop the war in one fell swoop."

Chapter Eleven:

"What do you mean, 'You've got a little job for me'?"

—HERCULES

"STEAL the Trophy back from Veygus. Just like that," Aahz grumbled for the hundredth time.

"We're doomed," Griffin prophesied grimly.

"Shut up, Griffin," I snarled.

It occurred to me I was picking up a lot of Aahz's bad habits lately.

"But I keep telling you, I don't know Veygus," the youth protested. "I won't be any help at all. Please, can't I go back to Ta-hoe?"

"Just keep walking," I sighed.

"Face it, son," Aahz smiled, draping a casual arm over our guide's shoulder. "We aren't going to let you out of our sight until this job's over. The sooner we get to Veygus, the sooner you'll be rid of us."

"But why?" Griffin whined.

"We've gone over this before," my mentor sighed. "This heist is going to be rough enough without Veygus hearing about it in advance. Now the only way we can be sure you don't tell anyone is to keep you with us. Besides, you're our passport through the Ta-hoe patrols if we meet any.''

"The patrols are easy to avoid,'' the youth insisted. "And I won't tell anyone about your mission, honest. Isn't there any way I can get you to trust me?''

"Well,'' Aahz drawled judiciously, "I guess there is one thing that might do the trick.''

"Really?'' our guide asked hopefully.

"What da ya think, Skeeve?'' my mentor called. "Do you feel up to turning our friend here into a rock or a tree or something until the job's over?''

"A rock or a tree?'' the youth gulped, wide-eyed.

"Sure,'' Aahz shrugged. "I wouldn't have suggested it myself. There's always a problem finding the *right* rock or tree to change back. Sometimes it takes years of searching. Sometimes the magician just gives up.''

"Can't you guys walk any faster?'' Griffin challenged, quickening his pace. "We'll never get to Veygus at this rate.''

"I guess that settles that,'' I smiled, winking at Aahz to show I appreciated his bluff.

"Steal the Trophy from Veygus,'' my mentor replied, picking up his witty repartee where he had left it. "Just like that.''

So much for changing the subject.

"C'mon Aahz, give me a break,'' I defended glibly. "You agreed to this before I proposed it.''

"I didn't say anything,'' he argued.

"You winked,'' I insisted.

"How do you know I didn't just get something in my eye?'' he countered.

"I don't,'' I admitted. "Did you?''

"No,'' he sighed. "I winked. But only because it looked like the only way out of the situation *you* got us into.''

He had me there.

"How we got into this spot is beside the point," I decided. "The real question is how are we going to steal the Trophy."

"I see," Aahz grunted. "When you get us into trouble, it's beside the point."

"The Trophy," I prompted.

"Well . . . " my mentor began slowly, rising to the bait. "We won't be able to make any firm plans until we see the layout and size up the guards. How 'bout it, Griffin? What are we liable to be up against? How good are these Veygans?"

"The Veygans?" our guide grimaced. "I wouldn't worry about them if I were you. They couldn't guard a pea if they swallowed it."

"Really inept, uh?" Aahz murmured, cocking an eyebrow.

"Inept? They're a joke," Griffin laughed. "There isn't a Veygan alive who knows how to spell strategy, much less use it."

"I thought you said you didn't know anything about Veygus," I commented suspiciously.

"Well . . . I don't actually," the youth admitted, "but I've seen their team play in the Big Game, and if that's the best they can muster . . . "

"You mean everything you've been saying was speculation based on the way their team plays?" Aahz interrupted.

"That's right," Griffin nodded.

"The same team that's been beating the pants off Ta-hoe for the last five years?"

Our guide's head came up as if he had just been slapped. "We won this year!" he declared fiercely.

"Whereupon they turned around and stole the Trophy right out from under your noses," my mentor pointed out. "It sounds to me like they may not be as inept as you'd like to think they are."

"They get lucky once in a while," Griffin muttered darkly.

"You might want to think it through a bit," I advised. "I mean, do you really want to go around claiming your team was beaten by a weak opponent? If Ta-hoe is so good and Veygus is so feeble, how do you explain five losses in a row? Luck isn't enough to swing the Game *that* much."

"We got overconfident," our guide confided. "It's a constant danger you have to guard against when you're as good as we are."

"I know what you mean," Aahz nodded. "My partner and I have the same problem."

Well, modesty has never been Aahz's strong suit. Still it was nice to hear him include me in his brash statements. It made me feel like my studies were finally bearing fruit, like I was making progress.

"Aside from the military, what are we up against?" my mentor asked. "How about the magik you keep mentioning? Do they have a magician?"

"They sure do," Griffin nodded vigorously. "Her name's Massha. If you have any troubles at all, it will be with her. She's mean."

"Is that 'mean' in abilities, or in temperament?" Aahz cross-examined.

"Both," our guide asserted firmly. "You know, I've never been totally convinced our magician is as good as he claims to be, but Massha's a real whiz. I couldn't even start to count the fantastic things I've seen her do."

"Um . . . what makes you think her temperament is mean?" I asked casually, trying to hide my sagging confidence.

"Well, let me put it this way," Griffin explained. "If there was a messy job to be done, and you could think of three ways to do it, she'd find a fourth way that was nastier than the other three ways combined.

She has a real genius for unpleasantness."

"Terrific," I grimaced.

"How's that again?" our guide frowned.

"Skeeve here always likes a challenge," Aahz explained hastily, draping a friendly arm around my shoulders.

I caught the warning, even without him digging his talons in until they nearly drew blood. He did it anyway, making it a real effort to smile.

"That's right," I laughed to hide my gasp. "We've handled heavyweights before."

Which was true. What I neglected to mention and tried hard not to think about was that we survived the encounters by a blend of blind luck and bald-faced deceit.

"Good," Griffin beamed. "Even if you don't manage to steal the Trophy, if you can take Massha out of action, Ta-hoe can win the war easily."

"You know, Griffin," Aahz commented, cocking an eyebrow, "for someone who doesn't know Veygus, you seem to know an awful lot about their magician."

"I sure do," our guide laughed bitterly. "She used to be Ta-hoe's magician until Veygus hired her away. I used to run errands for her and . . . " He suddenly stopped in mid-stride and mid-sentence simultaneously. "Hey! That's right," he exclaimed. "I can't go along with you if you're going to see Massha. She knows me! If the Veygans find out I'm from Ta-hoe, they'll think I'm a scout. I'd get torn apart."

"Don't worry," I soothed, "we aren't going anywhere near Massha."

"Yes, we are," Aahz corrected.

"We are?" I blinked.

"Kid, do I have to explain it to you all over again? We've got to check out the local magikal talent, the same as we did when we hit Ta-hoe."

"And look where that got us?" I muttered darkly.

"Look where *who* got us?" Aahz asked innocently. "I didn't quite hear that."

"All right! All right!" I surrendered. "We'll go see Massha. I guess I'll just have to whip up a disguise for Griffin so he won't be spotted."

"She'll recognize my voice," our guide protested.

"Don't talk!" I ordered, without clarifying if it was an immediate or future instruction.

"This time, I think he's right," Aahz interrupted thoughtfully. "It would probably be wisest to leave Griffin behind for this venture."

"It would?" I blinked.

"Hey! Wait a minute," Griffin interjected nervously. "I don't *want* to be a rock or a stone."

"Oh, I'm sure we can work out something a bit less drastic," my mentor smiled reassuringly. "Excuse us for a moment while we confer."

I thought Aahz was going to pull me aside for a private conversation, but instead he simply slipped off his translator pendant. After a bit of browbeating, Quigley had supplied us with an extra, so now we each had one. Removing them allowed us to converse without fear of being overheard, while at the same time keeping Griffin within arm's length. I followed suit and removed mine.

"What gives, Aahz?" I asked as soon as I was free of the pendant. "Why the change in plans?"

"The job's getting a little too complex," he explained. "It's time we started reducing our variables."

"Our what?" I puzzled.

"Look!" Aahz gritted. "We're going to have our hands full trying to elude the military and this Massha gal without trying to keep an eye on Griffin, too. He can't be any great help to us, and if he isn't a help, he's a hindrance."

"He shouldn't be too much trouble," I protested.

"Any trouble will be too much trouble," my men-

tor corrected firmly. "So far, he's an innocent bystander we've dragged into this. That means if we
take him into Veygus, we should be confident we can
bring him out again. Now, are you that confident?
Or don't you mind the thought of leaving him
stranded in a hostile town?"

Aahz doesn't give humanitarian arguments often,
but when he does, they always make sense.

"Okay," I sighed. "But what do we do with him?
You know I can't turn him into a rock or a tree. Not
that I would if I could."

"That's easy," Aahz shrugged. "You put a sleep
spell on him. That should keep him out of mischief
until we get back here."

"Aahz," I said gently, closing my eyes. "I don't
know how to cast a sleep spell. Remember?"

"That's no problem," my mentor winked. "I'll
teach you."

"Right now?" I questioned incredulously.

"Sure. Didn't you hear Quigley? It's easy," Aahz
declared confidently. "Of course, you realize it isn't
really a 'sleep' spell. It's more like suspended anima-
tion."

"Like what?" I blinked.

"It's a magikal slowing of the body's metabolism," he clarified helpfully. "If it were sleep as you
perceive it, then you'd run into problems of dehydra-
tion and . . . "

"Aahz!" I interrupted, holding up a hand. "Is the
spell easier than the explanation?"

"Well, yes," he admitted. "But I thought you'd
like to know."

"Then just teach me the spell. Okay?"

Chapter Twelve:

"Out of the frying pan, into der fire."
—THE SWEDISH CHEF

FORTUNATELY, the sleep spell was as easy to learn as Aahz had promised, and we left Griffin snoozing peacefully in a patch of weeds along the road.

We took the precaution of circling Veygus to enter the city from a direction other than Ta-hoe. As it turned out it was a pointless exercise. Everyone in Veygus was too busy with their own business to even notice us, much less which direction we were coming from.

"This is really great!" Aahz chortled, looking about the streets as we walked. "I could develop a real fondness for this dimension."

The war activities in Veygus were the same as we had witnessed in Ta-hoe, except the souvenirs were being made in red and white instead of blue and gold. I was starting to wonder if anyone was ever going to get around to actually fighting the war, or if they were all too busy making money.

"Look at that, Aahz!" I exclaimed, pointing.

There was a small crowd gathered, listening to a

noisy orator. From what I could hear, their complaint was the same one we heard back in Ta-hoe: that the government's withholding information about the war was hampering the odds-makers.

"Yeah. So?" my mentor shrugged.

"I wonder if they're bookies, too," I speculated.

"There's one way to find out," Aahz offered.

Before I could reply, he had sauntered over to someone at the back of the crowd and engaged him in an animated conversation. There was nothing for me to do but wait . . . and worry.

"Good news, kid," he beamed, rejoining me at last.

"Tell me," I pressed. "I could use some good news right about now."

"They're giving three-to-one odds against Ta-hoe in the upcoming war."

It took me a moment to realize that was the extent of his information. "That's it?" I frowned. "That's your good news? It sounds to me like we've badly underestimated Veygus's military strength."

"Relax, kid," Aahz soothed. "Those are the same odds they're offering in Ta-hoe against Veygus. Local bookies always have to weight the odds in favor of the home team. Otherwise no one will bet against them."

Puzzled, I shook my head. "Okay, so they're actually evenly matched," I shrugged. "I still don't see how that's good news for us."

"Don't you see?" my mentor urged. "That means the bookies are operating independently instead of as a combine. If we play our cards right, we could show a hefty profit from this mess."

Even though annoyed that Aahz could be thinking of money at a time like this, I was nonetheless intrigued with his logic. I mean, after all, he *did* train me.

"By betting?" I asked. "How would we know which side to bet for?"

"Not 'bet for,' bet against," Aahz explained. "And we'd bet equal amounts against both sides."

I thought about this a few moments, nodding knowingly all the while, then gave up. "I don't get it," I admitted. "Betting the same amount for—excuse me, against—both sides, all we do is break even."

Aahz rolled his eyes in exasperation. "Think it through, kid," he insisted. "At three-to-one odds we can't do anything but win. Say we bet a thousand against each team. If Ta-hoe wins, then we pay a thousand in Ta-hoe and collect three thousand in Veygus, for a net profit of two thousand. If Veygus wins, we reverse the process and still come out two thousand ahead."

"That's not a bad plan," I said judiciously, "but I can see three things wrong with it. First, we don't have a thousand with us to bet . . ."

"We could hop back to Klah and get it," Aahz countered.

"Second, we don't have the time . . ."

"It wouldn't take that long," my mentor protested.

"Third, if our mission's successful, there won't be a war."

Aahz's mouth was open for a response, and that's where it stayed—open, and blissfully noiseless as he thought about my argument.

"Got you there, didn't I, Aahz?" I grinned.

"I wonder what the odds are that there won't be a war," he mused, casting a wistful eye at the crowd of bookies.

"C'mon, Aahz," I sighed, tugging bravely at his arm, "we've got a heist to scout."

"First," he corrected firmly, "we have to check out this Massha character."

I had hoped he had forgotten, but then, this adventure was not being typified by its phenomenally good luck.

We picked our way across Veygus, occasionally stopping people to ask directions, and arrived at last outside the dwelling of the town magician. It was an unimposing structure, barely inside the eastern limits of the city, and exuded an intriguing array of aromas.

"Not much of a hangout for a powerful magician, eh, Aahz?" I commented, trying to bolster my sagging courage.

"Remember where you were living when we first met?" my mentor retorted, never taking his eyes from the building.

I did. The one-room clapboard shack where I had first studied magik with Garkin made this place look like a veritable palace.

"What I can't figure out is why Massha settled for this place," Aahz continued, talking as much to himself as to me. "If what Griffin said is true, she could have had any place in town to work from. Tell you what, kid. Check for force lines, will you?"

I obediently closed my eyes and stretched out my mind, searching for those invisible currents of magikal power which those in the profession tap for their own use. I didn't have to look hard.

"Aahz!" I gasped. "There are four . . . no, five . . . force lines intersecting here. Three in the air and two in the ground."

"I thought so," my mentor nodded grimly. "This location wasn't chosen by accident. She's got power to spare, if she knows how to use it."

"But what can we do if she's that powerful?" I moaned.

"Relax, kid," Aahz smiled. "Remember, the power's there for anyone to use. You can tap into it as easily as she can."

"That's right," I said, relaxing slightly, but not much. "Okay, what's our plan?"

"I don't really know," he admitted, heading for

the door. "We'll just have to play this by ear."

Somehow that phrase rang a bell in my memory. "Say—um—Aahz," I stammered. "Remembering how things went back in Ta-hoe, this time let's play it by *your* ear. Okay?"

"You took the words right out of my mouth," Aahz grinned. "Just remember to check her aura as soon as we get inside. It'll help to know if she's local or if we're dealing with imported help."

So saying, he raised his hand and began rapping on the door. I say "began" because between the second and third rap, the door flew open with alarming speed.

"What do you . . . well, hel-lo there, boys."

"Are . . . um . . . are you Massha, the magician?" Aahz stammered, both taken aback and stepping back.

"Can you imagine anyone else fitting the description?" came the throaty chuckle in response.

She was right. I had not seen anyone in Jahk— heck, in several dimensions—who looked anything like the figure framed in the open door. Massha was immense, in girth if not in height. She filled the door-way to overflowing—and it wasn't that narrow a door. Still, size alone doth not a pageant make. Massha might have been overlooked as just another large woman were it not for her garments.

Purple and green warred with each other across her tent-like dress, and her bright orange hair draped across one shoulder in dirty strings did nothing toward encouraging an early settlement. And jewelry! Massha was wearing enough in the way of earrings, rings and necklaces to open her own store. She wasn't a sample case, she was the entire inven-tory!

Her face was nothing to write home about—unless you're really into depressing letters. Bad teeth were framed by fleshy chapped lips, and her pig-like eyes peering from the depths of her numerous smile wrinkles were difficult to distinguish from her other skin blemishes.

I've seen some distinctive looking women in my travels, but Massha took the cake, platter, and table-cloth.

"Did you boys just come to stare?" the apparition asked, "or can I do something for you?"

"We . . . um . . . we need help," Aahz managed.

I wasn't sure if he was talking about our mission or our immediate situation, but either way I agreed with him wholeheartedly.

"Well, you came to the right place," Massha leered. "Step into my parlor and we'll discuss what I've got that you want—and vice-versa."

Aahz followed her into the building, leaving me no choice but to trail along. He surprised me, though, by dropping back slightly to seek my advice.

"What's the word, kid?" he hissed.

"How about 'repulsive'?" I suggested.

That earned me another dig in the ribs.

"I meant about her aura. What's the matter, did you forget?"

As a matter of fact, I had. Now that I had been so forcefully reminded, though, I hurriedly checked for magikal emanations.

"She's got—no, wait a minute," I corrected. "It isn't her, it's her jewelry. It's magikal, but she isn't."

"I thought so," Aahz nodded. "Okay. Now we know what we're dealing with."

"We do?" I asked.

"She's a mechanic," my mentor explained hurriedly. "Gimmick magik with her jewelry. Totally different than the stuff I've been teaching you."

"You mean you think I could beat her in a fair fight?"

"I didn't say that," he corrected. "It all depends on what kind of jewelry she's got—and from what we've seen so far, she's got a lot."

"Oh," I sagged. "What are we going to do?"

"Don't worry, kid," Aahz winked. "Fair fights have never been my specialty. As long as she doesn't know you're a magician, we've got a big advantage."

Any further questions I might have had were forgotten as we arrived at our destination. Having just left Quigley's dwelling, I was unprepared for what Massha used for an office.

To say it was a bedroom would be an understatement. It was the gaudiest collection of tassels, pillows, and erotic statues I had seen this side of the Bazaar at Deva. Colors screamed and clawed at each other, making me wonder if Massha were actually colorblind. As fast as the thought occurred to me, I discarded it. No one could select so many clashing colors by sheer chance.

"Sit down, boys," Massha smiled, sinking onto the parade-ground-sized bed. "Take off your things and we'll get started."

My life flashed before my eyes. While I had secretly dreamed of a career as a ladies' man, I had never envisioned it starting like this! If I had, I might have become a monk.

Even Aahz, with his vast experience, seemed at a loss. "Well, actually," he protested. "We don't have much time . . ."

"You misunderstand me," Massha waved, fanning the air with a massive hand. "What I meant was, take off your disguises."

"Our disguises?" I blurted, swallowing hard.

In reply, she held aloft her left hand, the index finger extended for us to see. The third—no, it was the fourth—ring was blinking a brilliant purple.

"This little toy says you're not only magicians, you're disguised," she grinned. "Now, I'm as sociable as the next person but I like to see who I'm doing business with. In fact, I insist!"

As she spoke, the door behind us slammed shut and locked with an audible click.

So much for our big advantage.

Chapter Thirteen:

"If you can't dazzle them with dexterity, baffle them with bullshit!"
—PROF. H. HILL

THERE was a long silent moment of frozen immobility. Then Aahz turned to me with an exaggerated shrug.

"Well," he sighed, "I guess she's got us dead to rights. There's no arguing with technology, you know. It never makes mistakes."

I almost missed his wink, and even then I was slow to realize what he was up to.

"With your permission, dear lady . . ." Making a half bow at Massha, he began making a series of graceful passes with his hand in the air in front of him.

It was all very puzzling. Aahz had lost all his magikal powers back when . . . Then it hit me. Massha thought we were *both* magicians! Aahz was trying to maintain the illusion and could very well pull it off—if I got busy and backed his move.

As inconspicuously as possible, I closed my eyes

and got to work stripping away his disguise.

"A Pervert!" Massha crowed in tribute to my efforts. "Well, whatdaya know. Thought you walked funny for a Jahk."

"Actually," Aahz corrected smoothly, "as a native of Perv I prefer to be called a 'Pervect.' "

"I don't care what ya *call* yourself," she winked lewdly, "I'm more interested in how ya act."

I was just beginning to enjoy my mentor's discomfort when Massha turned her attentions on me.

"How 'bout you, sport?" she pressed. "You don't say much, let's see what yer hiding."

I resisted an impulse to clutch wildly at my clothes, and instead set about restoring my normal appearance.

"A Klahd—and a young one at that," Massha proclaimed, cocking her head as she examined me. "Well, no matter, by the time old Massha's through with you . . . say!"

Her eyes suddenly opened wide and her gaze darted to Aahz, then back to me.

"A Klahd traveling with a Pervert . . . your name wouldn't be Skeeve, would it?"

"You've heard of me?" I blinked, both startled and flattered.

"Heard of you?" she laughed. "The last time I dropped into the Bazaar, that's all anyone was talking about."

"Really? What were they saying?" I urged.

"Well, the word is that you put together a team of six and used 'em to stop a whole army. It's the most effective use of manpower anyone's pulled off in centuries."

"It was actually eight, if you include Gleep and Berfert," I admitted modestly.

"Who?" She frowned.

"A dragon and a salamander," I explained. "It was such a successful venture I'd like to be sure everyone involved gets some credit."

"That's decent of you," Massha nodded approvingly. "Most folks I know in the trade try to hog all the glory when their plans work and only mention the help if they need someone to blame for failure."

"If you know Skeeve, here," Aahz smiled, elbowing his way into the conversation, "then surely you know who I am."

"As a matter of fact, I don't," Massha shrugged. "I heard there was a loudmouthed Pervert along, but no one mentioned his name."

"Oh, really?" Aahz asked, showing a suspicious number of teeth. "A loudmouthed Pervert, eh? And just who did you hear that from?"

"Um . . . in that case," I interrupted hastily, "allow me to introduce my friend and colleague, Aahz."

"Aahz?" Massha repeated, raising an eyebrow. "As in . . . "

"No relation," Aahz assured her.

"Oh," she nodded.

"Mind if I have some wine?" my mentor asked, gesturing grandly at the wine pitcher on a nearby table. "It's been a long dry trip."

This time I was ready, and covertly levitated the pitcher into his waiting hand. The thought of embarrassing him by leaving the wine where it was never entered my mind. We were still in a tight spot, and anything we could do to keep Massha off balance was a good gambit.

"So, what are a pair of big leaguers like you doing in Jahk?" Massha asked, leaning back into her silken pillows. "You boys wouldn't be after my job, would you?"

It occurred to me that all the employed magicians I was meeting shared a common paranoia about losing their jobs.

"I assure you," Aahz interjected quickly, "taking

your job away from you is the furthest thing from
our minds. If nothing else, we couldn't pass the
physical."

I almost asked "The physical what?" but re-
strained myself. Verbal banter was Aahz's forte, and
for the time being my job was to give him room to
operate.

"Flattery will get you everywhere," Massha
chuckled appreciatively, "except around a direct
question—and you haven't answered mine. If you
aren't looking for work, what are you doing here?"

That was a good question, and thankfully Aahz
had an answer ready.

"We're just on a little vacation," he lied, "and
dropped by Jahk to try to make some of our money
back in the gambling set."

"Gambling?" Massha frowned. "But the Big
Game is over."

"The Big Game," Aahz snorted. "I'll level with
you. We don't know enough about spectator sports
to bet on 'em, but we do know wars—and we hear
there's one brewing. I figure if we can't bet more intelligently than a bunch of yokels who haven't seen a
war in five hundred years, we deserve to lose our
money."

"That explains what you're doing in Jahk,"
Massha nodded thoughtfully, "but it doesn't say
what you're doing here—'in my office' here. What
can I do for you you can't do for yourselves?"

"I could give you a really suggestive answer,"
Aahz smirked, "but the truth is, we're looking for information. From where we sit, magik could swing the
balance one way or the other in this war. What we'd
like is a little inside information as to how much of a
hand you expect to have in the proceedings, and if
you expect any trouble with the opposition."

"The opposition? You mean Ta-hoe's magician?"
She threw back her head and laughed, "I guaran-

tee you, boys, I can handle . . . what's his name . . .
Quigley . . . with one hand. That is, of course, providing that one hand is armed with a few of my
toys."

She wiggled her fingers to illustrate her point and
the ring colors glittered and danced like a malevolent
rainbow."

"That's fine for the war," Aahz nodded. "But
how about here in town? What's to keep Ta-hoe
from stealing the Trophy back before the war?"

"Oh, I've got a few gizmos over at the Trophy
Building that'll fry anyone who tries to heist it—
especially if they try to use magik. Any one of 'em
alone is fallible, but the way I've got 'em set, disarm-
ing one means setting off another. Nobody's taking
that Trophy anywhere without my clearing it."

"Sounds good," my mentor smiled, though I noticed it was a little forced. "As long as you have total
control on the Trophy's security, it isn't likely anything will go wrong."

"Not total control," Massha corrected. "The
army's responsible for it when it's on parade."

"Parade?" I blurted. "What parade?"

"I know it's dumb," she grimaced. "That's why I
refuse any responsibility for it. In fact, I had it written into my contract. I don't give demonstrations and
I don't do parades."

"What parade?" Aahz repeated.

"Oh, once a day they carry the Trophy through the
streets to keep the citizens fired up. You'd think
they'd get tired of it, but so far everyone goes
screaming bonkers every time it comes in view."

"I assume it has a military escort," Aahz commented.

"Are you kidding? Half the army tags along when
it does the rounds. They spend more time escorting
that Trophy around than they do drilling for the
war."

"I see," my mentor murmured. "Well, I guess that tells us what we need to know. We should be on our way."

Before he could move, Massha was at the end of the bed, clasping his leg. "What's the hurry?" she purred. "Doesn't Massha get a little something in return for her information?"

"As a matter of fact," Aahz said, struggling to extract his leg, "there is something that might be valuable to you."

"I know there is," Massha smiled, pulling herself closer to him.

"Did you know that Quigley has summoned up a demon to help him?"

"He what?"

Massha released her hold on Aahz's leg to sit bolt upright.

"That's right," Aahz nodded, moving smoothly out of reach. "From what we hear, he's holding it captive in his workshop. I can't imagine any reason for his doing that unless he plans to use it in the war."

"A demon, eh?" Massha muttered softly, staring absently at the far wall. "Well, well, whatdaya know. I didn't think Quigley had it in him. I don't suppose you've heard anything about its powers?"

"Nothing specific," Aahz admitted, "but I don't think he'd summon anything weaker than he is."

"That's true," Massha nodded. "Well, I should be able to handle them both."

I recognized her tone of voice. It was the way I sound when I'm trying to convince myself I'm up to handling one of Aahz's plans.

"Say, Massha," my mentor explained, as if a thought had just struck him. "I know we're supposed to be on vacation, but maybe we can give you a hand here."

"Would you?" she asked eagerly.

"Well, it's really in our own best interest if we're betting money on the war," he smiled. "Otherwise we wouldn't get involved. As it is, though, I think we can get the demon away from Quigley, or at least neutralize it so it won't help him at all."

"You'd do that for me? As a favor?" Massha blinked.

"Sure," Aahz waved. "Just don't be surprised at anything we do and whatever you do, don't try to counter any of our moves. I won't make any guarantees, but I think we can pull it off. If we do, just remember you owe us a favor someday."

Anyone who knew Aahz would have been immediately suspicious if he offered to do anything as a favor. Fortunately, Massha didn't know Aahz, and she seemed both solicitous and grateful as she waved goodbye to us at the door.

"Well, kid," Aahz grinned, slapping me on the back. "Not bad for an afternoon's work, if I do say so myself. Not only did we scout the opposition, we neutralized it. Big bad Massha won't move against us no matter what we do, for fear of disrupting our plans against Quigley."

As I had restored our disguises before we emerged onto the street, Aahz's back slap didn't arrive on my back—and it hit me with more force than I'm sure he intended. All in all, it did nothing to improve my already black mood.

"Sure, Aahz," I growled. "Except for one little detail."

"What's that?"

"We can't steal Tanda away from Quigley because he'd lose his job and we promised we wouldn't do anything to jeopardize his position. Remember?"

"Skeeve, Skeeve," my mentor chuckled, shaking his head. "I haven't overlooked anything. *You're* the one who hasn't thought things through."

"Okay," I snapped. "So I'm slow! Explain it to me."

"Well, first of all, as I just mentioned, we don't have to worry about Massha for a while."

"But—" I began, but he cut me off.

"Second of all," he continued, "I said 'free or neutralize.' Now, we already know Quigley isn't about to use Tanda in the war, so Massha's going to owe us a favor whether we do anything or not."

"But we're supposed to be rescuing Tanda," I protested, "and that means stealing the Trophy."

"Right!" Aahz beamed. "I'm glad you finally caught on."

"Huh?" I said intelligently.

"You *haven't* caught on," my mentor sighed. "Look, kid. The mission's still on. We're going to steal the Trophy."

"But I can't bypass Massha's traps at the Trophy Building."

"Of course not," Aahz agreed. "That's why we're going to steal it from the parade."

"The parade?" I blinked. "In broad daylight with half the army and the whole town watching?"

"Of course," Aahz shrugged. "It's the perfect situation."

It occurred to me that either my concept of a perfect situation was way out of line, or my mentor had finally lost his mind!

Chapter Fourteen:

"As any magician will tell you—Myth Directions is the secret of a successful steal."

—D. HENNING

"DON'T you see, kid? The reason it's a perfect situation is that everyone's sure it can't be stolen!"

It was the same answer Aahz had given the last ten times I asked, so I gave him my usual rebuttal.

"The reason they're sure is because it *can't* be stolen. At least half the population of Veygus will be looking, Aahz, and they'll be looking right at the Trophy we're trying to steal! Someone's bound to notice."

"Not if you follow your instructions, they won't," my mentor winked. "Trust me."

I wasn't reassured. Not that I didn't trust Aahz, mind you. His ability to get me into trouble is surpassed only by his ability to bail me out again. I just had a hunch his bailing abilities were going to be tested to their limits this time.

I was about to express this to Aahz when a roar went up from the crowd around us, ending any hope for conversation. The Trophy was just coming into view.

We had chosen our post carefully. This point was the closest the procession came to the North wall of Veygus . . . and hence it was the closest the Trophy came to the gate opening onto the road to Ta-hoe.

In line with Aahz's plan, we waved our fists in the air and jumped up and down as the Trophy passed by with its military escort. It was pointless to shout, however. The crowd was making so much noise that two voices more or less went unnoticed, and we needed to save our lung power for the heist itself. Working our way to the back of the mob also proved to be no problem. By simply not fighting back when everyone else elbowed in front of us soon moved us to our desired position.

"So far, so good," Aahz murmured, scanning the backs in front of us to be sure we were unobserved.

"Maybe we should quit while we're ahead," I suggested hopefully.

"Shut up and start working," he snapped back in a tone that left no room for argument.

With an inward sigh, I closed my eyes and began making subtle changes in our disguises.

When I first learned the disguise spell, it was specifically to alter the facial features and body configurations of a being to resemble another. Later, after considerable practice, I learned to change the outward appearance of inanimate objects, providing they had once been alive. Aahz had seized this modification for a new application . . . specifically to change the configuration of our clothes. By the time I was done, we not only looked like Jahks, we were dressed in the uniforms of Veygan soldiers.

"Good enough, kid," Aahz growled, clapping me on the shoulder. "Let's go!"

With that, he plunged headlong into the crowd, clearing a path for me to emerge on the street behind the Trophy procession. Clearing paths through moveable objects, like people, is one of the things Aahz does best.

"Make way!" he bawled. "One side! Make way!"
Close behind him, I added my bellow to the din.

"Ta-hoers!" I called. "At the South wall! Ta-hoers!"

That's one of the things I do best—scream in panic.

For a moment, no one seemed to hear us. Then a few heads turned. A couple voices took up my call.

"Ta-hoers!" they cried. "We're being attacked."

The word spread through the crowd ahead of us like wildfire, such that when we reached the rear-guard of the procession, it had ground to a halt. The soldiers milled about, tangling weapons with bodies around them as they tried simultaneously to scan the crowd, rooftops, and sky.

"Ta-hoers!" I shouted, pushing in among them.

"Where?"

"The South wall."

"Where?"

"The South wall."

"Who?"

"Ta-hoers!"

"Where?"

This nonsense might have continued endlessly, except for the appearance of an officer on the scene. He was noticeably more intelligent than the soldiers around him . . . which was to say he might have won a debate with a turnip.

"What's going on here?" he demanded, his authoritative voice silencing the clamor in the ranks.

"Ta-hoers, sir!" I gasped, still a bit out of breath from my performance. "They're attacking in force at the South wall!"

"The South wall?" the officer frowned. "But Ta-hoe is north of here."

"They must have circled around the city," I suggested hastily. "They're attacking the South wall."

"But Ta-hoe is north of here," the man insisted. "Why would they attack the South wall?"

His slow-wittedness was exasperating. It was also threatening to totally disrupt our plan, which hinged on momentum.

"Are you going to stand here arguing while those yellow and blue idiots take the city?" Aahz demanded, shouldering his way past me. "If everybody gets killed because of your indecision, the council will bust you back to the ranks."

That possibility wasn't very logical, so, of course, the fool took it to heart. Drawing his sword, he turned to the men around him.

"To the South wall," he ordered. "Follow me!"

"To the South wall!"

The cry went up as the soldiers wheeled and dashed back down the street.

"To the South wall!" I echoed, moving with them.

Suddenly, a powerful hand seized my shoulder and slammed me against a wall hard enough to knock the air out of my lungs.

"To the South wall!"

It was Aahz, leaning back to keep me pinned between him and the wall as he waved the soldiers past.

At last, he turned his head slightly to address me directly.

"Where ya going?" he asked curiously.

"To the South wall?" I suggested in a small voice.

"Why?"

"Because the Ta-hoers . . . oh!"

I felt exceptionally stupid. I also felt more than slightly squashed. Aahz is no featherweight.

"I think better when I can breathe," I pointed out meekly.

The ground slipped up and crashed into me as Aahz shifted his weight forward.

"Quit clowning around, kid," he snarled, hauling me to my feet. "We've still got work to do."

As I've said before, Aahz has an enviable grasp of the obvious. A dozen soldiers were still clustered around the Trophy, its litter now resting on the ground. There was also the minor detail of the crowd of onlookers still milling about arguing over this latest change in events.

"What are we going to do, Aahz?" I hissed.

"Just leave everything to me," he retorted confidently.

"Okay," I nodded.

"Now here's what I want you to do . . . "

"What happened to 'leave everything to you'?" I grumbled.

"Shut up and listen," he ordered. "I want you to change my face and uniform to match that officer we talked to."

"But . . . "

"Just do it!"

In a moment the necessary adjustments were made and my mentor was on his way, striding angrily toward the remaining soldiers.

"What are you doing there?" he bawled. "Get to the South wall with the others!"

"But . . . we were . . . our orders are to guard the Trophy," the nearest soldier stammered in confusion.

"Defend it by keeping the Ta-hoers out of the city," Aahz roared. "Now get to the South wall! Anyone who tries to stay behind I'll personally charge with cowardice in the face of the enemy. Do you know what the punishment for that is?"

Apparently they did, even if I didn't. Aahz's question went unanswered as the soldiers sprinted off down the street toward the South wall.

So much for the Trophy's military escort. I did wonder, though, what my mentor planned to do about the milling crowd.

"Citizens of Veygus," Aahz boomed, as if in answer to my silent question. "Our fair city is under attack. Now, I know all of you will want to volunteer to help the Army in this battle, but to be effective you must be disciplined and orderly. To that end, I want all volunteers to line up here in front of me for instructions. Any who are unable to serve should return to their homes at this time, so the militia will have room to maneuver. All right, volunteers assemble!"

Within seconds, Aahz and I were left alone in the street. The crowd of potential volunteers had evaporated like water spilled on a hot griddle.

"So much for the witnesses," my mentor grinned, winking at me.

"Where'd they all go?" I asked, craning my neck to look around.

"Home, of course," Aahz smirked. "No one likes the draft—particularly when it affects them personally."

I wet my finger and tested the breeze. "There's not that much wind today," I announced suspiciously.

For some reason, this statement seemed to annoy my mentor. He rolled his eyes and started to say something, then changed his mind.

"Look, let's just grab the Trophy, okay?" he snarled. "That 'South wall' bit won't fool the Army forever, and I for one don't want to be here when they get back."

For once, we were in total agreement.

"Okay, Aahz," I nodded. "How do we get it out of the city?"

"That's easy," he waved. "Remember, I'm not exactly a weakling."

With that, he strode over to the Trophy and simply picked it up and tucked it under his arm, balancing it casually on his hip.

"But, Aahz . . . " I began.

"I know what you're going to say," he admonished, holding up a hand, "and you're right. It would be easier to steal a cart. What you're overlooking is that a cart is personal property, while the Trophy belongs to the whole city."

"But, Aahz . . . "

"That means," he continued hastily, "that everyone assumes someone else is watching the Trophy, so we can walk away with it. If we stole a cart, the owner would spot it in a minute and raise the alarm. Now, having successfully liberated the Trophy, it would be really dumb to get arrested for stealing a cart, wouldn't it?"

"I didn't mean how are we going to move it!" I blurted. "I meant how are we going to get it past the guards at the North gate?"

"What's that?" Aahz frowned.

"They aren't going to let us just walk past them carrying that Trophy, and I can't disguise it. It's a metal!"

"Hmmm . . . you're right, kid," my mentor nodded thoughtfully. "Well, maybe we can . . . oh, swell!"

"What is it?" I asked fearfully.

"The soldiers are coming back," he announced, cocking his head to listen. Aahz has exceptionally sharp hearing. "Oh, well, we're just going to have to do this the fast way. Break out the D-Hopper."

"The what?" I blinked.

"The D-Hopper!" he insisted. "We'll just take this back to Klah with us."

I hurriedly fumbled the D-Hopper out of my pouch and passed it to Aahz for setting.

"What about Tanda?"

"We'll use this gizmo to bring the Trophy back later and spring her," Aahz mumbled. "I hadn't figured on using this just now. There's always a possibility that . . . oh, well. Hang on, kid. Here we go."

I crowded close to him and waited as he hit the button to activate the Hopper.

Nothing happened.

Chapter Fifteen:

"—Or was it unlock the safe then swim to the surface?"

—H. HOUDINI

"NOTHING happened."

"I know it," Aahz groaned, glaring at the D-Hopper. "That's the trouble with relying on mechanical gadgets. The minute you rely on them, they let you down."

"What's wrong?" I pressed.

"The damn thing needs recharging," Aahz spat. "And there's no way we can do it before the Army gets here."

"Then let's hide until . . ."

"Hide where?" my mentor snapped. "Do you want to ask one of the citizens to hide us? They might have a few questions about the Trophy we're lugging along."

"Okay, you suggest something!" I snarled.

"I'm working on it," Aahz growled, looking around. "What we need is . . . there!"

Before I could ask what he was doing, he strode into a nearby shop, tugged an animal skin off the wall, and began wrapping it around the Trophy.

"Terrific," I observed dryly. "Now we have a furry Trophy. I don't think it will fool the guards."

"It will, once you disguise it," Aahz grinned.

"I told you, I can't," I insisted. "It's a metal!"

"Not the Trophy, dummy!" he snapped. "The skin. Get to work! Change it to anything. No . . . make it a wounded soldier!"

I wasn't sure it would work, but I closed my eyes and gave it a try. One wounded soldier—complete with a torn, bloodstained uniform and trailing feet.

"Not bad, kid," Aahz nodded, sticking the bundle under his arm.

As usual, I couldn't see the effects of my work. When I looked, I didn't see an officer of the guard with a wounded comrade under his arm. I saw Aahz holding a suspiciously lumpy package.

"Are you sure it's okay?" I asked doubtfully.

"Sure," Aahz nodded. "Just . . . oops! Here they come. Leave everything to me."

That had a suspiciously familiar ring to it, but I didn't have many other options at the moment. The soldiers were in sight now, thundering down on us with grim scowls set fiercely on their faces.

"That way! Quick! They're getting away."

Aahz's bellow nearly startled me out of my skin, but I held my ground. I'm almost used to his unexpected gambits—almost.

"After them!" Aahz repeated. "Charlie's hit!"

"Who's Charlie?" I frowned.

"Shut up, kid," my mentor hissed, favoring me with a glare before returning his attention to the soldiers.

They had slowed their headlong dash and were looking down the sidestreets as they came, but they hadn't changed course. The only fortunate thing was that the officer Aahz was impersonating was nowhere in sight.

"Don't you understand?" Aahz shouted. "They've got the Trophy! That way!"

That did it. With a roar of animal rage, the soldiers wheeled and started off in the direction Aahz had indicated.

"Boy," I murmured in genuine admiration. "I wouldn't want to be holding that Trophy when they caught up with me."

"It could be decidedly unpleasant," Aahz agreed. "So if you don't mind, could we be on our way? Hmmm?"

"Oh! Right, Aahz."

He was already on his way, eating up great hunks of distance with his strong, hurried stride. As I hastened to keep up with him, I resolved not to ask about his plans for getting past the guards at the North gate. I was only annoying him with my constant questions, and besides, the answers only unsettled me.

As we drew nearer to the gate, however, my nervousness grew stronger and my resolve weaker.

"Ummm . . . do you want me to change the disguise on the Trophy?" I asked tentatively.

"No," came the brusque reply. "But you could mess us up a little."

"Mess us up?" I blinked.

"A little dirt and blood on the uniforms," Aahz clarified. "Enough to make it look like we've been in a fight."

I wasn't sure what he had up his sleeve, but I hastened to adjust our disguises. That isn't as easy as it sounds, incidentally. Try closing your eyes and imagining dirty uniforms in detail while walking down a strange street at a near-trot. Fortunately, my life with Aahz had trained me to work under desperate conditions, so I completed my task just as we were coming up on the gate.

As a tribute to my handiwork, the guard didn't

even bother to address us directly. He simply gaped at us for a moment, then started hollering for the Officer of the Guard. By the time that member appeared, we were close enough to count his teeth as his jaw dropped.

"What's going on here?" he demanded finally, recovering his composure.

"Fighting in the streets," Aahz gasped in a realistic imitation of a weary warrior. "They need your help. We're your relief."

"Our relief!" the officer frowned. "But that man's unconscious and you look like . . . fighting, did you say?"

"We're fit enough for gate duty," Aahz insisted, weakly pulling himself erect. "Anything to free a few more able-bodied men for the fighting."

"What fighting?" the officer screamed, barely suppressing an impulse to shake Aahz back to his senses.

"Riots," my mentor blinked. "The bookies have changed the odds on the war and won't honor earlier bets. It's awful."

The officer blanched and recoiled as if he had been struck. "But that means . . . my life savings are bet on the war. They can't do that."

"You'd better hurry," Aahz insisted. "If the mobs tear the bookies apart, no one will get their money back."

"Follow me! All of you!" the officer bellowed, though it wasn't necessary. The guards were already on their way. Apparently the officer wasn't the only one with money in the bookies' care.

The officer started after them, then paused to sweep us with an approving stare.

"I don't know if you'll get a medal for this," he announced grimly, "but I won't forget it. You have my personal thanks."

"Don't mention it, turkey," Aahz murmured as the man sprinted off.

"You know, I bet he *won't* forget this . . . ever," I smiled.

"Feeling pretty smug, aren't you, kid?" Aahz commented, cocking a critical eyebrow at me.

"Yes," I confirmed modestly.

"Well, you should," he laughed, clapping me on the back. "I think, however, we'd best celebrate at a distance."

"Quite right," I agreed, gesturing grandly to the open gate. "After you."

"No, after you!" he countered, imitating my gesture.

Not wanting to waste additional time arguing, we walked side by side through the now unguarded North gate of Veygus, bearing our prize triumphantly with us.

That should have been it. Having successfully recaptured the Trophy, it should have been an easy matter to return to Ta-hoe, exchange the Trophy for Tananda, and relax in a celebration party back at Klah. I should have known better.

Any time things seem calm and tranquil, something happens to disrupt matters. If unforeseen outside complications don't arise, then either Aahz's temper flares or I open my big mouth. In this case, there were no outside complications, but there our luck ran out. Neither one of us was to blame—we both were. Aahz for his temper, me for my big mouth.

We were nearly back to the place where he had hidden Griffin, when Aahz made an unexpected request.

"Say, kid," he said, "how about dropping the disguises for a while?"

"Why?" I asked, logically.

"No special reason," he shrugged. "I just want to look at this Trophy that's caused everyone so much trouble."

"Didn't you see it back at Veygus?" I frowned.

"Not really," my mentor admitted. "At first I was

busy chasing away the soldiers and the civilians, and after that it was something big and heavy to carry. I never really stopped to study it.''

It took mere seconds to remove the disguises. They're easier to break down than to build, since I can see what the end result is supposed to look like.

''Help yourself,'' I announced.

''Thanks, kid,'' Aahz grinned, setting the Trophy down and hastily unwrapping it.

The Trophy was as ugly as ever; not that I had expected it to change. If anything, it looked worse up close, as Aahz was looking at it. Then he backed up and looked again. Finally he walked around it, studying the monstrosity from all angles.

For some reason, his silent scrutiny was making me uneasy.

''Well, what do you think?'' I asked, in an effort to get the conversation going again.

He turned slowly to face me, and I noticed his scales were noticeably darker than normal.

''That's it?'' he demanded, jerking a thumb over his shoulder at the statue. ''That's the Trophy? You got Tanda captured and put us through all this for a dismal hunk of sculpture like that?''

Something clicked softly in my mind, igniting a small ember of anger. I mean, I've never pretended to admire the Trophy, but it *had* been Tananda's choice.

''Yes, Aahz,'' I said carefully. ''That's it.''

''Of all the dumb stunts you've pulled, this takes the cake!'' my mentor raged. ''You neglect your studies, cost us a fortune, not to mention putting everybody's neck on the chopping block, and for what?''

''Yes, Aahz,'' I managed.

''And Tanda! I knew she was a bit dippy, but this! I've got a good mind to leave her right where she is.''

I tried to say something, but nothing came out.

"All I want to hear from you, apprentice, is why!"
He was looming over me now.

"Even feeble minds need a motive. What did you
two figure to do with this pile of junk once you stole
it? Tell me that!"

"It was going to be your birthday present!" I
shouted, the dam bursting at last.

Aahz froze stock-still, an expression of astonishment spreading slowly over his face.

"My . . . my birthday present?" he asked in a
small voice.

"That's right, Aahz," I growled. "Surprise. We
wanted to get you something special. Something no
one else had, no matter how much trouble it was.
Sure was stupid of us, wasn't it?"

"My birthday present," Aahz murmured, turning
to stare at the Trophy again.

"Well, it's all over now," I snarled savagely. "Us
feeble-minded dolts bit off more than we could chew
and you had to bail us out. Let's spring Tanda and go
home. Maybe then we can forget the whole thing—if
you'll let us."

Aahz was standing motionless with his back to me.
Now that I had vented my anger, I found myself suddenly regretful for having ground it in so mercilessly.

"Aahz?" I asked, stepping in behind him. "Hey!
C'mon, we've got to give it back and get Tanda."

Slowly he turned his head until our gazes met.
There was a faraway light in his eyes I had never seen
before.

"Give it back?" he said softly. "Whatdaya mean,
'Give it back'? That's my birthday present!"

Chapter Sixteen:

". . . and then the fun began."
— N. BONAPARTE

I HAD attended war councils before. I hadn't been wild about it as a pastime even then, but I had done it. On those occasions, however, our side was the only one with the vaguest skills in magik. This time, all three sides would have magicians in attendance. My joy knew definite bounds; in fact, I didn't want to be there at all.

"Maybe they won't come," I suggested hopefully.

"With their precious Trophy on the line?" Aahz grinned. "Not a chance. They'll be here."

"If they got the messages," I corrected. "Griffin may have just headed for the horizon."

My mentor cocked an eyebrow at me. "Think back to the days before you were an apprentice, kid," he suggested. "If a magician gave you a message to deliver, would you try to get away?"

"Well . . . " I conceded.

"They'll be here," he concluded firmly. "I just hope Quigley gets here first."

My last hope gone, I resigned myself to the meeting and turned my attention to our immediate surroundings.

"Can you at least tell me why we're meeting here?" I asked. "Why not in the forest where we'd have some trees to duck behind if things get ugly? What's so special about this statatorium?"

"That's stadium, kid," my mentor corrected, rolling his eyes. "And there're three good reasons to set up the meeting here. First of all, both the Veygans and the Ta-hoers know where it is. Second, they both acknowledge it as neutral ground."

"And third?" I prompted.

"You said it yourself," Aahz shrugged. "There's no cover. Nothing at all to hide behind."

"That's good?"

"Think it through, kid," my mentor sighed. "If we can hide behind a tree, so could someone else. The difference is, they have more people to hide."

"You mean they might try to ambush us?" I blinked.

"It's a possibility. I only hope that having the meeting in the open like this will lower the probability."

One thing I have to admit about Aahz. Any time I'm nervous, I can count on him to say just the right thing to convert my nervousness to near-hysteric panic.

"Um . . . Aahz," I began carefully. "Isn't it about time you let me in on this master plan of yours?"

"Sure," my mentor grinned. "We're going to have a meeting with representatives from both Veygus and Ta-hoe."

"But what are you going to say to them?" I pressed.

"You're missing the point, kid. The reason I'm meeting with both of them at once is because I don't want to have to repeat myself. Now, if I explain everything to you now, I'll only have to repeat myself at the meeting. Understand?"

"No," I announced bluntly. "I don't. I'm supposed to be your apprentice, aren't I? Well, how am I going to help out if I don't know what's going on?"

"That's a good point," Aahz conceded. "I wish you had raised it earlier. Because now it's too late. Our guests are arriving."

I turned to look in the direction he was pointing and discovered he was right. A small group had emerged from one of the entrances halfway up the side of the stadium and was filing down the stairs toward the field where we were waiting. Watching them descend, I was struck again by the enormity of the stadium. I had realized it was large when we first arrived and I saw the rows and rows of seats circling the field. Now, however, seeing how tiny the group looked in this setting made me all the more aware of exactly how large the stadium really was. As we waited, I tried to imagine the seats filled with thousands upon thousands of people all staring down at the field and the very thought of it made me uneasy. Fortunately, the odds of my ever actually seeing it were very, *very* low.

The group was close enough now for us to distinguish between individuals. This didn't do us much good, though, as we didn't *know* any of the individuals involved. I finally recognized Griffin in their ranks, and from that figured out it was the Ta-hoe delegation approaching. Once I realized that, I managed to spot Quigley bringing up the rear. I would have recognized him sooner, but he was disguised as a Jahk, which threw me for a moment. Actually, it made sense. I mean, Aahz and I were currently disguised as Jahks, so it was only logical that Quigley would also be hiding his extra-dimensional origins as well. Sometimes it bothers me that I seem to habitually overlook the obvious.

"That's far enough!" Aahz boomed.

The group halted obediently a stone's throw away.

It occurred to me it might be better if they were a little *more* than a stone's throw away, but I kept quiet.

"We're ready to discuss the return of the Trophy," one of the delegates called, stepping forward.

"We're not," my mentor retorted.

This caused a minor stir in the group and they began to mumble darkly among themselves.

"Aahz!" I urged.

"What I mean to say," Aahz added hastily, "is that what we have to say will wait until the other delegation arrives. In the meantime, I wish a word with your master magician."

There was a brief huddle, then Quigley came forward to join us. Even at a distance I could see he was upset.

"Hi, Quigley," Aahz grinned. "How's tricks?"

"I certainly hope you have an explanation for this," the ex-demon hunter snapped, ignoring the cordial greeting.

"Explanation for what?" my mentor countered innocently.

"You promised . . . or rather, Master Skeeve did . . . that you two wouldn't do anything to endanger my job."

"And we haven't," Aahz finished.

"Yes, you have!" Quigley insisted. "The council expects me to use my magik to get the Trophy away from you at this meeting. If I don't, I can kiss my job goodbye."

"Don't worry," my mentor soothed. "We've taken that into account."

"We have?" I murmured in wonder.

Aahz shot me a black look and continued.

"I guarantee that by the end of the meeting the council won't expect you to perform any magik against us."

"You mean you'll give the Trophy back voluntar-

ily?'' Quigley asked, brightening noticeably. "I must
say that's decent of you.''

"No, it isn't," Aahz corrected, "and we're not
going to give it back. All I said was they wouldn't expect you to get it for them with magik."

"But—"

"The reason I wanted to talk with you," Aahz interrupted, "was to clarify a little something from our
previous conversation.''

"What's that?" Quigley frowned.

"Well, you promised to release Tanda if the
Trophy was returned. Now, if Ta-hoe has a chance to
take the Trophy back, and then doesn't do it, is the
deal still on? Will you let her go?"

"I . . . I suppose so," the ex-demon hunter ac-
quiesced, gnawing his lip. "But I can't imagine them
not wanting it.''

"Wanting something and being able to take it are
two different things," Aahz grinned.

"But I'm supposed to be helping them with my
magik!''

"Not this time, you aren't," my mentor corrected.
"I've already told you that—''

"Is this a private chat, boys? Or can anybody join
in?''

We all turned to find Massha lumbering towards
us. The rest of the Veygus delegation waited behind
her, having apparently arrived while we were talking
to Quigley.

"Good God! What's that?" Quigley gasped, gap-
ing at Massha's approaching bulk.

"That's Massha," I volunteered casually. "You
know, the Veygans' magician!''

"That's Massha?" he echoed, swallowing hard.

"If you'll excuse us for a moment," Aahz suggested, "there are a few things we have to discuss
with her before the meeting.''

"Of course, certainly.''

The ex-demon hunter beat a hasty retreat, apparently relieved at being able to avoid a face-to-face meeting with his rival.

"The council there tells me that was Quigley you were just talking to," Massha announced, tracking his flight with her eyes. "Is that true?"

"Umm . . . yes," I admitted.

"You boys wouldn't be trying to double-cross old Massha, would you?" Her tone was jovial, but her eyes narrowed suspiciously.

"My dear lady!" Aahz gasped. "You wound me! Didn't we promise to neutralize Quigley's demon for you?"

"You sure did."

"And it would be extremely difficult to engineer that without at least being on speaking terms with Quigley. Wouldn't it?"

"Well . . . yes."

"So no sooner do we start working on the project than you accuse us of double-crossing you! We should leave right now and let you solve your own problems."

I had to suppress a smile. Aahz looking indignant is a comical sight at best. Massha, however, swallowed it hook, line and sinker.

"Now, don't be that way," she pleaded. "I didn't mean to get ya all out of joint. Besides, do you blame me for being a little suspicious after you up and made off with the Trophy?"

Aahz sighed dramatically. "Didn't we say not to be surprised at anything we did? Geez! I guess it's what we should expect, trying to deal with someone who can't comprehend the subtlety of our plans."

"You mean stealing the Trophy is part of your plan to neutralize the demon?" Massha asked, wide-eyed with awe.

"Of course!" Aahz waved. "Or it was. You see, Quigley got the demon to help get the Trophy away from Veygus. Now, if Veygus doesn't have the Trophy, he doesn't need the demon, right?"

"Sounds a little shaky to me," the sorceress frowned.

"You're right," Aahz acknowledged. "That's why I was so glad when the k . . . I mean, when Master Skeeve here came up with this new plan."

"I did?"

Aahz's arm closed around my shoulders in an iron grip which eliminated any thoughts of protest from my mind.

"He's so modest," my mentor explained. "You've heard what a genius tactician he is? Well, he's come up with a way to neutralize the demon . . . *and* give Veygus a good chance at retrieving the Trophy."

"I'm dying to hear it," Massha proclaimed eagerly.

"Me, too," I mumbled. Aahz's grip tightened threateningly.

"Then I guess we're ready to get started," he declared. "You'd better rejoin your delegation. Wouldn't want it to look like we're playing favorites. And remember . . . agree with us no matter what we say. We're on your side."

"Right!" she winked, and headed off.

"Say, um, Aahz," I managed at last.

"Yeah, kid?"

"If you're on Quigley's side *and* on Massha's side, who's on my side?"

"I am, of course."

I had been afraid he was going to say something like that. It was becoming increasingly clear that Aahz was going to come out of this in pretty good shape no matter how it ran. I didn't have much time to ponder the point, though.

Aahz was beckoning the groups forward to start the meeting.

Chapter Seventeen:

"I'm sure we can talk things out like civilized people."

—J. WAYNE

"I SUPPOSE you're all wondering why I called you here," my mentor began with a grin.

I think he intended it as a joke. I've gotten so I recognize his "waiting for a laugh" grin. Unfortunately, he was trying it on the wrong crowd. Jahks aren't generally noted for their sense of humor.

"I assume it's to talk about the Trophy," a distinguished individual from the Ta-hoe group observed dryly. "Otherwise we're wasting our time."

"Oh, it's about the Trophy," Aahz assured him hastily.

"Which you stole from us!" a Veygan contributed venomously.

"After you stole it from us!" the Ta-hoer speaker shot back.

"Only after you cheated us out of it at the Big Game."

"That call was totally legal! The rules clearly state. . . ."

"*That* rule hasn't been enforced for three hundred

119

years. There are four rulings on record which have since contradicted. . . ."

"Gentlemen, please!" Aahz called, holding up his hands for order. "All that is water under the drawbridge, as well as being totally beside the point. Remember, neither of you currently have the Trophy. *We* do."

There was a moment of tense silence as both sides absorbed this observation. Finally, the Ta-hoer speaker stepped forward.

"Very well," he said firmly. "Name your price for its return. The Ta-hoe Council is prepared to offer . . ."

"Veygus will top any offer Ta-hoe makes."

"And Ta-hoe will double any offer that Veygus makes," the speaker shot back.

This was starting to sound pretty good to me. Maybe I've been hanging around with Aahz too long, but the potential financial benefits of our situation impressed me as being exceptionally good. The only foreseeable difficulty was Aahz's insistence that he was going to keep his birthday present.

"If you try anything, our magician will . . ."

"Your magician! We fired her. If she tries anything, *our* magician will . . ."

The raging debate forced its way into my consciousness again. That last bit sounded like it could get very ugly very quickly. I snuck a nervous glance at Aahz, but as usual he was way ahead of me.

"Gentlemen, gentlemen!" he admonished, raising his hands once more.

"Who are you calling a gentleman?"

"And ladies," my mentor amended, squinting at the source of the voice. "What-da-ya know. ERA strikes again."

"What's an eerah?" the Ta-hoe spokesman frowned, echoing my thoughts exactly.

"It seems," Aahz continued, ignoring the question entirely, "that our motives have been misconstrued.

We didn't appropriate the Trophy to ransom it. Quite the contrary. It has been our intention all along to see that it goes to its rightful owners."

An ugly growl arose from the Veygans.

"Excellent!" beamed the Ta-hoe spokesman. "If you won't accept a reward, will you at least accompany us back to town as our guests. There's sure to be celebrating and . . ."

"I said 'the rightful owner.' " Aahz smiled, cutting him off.

The spokesman paused, his smile melting to a dangerous scowl. "Are you saying we aren't the rightful owners?" he snarled. "If you thought Veygus had a better claim, why did you steal it in the first place?"

"Let me run it past you one more time," my mentor sighed. "The Trophy's going to its *rightful* owner. That lets Veygus out, too."

That took the spokesman aback. I didn't blame him. Aahz's logic had me a bit confused, too . . . and I was on his side!

"If I understand it correctly," Aahz continued grandly, "the Trophy goes to the winning team—that wins the Big Game—as their award for being the year's best team. Is that right?"

"Of course," the spokesman nodded.

"Why do you assume the team that wins the Big Game is the best team?" Aahz asked innocently.

"Because there *are* only two teams. So it follows logically that . . ."

"That's where you're wrong," my mentor interrupted. "There *is* another team."

"Another team?" the spokesman blinked.

"That's right. A team that neither of your teams has faced, much less beaten. Now, we maintain that until that team is defeated, neither Ta-hoe nor Veygus has the right to declare their team the year's best!"

My stomach did a flip-flop. I was getting a bad feeling about this.

"That's ridiculous!" called the Veygus spokesman. "We've never *heard* of another team. Whose team is this, anyway?"

"Ours," Aahz smiled. "And we're challenging both your teams to a game, a three-way match, right here in thirty days . . . Winner takes all."

Bad feeling confirmed. For a moment, I considered altering my disguise and sneaking out with one of the delegations. Then I realized that option was closed. Both groups had stepped back well out of ear-shot to discuss Aahz's proposal. That put them far away, so that I couldn't join them without being noticed. With nothing else to do, I turned on Aahz.

"*This* is your plan?" I demanded. "Setting us up to play a game we know absolutely nothing about against not one but two teams who've been playing it for five hundred years? That's not a plan, that's a disaster!"

"I figure it's our best chance to spring Tanda *and* keep the Trophy," my mentor shrugged.

"It's a chance to get our heads beaten in," I corrected. "There's got to be an easier way."

"There was," Aahz agreed. "Unfortunately, you eliminated it when you promised we wouldn't do anything to endanger Quigley's job."

I hate it when Aahz is right. I hate it almost as much as getting caught in my own stupid blunders. More often than not, those two phenomena occur simultaneously in my life.

"Why didn't you tell me about this plan before?" I asked to hide my discomfort.

"Would you have gone along with it if I had?"

"No."

"That's why."

"What happens if we refuse your challenge?" the Ta-hoe spokesman called.

"Then we consider ourselves the winners by default," Aahz replied.

"Well, Veygus will be there," came the decision from the other group.

"And so will Ta-hoe," was the spontaneous response.

"If I might ask," the Ta-hoe spokesman queried, "why did you pick a date thirty days from now?"

"It'll take time for you to lay out a triangular field," my mentor shrugged. "And besides, I thought your merchants would require more than a week to prepare their souvenirs."

There were nods in both groups for that reasoning.

"Then it's agreed?" Aahz prompted.

"Agreed!" roared Veygus.

"Agreed!" echoed Ta-hoe.

"Speaking of merchandizing," the Ta-hoe spokesman commented, "what is the name of your team? We'll need it before we can go into production of the souvenirs."

"We're called 'The Demons,'" Aahz said, winking at me. In a flash I saw that his plan really was. "Would you like to know why?"

"Well . . . I would assume it's because you play like demons," the Ta-hoe spokesman stammered.

"Not 'like' demons!" my mentor grinned. "Shall we show them, partner?"

"Why not?" I smiled, closing my eyes.

In a moment, our disguises were gone, and for the first time the delegates had a look at what was opposing them.

"As I was saying," Aahz announced, showing all his teeth, "not 'like' demons."

It was a good gambit, and it should have worked. Any sane person would quake at the thought of taking on a team of demons. No sacrifice would be too great to avoid the confrontation. We had overlooked one minor detail, however. Jahks are not sane people.

"Excellent," the Ta-hoe spokesman exclaimed.

"What?" Aahz blinked, his smile fading.

"This should keep the odds even," the spokesman continued. "That's what we were discussing . . . whether you could field a good enough team to make a fight of it. But now . . . well, everyone will want to see *this* matchup."

"You . . . aren't afraid of playing against demons?" my mentor asked slowly.

Now it was the spokesman's turn to smile.

"My dear fellow," he chortled, "if you had ever seen *our* teams play, you wouldn't have to ask that question."

With that, he turned and rejoined his delegation as the two groups prepared to withdraw from the meeting.

"Didn't you listen in on their conversations?" I hissed.

"If you'll recall," Aahz growled back, "I was busy talking with you at the time."

"Then we're stuck," I moaned.

"Maybe not," he corrected. "Quigley! Could we have a word with you?"

The ex-demon hunter lost no time in joining us.

"I must say," he chortled. "You boys *did* an excellent job of getting me out of a tight spot there. Now it's a matter of pride for them to win the Trophy back on the playing field."

"Swell," Aahz growled. "Now how about your part of the deal? Ta-hoe has its chance, so there's no reason for you to keep Tanda."

"Mmm . . . yes and no," Quigley corrected. "It occurs to me that if I release her now, then you'll have the Trophy *and* Tanda, and would therefore have no motive to return for the game. To fulfill your promise, to give Ta-hoe a chance for the Trophy, the game will have to take place. *Then* I'll release Tanda."

"Thanks a lot," my mentor spat.

"Don't mention it," the ex-demon hunter waved as he went to rejoin his group.

"Now what do we do?" I asked.

"We form a team," Aahz shrugged. "Hey, Griffin!"

"What is it now?" the youth growled.

"We have one more job for you," my mentor smiled. "All you have to do is help us train our team. There are . . . a few points of the game that aren't very clear to us."

"No," said Griffin firmly.

"Now look, short stuff . . ."

"Wait a minute, Aahz," I interrupted. "Griffin, this time we aren't threatening you. I'm offering you a job at good wages to help us."

"What!?" Aahz shrieked.

"Shut up, Aahz."

"You don't understand," Griffin interrupted in turn. "Neither threats nor money will change my mind. I helped you steal the Trophy from Veygus, but I won't help you against my own team. I'd die before I'd do that."

"There are worse things than dying," Aahz suggested ominously.

"Let it drop, Aahz," I said firmly. "Thanks anyway, Griffin. You've been a big help when we needed you, so I won't fault you for holding back now. Hurry up. The others are waiting."

We watched as he trotted off to join his delegation.

"You know, kid," Aahz sighed at last, "sometime we're going to have to have a long talk about these lofty ideals of yours."

"Sure, Aahz," I nodded. "In the meantime, what are we going to do about this game?"

"What else can we do?" my mentor shrugged. "We put together a team."

"Just like that," I winced. "And where are we going to find the players, much less someone who can tell us how the game is played?"

"Where else?" Aahz grinned, setting the D-Hopper. "The Bazaar at Deva!"

Chapter Eighteen:

"What's the point-spread on World War III?"

—R. REAGAN

AT several other points in this tale, I've referred to the Bazaar at Deva. You may be wondering about it. So do I . . . and I've been there!

Deva is the home dimension of the Deveels, acknowledged to be the best traders anywhere. You may find references to them in your folklore. Deals with Deveels are usually incredible and frequently disastrous. I've dealt with only two Deveels personally. One got me hung (not hung-over from drink—but hung up by the neck!) and the other sold me my dragon, Gleep. I like to think that makes me even, but Aahz insists I'm batting zero—whatever that means.

Anyway, there is a year-round, rock-the-clock Bazaar in that dimension where the Deveels meet to trade with each other. Everything imaginable and most things that aren't are available there. All you have to do is bargain with the Deveels. Fortunately, the Bazaar is large enough that there is much duplication, and sometimes you can play the dealers off against each other.

I had been here twice before, both times with Aahz. This was, however, the first time I had been here when it was raining.

"It's raining," I pointed out, scowling at the overhanging clouds. They were a dark orange, which was quite picturesque, but did nothing toward making getting wet more pleasant.

"I know it's raining," Aahz retorted tersely. "C'mon. Let's step in here while I get my bearings."

"Here," in this case, was some sort of invisible bubble enveloping one stall which seemed to be doing an admirable job of keeping the rain out. I've used magik wards before to keep out unwelcome intruders, but it had never occurred to me to use it against the elements.

"Buying or looking, gentlemen?" the proprietor asked, sidling up to us.

I glanced at Aahz, but he was up on his tiptoes surveying the surroundings.

"Um . . . looking, I guess."

"Then stand in the rain!" came the snarling reply. "Force fields cost money, you know. This is a display, not a public service."

"What's a force field?" I stalled.

"Out!"

"C'mon, kid," Aahz said. "I know where we are now."

"Where?" I asked suspiciously.

"In the stall of the Bazaar's rudest dealer," my mentor explained, raising his voice. "I wouldn't have believed it if I hadn't heard him with my own ears."

"What's that?" the proprietor scowled.

"Are you Garbelton?" Aahz asked, turning his attention on the proprietor.

"Well . . . yes."

"Your reputation precedes you, sir," my mentor intoned loftily, "and is devastatingly accurate. Come, Master Skeeve, we'll take our business elsewhere."

"But, gentlemen!" Garbelton called desperately, "if you'll only reconsider . . ."

The rest was lost as Aahz gathered me up and strode off into the rain.

"What was that all about?" I demanded, breaking stride to jump a puddle. Aahz stepped squarely on it, splashing maroon mud all over my legs. Terrific.

"That? Oh, just a little smokescreen to save face. It isn't good for your reputation to get thrown out of places . . . particularly for not buying."

"You mean you hadn't heard of him before? Then how did you know his name?"

"It was right there on the stall's placard," Aahz grinned. "Sure gave him a turn, though, didn't I? There's nothing a Deveel hates as much as losing a potential customer . . . except for giving a refund."

As much as I care for Aahz and appreciate the guidance he's given me, he can be a bit stomach-turning when he starts gloating.

"We're still out in the rain," I pointed out.

"Ah, but now we know where we're going."

"We do?"

Aahz groaned, swerving to avoid a little old lady who was squatting in the middle of the thoroughfare chortling over a cauldron. As we passed, a large hairy paw emerged from the cauldron's depth, but the lady whacked it with her wooden spoon and it retreated out of sight. Aahz ignored the entire proceedings.

"Look, kid," he explained, "we're looking for two things here. First, we need to recruit some players for our team."

"How can we recruit for the team when we don't know the first thing about the game?" I interrupted.

"Second," my mentor continued tersely, "we have

to find someone who can fill us in on the details of the game."

"Oh."

Properly mollified, I plodded along beside him in silence for several moments, sneaking covert glances at the displays we were passing. Then something occurred to me.

"Say . . . ummmm, Aahz?"

"Yeah, kid?"

"You never answered my question. Where are we going?"

"To the Yellow Crescent Inn."

"The Yellow Crescent Inn?" I echoed, brightening slightly. "Are we going to see Gus?"

"That's right," Aahz grinned. "Gus is a heavy bettor. He should be able to put us in touch with a reliable bookie. Besides he owes us a favor. Maybe we can get him for the team."

"Good," I said, and meant it.

Gus is a gargoyle. He was part of the crew we used to stop Big Julie's army and I trust him as much as I do Aahz . . . maybe a little more. Anyone who's used the expression "heart of stone" to mean insensitive has never met Gus. I assume his heart is stone, the rest of him is, but he's one of the warmest, most sympathetic beings I've ever met. He's also without a doubt the stablest being that I've met through Aahz. If Gus joined our team, I'd worry a lot less . . . well, a little less. Then again, he might be too sensible to get involved in this madcap scheme. And as for the bookies . . .

"Hey, Aahz," I blinked. "What do we need a bookie for?"

"To brief us on the game, of course."

"A bookie from Deva is going to tell us how to play the game in Jahk?"

"It's the best we can do," Aahz shrugged. "You heard Griffin. Nobody in Jahk will give us the time of day, much less help us put a team together. Cheer up, though. Bookies are very knowledgeable in spectator sports, and the ones here in Deva are the best."

I pondered this for several moments, then decided to ask the question that had been bothering me since the meeting.

"Aahz? When you issued the challenge, did you really expect to play the game?"

My mentor stopped dead in his tracks and whirled to face me.

"Do you think I'd issue a challenge without intending to fight?" he demanded. "Do you think I'm a big-mouthed bluffer who'd rather talk his way out of trouble than fight?"

"It had crossed my mind," I admitted.

"Well, you're right," he grinned, resuming his stride. "You're learning pretty fast—for a Klahd. No, I really thought they'd back down when we dropped our disguises. That and I didn't think Quigley would see through the ploy and call our hand."

"He's learning fast, too," I commented. "I'm afraid he could become a real problem."

"Not a chance," my mentor snorted. "You've got him beat cold in the magik department."

"Except I've promised not to move against him," I observed glumly.

"Don't let it get you down," Aahz insisted, draping an arm around my shoulders. "We've both made some stupid calls on this one. All we can do is play the cards we're dealt."

"Bite the bullet, eh?" I grimaced.

"That's right. Say, you really are learning quick."

I still didn't know what a bullet was, but I was picking up some of Aahz's pet phrases. At least now I could give the illusion of intelligence.

The Yellow Crescent Inn was in sight now. I expected Aahz to quicken his pace . . . I mean, it *was* raining. Instead, however, my mentor slowed slightly, peering at a mixed group of beings huddled under a tent-flap.

"Hel-lo!" he exclaimed. "What have we here?"

"It looks like a mixed group of beings huddled under a tent-flap," I observed dryly, or as dryly as I could manage while dripping wet.

"It's a crap game," Aahz declared. "I can hear the dice."

Trust a Pervect to hear the sound of dice on mud at a hundred paces.

"So?" I urged.

"So I think we've found our bookie. The tall fellow, there—at the back of the crowd. I've dealt with him before."

"Are we going to talk to him now?" I asked eagerly.

"Not 'we,' " Aahz corrected me. "Me. You get in enough trouble in cleancut crowds without my taking you into a crap game. You're going to wait for me in the Inn. Gus should be able to keep an eye on you."

"Oh, all right."

I was disappointed, but willing to get out of the rain.

"And don't stop to talk to anyone between here and there. Do you hear me?"

"Yes, Aahz," I nodded, starting off at a trot.

"And whatever you do, don't eat the food!"

"Are you kidding?" I laughed. "I've been here before."

The food at the Yellow Crescent Inn is dubious at best. Even after dimension hopping with Tananda and seeing what was accepted as food elsewhere, I wouldn't put anything from that place in my mouth voluntarily.

As I approached, I could see through the door that the place was empty. This surprised me. I mean, from my prior experience, there was usually a good-sized crowd in there, and I would have expected the rain to increase the number of loiterers.

Gus wasn't in sight, either; but the door was open, so I pushed my way in, relieved to be somewhere dry again. I shouldn't have been.

No sooner had I gained entry when something like a large hand closed over the top of my head and I was hoisted bodily from my feet.

"Little person!" a booming voice declared. "Crunch likes little persons. Crunch likes little persons better than Big Macs. How do you taste, little person?"

With this last, I was rotated until I was hanging face to face with my assailant. In this case, I use the term "face" loosely. It had felt like I was being picked up by a big hand because I *was* being picked up by a big hand. At the other end of the big hand was the first and only troll it had been my misfortune to meet . . . and he looked hungry.

Chapter Nineteen:

"Why should I have to pay a troll just to cross a bridge?"

—B. G. GRUFF

WHILE I had never seen a troll before, I knew that this was one. I mean, he fit the description: tall, scraggly hair in patches, long rubbery limbs, misshapen face with runny eyes of unequal size. If it wasn't a troll, it would do until something better—or worse—came along.

I should have been scared, but strangely I wasn't. For some time now I had been ducking and weaving through some tight situations trying to avoid trouble. Now, Big Ugly here wanted to hassle me. This time, I wasn't buying.

"Why little person not answer Crunch?" the troll demanded, shaking me slightly.

"You want an answer?" I snarled. "Try this!"

Levitation is one of my oldest spells, and I used it now. Reaching out with my mind, I picked up a chair and slammed it into his face.

He didn't even blink.

Then I got scared.

"What's going on out here?!" Gus bellowed, charging out of the kitchen. "Any fights, and I'll . . . Skeeve!!"

"Tell your customer here to put me down before I tear off his arm and feed it to him!" I called, my confidence returning with the arrival of reinforcements.

I needn't have said anything. The effect of Gus's words on the troll was nothing short of miraculous.

"Skeeve?" my assailant gaped, setting me gently on my feet. "I say. Bloody good to make your acquaintance. I've heard so much about you, you know. Chumly here."

The hand which had so recently fastened on my head now seized my hand and began pumping it gently with each adjective.

"Ummm . . . a pleasure, I'm sure," I stammered, trying vainly to retrieve my hand. "Say, weren't you talking differently before?"

"Oh, you mean Crunch?" Chumly laughed. "Beastly fellow. Still, he serves his purpose. Keeps the riffraff at a distance, you know."

"What he's trying to say," Gus supplied, "is that it's an act he puts on to scare people. It's lousy for business when he drops in for a visit, but it does mean we can talk uninterrupted. That's about the only way you can talk to Chumly. He's terribly shy."

"Oh, tosh," the troll proclaimed, digging at the floor with his toe. "I'm only giving the public what it wants. Not much work for a vegetarian troll, you know."

"A vegetarian troll?" I asked incredulously. "Weren't you about to eat me a minute ago?"

"Perish the thought," Chumly shuddered. "Presently I would have allowed you to squirm free and run . . . except, of course, you wouldn't. Quite a spirited lad, isn't he?"

"You don't know the half of it," the gargoyle

answered through his perma-grin. "Why, when we took on Big Julie's army . . . "

"Chumly!" Aahz exclaimed, bursting through the door.

"Aahz," the troll answered. "I say, this is a spot of all right. What brings you . . . "

He broke off suddenly, eyeing the Deveel who had followed Aahz into the inn.

"Oh, don't mind the Geek here," my mentor waved. "He's helping us with some trouble we're having."

"The Geek?" I frowned.

"It's a nickname," the Deveel shrugged.

"I knew it," Gus proclaimed, sinking into a chair. "Or I should have known it when I saw Skeeve. The only time you come to visit is when there's trouble."

"If you blokes are going to have a war council, perhaps I'd better amble along," Chumly suggested.

"Stick around," Aahz instructed. "It involves Tanda."

"Tanda?" the troll frowned. "What has that bit of fluff gone and gotten herself into now?"

"You know Tanda?" I asked.

"Oh, quite," Chumly smiled. "She's my little sister."

"Your sister?" I gaped.

"Rather. Didn't you notice the family resemblance?"

"Well . . . I, ah . . . " I fumbled.

"Don't let him kid you," my mentor grinned. "Tanda and Chumly are from Trollia, where the men are Trolls and the women are Trollops. With men like this back home, you can understand why Tanda spends as much time as she does dimension hopping."

"That's quite enough of that," Chumly instructed firmly. "I want to hear what's happened to little sister."

"In a bit," Aahz waved. "First let's see what information the Geek here has for us."

"I can't believe I let you pull me out of a hot crap game to meet with this zoo," the Deveel grumbled.

"Zoo?" echoed Gus. He was still smiling, but then, he always smiled. Personally, I didn't like the tone of his voice.

Apparently Aahz didn't either, as he hastened to move the conversation along.

"You should thank me for getting you out," he observed, "before the rest of them figured out that you'd switched the dice."

"You spotted that?" the Geek asked, visibly impressed. "Then maybe it's just as well I bailed out. When a Pervert can spot me . . . "

"That's a Pervect!" Aahz corrected, showing all his teeth.

"Oh! Yes . . . of course," the Deveel amended, pinking visibly.

For his sake, I hoped he had some good information for us. In an amazingly short time he had managed to rub everyone wrong. Then again, Deveels have never been noted for their personable ways.

"So what can you tell us about the game on Jahk?" I prompted.

"How much are you paying me?" the Geek yawned.

"As much as the information's worth," Aahz supplied grimly. "Probably more."

The Deveel studied him for a moment, then shrugged.

"Fair enough," he declared. "You've always made good on your debts, Aahz. I suppose I can trust you on this one."

"So what can you tell us?" I insisted.

Now it was my turn to undergo close scrutiny, but the gaze turned on me was noticeably colder than the one Aahz had suffered. With a lazy motion, the Geek reached down and pulled a dagger from his boot and tossed it aloft with a twirl. Catching it with his other hand, he sent it up again, forming a glittering arch from hand to hand, never taking his eyes from mine.

"You're pretty mouthy for a punk Klahd," he observed. "Are you this mouthy when you don't have a pack of goons around to back your move?"

"Usually," I admitted. "And they aren't goons, they're my friends."

As I spoke, I reached out once more with my mind, caught the knife, gave it an extra twirl, then stopped it dead in the air, its point hovering bare inches from the Deveel's throat. Like I said, I was getting a little tired of people throwing their weight around.

The Geek didn't move a muscle, but now he was watching the knife instead of me.

"In case you missed it the first time around," Gus supplied, still smiling, "this 'punk Klahd's' name is Skeeve. The Skeeve."

The Deveel pinked again. I was starting to enjoy having a reputation.

"Why don't you sit down, Geek," Aahz suggested, "and tell the k . . . Skeeve . . . what he wants to know?"

The Deveel obeyed, apparently eager to move away from the knife. That being the case, I naturally let it follow him.

Once he was seated, I gave it one last twirl and set it lightly on the table in front of him. That reassured him somewhat, but he still kept glancing at it nervously as he spoke.

"I . . . um . . . I really don't have that much information," he began uncomfortably. "They only play one game a year, and the odds are usually even."

"How is the game played?" Aahz urged.

"Never seen it, myself," the Geek shrugged. "It's one of those get-the-ball-in-the-net games. I'm more familiar with the positions than the actual play."

"Then what are the positions?" I asked.

"It's a five-man team," the Deveel explained. "Two forwards, or Fangs, chosen for their speed and agility; one guard or Interceptor, for power; a goaltender or Castle, who is usually the strongest man on the team; and a Rider, a mounted player who is used both for attack and defense."

"Sounds straightforward enough," my mentor commented.

"Can't you tell us anything at all about the play?" I pressed.

"Well, I'm not up on the strategies," the Geek frowned. "But I have a general idea of the action. The team in possession of the ball has four tries to score a goal. They can move the ball by running, kicking, or throwing. Once the ball is immobilized, the try is over and they line up for their next try. Of course, the defense tries to stop them."

"Run, kick, or throw," Aahz murmured. "Hmmm . . . sounds like defense could be a problem. What are the rules regarding conduct on the field?"

"Players can't use edged weapons on each other," the Deveel recited. "Any offenders will be shot down on the spot."

"Sensible rule," I said, swallowing hard. "What else?"

"That's it," the Geek shrugged.

"That's it?" Aahz exclaimed. "No edged weapons? That's it?"

"Both for the rules and my knowledge of the game," the Deveel confirmed. "Now, if we can settle accounts, I'll be on my way."

I wanted to cross-examine him, but Aahz caught

my eye and shook his head.

"Would you settle for a good tip?" he asked.

"Only if it was a *really* good tip," the Geek responded dourly.

"Have you heard about the new game on Jahk? The three-way brawl that's coming up?"

"Of course," the Deveel shrugged.

"You have?" I blinked. I mean we had only just set it up!

"I have a professional stake in keeping up on these things."

"Uh-huh!" my mentor commented judiciously. "How are the odds running?"

"Even up for Ta-hoe and Veygus. This new team is throwing everyone for a loop, though. Since no one can get a line on them, they're heavy underdogs."

"If we could give you an inside track on this dark-horse team," Aahz said, looking at the ceiling, "would that square our account?"

"You know about the Demons?" the Geek asked eagerly. "If you do, it's a deal. With inside info, I could be the only one at the Bazaar with the data to fix the real odds."

"Done!" my mentor declared. "We're the Demons."

That got him. The Geek sagged back in his chair for a moment, open mouthed. Then he cocked his head at us.

"You mean, you're financing the team?"

"We *are* the team . . . or part of it. We're still putting it together."

The Deveel started to say something, then changed his mind. Rising silently, he headed for the door, hesitated with one hand on the knob, then left without saying a word.

Somehow, I found his reaction ominous.

"How 'bout that, kid," Aahz chortled. "I got the

information without paying a cent!"

"I don't like the way he looked," I announced, still staring at the door.

"C'mon. Admit it! I just got us a pretty good deal."

"Aahz?" I said slowly. "What is it you always told me about dealing with Deveels?"

"Hmmm? Oh, you mean, 'If you think you've made a good deal with a Deveel . . . !' "

He broke off, his jubilance fading.

" 'First count your fingers, then your limbs, then your relatives!' " I finished for him. "Are you *sure* you got a good deal?"

Our eyes met, and neither of us were smiling.

Chapter Twenty:

"What are friends for?"
—R. M. NIXON

WE were still pondering our predicament, when Chumly interrupted our thoughts.

"You blokes *do* seem to be having a bit of difficulty," he said, draping an arm around both of our shoulders. "But if it wouldn't be too much trouble, could you enlighten me as to what all this has to do with Tanda?"

Normally, this would sound like a casual request. When one pauses to consider, however, that the casual request was coming from a troll half again as tall as we were, and capable of mashing our heads like normal folks squash grapes, the request takes on a high priority no matter how politely it's phrased.

"Well, you know this game we're talking about?" Aahz began uneasily.

"Tanda's the prize," I finished lamely.

Chumly was silent. Then his grip on my shoulder tightened slightly.

141

"Forgive me," he smiled. "For a moment there I thought you said my little sister is the prize in some primitive, spectator brawl."

"Actually," Aahz explained hastily, trying to edge away, "the kid, here, was there when she was captured."

"But it was Aahz that got her involved in the game," I countered, edging in the other direction.

"You chaps got her into this?" the troll asked softly, his grip holding us firmly in place. "I thought you were trying to rescue her."

"Whoa! Everybody calm down!" Gus ordered, stepping into the impending brawl. "Nobody wrecks this place but me. Chumly, let's all sit down and hear this from the top."

I was pretty calm myself . . . at least, I wasn't about to start a fight. Still, Gus's suggestion was a welcome change in direction from the one the conversation was headed in.

This time, I needed no prompting to let Aahz do the talking. While he gets trapped in oversights from time to time, if given free rein, he can and has talked us out of some seemingly impossible situations. This was no exception. Though he surprised me by sticking to the truth, by the time he was done, Chumly's frozen features had softened to a thoughtful stare.

"I must say," the troll commented finally, "it seems little sister has done it to herself this time. You seem to have tried everything you could to effect her release."

"We could give the Trophy back," I suggested.

Aahz kicked me under the table.

"Out of the question," Chumly snorted. "It's Aahz's gift fair and square. If Tanda got herself in trouble acquiring it, that's bloody well her problem. You can't expect Aahz to feel responsible."

"Yes, I can," I corrected.

"No," the troll declared. "The only acceptable

solution is to trounce these blighters soundly at their own game. I trust you'll allow me to fill a position on your team?"

"I'd had my hopes," my mentor grinned.

"Count me in, too," Gus announced, flexing his stone wings. "Can't let you all go into a brawl like this without my steadying influence."

"See, kid?" Aahz grinned. "Things are looking up already."

"Say, Aahz," I said carefully. "It occurs to me . . . you know that Rider position? Well, it seems to me we'd have a big psychological advantage if our Rider was sitting on top of a dragon."

"You're right."

"Aw, c'mon, Aahz! Just because Gleep's a bit . . . Did you say 'you're right'?"

"Right. Affirmative. Correct," my mentor nodded. "Sometimes you come up with some pretty good ideas."

"Gee, Aahz . . ."

"But not that stupid little dragon of yours," he insisted. "We're going to use that monster we got with Big Julie's army."

"But, Aahz . . ."

"But, Aahz nothing! C'mon, Gus! Close up shop here. We're heading for Klah to pick up a dragon!"

Now, Klah is my home dimension, and no matter what my fellow dimension travelers say, I think it's a pretty nice one to live in. Still, after spending extensive time in some other dimensions, however pleasantly familiar the sights of Klah seem, they do look a little drab.

Aahz had surprised me by bringing us well north of Possiltum, instead of at our own quarters in the royal palace. I inquired about this, and for a change my mentor gave me a straight answer.

"It's all in how you set the D-Hopper," he explained. "You've got eight dials to play with, and they let you control both which dimension you're going to as well as where you are when you arrive."

"Does that mean we could use it to go from one place to another in the same dimension?" I asked.

"Hmmm," Aahz frowned. "I really don't know. It never occurred to me to try. We'll have to check into it sometime."

"Well then, why did you pick this arrival point?"

"That's easy," my mentor grinned, gesturing at our colleagues. "I wasn't sure what our reception at the palace would be like if we arrived with a troll and a gargoyle."

He had me there. At the Bazaar disguises had been unnecessary, and I had gotten so used to seeing strange beings around me it had completely slipped my mind that our group would be a strange sight to the average Klahd.

"Sorry, Aahz," I flushed. "I forgot."

"Don't worry about it," my mentor waved. "If it had been important I would have said something to you before we left the Bazaar. I just wanted to shake you up a little to remind you to pay attention to details. The real reason we're here instead of at the palace is, we want to see Big Julie, and I'm too lazy to walk the distance if we could cover it with the D-Hopper."

Despite his reassurances, I got to work correcting my oversight. To redeem myself, I decided to show Aahz I had been practicing during my tour with Tananda. Closing my eyes, I concentrated on disguising Gus and Chumly at the same time.

"Not bad, kid," Aahz commented. "They're a little villainous looking, but acceptable."

"I thought it would help us avoid trouble if they looked a little mean," I explained modestly.

"Not bad?" Chumly snarled. "I look like a Klahd!"

"I think you look cute as a Klahd," Gus quipped.

"Cute? CUTE?" Chumly bristled. "Who ever heard of a cute troll? I say, Aahz, is this really necessary?"

"Unfortunately, yes," my mentor replied, his grin belying his expression of sympathy. "Remember, you aren't supposed to be a troll just now. Just a humble citizen of this lower than humble dimension."

"Why aren't you disguised?" the troll asked suspiciously, obviously unconvinced.

"I'm already known around here as the apprentice of the court magician," Aahz countered innocently. "Folks are used to seeing me like this."

"Well," Chumly grumbled, "there'll be bloody Hell to pay if anyone I know sees me looking like this."

"If anyone you know sees you like this, they won't recognize you," I pointed out cautiously.

The troll thought about that for a moment, then slowly nodded his head.

"I suppose you're right," he conceded at last. "Let's off to find this Big Julie, hmmm? The less time I spend looking like this, the better."

"Don't get your hopes too high," Aahz cautioned. "We're going to do our training in this dimension, so you might as well get used to being a Klahd for a while."

"Bloody Hell," was the only reply.

True to his plans for retirement, Big Julie was relaxing on the lawn of his cottage, drinking wine when we arrived. To the casual observer, he might seem nothing more than a spindly old man basking in the sun. Then again, the casual observer wouldn't have known him when he was commanding the mightiest army ever to grace our dimension. This was probably just as well. Julie was still hiding from a particularly nasty batch of loan sharks who were very curious as to why he and his men gave up soldiering . . . and hence their ability to pay back certain old gambling debts.

"Aye! Hello, boys!" he boomed, waving enthusiastically. "Long time no see, ya know? Pull up a chair and have some wine. What brings you out this way, eh?"

"A little bit of pleasure and a lot of business," Aahz explained, casually gathering to his bosom the only pitcher of wine in sight. "We've got a little favor to ask."

"If it's mine, it's yours," Julie announced. "Whatdaya need?"

"Is there any more wine?" I asked hastily.

Long years of experience had taught me not to expect Aahz to share a pitcher of wine. One was barely enough for him.

"Sure. I got lots. Badaxe is inside now getting some."

"Badaxe?" Aahz frowned. "What's he doing here?"

"At the moment, wondering what *you're* doing here," came a booming voice.

We all turned to find the shaggy-mountain form of Possiltum's general framed in the doorway of the cottage, a pitcher of wine balanced in each hand. Hugh Badaxe always seemed to me to be more beast than man, though I'll admit his curly dark hair and beard when viewed in conjunction with his favorite animal skin cloak contributed greatly to the image. Of course, beasts didn't use tools, while Badaxe definitely did. A massive double-edged axe dangled constantly from his belt, at once his namesake and his favorite tool of diplomacy.

"We just dropped in to have a few words with Big Julie here," my mentor replied innocently.

"What about?" the general demanded. "I thought

we agreed that all military matters would be brought to me before seeking Big Julie's advice. I *am* the Commander of Possiltum's army, you know.''

"Now, Hugh,'' Julie soothed, "the boys just wanted to ask me for a little favor, that's all. If it involved the army, they would've come to you. Right, boys?''

Aahz and I nodded vigorously. Gus and Chumly looked blank. We had overlooked briefing them on General Badaxe and his jealousies regarding power.

"You see?'' Julie continued. "Now, then, Aahz, what sort of favor can I do for you?''

"Nothing much,'' my mentor shrugged. "We were wondering if we could borrow your dragon for a little while.''

"My dragon? What do you need my dragon for? You've already got a dragon.''

"We need a *big* dragon,'' Aahz evaded.

"A big dragon?'' Julie echoed, frowning. "It sounds like you boys are into something dangerous.''

"Don't worry,'' I interjected confidently, "I'll be riding the dragon in the Game, so nothing . . .''

"Game?'' Badaxe roared. "I knew it. You're going into a war game without even consulting me.''

"It's not a war game,'' I insisted.

"Yes, it is,'' Aahz corrected.

"It is?'' I blinked.

"Think about it, kid,'' my mentor urged. "Any spectator sport with teams is a form of wargaming.''

"Then why wasn't I informed?'' Badaxe blustered. "As commander of Possiltum's armed forces, any war games to be held fall under my jurisdiction.''

"General,'' Aahz sighed, "the game isn't going to be played in this kingdom.''

"Any military . . . oh!'' Badaxe paused, confused by this turn of events. "Well, if it involves any members of my army . . .''

"It doesn't," my mentor interrupted. "This exercise only involves a five-man team, and we've filled it without drawing on the army's resources."

A bell went off in my mind. I ran a quick check, which only confirmed my fears.

"Um . . . Aahz . . ." I began.

"Not now, kid," he growled, "You see, general, all your paranoid fears were . . ."

"Aahz!" I insisted.

"What is it?" my mentor snarled, turning on me.

"We haven't got five players, only four."

Chapter Twenty-One:

"We've got an unbeatable team!"
—SAURON

"FOUR?" Aahz echoed blankly.

"I count real good up to five," I informed him loftily, "and you, me, Gus and Chumly only make four. See? One, two, three . . ."

"All right! I get the message," my mentor interrupted, scowling at our two comrades. "Say Gus! I don't suppose Berfert's along, is he?"

"C'mon, Aahz," I chided, "we can't claim a salamander as a team member."

"Shut up, kid. How 'bout it, Gus?"

"Not this time," the gargoyle shrugged. "He ran into a ladyfriend of his, and they decided to take a vacation together."

"A lady friend?" Aahz asked, arching an eyebrow.

"That's right," Gus nodded. "You might say she's an old flame."

"An old flame," the troll grinned. "I say, that's rather good."

For a change, *I* got the joke, and joined Gus and Chumly in a hearty round of laughter, while Badaxe and Julie looked puzzled.

Aahz rolled his eyes in exasperation.

"That's all I need," he groaned. "One member short, and the ones I've got are half-wits. When you're all quite through, I'm open to suggestions as to where we're going to find a fifth team member."

"I'll fill the position," Badaxe said calmly.

"You?" I gulped, my laughter forgotten.

"Of course," the general nodded. "It's my duty."

"Maybe I didn't make myself clear," Aahz interjected. "Possiltum isn't involved in this at all."

"But its magician and his apprentice are," Badaxe added pointedly. "You're both citizens of Possiltum, and rather prominent citizens at that. Like it or not, my duty is to protect you with any means at my disposal—and in this case, that means me."

I hadn't thought of that. In a way, it was kind of nice. Still, I wasn't wild about the general putting himself in danger on our account.

"Ummm . . . I appreciate your offer, general," I began carefully, "but the game's going to be played a long way from here."

"If you can survive the journey, so can I," Badaxe countered firmly.

"But you don't understand!"

"Kid," Aahz interrupted in a thoughtful tone, "why don't you introduce him to his potential teammates?"

"What? Oh, I'm sorry. General Badaxe, this is Gus, and that's Chumly."

"No," my mentor smiled. "I mean *introduce* him."

"Oh!" I said. "General, meet the rest of our team."

As I spoke, I dropped the disguise spell, revealing both gargoyle and troll in their true forms.

"Gus!" Big Julie roared. "I thought I recognized your voice."

"Hi, Julie!" the gargoyle waved. "How's retirement?"

"Pretty dull. Hey, help yourself to some wine!"

"Thanks."

Gus stepped forward and took the two pitchers of wine from the general's nerveless grip, passing one to Chumly. It occurred to me that I was the only one of the crew who wasn't getting a drink out of this.

The general was transfixed, his eyes darting from gargoyle to troll and back again. He had paled slightly, but to his credit he hadn't given ground an inch.

"Well, Badaxe," Aahz grinned, "still want to join the team?"

The general licked his lips nervously, then tore his eyes away from Gus and Chumly.

"Certainly," he announced. "I'd be proud to fight alongside such . . . worthy allies. That is, if they'll have me."

That dropped it in our laps.

"What do you think, Skeeve?" Aahz asked. "You're the boss."

Correction. That dropped it in my lap. Aahz had an annoying habit of yielding leadership just when things got sticky. I was beginning to suspect it wasn't always coincidence.

"Well, Lord Magician?" Badaxe rumbled. "Will you accept my services for this expedition?"

I was stuck. No one could deny Badaxe's value in a fight, but I had never warmed to him as a person. As a teammate . . .

"Gleep!"

The warning wasn't soon enough! Before I could brace myself, I was hit from behind by a massive

force and sent sprawling on my face. The slimy
tongue worrying the back of my head and the accompanying blast of incredibly bad breath could only
have one source.

"Gleep!" my pet announced proudly, pausing
briefly in his efforts to reach my face.

"What's that stupid dragon doing here?" Aahz
bellowed, unmoved by our emotional reunion.

"Ask Badaxe," Julie grinned. "He brought him."

"He did?" my mentor blinked, momentarily
stunned out of his anger.

I was a bit surprised myself. Pushing Gleep away
momentarily I scrambled to my feet and shot a ques-
tioning glance at the general.

For the first time since and including our original
confrontation, Hugh Badaxe looked uncomfortable.
The fierce warrior who wouldn't flinch before army,
magician, or demon couldn't meet our eyes.

"He was . . . well, with you two gone he was just
moping around," the general mumbled. "No one
else would go near him and I thought . . . well, that is
. . . it seemed logical that . . ."

"He brought him out to play with my dragon,"
Julie explained gleefully. "It seems the fierce general
here has a weak spot for animals."

Badaxe's head came up with a snap. "The dragon
served the Kingdom well in the last campaign," he
announced hotly. "It's only fair that *someone* sees to
his needs—as a veteran."

His bluster didn't fool anyone. There was no
reason why he should feel responsible for my dragon.
Even if he did, it would have been easy for him to
order some of his soldiers to see to my pet rather than
attending to it personally as he had done. The truth
of the matter was that he liked Gleep.

As if to confirm our suspicions, my pet began to
frolic around him, waggling head and tail in movements I knew were reserved for playmates. The gen-

eral stoically ignored him . . . which is not that easy to do.

"Um . . . general?" I said carefully.

"Yes?"

I was fixed by a frosty gaze, daring me to comment on the dragon's behavior.

"About our earlier conversation," I clarified hastily. "I'm sure I speak for the rest of the team when I say we're both pleased and honored to have you on our side for the upcoming war game."

"Thank you, Lord Magician," he bowed stiffly. "I trust you will find your confidence in me is not misplaced."

"Now that that's settled," Aahz chortled, rubbing his hands together. "Where's the big dragon? We've got some practicing to do."

"He's asleep," Julie shrugged.

"Asleep?" Aahz echoed.

"That's right. He got into the barn, ate up over half the livestock in the place. Now he's sleepin' like a rock, you know? Probably won't wake up for a couple of months at best."

"A couple of months!" my mentor groaned. "Now what are we going to do? The kid's got to have something to ride in the game!"

"Gleep!" my pet said, rolling on the ground at my feet.

Aahz glared at me.

"He said it, I didn't," I declared innocently.

"Don't think we've got much choice, Aahz," Gus pointed out.

"If you aren't used to them, *any* dragon would seem rather frightening," Chumly supplied.

"All right! All right!" Aahz grimaced, throwing up his hands in surrender. "If you're all willing to risk it, I'll go along. As long as he doesn't drive me nuts by always saying . . . ."

"Gleep?" my pet asked, swiveling his head around

to see what Aahz was shouting about.

"Then we're ready to start practicing?" I asked hastily.

"As ready as we'll ever be, I guess," Aahz grumbled, glaring at the dragon.

"I know this isn't my fight," Big Julie put in, "but what kinda strategies have you boys worked up?"

"Haven't yet," my mentor admitted. "But we'll think of something."

"Maybe I can give you a hand. I used to be pretty good with small unit tactics. You know what I mean?"

The next few weeks were interesting. You notice I didn't say "instructive," just interesting. Aside from learning to work together as a team, there was little development among the individuals of our crew.

You could argue that with the beings we had on the team, there was little development to be done. That was their opinion. Nor was it easy to argue with them. With the exception of myself, their physical condition ranged from excellent to unbelievable. What was more, they were all seasoned veterans of countless battles and campaigns. From what we had seen of the Jahks, any one of our team was more than a match for five of our opponents—and together . . .

Maybe that's what bothered me: the easy assurance on everyone's part that we could win in a walk. I know it bothered Big Julie.

"You boys are over-confident," he'd scold, shaking his head in exasperation. "There's more to fighting than strength. Know what I mean?"

"We've *got* more than strength," Aahz yawned. "There's speed, agility, stamina, and with Gus along, we've got air cover. Then again, Skeeve there has a few tricks up his sleeve as a magician."

"You forgot 'experience,'" Julie countered. "These other guys, they've been playing this game for what? Five hundred years now? They might have a trick or two of their own."

With that stubborn argument, Julie would threaten, wheedle, and cajole us into practicing. Unfortunately, most of the practice centered around me.

Staying on Gleep's back was rough enough. Trying to keep my seat while throwing or catching a ball proved to be nearly impossible. Gleep was no help. He preferred chasing the ball himself or standing stock still while scratching himself with a hind leg to following orders from me. I finally had to cheat a little, resorting to magik to keep me upright on my mount's back. A little levitation, a little flying, and suddenly my riding skills improved a hundred fold. If Aahz suspected I was using something other than my sense of balance, he didn't say anything.

The problem of catching and throwing the ball was solved by the addition of a staff to my argument. Chumly uprooted a hefty sized sapling, and the general used his ever-present belt axe to trim away branches and roots. The result was an eleven foot club with which I could either knock the ball along the ground or swat it out of the air if someone had thrown or kicked it aloft. The staff was a bit heavier than I would have liked, but the extra weight moved the ball farther each time I hit it. Of course, I used a little magik to steer the ball, too, so I didn't miss often and it usually went where I wanted it to go.

Gleep, on the other hand, went where he wanted to go. While my club occasionally helped both to set him in motion and to institute minor changes in his direction once he was moving, total control had still eluded me when the day finally arrived for our departure.

The five of us (six including Gleep) gathered in the center of our practice meadow and said our goodbyes to Julie.

"I'm sorry I can't come with you, boys," he declared mournfully, "but I'm not as young as I used to be, you know?"

"Don't worry," Aahz waved, "we'll be back soon. You can come to our victory celebration."

"There you go again," Julie scowled, "I'm warning you, don't celebrate until after the battle. After five hundred years . . ."

"Right, Julie," Aahz interrupted hastily. "You've told us before. We'd better get going now or we'll miss the game. Wouldn't want to lose by default."

With that, he checked to see we were all in position and triggered the D-Hopper.

A moment later, we were back in Jahk.

Chapter Twenty-Two:

"No matter what the game, no matter what the rules, the same rules apply to both sides!"

—HOYLE'S LAW

THE stadium had undergone two major changes since the last time Aahz and I were here.

First, the configuration of the field had been changed. Instead of a rectangle, the chalk lines now outlined a triangle with netted goals at each corner. I assumed that was to accommodate a three-way instead of a two-way match.

The second change was people. Remember how I said I didn't even want to imagine what the staium would be like full of people? Well, the reality dwarfed anything my imagination could have conjured up. Where I had envisioned neat rows of people to match the military precision of the seats, the stands were currently a chaotic mass of color and motion. I don't know why they bothered providing seats. As far as I could tell, nobody was sitting down.

A stunned hush had fallen over the crowd when we appeared. This was understandable. Beings don't appear out of thin air very often, as we had assembled.

At Aahz's instruction, I had withheld any disguises

from our team in order to get maximum psychological impact from our normal appearance. We got it.

The crowd gaped at us, while we gaped at the crowd. Then they recovered their composure and a roar trumpeted forth from a thousand throats simultaneously. The bedlam was deafening.

"They don't seem very intimidated," I observed dryly.

I didn't expect to be heard over the din, but I had forgotten Aahz's sharp ears.

"*Ave Caesar. Salutes e moratorium*. Eh, kid?" he grinned.

I didn't have the foggiest what he was talking about, but I grinned back at him. I was tired of staring blankly every time he made a joke.

"Hey, boss. We've got company," Gus called, jerking his head toward one side of the stadium.

"Two companies, actually," Chumly supplied, staring in the opposite direction.

Swiveling my head around, I discovered they were both right. Massha was bearing down on us from one side, while old Greybeard was waddling forward from the other. It seemed both Veygus and Ta-hoe wanted words with us.

"Hell-o boys," Massha drawled, arriving first. "Just wanted to wish you luck with your . . . venture."

This might have sounded strange coming from a supporter of the opposition. It did to me. Then I remembered that Massha thought we were out to neutralize Quigley's "demon." Well, in a way we were.

Aahz, as usual, was way ahead of me.

"Don't worry, Massha," he grinned. "We've got everything well in hand."

It never ceases to amaze me the ease with which my mentor can lie.

"Just be sure you stay out of it," he continued

smoothly. "It's a rather delicate plan, and any miscellaneous moving parts could foul things up."

"Don't worry your green little head about that," she winked. "I know when I'm outclassed. I was just kinda hoping you'd introduce me to the rest of your team."

I suddenly realized that throughout our conversation, she hadn't taken her eyes off our teammates. Specifically, she was staring sideways at Hugh Badaxe. This didn't change as Aahz made the proper introductions.

"Massha, this is Gus."

"Charmed, madam," the gargoyle responded.

"And Chum—er—Crunch."

"When fight? Crunch likes fighting," Chumly declared, dropping into his troll act.

Massha didn't bat an eye. She was busy running both of them up and down the general's frame.

"And this is Hugh Badaxe."

With a serpentine glide, Massha was standing close to the general.

"So pleased to meet cha, Hugh . . . you don't mind if I call you Hugh, do you?" she purred.

"Harmmph . . . I . . . that is," Badaxe stammered, visibly uncomfortable.

I could sympathize with him. Having Massha focus her attention on one was disquieting to say the least. Fortunately, help arrived just then in the form of the Ta-hoe delegate.

"Good afternoon, gentlemen," he chortled, rubbing his hands together gleefully. "Hello, Massha."

"Actually," she returned icily, "I was just leaving."

She leaned forward and murmured something in the general's ear before departing for her seat in the stands. Whatever it was, Badaxe flushed bright red and avoided our eyes.

"We were afraid you wouldn't arrive in time,"

Greybeard continued, ignoring Massha's exit. "Wouldn't want to disappoint the fans with a default, would we? When are you expecting the rest of your team?"

"The rest of our team?" I frowned. "I thought the rules only called for five players plus a riding mount."

"That's right," Greybeard replied, "but . . . oh, well, I admire your confidence. So there're only the five of you, eh? Well, well. That will change the odds a bit."

"Why?" I demanded suspiciously.

"Are the edges on that thing sharp?" the spokesman asked, spying the general's axe.

"Razor," Badaxe replied haughtily.

"But he won't use it on anyone," I added hastily, suddenly remembering the "no edged weapons" rule. I wasn't sure what the general's reaction would be if anyone tried to take his beloved axe away from him.

"Oh, I have no worries on that score," Greybeard responded easily. "As with all games, the crossbowmen will be quick to eliminate any player who chooses to ignore the rules."

He waved absently at the sidelines. We looked in the indicated direction, and saw for the first time that the field was surrounded by crossbowmen, alternately dressed in the blue and yellow of Ta-hoe and the red and white of Veygus. This was a little wrinkle the Geek had neglected to mention. He had told us about the rules, but not how they were enforced.

At the same time, I noticed two things which I had previously missed while scanning the stands.

The first was Quigley, sitting front and center on the Ta-hoe side. What was more important was that he had Tananda with him. She was still asleep, floating horizontally in the air in front of him. Apparently he didn't want to miss the game, and didn't trust us enough to leave her unguarded back at his workshop.

He saw me staring and waved. I didn't wave back. Instead, I was about to call Aahz's attention to my find when I noticed the second thing.

Griffin was at the edge of the field, jumping up and down and frantically waving his arms to get my attention. As soon as he saw I was watching him, he began vigorously beckoning to me.

Aahz was engrossed in conversation with the Tahoe spokesman, so I ambled off to see what Griffin wanted.

"Hello, Griffin," I smiled. "How've you been?"

"I just wanted to tell you," he gasped, breathless from his exertions, "I've changed sides. If there's anything I can do to help you, just sing out."

"Really?" I drawled, raising an eyebrow. "And why the sudden change of heart, not to mention allegiances?"

"Call it my innate sense of fair play," he grimaced. "I don't like what they're planning to do to you. Even if my old team is involved, I don't like it."

"What are they planning to do to us?" I demanded, suddenly attentive.

"That's what I wanted to warn you about," he explained. "The two teams had a meeting about this game. They decided that however much they hated each other, neither side wanted to see the Trophy go to a bunch of outsiders."

"That's only natural," I nodded, "but what . . ."

"You don't understand!" the youth interrupted hastily. "They're going to double-team you! They've declared a truce with each other until they've knocked you off the field. When the game starts you'll be up against two teams working together against your one!"

"Kid! Get back here!"

Aahz's bellow reminded me there was another conference going on.

"I've got to go, Griffin," I declared. "Thanks for the warning."

"Good luck!" he called. "You're going to need it."

I trotted back onto the field, to find the assemblage waiting for me with expectant expressions.

"They want to see the Trophy," Aahz informed me with a wink.

"As per our original agreement," the Ta-hoe spokesman added stiffly. "It should be here to be awarded to the victorious team."

"It *is* here," I announced firmly.

"I beg your pardon?" Greybeard blinked, looking around.

"Show him, kid," my mentor grinned.

"All right," I nodded, "everybody stand back."

In many ways it was harder to produce the statue using magik than it would have been to do it with physical labor. I had to agree with Aahz, though, that this way was far more dramatic.

Stretching my levitation capacities to their utmost, I went to work. A large hunk of turf was lifted from the center of the field and set aside. Then the exposed dirt was shoved aside, and finally the Trophy rose into view. I let it hover in midair while I rearranged the dirt and replaced the turf, then let it settle majestically to rest in all its magnificent, ugly splendor.

The crowd roared its approval, though whether for my magik or the Trophy itself I wasn't sure.

"Pretty good," Aahz exclaimed, slapping me gently on the back.

"Gleep," my pet exclaimed, adding his slimy tongue to the offered congratulations.

"Very clever," Greybeard admitted. "We never thought to look there. A little rough on the field, though, isn't it?"

"It'll get torn up this afternoon anyway," my

mentor shrugged. "Incidentally, when's game time?"

As if in answer to his question, the stands exploded in bedlam. I hadn't thought the stadium could get any noisier, but this was like a solid wall of sound pressing in on us from all sides.

The reason for the jubilation was immediately obvious. Two columns of figures had emerged from a tunnel at the far end of the stadium and were jogging onto the field.

The blue and yellow tunics of one column contrasted with the scarlet and white tunics of the other, but served nicely to identify them as our opponents. This, however, was not their most noteworthy feature.

The Ta-hoe team was wearing helmets with long, sharp spikes on the top, while their counterparts from Veygus had long, curved horns emerging from either side of their helmets giving them an animalistic appearance. Even more noticeable, all the players were big. Bigger than any Jahk I had encountered to date. Easily as big as Chumly, but brawnier with necks so short their heads seemed to emerge directly from their shoulders.

As I said earlier, I count real good up to five, and there were considerably more than five players on each team.

Chapter Twenty-Three:

"Life is full of little surprises."

—PANDORA

AS I was prone to do in times of crises, I turned to my mentor for guidance. Aahz, in turn, reacted with the calm levelheadedness I've grown to expect.

Seizing the Ta-hoe spokesman by the front of his tunic, Aahz hoisted him up until his feet were dangling free from the ground.

"What is this!!" he demanded.

Glaah . . . sakle . . ." the fellow responded.

"Um . . . Aahz?" I intervened. "He might be a little more coherent if he could breathe."

"Oh! Right," my mentor acknowledged, lowering the spokesman until he was standing once more. "All right. Explain!"

"Ex . . . explain what?" Greybeard stammered, genuinely puzzled. "Those are the teams from our respective cities. You can tell them apart by their helmets and . . ."

"Don't give me that!" Aahz thundered. "Those

aren't Jahks. Jahks are skinny or overweight!''

"Oh! I see," the spokesman said with dawning realization. "I'm afraid you've been misled. Not all Jahks are alike. Some are fans, and some are players—athletes. The fans are . . . a little out of shape, but that's to be expected. They're the workers who keep the cities and farms running. The players are a different story. All they do is train and so on. Over the generations, they've gotten noticeably larger than the general population of fans.''

"Noticeably larger?" Aahz scowled, glaring down the field. "It's like they're another species!''

"I've seen it happen in other dimensions," Gus observed, "but never to this extent.''

"Well, Big Julie warned us about over-confidence,'' Chumly sighed.

"What was that?" Greybeard blinked.

"Want fight," Chumly declared, dropping back into character. "Crunch likes fight.''

"Oh," the spokesman frowned. "Very well. If there's nothing else, I'll just . . .''

"Not so fast," I interrupted. "I want to know why there are so many players. The game is played by five-man teams, isn't it?''

"That's right," Greybeard nodded. "The extra players are replacements . . . you know, for the ones who are injured or killed during the game.''

"Killed?" I swallowed.

"As I said," the spokesman called, starting off, "I admire your confidence in only bringing five players.''

"Killed?" I repeated, turning desperately to Aahz.

"Don't panic, kid," my mentor growled, scanning the opposition. "It's a minor setback, but we can adapt our strategies.''

"How about the old 'divide and conquer' gambit?" Badaxe suggested, joining Aahz.

"That's right," Gus nodded. "They're not used to

playing a three-way game. Maybe we can play them off against each other.''

"It won't work," I declared flatly.

"Don't be so negative, kid," Aahz snapped. "Sometimes old tricks are the best."

"It won't work because they won't be playing against each other . . . just us."

I quickly filled them in on what Griffin had told me earlier. When I finished, the team was uncomfortably silent.

"Well," Aahz said at last, "things could be worse."

"How?" I asked bluntly.

"Gleep?"

My dragon had just spotted something the rest of us had missed. The other teams were bringing their riding beasts onto the field. Unlike the players, the beasts weren't marked with the team colors . . . but then, it wasn't necessary. There was no way they could be confused with each other.

The Veygus beast was a cat-like creature with an evilly flattened head—nearly as long as Gleep, it slunk along the ground with a fluid grace which was ruined only by the uneven gait of its oversized hindlegs. Though its movements were currently slow and lazy, it had the look of something that could move with blinding speed when it wanted to. It also looked very, very agile. I was sure the thing could corner like . . . well, like a cat.

The Ta-hoe mount was equally distinctive, but much more difficult to describe. It looked like a small, armored mound with its crest about eight feet off the ground. I would have thought it was an oversized insect, but it had more than six legs. As a matter of fact, it had hundreds of legs which we could see when it moved, which it seemed to do with equal ease in any direction. When it stopped, its armor settled to the ground, both hiding and guarding its tiny legs. I couldn't figure out where its eyes were, but I noticed it never ran into anything . . . at least accidentally.

"Gleep?"

My pet had pivoted his head around to peer at me. If he was hoping for an explanation or instructions, he was out of luck. I didn't have the vaguest idea of how to deal with the weird creatures. Instead, I stroked his mustache in what I hoped was a reassuring fashion. Though I didn't want to admit it to my teammates, I was becoming less and less confident about this game . . . and I hadn't been all that confident to begin with.

"Don't look now," Gus murmured, "but I've spotted Tanda."

"Where?" Chumly demanded, craning his neck to see where the gargoyle was pointing.

Of course, I had seen Tananda earlier and had forgotten to point her out to the others. I felt a little foolish, but then, that was nothing new. To cover my embarrassment, I joined the others in staring towards Tananda's floating form.

Quigley noticed us looking his way and began to fidget nervously. Apparently he was not confident enough in his newfound powers to feel truly comfortable under our mass scrutiny. His discomfort affected his magik . . . at least his levitation. Tananda's body dipped and swayed until I was afraid he was going to drop her on her head.

"If that magician's all that's in our way," Gus observed, "it occurs to me we would just sashay over there and take her back."

"Can't," Aahz snapped, shaking his head. "The kid here promised we wouldn't do anything to make that magician look bad."

"That's fine for you two," the gargoyle countered, "but Chumly and I didn't promise a thing."

"I say, Gus," Chumly interrupted, "we can't go against Skeeve's promise. It wouldn't be cricket."

"I suppose you're right," Gus grumbled. "I just thought it would be easier than getting our brains beaten out playing this silly game."

I agreed with him there. In fact, I was glad to find something I could agree with. Chumly's argument about crickets didn't make any sense at all.

"It occurs to me, Lord Magician," Badaxe rumbled, "that the promise you made wasn't the wisest of pledges."

"Izzat so?" Aahz snarled, turning on him. "Of course, general, you speak from long experience in dealing with demons."

"Well . . . actually . . ."

"Then I'd suggest you keep your lip buttoned about Lord Skeeve's wisdom *and* abilities. Remember, he's your ticket back out of here. Without him, it's a long walk home."

Chastised, the general retreated, physically and verbally.

"Gee, thanks, Aahz."

"Shut up, kid," my mentor snarled. "He's right. It was a dumb move."

"But you said . . ."

"Call it reflex," Aahz waved. "A body's got to earn the right to criticize my apprentice . . . and that specimen of Klahdish military expertise doesn't qualify."

"Well . . . thanks, anyway," I finished lamely.

"Don't mention it."

"Hey, Aahz," Chumly called. "Let's get this . . . Trophy out of the center of the field and put it somewhere safe."

"Like where?" my mentor retorted. "We're the only ones in the stadium I trust."

"How about in our goal?" Gus suggested, pointing to the wide net at our corner of the triangle.

"Sounds good," Aahz agreed. "I'll be back in a second, kid."

I had gotten so used to the bedlam in the stadium that I barely noticed it. As my teammates started to move the Trophy, however, the chorus of boos and catcalls that erupted threatened to deafen me. My colleagues responded with proper aplomb, shaking fists and making faces at their decriers. The crowd loved it. If they loved it any more, they'd charge down onto the field and lynch the lot of us.

I was about to suggest to my comrades that they quit baiting the crowd, when General Badaxe beckoned me over for a conference.

"Lord Magician," he began carefully, "I hope you realize I meant no offense with my earlier comments. I find that I'm a trifle on edge. I've never fought a war in front of an audience before."

"Forget it, Hugh," I waved. "You were right. In hindsight it *was* a bad promise. Incidentally . . . it's Skeeve. If we're in this mess together, it's a little silly to stand on formality."

"Thank you . . . Skeeve," the general nodded. "Actually I was hoping I could speak with you privately on a personal matter."

"Sure," I shrugged. "What is it?"

"Could you tell me a little more about that *marvelous* creature I was just introduced to earlier?"

"Marvelous creature?" I blinked. "What marvelous creature?"

"You know . . . Massha."

"Massha?" I laughed. Then I noticed the general's features were hardening. "I mean, oh, *that* marvelous creature. What do you want to know?"

"Is she married?"

"Massha? I mean . . . no, I don't think so."

The general heaved a sigh of relief. "Is there a chance she'll ever visit us in Possiltum?"

"I doubt it," I replied. "But if you'd like I could ask her."

"Fine," the general beamed, bringing a hand

down on my shoulder in a bone-jarring display of friendship. "I'll consider that a promise."

"A what?" I blinked. Somehow the words had a familiar ring to them.

"I know how you honor your promises," Badaxe continued. "Fulfill this pledge, and you'll find I can be a friend to prize . . . just as I can be an enemy to be feared if crossed. Do we understand each other?"

"But I . . ."

"Hey, kid," Aahz shouted. "Hurry up and get on that stupid dragon! The game's about to start!"

I had been so engrossed in my conversation with Badaxe I had completely lost track of the other activities on the field.

The teams from Ta-hoe and Veygus had retired to the sidelines, leaving five players apiece on the field. The cat and the bug each had riders now, and were pacing and scuttling back and forth in nervous anticipation.

At midfield, where the Trophy had been, a Jahk stood wearing a black and white striped tunic and holding a ball. I use the word *ball* rather loosely here. The object he was holding was a cube of what appeared to be a black, spongy substance. A square ball! One more little detail the Geek had neglected to mention.

Without bothering to take my leave from the general, I turned and sprinted for Gleep. Whatever was about to happen, I sure didn't want to face it afoot.

Chapter Twenty-Four:

*"This contest has to be the dumbest
thing I've ever seen."*

—H. COSELL

I WAS barely astride Gleep when the Jahk at midfield
set the ball down and started backing toward the
sidelines.

"Hey, Aahz!" I called. "What's with the guy in
the striped tunic?"

"Leave him alone," my mentor shouted back.
"He's a neutral."

Actually, I hadn't planned on attacking him, but it
was nice to know he wasn't part of the opposition.

I was the last of the team to get into place. Aahz
and Chumly were bracketing me as the Fangs, Gus
was behind me, waiting to take advantage of his extra
mobility as Guard; and Badaxe was braced in the
mouth of the goal as Castle. We seemed about as
ready as we would ever be.

"Hey, kid!" Aahz called. "Where's your club?"

I was so engrossed in my own thoughts it took a
minute for his words to sink in. Then I panicked. For

171

a flash moment I thought I had left my staff back in Klah. Then I spotted it lying in the grass at our entry point. A flick of my mind brought it winging to hand.

"Got it, Aahz!" I waved.

"Well, hang onto it, and remember . . ."

A shrill whistle blast interrupted our not-so-private conference and pulled our attention down-field. The cat and the bug were heading for the ball at their respective top speeds, with the rest of their teammates charging along in their wakes.

The game was on, and all we were doing was standing around with our mouths open.

As usual, Aahz was the first to recover.

"Don't just stand there with your mouth open!" he shouted. "Go get the ball."

"But I . . ."

"GLEEP!"

What I had intended to point out to Aahz was that the cat was almost at the ball already. Realizing there was no way I could get there first, I felt we should drop back and tighten our defense. My pet, however, had other ideas.

Whether he was responding to Aahz's command to "get the ball" (which was unlikely), or simply eager to meet some new playmates (which was highly probable), the result was the same. He bounded forward, cutting me off in mid-sentence and setting us on a collision course with the cat.

The crowd loved it.

Me, I was far less enthusiastic. The cat's rider had the ball now, but he and his mount were holding position at midfield instead of immediately advancing on our goal. Presumably this was to allow his teammates to catch up, so he could have some cover. This meant he wouldn't have to venture among us alone.

That struck me as being a very intelligent strategy.

I only wished I could follow it myself. Gleep's enthusiasm was placing me in the position I had hoped to avoid at all costs—facing the united strength of both of the opposing teams without a single teammate to support me. For the first time since our opponents had taken the field, I stopped worrying about surviving until the end of the game. Now I was worried about surviving until the end of the first play!

My hopes improved for a moment when I realized we would reach the cat and its rider well ahead of their teammates. The feeling of hope faded rapidly, however, as my rival uncoiled his weapon.

Where I was carrying a staff, he had a whip . . . a long whip. The thing was twenty feet long if it was an inch. No, I'm not exaggerating. I could see its length quite clearly as the rider let it snake out toward my head.

The lash fell short by a good foot, though it seemed much closer at the time. Its sharp crack did produce one result, however. Gleep stopped in his tracks, throwing me forward on his neck as I fought to keep my balance. An instant behind the whip attack, the cat bounded forward, its teeth bared and ears flat against its skull, and one of its forepaws darted out to swat my dragon on the nose.

Though never noted for his agility, Gleep responded by trying to jump backwards and swap ends at the same time. I'm not sure how successful he was, because somewhere in the middle of the maneuver, he and I parted company.

Normally such a move would not have unsettled me. When Gleep had thrown me in practice, I had simply flown clear, delicately settled to the ground at a distance. This time, however, I was already off balance and the throw disoriented me completely. Realizing I was airborne, I attempted to fly . . . and succeeded in slamming into the turf with the grace of a bag of garbage. This did nothing toward improving my orientation.

Lying there, I wondered calmly which parts of me would fall off if I moved. There was a distant roaring in my ears, and the ground seemed to be trembling beneath me. From far away, I could hear Aahz shouting something. Yes, just lying here seemed like an excellent idea.

"Up, kid!" came my mentor's voice. "Run!"

Run? He had to be kidding. My head was clearing slowly, but the ground was still shaking. Rolling over, I propped one eye open to get my bearings, and immediately wished I hadn't.

It wasn't in my head! The ground really was shaking! The bug was bearing down on me full tilt, displaying every intention of trampling me beneath its multiple tiny feet. It didn't even occur to me that this would be a ridiculous way to go. All that registered was that it was a way to go, and somehow that thought didn't appeal to me.

I sprang to my feet and promptly fell down again. Apparently I hadn't recovered from my fall as much as I thought I had. I tried again and got as far as my hands and knees. From there I had a terrific view of my doom thundering down on me, and there was nothing I could do about it!

Then Aahz was there. He must have jumped over me in mid-stride to get into position, but he was there, half-way between the charging bug and me. Feet spread and braced, knees bent to a crouch, he faced the charge unflinching. Unflinching? He threw his arms wide and bared his teeth in challenge.

"You want to fight?" he roared. "Try *me.*"

The bug may not have understood his words, but it knew enough about body language to realize it was in trouble. Few beasts or beings in any dimension have the courage or stupidity to try to face down a Pervect when it has a full mad on, and Aahz was mad. His scales were puffed out until he appeared twice his normal breadth, and they rippled dangerously from the tensed muscles underneath. Even his color was a darker shade of green than normal, pulsing angrily as my mentor vented his emotions.

Whatever intelligence level the bug might possess, it was no fool. It somehow managed to slow from a full charge to a dead stop before coming within Aahz's reach. Even the frantic goadings from its rider's hooked prod couldn't get it to resume its charge. Instead, it began to cautiously edge sideways, trying to bypass Aahz completely.

"You want to fight?" my mentor bellowed, advancing toward the beast. "C'mon! I'm ready."

That did it! The bug put it into reverse, scuttling desperately backward despite the frantic urgings of its rider and the hoots from the crowd.

"I say, you lads seem to have things in hand here."

A powerful hand fastened on my shoulder and lifted. In fact, it lifted me until my feet were dangling free from the ground.

"Um . . . I can walk now, Chumly," I suggested.

"Oh, terribly sorry," the troll apologized, setting me gently on the ground. "Just a wee bit distracted is all."

"Gleep!"

A familiar head snaked into view from around Chumly's hip to peer at me quizzically.

"You were a big help!" I snarled, glad for the chance to vent my pent-up nervous energy.

"Gleep," my pet responded, hanging his head.

"Here, now," the troll chided. "Don't take it out on your mate, here. He got surprised, that's all. Can't blame him for getting a little spooked under fire. What?"

"But if he hadn't . . . " I began.

"Now are you ready to get rid of that stupid dragon?" Aahz demanded, joining our group.

"Don't take it out on Gleep," I flared back. "He just got a little spooked under fire is all."

"How's that again?" my mentor blinked.

"Gleep!" proclaimed my pet, unleashing his tongue in one of his aromatic, slimy licks. This time, to my relief Aahz was the recipient.

"Glaah!" my mentor exclaimed, scrubbing at his face with the back of his hand. "I may be violently sick!"

"The beast's just showing his appreciation for your saving his master," Chumly laughed.

"That's right," I agreed. "If you hadn't . . ."

"Forget it," Aahz waved. "No refugee from a wine-making festival's going to do his dance on my apprentice while I'm around."

For once, I knew what he was talking about. " 'Refugee from a wine-making festival'—that's pretty good, Aahz," I grinned.

"No, it wasn't," my mentor snarled. "In fact, so far this afternoon, *nothing's* been good. Why are we standing around talking?"

"Because the first play's over," Chumly supplied. "Also, I might add, the first score."

We all looked down field toward our goal. The field was littered with bodies, fortunately theirs, not ours. Whatever had happened, we had given a good accounting of ourselves. Stretcher bearers and trainers were tending to the fallen and wounded with well practiced efficiency. The players still on their feet, both on the field and on the sidelines, were dancing around hugging each other and holding their index fingers aloft in what I supposed was some sort of religious gesture to the gods. Badaxe was sagging weakly against one of our four goalposts while Gus fanned him with his wings.

"The score," the troll continued casually, "is

nothing to nothing to one . . . against us. Not the best of starts, what?''

For one instant I thought we had scored. Then I remembered that in this game, points are scored *against* a team. Therefore "nothing to nothing to one" meant we were behind by a point.

"Don't worry," Aahz snarled. "We'll get the point back, with interest! If they want to play rough, so can we. Right?"

"Quite right," Chumly grinned.

"Ummm . . ." I supplied hesitantly.

"So let's fire up!" my mentor continued. "Chumly, get Gus and Badaxe up here for a strategy session. Kid, get back on that dragon—and this time try to stay up there, huh?"

I started to obey, then turned back to him. "Ummm . . . Aahz?"

"Yeah, kid?"

"I didn't say it too well a minute ago, but thanks for saving me."

"I said forget it."

"No, I won't," I insisted defiantly. "You could have been killed bailing me out, and I just wanted you to know that I'll pay you back someday. I may not be very brave where I'm concerned, but I owe you my life on top of everything else and it's yours anytime you need it."

"Wait a minute, kid," my mentor corrected. "Any risks I take are mine, understand? That includes the ones I take pulling your tail out of the fire once in a while. Don't mess up my style by making me responsible for two lives."

"But, Aahz . . ."

"If I'm in trouble and you're clear, you skedaddle. Got it? Especially in this game. In fact, here . . ."

He fumbled in his belt pouch and produced a familiar object.

"Here's the D-Hopper. It's set to get you home.

You keep it and use it if you have to. If you see a chance to grab Tanda and get out of here, take it! Don't worry about me."

"But . . ."

"That's an order, apprentice. If you want to argue it, wait until we're back in Klah. In the meantime, just do it! Either you agree or I'll send you home right now."

Our eyes locked for long moments, but I gave ground first.

"All right, Aahz," I sighed. "But we're going to have this out once we get home."

"Fine," he grinned, clapping me on the shoulder. "For now though, get on that stupid dragon of yours and try to keep him pointed in the right direction. We've got some points to score!"

Chapter Twenty-Five:

"If you can't win fair, just win!"
—U. S. GRANT

WE needed to score some points, and to do that, we needed the ball.

That thought was foremost in my mind as we lined up again. One way or another, we were going to get that ball.

When the whistle sounded, I was ready for it. Reaching out with my mind, I brought the ball winging to my grasp. Before our team could form up around me, however, the whistle sounded again and the Jahk in the striped tunic came trotting toward us waving his arms.

"Now what?" Aahz growled. Then aloud, he called, "What's wrong, Ref?"

"There's been a protest," the referee informed him. "Your opponents say you're using magik."

"So what?" my mentor countered. "There's no rule against it."

"Well, not officially," the ref admitted, "but it's

179

been a gentleman's agreement for some time.''

"We're not gentlemen," Aahz grinned. "So get out of our way and let us play."

"But if you can use magik, so can your opponents," the striped tunic insisted.

"Let 'em," Aahz snarled. "Start the game."

A flash of inspiration came to me. "Wait a minute, Aahz," I called. "Sir, we're willing to allow the use of magik against us *if*, and only if, the magicians do it from the field."

"What?" the ref blinked.

"You heard him," Aahz crowed. "If your magicians join the team and take their lumps like our magician does, then they're free to use whatever skills and abilities they bring onto the field with them. Otherwise they can sit in the bleachers with the spectators and keep their magik out of it."

"That seems fair," the Jahk nodded thoughtfully. "I'll so inform the other teams."

"I say," Chumly commented as the referee trotted off. "That was a spot of clear thinking."

"Tactically superb," Badaxe nodded.

"That's the kind of generalship that beat Big Julie's army," Gus supplied proudly.

I waved modestly, but inside I was heady from the praise.

"Let's save the congratulations until after the game, shall we?" Aahz suggested icily.

It was an annoyingly accurate observation. There was still a long battle between us and the end of the game, and the other teams were already lining up to pit their best against our clumsy efforts. In grim silence, we settled down to go to work.

I won't attempt to chronicle the afternoon play by play. Much of it I'm trying to forget, though sometimes I still bolt upright out of a sound sleep sweating at the memory. The Jahks were tough and they knew their business. The only thing holding them at bay

was the sheer strength and ferocity of my teammates
and some inspired magik by yours truly.

However, a few incidents occurred prior to the
game's climax which would be criminal neglect to
omit from my account.

Gleep came of age that afternoon. I don't know
what normally matures dragons, but for my pet
adulthood arrived with the first play of the afternoon. Gone was the playfulness which led to my
early unseating. Somewhere in that puzzling brain of
his, Gleep thought things over and arrived at the conclusion that we had some serious business on our
hands.

I, of course, didn't know this. When the ball ended
up in my hands, I was counting on my other teammates for protection. Unfortunately, our opponents
had anticipated this and planned accordingly. Three
players each swarmed over Aahz and Chumly, soaking up incredible punishment to keep them from
coming to my support. The two Riders converged on
me.

I saw them coming and panicked. I mean, the cat
was faster than us and the bug seemed invulnerable.
Frantically, I looked around for some avenue of
escape. I needn't have worried.

Instead of bolting, Gleep stood his ground, his
head lowered menacingly. As the cat readied itself
for a pounce, my pet loosed a jet of fire full in its
face, singeing its whiskers and setting it back on its
haunches.

I was so astonished I forgot to watch the bug moving up on our flank. Gleep didn't. His tail lashed out
to intercept the armored menace. There was a sound
like a great church bell gonging, and the bug halted
its forward progress and began wandering aimlessly
in circles.

"Atta boy, Gleep!" I cheered, balancing the ball
on his back for a moment so I could thump his side.

That was a mistake. No sooner had I released the hold on the ball when one of the Jahks leaped high to pluck it from its resting spot. I took a wipe at him with my staff but he dodged to one side and I missed. Unfortunately for him, the dodge brought him within Chumly's reach.

The troll snaked out one of his long arms over the shoulder of a blocker, picked up the ball carrier by his head, and slammed him violently to the ground.

"Big Crunch catch," he called, winking at me.

The ball carrier lay still, and the stretcher team trotted onto the field again. The lineup of players on the sideline had decreased noticeably since the game started. In case you haven't noticed, things were pretty rough on the field.

"Tell me I didn't see that," Aahz demanded, staggering to my side.

"Um . . . Chumly's tackle or Gleep stopping the two Riders?" I asked innocently.

"I'm talking about your giving the ball away," my mentor corrected harshly. "Now that the dragon's coming through for us, you start . . . "

"Do you really think he's doing a good job?" I interrupted eagerly. "I always said Gleep had a lot of potential."

"Don't change the subject," Aahz growled. "You . . . "

"C'mon, you two," Gus called. "There's a game on."

"Got to go," I waved, guiding my pet away from my sputtering mentor. "We'll talk after the game."

Our defense finally solidified, and we meted out terrible punishment to any Jahk foolish enough to head for our goal with the ball in his arms. We even managed to score some points, though it took a little help from my magik to do it.

The first point we scored was against the Veygans. It was a variation of Aahz's original "divide and conquer'' plan. The Veygans had the ball and were bringing it down-field when we plowed into them at midfield. As per my instructions, I waited until the brawl was getting heated, then used a disguise spell on Gus, altering his appearance so he looked like one of the Ta-hoe players, complete with a spiked helmet. Having been forewarned, the change didn't startle him at all. Instead, he started dancing around, waving his arms wildly.

"Here!" he shouted. "I'm open! Over here!"

The ball carrier was zig-zagging desperately with Aahz in hot pursuit. He saw an ally in a position to score and lobbed the ball to him without breaking stride. Gus gathered the ball in and started for the Veygus goal.

"Double-cross!"

The first shout was from Chumly, but the Veygus players quickly picked it up. Spurred by indignation, they turned on the Ta-hoe players who a moment ago had been their allies. The Ta-hoers were understandably surprised, but reacted quickly, defending themselves while at the same time laying down a blocking pattern for Gus.

The Veygan Castle had been up-field when the play broke, but the goal-tender braced himself as Gus swept down on him. The only pursuit close enough to count was Chumly, who appeared intent on hauling down the ball carrier from behind. At the crucial moment, however, he charged past the gargoyle and piled into the goal-tender. Gus scored untouched.

"That's zero to one to one now!" I crowed.

"Before you get too caught up in celebrating," Aahz advised, "you'd better do something about *that*!"

I followed his finger and realized that fights were breaking out throughout the stands. It seemed the fans didn't like the double-cross any more than the players had.

To avert major bloodshed, I removed Gus's disguise as he came back up the field. Within seconds, the fans and the opposing teams realized they had been had. Hostilities between the rival factions ceased immediately. Instead, they focused their emotions on us. Terrific.

The uniform change bit had been effective, but with the new attentiveness in the opposition, I was pretty sure it wouldn't work twice.

I'm particularly proud of our second goal, in that it was my idea from start to finish. I thought it up and executed it without the help or consultation of my teammates. Of course, that in itself caused some problems . . . but I'm getting ahead of myself.

The idea occurred to me shortly after my staff broke. I was swinging at the ball when one of the Tahoe players somehow got his head in the way. He was sidelined, but I was left with two pieces of what used to be a pretty good club. As we waited for play to resume, I found myself marveling anew at the sheer size of our opponents and wishing we had bigger players on our side. It occurred to me, too late of course, that I could have used disguise spells to make our team seem bigger when we first appeared. Now our rivals already knew how big, or to be specific, how small we were, so that trick wouldn't work.

I was starting to berate myself for this oversight, when the idea struck. If a disguise spell could make us look bigger, it could also make us look smaller. It was almost a good idea, but not quite. If one or all of us "disappeared" our opponents would notice immediately. What we needed was a decoy.

I found myself considering the two pieces of broken staff I was holding. There was a stunt I pulled once when we were fighting Big Julie. Then it had been a desperation gambit. Of course, we weren't exactly cruising along now.

"Get the ball to me!" I called to my teammates.
"I've got an idea."

"What kind of an idea?" Aahz asked.

"Just get me the ball," I snapped back.

I didn't mean to be short with him, but if this plan
was going to work, I needed all my concentration,
and Aahz's banter wasn't helping.

Closing my eyes, I began to draw and focus power.
At the same time, I began forming the required
images in my mind.

"Head's up, kid!" Aahz shouted with sudden
urgency.

My eyes popped open . . . and the ball was there. I
wasn't quite as ready as I would have liked to have
been but the time was now and I had to go for it.

I'll detail what happened next so you can appreciate the enormity of my accomplishment. In live
time, it took no longer than an eyeblink to perform.

Dropping the two halves of the staff, I caught the
ball with my hands. Then, I cast two spells simultaneously. (Four, actually, but I don't like to brag.)

For the first, I shrank the images of Gleep and
myself until we were scant inches high. Second, I
changed the appearance of the two staff halves until
what was seen was full sized reproductions of me
astride my pet.

Once that was accomplished, I used my remaining
energy to fly us toward the Ta-hoe goal. That's right,
I said "fly." Even in our diminutive form, I wanted
us well above the eye-level of our opponents.

Flying both Gleep and myself took a lot of effort.
So much, in fact, that I was unable to animate the
images we left behind. I had realized this before I
started, but figured that suddenly stationary targets
would only serve as a diversion for our real attack.

It seemed to work. We were unopposed until we
reached the Ta-hoe goal. Then my mischievous sense

of humor got the better of me. Landing a scant arm's length from the goalie, I let our disguises drop.

"Boo!" I shouted.

To the startled player, it appeared that we suddenly popped out of thin air. A lifetime of training fell away from him in a second, and he fainted dead away.

With a properly dramatic flourish, I tossed the ball into the goal.

One to one to one! A tie game!

The team was strangely quiet when Gleep and I triumphantly returned to our end of the field.

"Why the long faces?" I laughed. "We've got 'em on the run now!"

"You should have told us you had a gambit going," Gus said carefully.

"There wasn't time," I explained. "Besides, there's no harm done."

"That's not entirely accurate," Chumly corrected, pointing up field.

There was a pile of Jahks where I had left the staff pieces. The stretcher teams were busy untangling the bodies and carting them away.

"He was trying to protect you . . . or what he thought was you," Badaxe observed acidly.

"What . . . "

Then I saw what they were talking about. At the bottom of the pile was Aahz. He wasn't moving.

Chapter Twenty-Six:

"Winning isn't the most important thing; it's the only thing!"

—J. CAESAR

"HE'LL be all right," Gus declared, looking up from examining our fallen teammate. "He's just out cold."

We were gathered around Aahz's still form, anxiously awaiting the gargoyle's diagnosis. Needless to say, I was relieved my mentor was not seriously injured. General Badaxe, however, was not so easily satisfied.

"Well, wake him up!" he demanded. "And be quick about it."

"Back off, general," I snarled, irritated by his insensitivity. "Can't you see he's hurt?"

"You don't understand," Badaxe countered, shaking his head. "We need five players to continue the game. If Aahz doesn't snap out of it . . . "

"Wake up, Aahz!" I shouted, reaching out a hand to shake his arm.

It was bad enough that my independent scoring

drive had resulted in Aahz getting roughed up. If it cost us the game . . .

"Save it, Skeeve," Gus sighed. "Even if he woke up, he wouldn't be able to play. That was a pretty nasty pounding he took. I mean, I don't *think* there's anything seriously wrong with him, but if he tried to mix it up with anyone in his current condition . . ."

"I get the picture," I interrupted. "And if we wake him up, Aahz is just stubborn enough to want to play."

"Right," the gargoyle nodded. "You'll just have to think of something else."

I tried, I really did. The team kept fussing over Aahz to stall for time, but nothing came to me in the way of a plan. Finally the referee trotted over to our huddle.

"How's your player?" he asked.

"Ah . . . just catching his breath," Badaxe smiled, trying to keep his body between the official and Aahz.

"Don't give me that," the stripe-tunicked Jahk scowled. "I can see. He's out cold, isn't he?"

"Well, sort of," Gus admitted.

" 'Sort of' nothing," the ref scowled. "If he can't play and you don't have a replacement, you'll have to forfeit the game."

"We're willing to play with a partial team," the gargoyle suggested hastily.

"The rules state you must have five players on the field. No more, no less," the official declared, shaking his head.

"All right," Badaxe nodded. "Then we'll keep him on the field with us. We'll put him off to one side where he won't get hurt and then we'll play with a four-man team."

"Sorry," the ref apologized, "but I can't let him stay on the field in that condition. It's a rough game, but we do have some ethics when it comes to the safety of the players.''

"Especially when you can use the rules to force us out of the game," Gus spat.

I thought the slur would draw an angry response from the official, but instead the ref only shook his head sadly.

"You don't understand," he insisted. "I don't *want* to disqualify your team. You've been playing a hard game and you deserve a chance to finish it. I hate to see the game stopped with a forfeit . . . especially when the score's tied. Still, the rules are the rules, and if you can't field a full team, that's that. I only wished you had brought some replacements."

"We've got a replacement!" I exploded suddenly.

"We do?" Gus blinked.

"Where?" frowned the ref.

"Right there!" I announced, pointing to the stands.

Tananda was still floating in plain sight in front of Quigley.

"The captive demon?" the official gasped.

"What do you think we are? Muppets?" Gus snarled, recovering smoothly.

"Muppets? What . . . I don't think . . . " the ref stammered.

"You don't have to," I smiled. "Just summon the Ta-hoe magician and I'm sure we can work something out."

"But . . . Oh, very well."

The official trotted off toward the stands while the rest of the team crowded around me.

"You're going to have a woman on the team?" Badaxe demanded.

"Let me explain," I waved. "First of all, Tanda isn't . . . "

"She's not actually a woman," Chumly supplied.

"She's my sister. And when it comes to the old rough and tumble, she can beat me four out of five times."

"She isn't? I mean, she is?" Badaxe struggled. "I mean, she can?"

"You bet your sweet axe she can," Gus grinned.

"Gleep," said the dragon, determined to get his two cents worth in.

"If you're all quite through," I said testily. "I'd like to finish. What I was about to say was that Tanda isn't going to play."

There was a moment of stunned silence as the team absorbed this.

"I don't get it," Gus said at last. "If she isn't going to play, then what . . . "

"Once she's here and revived, we're going to grab her and the Trophy and head back for Klah," I announced. "The ref's about to hand us the grand prize on a silver platter."

"But what about the game?" Badaxe scowled.

I closed my eyes, realizing for a moment how Aahz must feel when he has to deal with me.

"Let me explain this slowly," I said carefully. "The reason we're *in* this game is to rescue Tanda and grab the Trophy. In a few minutes we're going to have them both, so there'll be no reason for us to keep getting our heads beaten in. Understand?"

"I still don't like quitting the field before the end of a battle," the general grumbled.

"For crying out loud!" I exploded. "This is a game, not a war!"

"Are we talking about the same field?" Chumly asked innocently.

Fortunately, I was spared having to formulate an answer to that one as Quigley chose that moment to arrive, Tananda floating in his wake.

"What's this the ref says about using Tanda in the game?" he demanded.

"That's right," I lied. "We need her to finish the game. Now if you'll be so good as to wake her up, we'll just . . . "

"But she's my hostage," the magician protested.

"C'mon, Quigley," I argued. "We aren't taking her anyplace. She'll be right here on the field in full sight of you and everybody else."

"And you can all skip off to another dimension any time you want," Quigley pointed out. "No deal."

That was uncomfortably close to the truth, but if there's one thing I've learned from Aahz, it's how to bluff with a straight face.

"Now, look, Quigley," I snarled. "I'm trying to be fair about this, but it occurs to me you're taking advantage of my promise."

"Of course," the magician nodded. "But tell you what. Just to show you I'm a sport, I'll let you have Tanda."

"Swell," I grinned.

"If . . . and I repeat, *if* you let me keep Aahz in exchange."

"What?" I exclaimed. "I mean, sure. Go ahead. He's already out cold."

"Very well," he nodded. "This will just take a few seconds."

"What does this do to our plans?" Gus asked, drawing me aside.

"Nothing," I informed him through gritted teeth. "We go as soon as it's clear."

"What?" the gargoyle gaped. "What about Aahz?"

"It's his orders," I snarled. "Before the game started he made me promise that if he got in trouble I wouldn't endanger myself or the team trying to save him."

"And you're going to skip out on him?" Gus

sneered. "After all he's done for you?"

"Now don't you start on me, Gus!" I grimaced. "I don't want to . . . "

"Hi, handsome," Tananda chirped, joining our discussion. "If it isn't too much trouble, could someone fill me in as to why this august assemblage has assembled, why we're standing in the middle of a pasture, and what all these people are doing staring at us? And where's Quigley going with Aahz?"

"There's no time," I declared. "We've got to get going."

"Get going where?" she frowned.

"Back to Klah," Gus grumbled. "Skeeve here is in the middle of abandoning Aahz."

"He's what?" Tananda gasped.

"Gus . . ." I warned.

"Save it, handsome. I'm not budging until someone tells me what's going on, so you might as well start now."

It took surprisingly little time to bring her up to date once I got started. I deliberately omitted as many details as possible to keep from getting Tananda riled. I had enough problems on my hands without fighting her, too! It seemed to work, as she listened patiently without comment or frown.

" . . . and so that's why we've got to get out of here before play resumes," I finished.

"Bull feathers," she said firmly.

"I'm glad you . . . how's that again?" I sputtered.

"I said 'Bull feathers,' " she repeated. "You guys have been knocked around, trampled, and otherwise beaten on for my sake and now we're going to run? Not me! I say we stay right here and teach these bozos a lesson."

"But . . . "

"I don't know if your D-Hopper can move the whole team," she continued, "but I'll bet it can't do the job if we aren't cooperating."

"That's telling him," Gus chortled.

" . . . so retreat is out. Now, if you're afraid of getting hurt, just stay out of our way. We aren't leaving until we finish what you and Aahz started."

"Well said," Badaxe nodded.

"Count me in," the gargoyle supplied.

"You'll be the death of me yet, little sister," Chumly sighed.

I managed to get a grip on Gleep's nose before he could add his vote to the proceedings.

"Actually," I said slowly, "Aahz had always warned me about how dangerous it is to travel dimensions alone. And if I'm going to stay here, it occurs to me the safest place would be surrounded by my teammates."

"All right, Skeeve!" Gus grinned, clapping me on the back.

"Then it's decided," Tananda nodded. "Now, then, handsome, what's the plan?"

Somehow, I had known she was going to say that.

"Give me a minute," I pleaded. "A second ago the plan was to just split, remember? These plans don't just grow on trees, you know."

I plunged into thought, considering and discarding ideas as they came to me. That didn't take long. Not that many ideas were occurring to me.

I found myself staring at Chumly. He was craning his neck to look at the stands.

"What are *you* doing?" I asked, irritated by his apparent lack of concern with our situation.

"Hmmm? Oh. Sorry, old boy," the troll apologized. "I was just curious as to how many Deveels were in the crowd. There's a lot of them."

"There are?" I blinked, scanning the crowd. "I don't see any."

"Oh, they're disguised, of course," Chumly shrugged. "But you can see their auras if you check. With the odds that were being given on this bloody game, it was a sure thing they'd be here."

He was right. I'd been so preoccupied with the game I had never bothered to check the stands. Now that I looked, I could see the auras of other demons scattered throughout the crowd.

"It's too bad we can't cancel their disguises," I muttered to myself.

"Oh, we could do that easy enough," the troll answered.

"We could?"

"Certainly. Deveels always use the cheapest, easiest disguises available. I know a spell that would restore their normal appearance quick enough."

"You do?" I pressed. "Could it cover the whole stadium?"

"Well, not for a terribly long time," Chumly said, "but it would hold for a minute or two. Why do you ask?"

"I think I've got an idea," I explained. "Be back in a minute."

"Where are you going?" the troll called after me as I started for the sidelines.

"To talk to Griffin," I retorted, not caring that the explanation didn't really explain anything.

Chapter Twenty-Seven:

"Ask not for whom the bell tolls—"
                                    —M. ALI

THE ball carrier was somewhere under Gleep when the whistle blew. That wouldn't have been too bad, if it weren't for the fact that Chumly had already thrown the ball carrier to the ground and jumped on him prior to my pet joining in the fracas. As I said before, Gleep had *really* gotten into the spirit of things.

"I say," came an agonized call from the troll, "do you mind?"

"Sorry!" I apologized, backing the dragon onto more solid footing.

"Say, Skeeve," Gus murmured, sliding up beside me, "how much longer until we're set for the big play?"

"Should be any minute now," I confided. "Why do you ask?"

"He's afraid of additional casualties you and that dragon will inflict on the team while we're stalling for

195

time," Badaxe chimed in sarcastically.

"Gleep," my pet commented, licking the general's face.

"You might as well forget the hard guy act, Hugh," the gargoyle observed. "The dragon's got you pegged as a softie."

"Is that so?" Badaxe argued, gasping a bit on Gleep's breath. "Well, allow me to point out that with the master plan about to go into effect, we don't have the ball!"

"Skeeve'll get it for us when we need it," Tananda protested, rising to my defense. "He always comes through when we need him. You've just never followed him into battle before."

"I believe I can testify," Chumly growled, limping back to join us, "that it's safer to be following him than in front of him."

"Sorry about that, Chumly," I winced. "It's just that Gleep . . . "

"I know, I know," the troll interrupted. " 'Spooked under fire' . . . remember, *I* gave you that excuse originally. He seems to have recovered admirably."

"I hate to interrupt," Gus interrupted, "but isn't that our signal?"

I followed his gaze to the sidelines. Griffin was there waving his arms wildly. When he saw he had my attention, he crossed the fingers on both hands, then crossed his forearms over his head. That was the signal.

"All right," I announced. "Fun time is over. The messages have been delivered. Does everyone remember what they're supposed to do?"

As one, the team nodded, eager grins plastered on their faces. I don't know what they were so cheerful about. If any phase of this plan didn't work, some or all of us would be goners.

"Tanda and Chumly make one team. Badaxe, you

stick with Gus. He's your ticket home," I repeated needlessly.

"We know what to do," the general nodded.

"Then let's do it!" I shouted, and wheeled Gleep into position.

This time, as the ball came into play, we did not swarm toward the ball carrier. Instead, our entire team back-pedaled to cluster in the mouth of our goal.

Our opponents hesitated, looking at each other. We had emptied over three quarters of their reserve teaching them to respect our strength, and now that lesson was bearing fruit. No one seemed to want to be the one to carry the ball into our formation. They weren't sure what we were up to but they didn't want any part of it.

Finally, the ball carrier, a Ta-hoe player, turned and threw the ball to his Rider, apparently figuring the bug had the best chance of breaking through to the goal. That's what I had been waiting for.

Reaching out with my mind, I brought the ball winging, not to me, but to Hugh Badaxe. In a smooth, fluid motion, the axe came off the general's belt and struck at the missile. I had never seen Hugh use his axe before, and I'll admit I was impressed. Weapon and ball met, and the weapon won. The ball fell to the ground in two halves as the axe returned to its resting place on the general's belt.

The crowd was on its feet, screaming incoherently. If they didn't like that, they didn't really get upset over our next move.

"Everybody, mount up!" I shouted.

On cue, Tananda jumped on Chumly's back and Badaxe did the same with Gus. I levitated half the ball to each twosome, then did a fast disguise spell.

What our opponents saw now was three images of me astride three images of Gleep. Each image of me had half a ball proudly in its possession.

The more mathematically oriented of you might realize that that adds up to three halves. Very good. Fortunately for us, Jahks aren't big on math. The question remains, however, where did the third half come from?

You don't think I was standing by idly while all this was going on, do you? While my teammates were mounting up, I took advantage of the confusion to do one more levitation/disguise job. As a result, the Trophy was now resting in front of me on Gleep's back disguised as half a ball. It was the same stunt I had pulled in Veygus, but this time I draped my shirt over it.

"Chumly!" I called. "Start your spell!"

"Done!" he waved back.

"We meet back in Klah!" I shouted.

"Now go for it!"

My teammates started up opposite sidelines, heading for both our opponents' goals simultaneously. I waited a few beats for them to draw off the tacklers, then started for my objective. Gleep and I were going for Aahz.

With all due modesty, my plan worked brilliantly. The appearance of Deveels throughout the crowd sent the Jahks into a state of panic. The crossbowmen were too busy trying to get a shot of these new invaders to pay any attention to me, but they were poorly aimed. For some reason the beings shooting at me seemed a bit rattled.

I caught sight of Quigley, standing on his seat and waving his arms. Catchy phrases like "Begone foul spirits!" and "I vanquish thee!" were issuing from his lips as he did his routine.

This didn't surprise me. Not that I felt Quigley was particularly quick thinking in a crisis. It had to do with the messages I had sent to both him and Massha before the play started.

The messages were simple:

STAND BY TO REPEL AN INVASION OF
DEMONS!
P.S. GO THROUGH THE MOTIONS. I'LL
TAKE CARE OF THE DEMONS.

                                    SKEEVE

I caught his eye and winked at him. In return, one
of his "demon dispelling" waves got a little limp-
wristed as he nodded slightly, bidding me adieu. In
the middle of saving his employers from an invasion
of demons, who could blame him if a few departed
who were supposed to stay put.

Aahz's unconscious body came wafting toward us
in response to my mental summons. Gleep stretched
out his long neck and caught my mentor's tunic in his
mouth as he floated by.

It wasn't quite the way I planned it but I was in no
position to be choosy. Tightening my legs around
Gleep's middle, I hit the button on the D-Hopper,
and . . .

The walls of my room were a welcome change
from the hostile stadium.

"We did it!" I exclaimed, then was startled by the
volume of my voice. After the din of the stadium, my
room seemed incredibly quiet.

"Kid," came a familiar voice, "would you tell
your stupid dragon to put me down before I die from
his breath?"

"Gleep?" my pet asked, dropping my mentor in
an undignified heap.

"Aahz?" I blinked. "I thought you were . . ."

"Out cold? Not hardly. Can you think of a better
way to get Tanda out on the field? For a while there I
was afraid you wouldn't figure it out and call for a
replacement."

"You mean you were faking all along?" I demanded. "I was scared to death! You could have warned me, you know."

"Like you warned me about your vanishing act?" he shot back. "And what happened to my orders to head for home once Tanda was in the clear?"

"Your orders?" I stammered. "Well . . ."

There was a soft *BAMF* and Gus and Badaxe were in the room. Gus was holding the general cradled in his arms like a babe, but they both seemed in good spirits.

"Beautiful!" Hugh chortled, hugging the gargoyle around the neck. "If you ever need a back-up man . . ."

"If you ever need a partner." Gus corrected, hugging him back. "You and I could . . ."

BAMF!

Chumly and Tananda appeared sprawling on the bed. Both her nostrils were bleeding, but she was laughing uproariously. Chumly was panting for breath and wiping tears of hilarity from his big moon eyes.

"I say," he gasped. "That *was* a spot of fun. We haven't double-teamed anyone like that since the last family reunion, when Auntie Tizzie got Tiddley and . . ."

"What happened?" I bellowed.

"We won!" Gus cheered. "One and a half to one and a half to one! They never knew what hit 'em."

"It's one for the record book," Tananda agreed, dabbing at her nose.

"For the record book?" Gus challenged. "This game'll fill a book by itself."

"Aahz, old bean," Chumly called. "Do you have any wine about? The assemblage seems up for a celebration."

"I know where it is," Badaxe waved, starting for the barrels we had secreted under the work table.

"Hold it!" Aahz roared. "Halt, stop, desist, and TIME OUT!!"

"I think he wants our attention," Tananda told the group.

"If you're all *quite* through," my mentor continued, shooting her a black look. "I have one question."

"What's that?" Tananda asked in her little girl voice.

"Quit bleeding on the bed," Aahz scowled. "It lacks class. What I want to know is, did any of you superstars think to pick up the Trophy? That was the objective of this whole fiasco, you know."

The team gestured grandly at me. With a grin, I let the disguise drop away from the Trophy.

"Ta-da!" I warbled. "Happy birthday, Aahz."

"Happy birthday!!" the team echoed.

Aahz looked at their grins, then at the Trophy, then at their grins again.

"All right," he sighed. "Break out the wine."

The roar of approval for this speech rivaled anything that had come from the stands that afternoon as the team descended on the wine barrels like a swarm of hungry humming mice.

"Well, Aahz," I grinned, levitating the Trophy to the floor and sliding from Gleep's back. "I guess that just about winds it up."

I was starting for the wine barrels when a heavy hand fell on my shoulder.

"There are a *few* loose ends to be tied up," my mentor drawled.

"Like what?" I asked fearfully.

"Like the invitation you gave Massha to drop by for a visit."

"Invitation?" I echoed in a small voice.

"Badaxe told me about it," Aahz grimaced. "Then there's a little matter of a quick trip to Deva."

"To Deva?" I blinked. "What for? I mean, swell, but . . . "

"I've got to pick up our winnings," my mentor informed me. "I took the time to place a few small bets on the game while we were there. Profits don't just happen, you know."

"When do we start?" I asked eagerly.

"We don't," Aahz said firmly. "This time I'm going alone. There's something about you and the Bazaar that just don't mix well."

"But Aahz . . . "

"And besides," he continued, grinning broadly, "there's one more loose end from this venture that will be occupying your time. One which only you can handle."

"Really?" I said proudly. "What's that?"

"Well," my mentor said, heading for the wine, "you can start thinking about how we're going to get that stupid dragon out of our room. He's too big to fit through the door or window."

"Gleep!" said my pet, licking my face.